I0672416

# Will You Marry Me My T Girl?

## *And Other Stories*

# Dr. Lynette Hlongwane

PROUDLYAFRIKAN

ISBN- 13: 978-0-620-73233-8


Second edition


Logo Design: Sifiso Hlongwane


Email: info@proudlyafrikan.org
        drlynettehlongwane@hotmail.com

*I dedicate this book to all members of my family, and to life.*

## Also by Dr. Lynette Hlongwane

White Goat for the White House: Saved by Synchronicity

Upon These Ashes: Poems and Reflections

# Contents

# Introduction

The short story titled, *Joan Random is Dead,* was first published in *The Big Issue* magazine which supports the homeless, and is sold by the homeless on the streets of Cape Town, in South Africa. The December 28, 2007 edition which featured my short story, was specifically titled, *The Big Issue's Fiction Issue.*

Little did I know that completely out of the blue, the beginning of December, 2008, would catapult me into the most unforgettable experience of my life! I'd embark on a truly life-changing journey. The year 2010 began the most challenging period of that ordeal.

But the muse and Universe threw me a life line, I could say, in hindsight. I found myself using blocks of time engaged in writing the short stories now published in the book in your hand. This process offered me some respite, a breather, an escape.

The rest of the short stories followed, one after the other, after I wrote, *Will You Marry Me T Girl?* None of them were even drawn from my personal life experience. I'm still amazed that in the midst of my difficult saga, I could focus on writing fiction!

The setting for all the short stories is the democratic South Africa, with occasional flashbacks to the Apartheid era. As I worked on the short stories, I began to notice a theme running through them. Love relationships. Nothing syrupy, really. Just the lived life of coupled love.

Most of the stories are fairly long. Some almost pass as novellas. The length thus provides the reader ample time to delve deeper into the plot and the characters.

I enjoyed writing this collection which covers an interesting range, across age, race, class, sexual orientation and geographical location. I have a broad smile on my face, each time the characters pass through my mind - what they say, think and do. I hope you'll enjoy reading the short stories, and most importantly, find something valuable in them, a keepsake of sorts.

This collection includes expanded versions of two previously published short stories: *Joan Random is Dead* and *Will You Marry Me T Girl?* In this edition, the latter story is titled, *Will You Marry Me My T Girl?*


Lynette Hlongwane

# Joan Random is Dead

When Joan Random's body was found floating in the middle of the mighty Sibika Dam, a grim wave of electric shock embraced the Sibika community, and later reverberated throughout the country. Given suicide incidents, infanticides and family killings that had gripped the nation in oversized collective pliers, many began to draw conclusions as to the cause of Joan's rendezvous with death.

The whole of Joan's glorious life was now untidily packed together in a floating mass. The life that many would remember her by had wilted and exited. Her unique laugh. Her gentle big brown eyes. Her peculiar gait, which one quickly got used to, however. How her pants sat on her behind. Her fair yet problem skin. Her gentle yet strong hands. All of this now lay in a bundle wrapped in death's dark cold and wet blanket.

Some remembered how sociable she was, and how she quickly made one feel at ease about the limp in her step. She'd simply tell the story that began, "It was polio. Mother thought immunization is optional." And so, Joan nipped in the bud the pity, sadness and awkwardness, always making it a point to highlight her gratefulness, "I'm alive, my China. That's all that matters. And religiously, every day, I count my blessings."

"Another flame extinguished," remarked the constable who led the team called to the scene.

"Mr. Random, as Joan's husband, and the last person who saw her alive, we will need your full cooperation. Was she pushed from behind? Did she take the decision to jump? Was she aided in the sad exercise? Did she fight hard as best she could to save her life? Had there been a fight? Had you quarrelled?"

The constable with short curly hair put his hand gently on Mr. Random's shoulder, and continued, "These are always difficult procedures for us, and particularly, for the next-of-kin. But please bear with us, Mr. Random. We need your full cooperation, sir, as we grapple with these questions in our investigation, a journey with one acceptable destination - the whole truth."

The third constable - elderly, the frown on his forehead clearly exhibiting masses of experience in his work, added, "So that the law can take its course. And most importantly, Mr. Random, closure for family and friends of the deceased."

"Gentlemen, I'm just as baffled. No-one needs answers to those questions more than I do. God knows," responded red-eyed Tony. He knew he was instantly suspect number one. This was written all over the constables' long faces, the way they occasionally looked through him. The moments of long uncomfortable silence that shaped that first questioning.

"My only hope is the community - if anyone witnessed what happened. I say this is my Joan, my dearest wife and friend!" Tony's voice began to shake. His mind a casualty of uncontrollable emotions at this point, Tony seamlessly switched from talking to the police, to talking to himself. "Sweetheart what happened? Tell me now?" His hands were firmly clasped on his head as he impatiently stamped his one foot on the ground. His face was child-like bewilderment itself.

It told the story that began as the police knocked on the front door of their house. They were carrying a pair of beautiful gold earrings. Definitely far more than 9 karat gold. When the awkward silence finally penetrated his psyche, Tony took a closer look at the earrings. He was aware of the look on the face of the policeman who stood at the door, with his cop cap in hand; human nature and respect for the dead, competing with duty and training.

"Yes, sir, I do recognize these. They are my wife's." Tony had bought the earrings as Joan's birthday gift, two months before. These are the earrings he'd touched and played with a countless times. These same earrings were now the bearer of bad news.

"Almost one hundred percent of the time you will know if the suspect is guilty or not. Trust your instincts. Don't be a heartless monster, unnecessarily." So they were reminded at the Police College. The police continued to quietly study Tony's behaviour, searching for telling clues.

In a hoarse voice, Tony asked, "Where's she? But why? But why, dear Lord? Why us? Why me, Lord? Was it an accident? In which hospital is she? When did it happen? How did it happen?" When Tony Random's own barrage of questions tapered to an end, the police knew that reality had begun to sink in. He eventually understood.

Tony turned his back from the tiny audience, and leaned against the wall. When he turned to face the bearers of the bad news, he battled to keep a tearless face. He could hardly open his eyes now from the glare of the pain. The highly polished metal blue and gold plate etched on their front door, exacerbated matters: "Welcome to the warm home of Joan and Tony Random."

The unbearable burden of pain weighed Tony down. Even if someone tried to puncture the stubborn bubble of sadness that engulfed him, it would remain supple yet intact. He felt dizzy. One constable quickly came to his rescue, and held him firm.

"She left here to drop off these earrings at the jeweller's, to be engraved. She'd take a walk to the dam after that, like she does most afternoons or early evenings in the summer."

"We are very sorry, sir. This is a part of our job we loathe, being the bearer of bad news." The words of his lecturer at the Police College filled up the constable's mind. "Someone has to do it. Someone has to do it."

"You can come with us to identify the body at Sibika Dam, before we move it to the mortuary, for forensic tests."

"My God, Sibika Dam? How? How on earth? I'm shocked!" Tony felt a surge of anger mixed with disbelief that his vibrant Joan, the joy in his life, was now a mere body. Her favourite dam had killed her! "Life is so ridiculous!" He said in a barely audible whisper.

As he entered the police vehicle Tony realized he was walking barefoot. He took a few steps back to the house and found a pair of blue flip-flops in the patio. Absentmindedly, he noted a bit of discomfort, and realized these flip-flops were Joan's.

He shoved the earrings in his back pocket, remembered to lock the front door this time, and finally sat on the edge of the back seat, head bowed, his house keys dangling carelessly from his hand – clearly an extra weight. The policeman took away the keys and put them on the dashboard.

Tony rested his flushed face in the palms of his hands, quietly staring into space. The faces of people they passed along the way had an air of curiosity, suspicion and pity.

They could have walked to Sibika Dam. It was a very short distance. Indeed, it was this very feature that had helped Joan and Tony decide to buy their home. Its proximity to nature, the dam, and the hills.

The dam was an immediate attraction for Joan. Frequent brisk walks, almost daily, replaced public gym, "until differently-abled people like me are thought of more seriously, and catered for," she'd say. But who wanted to walk on this fateful day, putting one foot in front of the other - a life rule, otherwise, but not in such mysterious circumstances?

Half muttering to himself, Tony remembered and unintentionally shared their last moments together. He was least concerned that whatever he said and did might serve as evidence against him. "Just the evening before last we had a romantic dinner, with flowers, aromatic candles, good wine and perfect roast beef."

"Oh! Those are life-saving memories to savour, Mr. Random." Tony continued, as if oblivious to that comment from one of the policemen. His nerves and soul remained raw and jagged. In a tired voice Tony continued, "It was a fun evening. After dinner we took a big bowl of grapes upstairs to munch as we watched Television. We cuddled, and became so child-like, throwing a grape into each other's open mouth."

It was quiet in the car. One constable simply nodded his head, respectfully. "Life! Who knew that was our last good time together?"

Tony did not want to talk about the rest of that romantic night. His hands instinctively moved to his nether regions, as he wondered who will ask him again: "Give me my African potatoes, sweetheart. I just like to hold them ...."

The police vehicle slowed down as it now negotiated the narrowing and meandering road leading in a very short stretch to Sibika Dam. Within view were a police van, a boat, and some constables who had already secured the crime scene.

Tony alighted reluctantly. His pain-riddled body was a ton of bricks. His legs felt as if they were tied up in heavy irons. He feared the inevitable; contact with the reality of what he felt was cruel abandonment. Stories he'd read and heard, came tumbling all over him. "He just left me." He felt the dizziness again, but took a deep breath and trudged on.

She was all bloated and ballooned to double her size, the well-defined biceps and triceps, ironed out by the mighty waters of Sibika. "Yes, the lion head tattoo is Joan's. But why, Joan?"

The body was put in the body bag and wheeled into the police van they found at the crime scene. The team leader explained, "As you might know, forensic experts will throw more light on this matter. With DNA testing and all the new technologies, we'll get to the bottom of this crime."

The police watched as Tony took a little walk down into the woods. They knew he needed to be alone. Meanwhile, they scoured the area for all possible evidence. Tony had to be fetched from the woods. He was gripped and almost aged by grief. He was sobbing uncontrollably.

———————

The telephone call he'd long awaited, came. "The certificate is ready for pick up. When can we expect you?"

"Within the next hour."

Sweat pouring all over Tony's body defied the air-conditioned office. His handkerchief was now soaking wet. After a weak clammy handshake, Tony followed the District Surgeon to his office.

"Did your wife have a heart condition, Mr. Random? I noted she had diabetes."

"Her diabetes was under control."

Tony struggled to steady his hand as he received and read the certificate. "Heart seizure? I don't understand. Joan was a health fanatic. And we were happy."

"At least, your children will be a source of comfort, Mr. Random."

"We were not blessed with children."

"I'm sorry, Mr. Random. But you know, we are in the same boat. I divorced my wife. I truly believe cheating in marriage is a form of death, you know."

"That's different," Tony responded.

"As Christians like to say, 'God doesn't make a mistake.'" The doctor grinned and continued, "And if you need to talk, I'll be more than ...."
Tony had stormed out.

Another call came through that day. "Any news, Tony?"

"It was heart seizure, mom, strange as this will sound. The whole thing is so senseless. I am trying to piece together Joan's last moments. I assume she had heart seizure while dipping her legs and feet in the water, a free water treatment for her bad foot, as she liked to say."

"It's inexplicable. But you have been exonerated."

"I know, mom. But how will I cope with this reality?"

Indeed, the almost palpable presence of Joan's absence, took a toll on Tony.

"This ends our counselling sessions, Mr. Random. I've done my best. The rest is up to you, to defy your grief, beg yourself to successfully summon up the courage and willingness to live." The psychologist closed the file and left.

Tony became a familiar figure. Haggard. Talking to himself. He'd be seen shaking his head, his thin long arms occasionally outstretched, as if begging to be crucified on the cross he could no longer bear.

Here was an iceberg dislodged from its familiar surroundings, drifting. Here was a lonesome troubled feather, gliding awkwardly on the wings of a ruthless gale wind.

Tony became a landmark. "Sibika Dam is easy to find. As you turn into Sibika Street, drive slowly. You'll encounter a mentally unstable man standing in the middle of the street. The dam will be a few minutes away."

Could Tony live life fully, all over again? Would he? How? Why?

———————

"The medical doctors say you shorten your life if you don't sleep well, night after night, Tony. I'm worried about you."

"I know, mother. I simply can't help it. And *you* should still be in bed. It is 6 am on a Sunday, mom!" She simply ignored his efforts to fuss about her.

"What is still giving you sleepless nights, son?" Tony did not answer. He had woken up with a headache again that morning. But with his mother forcing him to talk about a subject he'd rather leave alone, the throbbing increased. He had a question for his mother. "Why should I live life fully, again? Just tell me, mother." But he did not want to share this burden.

"Mother, must you really know?"

"Would I have posed the question, if I did not want an

16

answer, dear?" Tony noted his mother's feisty nature, even so early in the morning. He gave up hiding his feelings from her. He sighed. "I still miss my wife."

"Oh! Christ! Don't do this to yourself, child. Our dearest Joan has been gone for over 3 years now."

"Well, mom, to me it feels like it was just yesterday Joan left us."

"I've watched you, son, slowly becoming a walking dead."

"I can't help it, mother!" Stress, sadness and anger were hanging onto the tone of Tony's voice.

"You've allowed grief to drive you nuts, son. I don't think this is how Joan would have wanted you to live the rest of your life! Wasting it like this?" Tony did not respond. "You are slowly dying on me, Tony! Slow poison it is. Self-inflicted slow poison, my son. This is too much. I can't handle the torment anymore." Tony heard his mother begin to sniff on the phone. A soft cry followed.

"Mother, are you crying now? Don't do this to yourself. Please." His voice began to shake. The line went dead. "Mother, you've actually hung up on me!"

This, indeed, was one of countless conversations Tony had had with his mother. The subject was always the same. It is difficult to watch a loved one die in the midst of one precious gift. Life! Tony's mother could not give up on her son, though. Year in and year out, she pleaded with him to embrace life, again.

Tony was sad and embarrassed that his mother had hung up on him on this early morning. She had never done this before. Clearly, his pain and his reluctance to release it, were taking a heavy toll on his mother. He had to call her back and apologize. In the quiet of his bedroom, through the volley of tears streaming down his face, he vented out: "I'm sorry, mother, for the burden I've become in your life. But how can I live a full life again? My beloved Joan is gone, mother! We were so happy together. I do not deserve to be happy alone."

Tony picked up the phone. But what was he going to tell his mother? He decided he'd call her a bit later. He needed time to compose himself. He also needed to give his mother some time for her raw emotions to ebb.

But on this Sunday morning, Tony began to collect his thoughts in ways he'd not done before. He had to dare himself, he realized. Something had to change. He summoned the courage to turn over a new leaf. It was time.

So, that same Sunday morning Tony took a walk to Sibika Dam. It was his very first walk in that direction, since Joan's passing. His Joan in a body bag. The memory of that sad day was still fresh. But he kept walking until he reached the edge of the water.

With his bare hand he cleared a bit of sand on a small patch. With a little groan he slowly bent forwards to roll up his pants, and take off his sandals. Then he moved and sat on the edge of the dam. He took a moment to look around. The little bush was still there. This is where he'd gone to be alone with his thoughts on that fateful day.

As Tony dipped his feet in the cold water, birds chirped happily, as if urging him to join in and make merriment. Toes went in first, a bit hesitantly. And then his whole feet were fully immersed in the water.

In the stillness of the hills and the peace inherent in untroubled waters, Tony felt Joan's presence by his side, with her feet also in the water. He heard her calm and gentle voice, whispering in his ear, "I'm okay, Tony. I'm alright, my China." For one entire year, Tony never missed even one Sunday of this crack of dawn ritual.

———————

"The waters of Sibika Dam finally released his pain, and returned Tony, to Tony Random. A round of applause to my beloved son, here. I'm so proud of him! Ladies and gentlemen, I give you, Tony Random!" This is how Mrs. Random, senior, ended her speech. Indeed, her son was getting married again. Exactly five years after Joan's passing, Tony Random had eventually come to.

As he stood up and buttoned his jacket to take a few steps to the podium, Iris, his new wife, accompanied him. She held his hand and stayed by his side, as Tony struggled for a long moment, to find words to begin his speech.

# Two Girls

It was 6.00 am on a young morning in Bonzotown. I liked taking long walks when the weather was agreeable for walking. I have never liked the unholy baptismal by the scotching sun of African summers, when the sun seems to have been demoted from its lofty position, and is forced to hang out with us mere mortals, down here.

When the temperature reaches unbearably high levels, even confusing air conditioners on their otherwise well-mastered responsibilities, I wish I could ask the sun: "Why do you choose to park your piping hot bum right in the middle of my head, cooking my brain to an undesirable mushy blob? During such times a greater part of my day is ruined. I'm lethargic, frustrated and pathetically fatigued.

On this pleasant morning, however, it actually even looked like rain! The air was so crisp I could crunch it with my teeth! My mouth began to water as I thought about the crunchy fresh lettuce salad I'd have for lunch.

Taking walks alone gives the mind some free time to wander sometimes. Mind reminisces. Mind plots. Mind develops great, and at times too far-fetched ideas. And this morning was no different. Just six hours into the new day, my mind embarked on a very interesting journey. It bought a return air ticket and booked an air conditioned car at the destination.

The rendezvous of all these mind activities was Tuna Bay, the small quiet coastal town where I'd spent my last holiday. As my body did the walking in Bonzotown, my mind was back in Tuna Bay. At the gentle coaxing of my mind, my nostrils opened wide and greedily sucked in as much as they could, of the smell of the sea. My mouth became this swiftly swelling well of saliva. Clear pictures of delicious plate after plate of the well-loved fish I had enjoyed daily, cleared all mind traffic and debris, so that I could selfishly enjoy a special and quiet memory stretch.

It's funny that the trip began with the waiter who usually took my breakfast order, how he grew to know my specialty: grilled fish and warm water with lots of lemon.

"The fish comes with eggs, a choice of baked beans, mushrooms, tomato slices and two slices of toasted bread, madam," he had politely advised me the first time. I believe he was concerned that I was robbing myself of a full meal on offer, for all that money.

Typical of a small country town with few local job opportunities, tourists were made to cover the shortfall in revenue. Eating out was thus fairly pricy, unless one booked a self-catering apartment. Nevertheless, the high costs came with enjoying the breathtaking beauty that abounded in Tuna Bay.

"Sir," I'd responded to the waiter, my voice deepening for faked seriousness, "There's another choice you've not mentioned." A frown formed on my forehead, for effect. His eyebrows came closer in puzzlement. I watched them almost looping to make some stitch some-one in the world of knitters might recognize. He cocked his head as he listened. I smiled and sniffed the sea breeze that was blowing my hair slightly, with the grace of a ballerina.

"I'll have my fish with this beautiful fresh morning breeze. This is your free specialty, Tuna Bay!" It was the weirdest thing he'd heard since his training as a waiter, I was sure. But he didn't argue with me as he subdued a hearty guffaw. "Understood, madam. Just fish and lemon water from our kitchen," he confirmed my order. "That's right. The rest is already served," I added, giving him a thumbs up. He walked away.

I knew he had shared our conversation with his colleagues, because when I was attacking the remaining half of the delectable fish on my plate, the manager passed by and asked, "Is everything still alright, madam?" He had a broad smile on his face. I assured him that I was enjoying my breakfast. I continued the small talk. "Your servings are quite generous, I must say. I'm not complaining. Just amazed and grateful."

"Is this your first visit to our Tuna Bay, ma'am?" I simply nodded a positive response. I had just tightly packed and carefully slid into my mouth, a folk heavily laden with a morsel of the great fish.

"Well, do enjoy the rest of your stay, and come back again next year, madam." I took an exaggerated gulp of the tasty breeze and smiled back at him. At that moment rays from the sun landed on the side of his face, highlighting his ebony skin. "He looks southern Sudanese," I thought to myself, only pretending to understand how far he might have travelled to get here.

Tuna Bay was a serene best kept secret for retirees, where a normal day for most inhabitants began with an early morning stint at the beach. I moved my hands to feel the improved tightening of my bottoms, as I remembered the newspaper headlines and subsequent meeting in the Town Hall, at Tuna Bay. A hot topic was being debated.

It was whether to allow a certain section of the beach to be set aside for nude bathing! I remembered the amusing debate on radio where the residents had to vote on whether they wanted to increase the revenue of Tuna Bay, by allowing nudity on their beaches, or preferred to keep Tuna Bay struggling economically. The advocates of this proposal were trying hard to convince all and sundry, that such nude bathing would be a sure way to boost tourism, and profit the small town.

I'd long noticed that most citizens were retired. So I wanted to write a provoking article while I was there, to make the point that the great line from John Keats' poem, *A Thing of Beauty is a Joy Forever*, would not apply among most of the senior citizens of this town. And if nude bathing saw the light of day, visitors would have to be content watching a lot of flab, cellulite and sagging parts; and maybe even grow to admire this definite eyesore.

I'd planned to end my article with a warning: "Forced to admire not so young nude bathers, tourists to this town will slowly develop a lopsided sense of aesthetics. Is this what you want, Tuna Bay? Think of the effects and repercussions thereof."

The potential nude bathers of Tuna Bay were quite a sight to watch. Some ladies in bikinis, and most men in the skimpiest of shorts. All shades of skin colour. From artificial to natural suntans. I had to ask myself if these older folks did not know about the mighty force of gravity! I wondered what it had taken to let them bask so joyfully in the conviction that the forceful power of gravity can be successfully and permanently defied.

It was easy to tell from the self-confidence the senior citizens displayed, that they truly believed whatever their chronological age was, they looked ten or twenty years younger! The ladies swayed their hips from side to side. I suspected that some of them were new replacements. I couldn't believe what I saw. How amazing that these seniors appeared to believe the crap that 60 is the new

50; 90, the new 80! They needed some-one brave enough to rough handle their collective egos a bit, I thought.

For a fleeting moment of a reluctant return to Bonzotown, I noticed how I'd become quite oblivious of the people I met and sounds I heard, on this early morning walk. Yes, this was Bonzotown, where parks were so few and far between, that nature lovers had learnt to embrace and worship any semblance of green, in the midst of hard concrete.

Back to Tuna Bay. These old folks needed some-one to tell them their bodies were absolutely no comparison to those of younger people. I wanted to ask the seniors of the beaches of Tuna Bay, if they hadn't noticed how younger people unwittingly and unconsciously displayed their pleasantly toned youthful wares on other beaches. And they weren't even considering flaunting their stuff by bathing in the nude, except in their private baths. Then I imagined reading angry responses to my article. I knew that on reading it, some old timers would even accuse me of age discrimination.

My mind took me back to my walks on the white beach sands of Tuna Bay. The sand particles were so fine. They formed a gentle layer on the top of my feet and stayed put, instead of rolling off with every step I took, as I deliberately kicked the sand.

I was thinking about sweet nothing, at the best of times. But I also recalled times on these beach walks when thoughts took the liberty to mar my happiness. Don't you hate it when work stuff you've left behind sneaks in and encroaches on your holiday, when you'd decided as you locked your office door, that you would be leaving everything behind?

So, here was gloom I thought I'd left behind in my office in Bonzotown. It was walking stealthily right behind me in Tuna Bay! The raise I deserved. But, alas, even on this early morning, I still lacked the guts to ask for it.

In my reverie, I heard sea gulls of Tuna Bay distinctly in my ears, as my feet pounded the cement of Bonzotown. The smell of fried fish and potato chips piping hot and dripping with tomato sauce, haunted me. I remembered fishermen proudly displaying their fresh fish, drenched delightfully in the smell of the sea from which it came. The small talk I used to have with them those mornings.

My mind travelled to other coastal cities of Africa I've visited, where the women would already have bought some of the fish, and cooked it for regular customers. The fishermen of Tuna Bay should do the whole package, I thought. There I was, pretending to be a smart business enhancer.

On this freshening early morning in Bonzotown, my mind unashamedly continued to indulge in its mental visit trip back in Tuna Bay. Like a happy seal I was rolling on my back, enjoying the mental delight of being back in that small town. It was loads of fun. I knew I had to find an excuse to return to Tuna Bay, and maybe actually write the article this time.

I was still consciously relishing the moment – daydreaming, when I was rudely dragged, mind body and soul, back to Bonzotown! And in real time.

Damn! How could this wretched car rudely and abruptly end my Tuna Bay spree like this? It screeched to a halt. I didn't pay much attention. I assumed that these were just jaywalkers receiving an important life-saving lesson, that street lights are the only safe points to cross. And, only when the lights turn green. In a few short minutes, traffic was still going to be the usual bumper to bumper, on that stretch of the road.

I was concentrating now on my exercise, making sure to get the maximum of energy burnt, as I approached my usual spot. Here, by this coffee shop, I knew I had covered my 30 minutes of walking. Thirty minutes times two, equals an hour of walking. According to experts, this is enough daily exercise to maintain a healthy, good looking body - toned and reasonably trim.

How much brisk walking did I achieve on this morning, though? It truly was an unknown quantity. I'd spent so much mental time lazily strolling in Tuna Bay, that my body mechanically walked on autopilot, except for the few times I landed back in Bonzotown. Well, I took off again, in a split second.

Then I saw out of the corner of my eye, traffic police cars stopping abruptly, once they located the scene. Obviously all of them had received the emergency call. They'd stopped everything and then rushed here. I was quite aware now of how I might have cheated my body on this walk. So, I was trying to make up to it, on my way back home. But I reluctantly forced myself to stop and take in the goings on. There were six traffic police cars now. One traffic police woman was directing the early morning traffic. Indeed, it was beginning to get heavier by this time, as I'd predicted earlier.

My goodness! It was an accident. The area of the accident was being cordoned off. For quite a while, I could hear sirens from ambulances. I knew they were navigating traffic, to get to the accident scene as speedily as drivers on the road made it possible. In no time at all, two paramedics had arrived. They were out with their bags, stretcher and stethoscopes.

Then I noticed a human form dressed in khaki shirt and pants on the tarmac, virtually motionless. I said a little prayer and crossed my chest, that the mouth-to-mouth respiration effort would yield positive results.

"Pedestrian. Drunk." This is was what I heard when I asked one person who walked past me. "Is he still alive?"

"I don't know. Let's hope so. I personally would hate to die on such a pleasant morning," he responded. Genuine concern was apparent in his voice. Sweat beads had already formed on his forehead and tip of his nose. He probably always walked to work, I surmised. The man proceeded on his way, his lunch box tucked neatly under his armpit.

The paramedics were bent over the form on the ground for quite a while, taking turns and willing the man's chest to heave, as they applied mouth-to-mouth respiration. I was beginning to lose hope that there would still be even an ounce of life in there.

I imagined how it must feel for paramedics to start their day like this - failing to resuscitate a fellow human being. I pondered on the general lives of paramedics. Good and bad experiences. This accident was a perfect way to start a disappointing day, I thought. But then, the next ten incidents might be good life-saving stories.

Rushing an old lady to the nearest hospital, for doctors to help flush out of her system inedible oil she had mistaken for olive oil, drizzled on her salad and ate. Possibilities of an attempted suicide hovering over the minds of the paramedics for the rest of the day. In another happily ending incident, paramedics giving life-saving first aid to a two-year old that is chocking from a swallowed crayon or piece of plastic.

Ah! With my imagination thoroughly having great fun creating all crises scenarios, I wondered what paramedics did when they retired. Did they write any books based on their experiences? Would that not be disallowed? Maybe perceived as a morally wrong infringement on the public's private spaces? Fishing on easily available waters, instead of diving to the deeper parts of rivers and oceans of creative writing, for story content? Again, I wondered how many of the paramedics stayed on this job until they reached retirement age. I had a bit of a writer's block since the day before, and I salivated at the experiences of these paramedics, how they could yield several volumes of books.

As if this accident was not enough for one morning, we all held our collective breath as about twenty minutes later, two teenage girls ran across this same busy road. These young ladies actually darted across like toddlers excitedly and mindlessly running onto the street, too young and too free to understand any sense of danger. One of these teenage girls had a white bundle in her arms. It looked like a newly-born baby. It was wrapped in a coarse cotton blanket, from what I could see.

Anyway, these two girls seemed proud to have made it across the street. They were laughing bashfully, aware that all eyes that could interact with theirs, were amazed at their luck, as well as their foolishness.

Then the young ladies began to walk slowly. It appeared they were not aware of the accident. It was a wide road with several lanes. I had joined the crowd of onlookers by this time, my brisk walk abandoned. Look, one life hung by the thread. I couldn't proceed as if this was a "business-as-usual" kind of walk. Why were the paramedics still bent over the form lying on the tarmac, for so long?

Was there still a sign of life there? There was no pull of blood around the form, however. That gave me hope. But still, a worst case scenario was a possibility. Internal bleeding can be fatal. I didn't wish to be there were a time to come when the paramedics had to finally give up and declare the man deceased. How I wished this sad early morning story in our Bonzotown had a happy ending!

Then those in the front began to applaud. I craned my neck to see. What was worth celebrating now? The injured man was still lying on the ground, but he had begun to move and then speak. His speech was slurred. He uttered something which I couldn't hear from where I was standing.

Then word spread through the crowd like a smell. He says he wants his baby back. That was the first thing he said. As he slowly stood up, his voice became loud enough for all to hear, "I want my baby back! I want my baby back!" There was urgency and panic in his voice. But his body was still struggling to get itself coordinated enough to match the desperately urgent message.

He was pleading with the paramedics. As if they knew anything about his baby. "I want my baby back." As he slowly became aware of the crowd, he seemed to be pleading with anyone within earshot. The man was almost in tears. He apparently had just one thing uppermost in his mind, as we all marvelled at the fact that he had been given another chance at life. He seemed a bit careless with this precious gift. Life! I thought this could have been his tenth chance to continue living *on* the earth, and not dead and buried *under* it.

Because I was standing a bit far yet close enough to take in more of the surrounding activities, I saw what most people probably couldn't see, especially those concentrating on the drunken man, uttering such a sobering spine chilling plea. I admit I'm always drawn to girls. Indeed, I'm a feminist, if you like! Something had struck me about these two careless girls, who seemed not to value the life of the baby one of them was carrying. I made a long study of the young ladies as they approached me.

They both looked about 17 or 18 years old, just the age for completion of high school, if things went normally in their schooling lives. For example, if they started school at age 6. Did not repeat a class. Didn't take a year off to nurse a dying parent. Didn't fall pregnant. Didn't surrender to other vicissitudes of life that tend to swallow, siphon and destroy the precious young lives of teenagers. Especially those of teenage girls.

No, they could not be baby-sitters! No parent in their right mind, would trust their little one with such careless and irresponsible girls!

The one holding the baby had a very flat tummy. It was obvious that it's the other girl that had recently given birth. Her tummy still had the shape of a pregnant woman. She was probably the mother of the tiny baby. I'd absentmindedly observed her gait. She was walking very slowly, as if the earth beneath her feet was fragile. With every step she took, she grimaced. I knew that dashing across the road had definitely not been fun for her.

I was talking from experience. I've been to the maternity ward to give birth. The first few days and weeks aren't meant to be remembered with glee, and added to the list of joys that motherhood brings. It feels like body parts have been pulled apart and then panel beaten.

The young teenage mother was struggling to put on a show of reasonable wellness, though. But the pain denied her this dignified passage in a crowd of strangers.

I wondered if she had had a caesarean section. I thought it was also likely that she had sustained a bad tear as she made that final push and delivered the baby to the world. She was just a baby herself, I reasoned. Every part of her anatomy and physiology had yet to fully mature. And there, she'd busted it, unfortunately. How does a puppy become a mother, and give birth to other puppies?

My own experiences in the labour ward continued to come fast and furious. I was surprised at the sharpness of my memory, because the last person I'd had to push out was now thirty years old. He was a ripe old man ready to have a wife to do the pushing of their own baby they'd make together. Cycles of life!

The girls had begun to slow their steps as they approached the scene of the accident. They gave me stealthy looks. I suppose they'd become aware of my concentration on them. As they came closer they became even more uncomfortable with the way I stared at them. If only they knew what I was occupied with mentally, as regards their careless selves. But my eyes told a clear story of total disapproval. I hoped that they could read "flabbergasted" in large print, spread out from one end of my sweaty forehead to another. They should have suspected of course that here was one more mama who strongly disapproved of children giving birth to other children. Let alone carelessly and irresponsibly bring their children up.

I could not see the baby's face. I wondered how it was supposed to be breathing in and out! Suffocating in the blanket was a grim possibility. This living and fighting to stay alive was still so new to him or her. I didn't trust these girls with more sense of judgment than that of a deranged bat. Slight panic rose up my spine. I imagined these unschooled arms failing to feel and distinguish between the blanket and the tiny baby wrapped in it, the precious contents of the bundle slipping unnoticed, and landing on the hard tarmac, with the splash of a soft rotten orange falling from the tree, its insides forming an untidy patch.

By this time the man had been up for some time, but he was still staggering. Although the paramedics held him by the shoulders, his head continued to lean forward and downwards. He was struggling to control the saliva that oozed out of his mouth, from time to time.

I was watching the two girls when they froze and made a dead stop. It was clear they now recognized the man who was struggling to stand erect, even with the help of the strong and healthy paramedics.

This sudden stop by the girls made me pay a little more attention to the object of the girls' concentration now, the man who'd just escaped a fatal accident. He was of very small built. He looked drawn and haggard. His lips were parched. That he was drunk didn't help give him a more decent demeanor. But here he was. A survivor! Thank God, he'd lived.

I hoped he'd have many more years to repeatedly tell the tale. Maybe better still, become an effective ambassador for our struggling, "Arrive Alive" Campaign here in Bonzotown. He'd have to emphasize the point that the campaign includes both careless drivers *and* careless pedestrians! The statistics never differentiate. It's all unfortunate loss of lives on our country's roads.

"It's him!" I heard the mother of the baby say. The girls nudged each other. Shock began to cover their faces. They still wanted to make sure, as I watched them scrutinize the man, up and down.

The man was probably in his mid-twenties. No, probably eighteen or seventeen. Intoxicating drink ages one prematurely. His lunch box of rice and fried cabbage was scattered on the road. The cabbage fumes had long generously reached as many nostrils as possible. So, we'd all virtually shared what would have been his lunch. He didn't seem to remember he had a lunch box on him, though, after he was hit by the car.

Most probably he was still too dazed and disoriented to remember all of the nitty-gritty about his life. Who he was. What he had on him. Where he was from. Where he was going when he jaywalked in a drunken state and nearly met his Maker before the heaven-scheduled time. Except, we all knew by now, what had been on his mind. His baby! How upset he was. All he knew instantaneously was his baby that he wanted back. It seemed this is all the memory part of his brain had space for then. His baby. Some-one had his baby. Who was it? Why?

"Where is your baby?"

"I want my baby."

"What happened to your baby?"

"I want my baby."

This had become a seesaw. Back and forth, between the paramedics and the man they'd just saved.

It seemed the girls were still contemplating what to do next as soon as they recognized the drunken man. I surmised that the three of them had something to do with one another. The girls clearly knew him. I began to toy with the idea that they all probably had left home, different homes maybe, to get to one destination in the vicinity of where they were now. The three weren't keeping the same appointment. This was clear from the way the girls furtively eyed the young man.

This road they'd crossed so dangerously wasn't a rendezvous for this threesome. Yet they'd all crossed it around the same time! The man was pining for his baby. The girls had a baby with them. Was this the baby the girls nearly got killed while jaywalking? Was the jaywalking a calculated and deliberate attempt at ending their lives, all three of them, including the man who was actually hit by the car earlier on? No, not the man. He wanted to live! He wanted his baby alive.

As I tried to construct the story of these three, it seemed the young man had an idea that it would be hereabouts that he could find and hopefully retrieve his baby, and maybe take the live bundle home with him. Maybe his destination was this vicinity. Maybe the girls' destination as well?

The interest and curiosity on the accident scene was beginning to wane with some of the onlookers standing by. The crowd was becoming thinner as people shook their minds, remembered where they were, where they were going, and then actually proceeded on their respective journeys.

The man had lived after all. He had been carried back to life by the silent prayers and well wishes of all the bystanders. He had lost consciousness for a good while on impact. But luckily he was one of those who would live to tell the tale that he emerged unscathed, except for the bruises on his forehead, arms and legs. Even those had hardly drawn much blood. Lucky fish!

"Is this the baby you are crying about so much?" The paramedics had now spotted the two young ladies carrying a baby. I could tell for the paramedic asking the question, that this was just a rhetorical question to while away the time, as they waited for the man to sober up a bit more, before they left him to proceed on his journey as well.

He wasn't fully alert, fully present, to draw out of him more about the baby story. However, instead of keeping his head bent and repeating, "I want my baby," the man actually looked up, when the paramedics drew his attention to the baby in a white baby blanket.

I'll not forget any time soon, what I saw then. "Yes," his limp forefinger was out pointing at the two girls and the baby, "This is my baby! She wants to kill my baby! Please stop her, please!" A long thick vein went down the middle of his forehead. He tried to take a few steps to lunge at the girls and grab the baby, but he was not stable enough to coordinate and summon all the parts to institute that action.

The paramedics caught him just in time before he landed on the ground. "I want my baby! I want my baby!" I have never heard a man wail like that before. Tears, mucus and saliva all competed to cover his face in a sorry slime, now that the baby he so agonized about was within reach.

"Oh, mother of this baby! Where's your beautiful kind heart?" This was my silent plea. Little baby, how unfair to be a witness to a war with you as the weapon of war. Just a few days old on planet earth. You did not ask to be conceived. Neither did you ask to be born to subconsciously witness this sad tug of war around your innocent soul.

What a sad point of reference to the rest of your life! Whatever is left of it? Indeed, who knew what cards destiny was shuffling in the life of this baby? I could not help these sad thoughts. There was no telepathy between my thoughts and those of the two girls, however.

Strange enough, the girls simply stood there, their teenage minds apparently swirling in a new pool of confusion and indecision. But there was, it appeared, an element of cold, schooled and seasoned defiance, as the girls watched the man pointing at them, and making desperate attempts to have his baby in his arms again.

The girls' faces wore this mixture of a cruel sneer and revenge, as they watched the man. Their hearts seemed to have long stiffened like a rod. Such young girls. Hardened by life? Already? Not that I trusted their inexperienced arms with this baby.

"Here, give the baby to me before he does something stupid." The girl I assumed was the mother reached out to take the baby from her friend's arms. She seemed to trust her capabilities at protecting her baby more than her physical condition allowed. Motherly instinct, I suppose. The other girl ignored the command from the mother and continued to hold the baby.

One traffic officer, among the three who were in charge of controlling the crowd, urged the teenage girls to come closer to the wailing man. The traffic officer had picked up something in this exchange. He had now put on his cloak as a detective, I observed.

It was clear there was more to investigate among these three. Four, with the baby. There was more to this 'coincidence' than met the eye, I thought, as I continued to wonder and try like a journalist, to piece together a likely story. Maybe a case of love gone painfully wrong.

The girls tried to resist. But the traffic inspector's professional training was plain to see. Without having to try hard, or even raise his voice and create an ugly scene, he made the girls take the few necessary steps for all parties to come closer. The baby began to cry.

"Do you know these girls and this baby?"

"She wants to sell my baby! She wants to sell my baby! I want my baby."

"What's the story, girls? Is he the father of this baby?"

"What the hell! Feed the baby, child." The baby was crying uncontrollably now.

"He doesn't take breast milk," the mother of the baby responded, looking at me like I'm mad to have instructed her on what to do with *her* baby. Worse still, drawing more of the unwanted onlookers' attention on her.

"Give him the bottle then, for God sake," I yelled back. A small bottle filled with a liquid that looked like water came out of the backpack which had school subjects written in large blue and red letters all over one side. Then after a bit of fumbling and groping another small bottle came out of this school bag. Its contents looked like black tea.

These young ladies had nothing else on them for the baby. I saw no bigger baby bag for diapers and change of clothing. I couldn't believe my eyes. The other girl absentmindedly swayed a bit. No doubt, this was a half-hearted, absentminded and reluctant attempt to keep the baby quiet. The small baby bottle of what looked like tea, was in the hands of the mother. The baby hadn't even taken one sip.

The girls' full attention was on the young man. This is where they devoted their gaze. Their eyes were concentrating on him, like those of a boxer in the ring, unblinkingly sizing up his opponent, figuring out the opponent's possible next move, and how to respond. The girls stood there firmly balanced, with legs apart, as if ready to engage in a warfare, if the man started one. Never mind that there was the traffic officer who was closely monitoring their every move.

"Mazipho, I told you where I'm taking the baby. Didn't I? I want to be free. I want to go back to school. I want to start over. I want to be somebody in life."

"I want my baby back, Bavumile!" The man's voice was lower now. "This boy is a Mhawu, through and through. I told you that." The young man's head was strong again. He was more balanced on his feet and more coherent in his speech. "Call my grandmother here, and at first sight she'll declare this is a Mhawu. I told you that. Didn't I?"

"After denying that this is your flesh and blood? Right? After dragging my name in the mud of the entire squatter camp, labelling me a slut, a whore who doesn't even know who of the several men I slept with, was the father of this poor baby?"

"Please, Bavumile, please, give me back my baby. How else do you want me to beg you? What more should I say to you to drum into your head that I want my baby back." His hands were outstretched, ready to receive the living bundle. A source of joy to some. But to this couple, a source of contestation. And to the teenage girls, apparently an inconvenience about to be a good riddance.

"Poor baby," I muttered to myself.

"I'll bring him up myself. This is my flesh and blood, my first born son, the one to carry the family name. Look,

I nearly died just now for him, and because of him." The young man appreciated that he was alive. And he wanted to carry on living with his baby. How moving!

"Does the baby have a name?" The traffic officer asked.

"Melikhaya," the father responded.

"What? Anyway, no point in giving him a name. Others will. I don't want to be tortured by the memory of a baby with a name till my dying day, Mazipho." I heard pain in the young mother's voice. Her private thoughts were out in the open now. The mother of the baby and the question of naming seemed to cut her soul in half.

She was trying hard to avoid any bonding with her baby, because she couldn't handle breaking that bond. Is this why she didn't even try breastfeeding the baby? Fear of bonding? And why would it haunt her so much? My heart was pumping furiously, as I thought, "What mother speaks like this on God's earth?"

"It's Melikhaya! This is his name! Melikhaya Mhawu!" The man's authority was returning. Maybe too little, too late. "Give my son back to me, you evil woman. You are cruel to do this. No motherly feelings in you, whatsoever! *Amantombazana*? [Girls?] *Awasafani!* [How they've changed!]"

I noticed that being branded a cruel woman by the father, weakened the mother of the baby. I could see she was trying to be strong. But tears defied her efforts. They came tumbling down. She allowed them a free generous flow, as her attempts at putting on a strong face failed as well.

The paramedics and the last of the state vehicles were parked outside the yellow line by now. The girls and the man were assembled there. The few of us still there had followed slowly at a decent distance. The mother of the baby was beginning to stumble. Anytime her legs would give in, I noticed and got closer.

"She needs to sit down. She's very weak, it appears, sir," I told the traffic officer. "Someone must also please examine this baby. I'm worried about him or her. How does a newly-born baby survive on just water? I don't even want to talk about the strange liquid that looks like tea! This is insane, girls."

"It's a baby boy, according to the father." The traffic officer quickly reminded me. As if the matter of gender was of paramount importance. As if he was happy that one more male had arrived to even out the number of males and females in our country. Females were still tipping the scales at 54%, according to statistics.

"I don't have breast milk."

"What?" I just gasped. "Did you try to express milk? Did you apply a hot cloth on your breasts and nipples to soften them? Did you try all that? Who do you live with? Where's your mother?" I knew I was deeply involving myself in a matter that had nothing to do with me, except that I was a human being and a mother. By the time I asked the last of those questions I'd realized I was just talking to myself. The young mother wouldn't be bothered by my concern or nosy questions.

The father kept following with his eyes what was going on. It seemed to me he was relying on the paramedics, traffic police and the crowd to help change the mind of the baby's mother. With cups of coffee volunteered from a flask of a bystander, the liquor seemed to evaporate even quicker by this time.

Time passed and the baby hadn't sucked on any bottle. He seemed too weak for any of this. I worried the baby had stopped crying, not because the swaying had shushed him, but because he was weak and possibly dehydrated. God forbid he was on his deathbed right in the presence of the woman who had brought him here.

Endless visits to gynaecologists. Sperm banks. Ovary donors. Test tube babies. Surrogate mothers. Prayers. I shook my head as I recalled some stories about the pain of yearning for a baby, and the inability to conceive.

One of the paramedics began to take a closer look at the baby boy's little body, after pleading with the teenage girls to be allowed just to take a look. The paramedic gingerly parted the blanket and slowly examined the baby with his eyes, while the girl held him. The girl holding the baby wouldn't let it go.

"When did you give birth to this baby? Where did you give birth? Who cut the umbilical cord? Has he had any milk since birth? Look, Ike. Just look. Oh! My God." The paramedic shook his head.

The next time I looked, Bavumile had her head bowed. The sorry condition of her baby embarrassed her. She knew what she had done was wrong. But this was still her baby and bonding with him was inevitable. Even animals bond with their young ones. For some reason, she had decided to act against Mother Nature.

Then she looked up. "Mazipho, how are you going to look after the baby? You couldn't even maintain me while I was pregnant."

"His name is Melikhaya Mhawu!"

"The school feeding scheme came to my rescue. Look how tiny this baby is. I never had decent nourishing food. Now, how are you going to change this?"

"Let's go, Bavumile. Let's go. I see you want to change your mind now. You brought me here to make sure you didn't. No-one will ever know from now on that this is a Mhawu baby. Come on, let's go. Don't let this rascal change your mind."

Bavumile's friend wanted to complete the agreed upon task. She turned to address the boy's father, "As for you, Mazipho, so-called father of Melikhaya! You can always make more babies with other stupid girls. But your life and connection with Bavumile and this baby is over. Do you hear me?"

"Don't be a fool, *wena* [you]! Giving your baby to that scoundrel? Men are dogs. He made you pregnant and denied he was the father. Now he throws himself onto oncoming traffic, hoping to die, shirking his responsibility one more time."

The man turned as we all did, to look at the woman who was ranting. The stares urged her on. "Then when you don't die, God sending you back to face your sins, you pretend to want this baby. My young sister, don't be a stupid idiot. Don't give him that baby. Let him suffer for the rest of his days for what he has done to you." Then she shouted even louder as she continued to lecture Bavumile.

"You should have done what I usually do. Abort them. Eat his money and abort this thing. Don't feel guilty about it, honestly. Let the holy ones condemn us till kingdom come. Me. I don't care. Simple as that. Come to me next time. I'll teach you how to survive as a young girl on these mean streets and mean people. This is Bonzotown! Live smart my sista!"

The woman's middle finger was raised and moving like the flat head of a cobra, ready to attack. I thought to myself, "Honestly now, who needed this very unhelpful foul-mouthed contribution?"

As I watched the woman talk in such a misleading manner, my usual habit kicked in. Call it passion, pastime or occupation. Studying the lives of girls. Except this one was a much older girl.

Instantly I knew she needed rehab and a health farm. I noticed how her lips, her mouth and maybe her entire gut seemed to have been badly corroded by who knows what, in her travels as a female. The world of hard knocks had torn her life into shreds. Some were visible. Others were not.

I wouldn't go near her as a man in search of love. I thought of mothers and their beloved sons. I said a little prayer. A lamentation came up. It appeared to have some potential. Might it grow up to be a poem? Was my writer's block receding?

> *Oh! How we carry our sons for nine*
> *months, bring them here; with love*
> *raise them. Then in moments of desire*
> *their thinking faculties retire*
> *level-headedness expires*
> *as mind shuts down*
> *they let us down*

I could say the same about our daughters. For this teenage mother was someone's daughter. She too had been carried in a womb for nine months. That was certain.

As for the woman dishing out such unhelpful advice! How had she been brought up? How had she been let down by her parent(s)? Or how had she let herself down? Only she could tell her story of fault and folly. One thing certain was that life had run her aground, and thoroughly hardened her.

Her other name could easily have been Helter-Skelter. Things seemed so helter-skelter about her. My heart bled for her. I prayed that the young mother who wanted to go back to school knew not to heed any advice from Helter-Skelter. The young mother had said she wanted to be free. I hoped her idea of freedom was more responsible than that of Helter-Skelter.

"What are you still waiting for, Bavumile? Let's go, please." This was the other girl expressing an impatience when only patience and reason would save the characters in this reluctant drama.

Bavumile took a few slow steps towards the father of their baby son. Her friend removed the blanket from the baby's face and showed it to the father. Bavumile's head and body were shaking visibly as she began to address the father of the baby boy, "Here, take the last look. Notice the birth mark on the tip of his nose. If it doesn't disappear, that's how you'll identify him. This will be many years later, when this boy's search for his biological father is over. And with some luck and hard work, you two meet for the first time after today."

The father looked at his baby from that calculated distance. I noticed that Bavumile had made sure he remained near enough to view, but distant enough not to lunge forward and try to grab the baby. The boy's father's condition wasn't helping either, although it had improved significantly by this time. Any strong man could easily have finally won the tug of war, if the baby didn't become a fatal casualty in the process.

Unlike the rough looking, street-wise abortionist, the baby's father couldn't say much else, besides pleading to be given back his son. This was one time I realized that men's lack of eloquence was their undoing.

As I replayed the whole morning drama, I genuinely felt the father's pain. Just a few people were still there. I guess the saga became more soul-sensitive as it unfolded and too much to bear for most of the people. "Isn't there anything that can be done?" I asked the paramedic that had been addressed as Ike. How could the law intervene and help the young man?

The girls left. The young father seemed sapped of all his energy to fight. I concluded that the rest would be a matter for the courts, for this gentleman known as Mazipho, the young lady, Bavumile, and Melikhaya, the baby. His young parents had made him in happier times.

I followed the girls at a safe distance. I refrained from coming closer. Bavumile's friend had an element of roughness and uncouthness about her. I hadn't brought my whistle or pepper spray with me. I was stupidly unarmed to venture close enough to these teenage girls, far from the watchful eye and secure presence of the traffic officer and paramedics. When the two girls disappeared from my view, I picked up my steps. I was concerned I'd lose them for good.

Several times I observed them stopping and then starting to walk again, towards a certain window. Passers-by stopped and watched briefly as they cast a glance at that window. They seemed to know and understand the young mother's dilemma.

I slowed down with a tint of relief when I saw the two girls coming back. They were walking painfully slowly, as if retracing their steps would lead to an undesired destination. The mother of the baby was crying now. I could tell even from a distance. The friend was trying to comfort the mother.

It appeared Bavumile wasn't done deciding what to do next. Judging by the way she had spoken to the baby's father, this day would be a point of no return, when she finally surrendered their son to whatever was on her mind, with her friend the more determined that the baby reached its final destination.

I turned back briefly to roughly calculate how far I had walked from the accident scene. Then I saw him coming towards me. He was walking slowly. He was limping. He was crying. I prayed that the girls didn't spot him until he was close enough to plead with the mother of his baby, one more time. Then he spoilt it all when he spotted them. He shouted, "Bavumile, don't do it! Please, don't do it!" It was not intentional, I thought. He was too distraught and in too much pain to plot and execute smart tactics.

The girls turned back and hastened to their destination. I sensed that their resolve had picked up strength, courage and speed, as the father of the boy followed and pleaded. The friend gave back the baby to the mother, as if to say, "It must be your own hands that do it." Then I heard an even louder cry. "I say, you'll regret this for the rest of your life, Bavumile. This is our son. Don't do it!" I prayed that the father's appeal to Bavumile's conscience and good heart would be persuasive enough to make a dent, in favour of father and son.

Unfortunately, those desperate words of pleas and threats propelled Bavumile forward, even as she also continued to sob uncontrollably. It was apparent that Melikhaya's mother could not change her mind. Had she brought the friend along to police her resolve? So that Bavumile wouldn't cave in? Motherly instinct is strong. I'm a mother. I was almost certain the story I'm narrating here would be different, if the friend hadn't come along to harden the soft place that comes with becoming a mother. But it was at Bavumile's plea that the friend came.

The teenage mother's cry was hardly audible as the two young ladies neared the destination. It was her whole body that cried the loudest. I imagined Bavumile pleading with her resolve that it shouldn't and indeed couldn't let her down at the crucial moment. "It's now or never. Come what may." I imagined this was her mantra during the final moments. Just a few more short steps would seal the demise of this threesome.

I turned to see how far the father was from this drama, the last act of the last scene, it appeared, if destiny is dead. He was walking slowly. Had he given up, anticipating the inevitable? The teenage mother seemed to hesitate again. She was holding tightly onto the baby now. But the sight of her boyfriend urged her on, to do the damnable.

She had her head turned, so I couldn't see her face. The mother of the baby lifted the flap of the large window. I guessed her eyes were also closed as she slid the white bundle carefully onto something. The flap closed automatically, when the deed was done. Literally an open and shut case for Melikhaya. His point of no return.

Bavumile's friend? How was she feeling? Was this the moment to jump up and down, mission accomplished? She had seemed a strong champion of this decision. I saw her turn away from the window and cover her face with both hands. The friends found each other's hands and walked away. Gentle sobs like a soft drizzle accompanied every step they took. They did not look back. I imagined that the father's words must have been weighing heavily on Bavumile's conscience. Their eyes dared not meet after this.

I continued to walk, until I reached the window. It's strange that I had not noticed it before. It took me a while to figure out the mission of this house, the service it offered. I couldn't help concluding that it was a very well-thought out convenience for women like Bavumile, once they'd made the final decision, to give up the baby.

The woman did not have to knock on the front or back door of this house, with the live bundle in her arms. She did not have to show her face to anyone at this house. She did not have to tell any story or explain anything to staff here. The woman did not have to convince anyone that she felt this was the right decision for her at that particular time.

Neither did the woman have to endure a long lecture from a nurse, a priest or social worker, trying to convince her to go back to wherever she'd come from with the baby, and rethink her decision and repercussions thereof. No one would force the woman to embark on a guilt trip, except at the will or demand of her own conscience.

When the mother of the baby reached the already opened window, she simply lifted the flap and lay her live bundle there. I imagined there was a receiver for the baby. Maybe a cot bed. Maybe a basket like the one Pharaoh's daughter found Moses in, along the River Nile, in Egypt. The flap immediately closed. The woman turned her back and walked away for good, from her baby.

I forced my mind to imagine a baby older than our newly-born Melikhaya here, going through this dumping session. A baby old enough to recognize the mother's voice, the feel of her body, her arms, and her hands. I imagined the heart-tearing baby's cry as the woman severed the natural bond between mother and child. How could the mother ever wipe off the memory of that last knowing cry from her baby?

I sat down on the pavement. I was weakened by what I'd seen. The brutally painful last scene of the very last scene. How I hoped it wasn't. My head was bowed. My towel was damp. Tears. I couldn't stop them. Oh, what I'd witnessed on what I assumed to be my routine one hour walk, on a familiar stretch in Bonzotown!

Just then, a hand gingerly found the nape of my neck and rubbed it gently. Who was this? I slowly looked up, a bit embarrassed. It was the traffic inspector who had held the two girls hands and brought them to the father of the Mhawu boy. Here he was now, holding the hand of the boy's father.

Mazipho wasn't crying loudly now. But the tears kept coming. He was crying from the more silent yet so unmistaken deepest depths of his heart and soul. How would anyone begin to console him?

The white bundle? "I eat their money and abort the thing..." That could have been the apple of the parents' eyes. That could have been a bouncing baby, gurgling and smiling, as mother and son continued to bond, with breast milk as a conduit. That could have been a happy healthy toddler the father loved to bath, play with and kiss his soft cheeks good night, as he tucked him into bed.

That could have been the parents' pride and joy, as Melikhaya Mhawu's name was called to walk on stage and receive his certificate for this university diploma and that degree. That could have been the young man from a warm loving home of his biological parents who would find love at the right time, and weep tears of joy as the blushing bride walked down the aisle on the arm of her father, for bride and groom to say, "I do". And the young couple would soon baptize Melikhaya's parents, Bavumile and Mazipho, with the new precious names of grandmother and grandfather.

Melikhaya means representative of the family, the clan. How ridiculous a name for one Melikhaya Mhawu, though! That identity lasted as long as the drama. Beyond the window, Melikhaya was going to be Baby X, except in the heart of his father, and when guilt conscience visited the mother.

My mind galloped into the future. What would Bavumile say to her new boyfriend who wanted to marry her and start a family?

"This flat tummy once carried a baby for nine months."

"Really? Tell me more."

Maybe that's when and where the promise of a life partner would end. I also imagined another scenario.

"I was a teenager. I shouldn't have given away the baby. Not a single day ends without Melikhaya passing through my mind."

"Thanks for telling me the truth." He takes her hand and locks it in two of his. He calls her name, "Bavumile," and patiently waits for her to compose herself and lift up her face, buried in her chest. Then he looks deep into her red eyes and assures her, "Vumi, my love, I love you more than all the mistakes you've made, and will still make." She responds in a quiet sob, I imagine.

"Maybe we'll meet Melikhaya and Mazipho, one day, and invite them to be a part our family. I believe in destiny, Vumi. No, destiny never dies." He kisses her softly on the cheek.

Feeling safe and secure in his loving arms, Vumi sleeps like a baby that night.

"I'm sorry you had to witness something as painful as this." The traffic officer apologized on behalf of fate. I simply nodded, unable to speak. "I'm taking this young man to a social worker close by. If we are lucky, we'll find the girls and try to persuade the young mother as well to join us. He knows her identity number. I believe some good can still come of this. This is not the end of this tragedy. My car is parked across the street. Are you going to be alright? I could arrange for a colleague to give you a ride back to wherever you came from, while we try to locate the girls."

I thanked the traffic officer for his kindness to rescue the devastated young father from being devoured and destroyed by his own pain. "The girls are just as broken. Deep inside. This much I can tell you, Officer. The last few minutes of giving up the baby were not easy. I'm a mother. I felt the severe agony of breaking such natural ties. This pain will live with me until I die."

"Maybe you also need help. You are visibly shaken. I can see that." The officer's kind insistence was gratifying.

"No. I don't need help. Any possibility of a recourse? Any window of an opportunity? This has been so heart-crunching! I tell you, Officer." My voice was breaking. I composed myself and assured him, "I'm old enough to contain the pain of this experience. Worse things have happened to me in my 60 years of living on this planet."

"Wow! You look very young for 60!"

"Thank you," I acknowledged the compliment. I could not think of anything else nice to say in return. The moment was awkward. The words came later, "You are very kind." The two men were no longer within earshot. I was in awe of human nature that still finds such light-hearted asides in the midst of tragedies like the one we had witnessed that morning. God's way to help us survive, I suppose.

Even the father of the little boy had raised his eyebrows and given me a good look up and down, when he learnt I'm 60. I marvelled that even he, still had a positive reserve left within him to tap into, as he silently complimented me on my youthfulness.

Wasn't his beloved Melikhaya now surely a nameless abandoned baby? A sad moment subconscious mind would surely store. This is how his new life would begin. He'd have a new file. A new name would be on it. The staff was registering him. They would soon give him a bath and feed him.

The comment that I look younger than my age, carried me all the way home. For the first time it dawned on me what the folks of Tuna Bay were about, with the town's proposal for nude bathing. I needed to write an article, open up about the mockery I'd made of them, and apologize.

Wasn't I one old timer now, bashfully yet a bit coquettishly basking in the comment that I looked youthful for my age? Wasn't I going to hang onto that compliment for a pretty long while? I concluded that John Keats, the great English Romantic poet, must have spent time within the vaults deep down in the basement that holds the cardinal points of our lives, the deeper secrets of life. And he had been wizened enough to write:

> *A thing of beauty is a joy forever:*
> *Its loveliness increases; it will never*
> *Pass into nothingness;*

How could I not forever be grateful to the poet, for these perfect lines? And, coming to think of it, isn't life itself *"a thing of beauty, that is a joy forever?"* Handled wisely, that is. Warts and all, though?

But, wasn't it easy for me to add warts and all, speaking from where I was sitting, as one somewhat lucky soul? Here I was lumping all of life vicissitudes as warts. What warts did I have in mind?

I thought about the girls, especially Bavumile, the baby boy, Melikhaya, and his dad, Mazipho Mhawu. They parted before Melikhaya could call him "dada".

There were unsightly warts spoiling the precious skin of the soul there. Loss of original identity and organic community for the poor little boy. An orphanage, for the boy? Most likely. Adoption? Who knew? Thus began a void Melikhaya could never explain. The void would develop into a compulsion he couldn't shake off. An endless search for something he couldn't even articulate in words. A life that felt forever half-full, no matter how full it seemed, in the eyes of the world.

Perpetual guilt, sadness and emptiness for Mazipho and Bavumile. They could never shed the label that they were parents of Melikhaya. Is it not possible to live with warts, enjoy other smooth parts of our soul skins, as life moves on?

What a jolting separation of what could have been in different circumstances, a lovely beginning of a nuclear family, for these three.

A childhood memory returned, when we travelled to and from primary school by train. The unnerving sound of the coach as it was separated from the rest of the goods train, played loudly in my ear. It violently shook my mind.

# Gertrude and Zabalaza

It was holiday season again. I hadn't saved enough money to travel overseas this time. It was a forced choice, so to speak.  It was either I kept for another year, the car that was becoming more of a migraine headache than a convenience, and travel overseas, or I bought another car and braced myself for a miserable holiday here at home. With my mind not made up, I was feeling completely gutted. I was tired of the city, tired of malls, tired of spending exorbitant amounts of money on plane fares and holiday accommodation during the Christmas season.

For a greater part of December I was miserable, not knowing what I'd do with myself. But thank God, by the time of our Christmas party at work, I had figured out where I'd be going. My old folks! Time with them would be well-spent. And the little money I had left, after buying the car, would be enough to make the holiday with my grandparents, very special.

It was the last of several Christmas parties. My colleagues were spewing out exotic destinations: Cape Town, Margate, Umhlanga, Maputo, Nairobi, Mombasa, Victoria Falls, London, New York, Zurich, Cairo. Some would be home seeing to upgrades and renovations.

But there were plenty raised eyebrows when I told my colleagues where I'd be spending *my* holidays. Siyahamba Township in KwaZulu-Natal! Little had I known that I'd have to pull out imaginary maps, on which I'd attempt to pinpoint Siyahamba's location on planet earth. My colleagues had no clue of such a place. They ended up with some idea, albeit in the middle of nowhere.

Siyahamba Township. "Siyahamba" translates to "we are leaving" in English. In the context of residents of

Siyahamba Township, however, the meaning connoted a strong resolve. *We are leaving! We are not going to stay here!* This was the collective spirit of both anger and defiance, as my grandparents and the entire community were forcefully removed from their ancestral land. Masangweni.

This was a very old community. The first residents had settled there in the aftermath of troubles with King Shaka. But all of a sudden, picturesque and fertile Masangweni was too good a place to be owned by indigenes. They no longer deserved it.

Bulldozers arrived one day at 5 am. Belongings were piled untidily on apartheid government trucks. Homes were raised to the ground. Trees that had been very generous with fruit were felled and uprooted. Masangweni became a "white area." Whatever that means in Africa! It remained a "white area". Masangweni was given a new name. Mazangue. It seems the new inhabitants lacked enough imagination to think of a totally different name. But the people of Masangweni vowed that they'd leave the new place the apartheid government relocated them to. They'd find a way to return to their ancestral land, no matter what it would take.

But alas, decades later, they still spoke fondly of Masangweni. But pride of belonging dried up and dwindled mid-sentence. Nothing of their vows to leave and return to Masangweni had materialized. The pain of referring to their ancestral land as *emanxiweni*, the old plots where homes once stood, is always a sad reminder of great loss. Natural wealth and beauty, and most importantly graves of loved ones. How every year, families wished for an opportunity to visit the graves, just to see if their loved ones are still safe from the elements.

But the same graves of the silent dead became and remained a monument of defiance. They could suffer the indignity of being desecrated. This was apartheid South Africa! But move them? Who would dare? Thus the graves became a perpetual reminder and eyesore to the new occupants. The dead spoke even in their cold silence, "Who are *you*? Where are *our* families? *We* are the owners of Masangweni!"

It was a long drive in my 'new' used car. I'd imagined it would be a peaceful drive that early in the morning. But motorists are motorists, especially in South Africa, during any holiday season. There were more insane, impatient, selfish and downright rude ones on this trip. But thank God, I finally entered the precinct of Siyahamba Township, without a nasty incident or accident.

I instantly noticed that the happy ambience created by the glitz, glitter and music of big cities was missing in the little shops at Siyahamba Township. Here and there were old electioneering posters. Their bright colours had now faded from being tortured and then despised by the elements, as seasons changed. I wondered if the promises from those who had canvassed for votes were delivered to those who'd done their expected share with an X on the ballot box. I hoped it was fair trade.

But despair was written in large print in some sections of the Township. Suffering and want were unashamedly paraded, right at the front gates that hung literally by a few rusty wires, on rusty rickety frames.

I recalled my days of childhood and youth. High school days. I remembered the boys that were identified and deemed streetwise by some male teachers at my high school. They trusted these boys to slip out during lunch time to buy them a nip of brandy or vodka at one of the closest shebeens, the Township drinking holes, now known as taverns. I thought about lots of teachers that were known alcoholics those days. Many are long deceased.

What was the cause? I've at times wondered if it wasn't the frustration that came with the forcefully imposed glass ceiling of apartheid. Canned intelligent minds. The teachers looked deep into the bottle in an effort to both manage and release the pain of humiliating oppression. Their dreams and aspirations were contained, if not squashed with the heavy boot of apartheid on their necks.

I noticed, as I kept getting lost on the streets of Siyahamba, that those with less means had a stubbornly tenacious sense of dignity. Their determination to defy odds was strong. The spirit of the liberation struggle still moved them, I thought. The 'I deserve better' mantra couldn't be missed. It was everywhere. Bold signs of it were displayed on deferred dreams. I could tell from some of the homes I passed that plans to extend the four-roomed Township house had only been suspended, certainly not aborted.

Additional rooms and garages. Some were up to window level. Others were still at the foundation. I passed several small mounds of broken bricks and building blocks. They were competing for the limelight with tufts of grass growing in the middle of what would perhaps one day be an extra bedroom, maybe for teenage sons.

Life continued. Being defiantly happy, regardless of unfortunate circumstances, is a choice. Not easy. But a choice, all the same. Boys in their very early teens were playing soccer on the streets of Siyahamba. I had to hoot several times for them to notice me, hold the ball, and let me drive through. Then I stopped to ask for directions to Sondombili Street. Everybody was eager to help. They knew the street well and the home of the retired teachers who lived there. I concluded that their older siblings must have all passed through the hands of my grandparents.

I passed a four-year old proudly sweeping the front of their yard with the short traditional grass broom, *umshayelo*. Her grandmother seemed to be supervising the little arm and hand, guiding the young lady. I waved at both ladies. They waved back.

There were the rowdy groups I passed in the vicinity of the beer hall. Some were peeing on the street. Others were beginning the journey somewhere else. I watched them stagger several times. The shots of whatever liquid they'd enjoyed, had clearly shot past their capacity to hold down intoxicating liquor.

The mechanics business seemed the most popular at Siyahamba Township. Almost on every street I passed, there was a man or men in overalls, bent over the engine of some car. But some cars were obviously a lost dream. Little children were in and out, playing in them. Other vehicles had become fowl runs. Different colors of old and fresh chicken poop made unique works of art on the bodies of these once automobiles.

I also passed churches where women were assembled for prayer and fellowship. They were all dressed in their denomination uniforms. Undoubtedly, their collective faith was strong. They still believed in the God of unbroken promises. The God who delivers on promises. I thought to myself, as I caught whiffs of their singing, these women and congregations still hold the candle of hope for Siyahamba Township residents, although their collective lives were compromised by circumstances of both oppression and freedom.

My depressing thoughts were beginning to get the better of me, when I finally found myself in an area that seemed familiar. Here was my grandparents' Lutheran Church. It needed some paint work.

Here was the higher primary school granddad last headed before he retired. It looked forlorn without the usual inhabitants. The lawn was still struggling to form a nice carpet. Tufts of long grass were beginning to pass for a hedge as they climbed enthusiastically on each side of the tall net wire fence that defined the school boundaries.

I remembered that when our primary school reopened, we had to use sickles to cut the grass. I still have a scar on the front of my leg from a sickle. The pointed end got me instead of the grass I was cutting.

But I was getting closer and closer now to my destination, I realized. I already had figured out where grandmother's lower primary school was located, also the last one she headed, before she retired.

My grandparents' retirement farewell functions. The memory of this time returned. The staff at each school had extended the invitation to the spouse of the retiring principal. Grandma had told me that initially they'd both been reluctant to honor the invitations. They were wary of intruding into each other's work spaces and interfere with the rapport each spouse had developed with their staff, over time. But they changed their minds, and joined in the festivities for each other. How well this worked out.

My grandparents marvelled at how big these farewell functions turned out to be. School Inspectors and even the Circuit Inspector made time to honour the invitations from staff. Praises and gratitude paid to each one of them, taught my grandparents something more about each other. Testimonies reflective of their contributions within the school and in the community humbled my grandparents. "We were just ordinary teachers, my grandchild. We'd never thought we were doing anything out of the ordinary," I remembered grandmother telling me, obviously still in disbelief.

Then I remembered boxes and boxes of gifts granddad and grandma received during their respective farewell parties. Different varieties of cakes of toilet soap. Cups and saucers. Different shapes and sizes of drinking glasses. Serving trays. Doilies. Table cloths. Full aprons for grandmother, the ones in-style that particular year, with fancy frills, lace and zigzag decorations. Wood carvings of animals. Flower vases. Tea and dinner sets from staff for grandma. An expensive briefcase for granddad, "when he collects his pension," the vice principal had said as he handed the gift. And a lovely leather handbag for grandma, for the same purpose.

For parents who couldn't attend the farewell functions, gifts, big and small, sent with their children, had been quite humbling. Other parents came home to personally present their gifts. I remembered how my grandparents had been moved to tears as they showed me the gifts, and related to me the highlights of their farewell parties.

I had these thoughts seating on the passenger seat. How long they'd been kindly keeping me company, as they yap yapped nonstop! But I noticed another thought demanding my attention. I'd haul out the boxes packed with gifts from under the beds, on top of the wardrobes, and wherever else they were stored. I'd arrange them nicely in a display cabinet I'd buy my grandparents as a Christmas present. How about that?

But it was time to bid good-bye to these reflections and memories as my companion. Something better was upon me. Here I was on Sondombili Street! Finally! I could see granddad as I drove round the sharp bend. My cellphone rang. It was him. I said, with heart-felt joy and relief, "Don't waste your airtime any longer, granddad. I can see you now. The car you see approaching is mine."

As I began to slow down, there was grandpa! He was still standing straight and tall. He was dressed in a white shirt and khaki pants. His light brown cap was smartly tilted at just the right angle to give him a 'man-about-town' look. The gold watch, the most expensive retirement gift he'd received from the Inspectorate so long ago, glistened brightly in the sun. Granddad hadn't gained any weight since my last time there.

And now he had dark brown suspenders on. Did he need these? Was his body frame shrinking slightly and giving in? Or was it a fashion statement? Most probably the latter. His suspenders matched his very stylish pair of dark brown shoes. Although I don't know much about good men's shoes, they looked a designer brand. One of those designers that have been around for decades, serving men who love quality. I wondered, as my eyes did a bit of a quick study of the shoes, if he had other pairs in different colors. They were so smart!

I thought to myself how bright my grandfather would look in his Sunday white shirt and red suspenders. How this combination would complement his dark smooth skin! Red suspenders? Why not? Gone were the days of dingy grey and all sorts of neutral colors for older people.

Hell. No! This was just the time to brighten their days with some vivacious colors.

More importantly, these would help offset any regret parties that loudly played bad music, and gave old folks plenty headaches and heartaches. Bright colors would warm up their joy. Lively colours would definitely even lull to deep sleep the occasional aches and pains that my General Practitioner cousin referred to once as "regular wear and tear we can virtually do nothing about, for this age group."

While on the color discussion for older folks, I received a brainwave. I'd set up a boutique for our valuable seniors. How about that? The viability of such a venture excited me. I entertained the idea of stocking up on merchandise by internationally acclaimed designers.

But a party spoiler crept in to end my excellent vision show. The reality of costs and affordability for old folks. Most only have government pension as source of income. Where would pensioners find the money? That thought went into homework basket, though. It was too brilliant to be shelved for an indefinite later, or thrown right out as completely unfeasible.

Anyway, here was granddad. He was all smiles as he gave me a brief hug. Awkward nevertheless, for both of us. Not surprising. This hugging thing is fairly new. Some older folks are struggling to get used to it. I'm still struggling with it myself, except when it's for little kids. Our parents and grandparents brought us up on handshakes.

I still remember my grandfather's voice that day. It was loaded with loads of praises. They came tumbling all over me. How lovely and healthy I looked. What a beauty, my new car was. He was giving it a good look, both inside and out. He was admiring the brand new tyres. He loved the unusual leather cover for the steering wheel. By the time he took a pause he was almost out of breath, from lavishing his granddaughter with a rain of compliments. I couldn't doubt the welcome. It was warm like breakfast toast on a cold morning.

For a second I wondered where grandmother was, as I helped granddad move my luggage into the house. But there she was waiting for me at the front door. Her arms were already outstretched to give me a warm hug. Maybe between women hugs aren't as awkward.

My grandmother aging? Says who? She still looked the same. Grandmother was also tall, maybe just 4 inches shorter than her husband. She was of medium built with some strong facial features. Her cheek bones were pronounced. They gave her face a slim look that tapered into a sharp chin, and an overall reluctant V-shape. My grandmother wouldn't pass for pretty. Neither was she plain. Just likeable, charming, especially when she smiled. Her dimpled cheeks added an unexpected plus to her looks. If grandmother had been born a boy she would have worn well the label of 'somewhat handsome'. Besides her sharp facial features, the rest of her body features tended to be minimalist. Her legs were very well-shaped.

Grandmother's body was definitely suited for competitive sport. She excelled at basketball. She'd usually tell me this after the girls' team at the school she headed had been beaten by a visiting school. No wonder she had been a popular girl at school, with lots of friends. I always wondered what happened the next day to the teacher who coached the girls! Maybe an aside little talk from the Headmistress, about what to improve and how, so that grandmother's school won the next match.

I didn't like grandmother's new teeth, though, on this Christmas visit. Her natural set had given her a wickedly beautiful smile. It paired so well with her dimples. What happened? She'd lost all of her teeth? Gum problem? For a fleeting moment I felt sad, knowing that if I've taken after her, I'll probably end up with a similar situation as well. But all I could do was hope the disease wasn't hereditary. Mom was still fairly young. It was thus still too early to rule out that gum condition for her. It would thus be futile and stupid of me to pin any hopes on being safe.

Grandma had a beautiful head shape. While in active service as a teacher and Headmistress she had her hair braided. It lowered her age by decades. I have a mental picture of her as today's young woman. Short hair or shaven head. Nice size hoop earrings for a balanced look.

I always itched to make up her face. She had straight but faint eyebrows. They'd have come alive with an eyebrow brush or pencil.

Grandmother was very fair in complexion. As I compared my grandparents, some years back, I mischievously concluded it was perhaps her fair complexion and intelligence that had attracted granddad to her.

Grandmother's background had also given her some edge, I'd thought. She was the daughter of a priest, one that was well-known and highly respected in the Masangweni community. He had singled himself out by demonstrating the teachings of the Gospel in very practical ways, with his keen sense of tireless service to the community, seven days a week. Yes, that's right. Seven days a week.

Granddad's parents were not as well-known in the community. But they were decent citizens. Most importantly I will always admire my paternal and maternal great-grandparents for understanding the value of giving their children a good education. Both boys and girls. And here were my grandparents, truly a cut above the rest, for African people at their age, who suffered from being undermined by colonialism and apartheid.

When my luggage was neatly parked in some corner of the bedroom my old folks had prepared for me, grandfather sort of quietly retreated and allowed grandmother to take over from then, as she led me on a tour of the house. It all began with the usual first thing visitors ask for. The loo.

I'd noticed as I first entered the house that my old folks had made major changes. I thought how lovely that they were still fairly young retirees. They had many good years to enjoy their comfortable home.

"We raised the roof in the entire house and replaced the asbestos roof with tiles, Bakhona."

"This apartheid government asbestos thing, grandma? Did the regime want us all to die from cancer? Slow elimination or annihilation?"
Grandmother grunted as she continued, "We extended the outer walls all around to give each room ample space. I wasn't quite keen on this, wondering if this change would make a significant difference."

I asked, "Is it granddad who insisted."

"Yes, indeed. And he was right. For once." I smiled at the jab women like to use on men in their lives. The house was roomy. No doubt about it.

"To think that bedrooms came with no doors in those four-roomed apartheid government houses, grandma?"

"They thought we didn't need privacy, I suppose, Bakhona. We were fine to sleep like animals in sheds?"

"Imagine, grandma! Most people simply used curtains to get some privacy. We did for a long time in our house. No privacy even in the main bedroom, coming to think of it!" Grandmother nodded. I read a naughty smile on her face. My parents' bedroom with just curtains for privacy? What was on my mind?

"Whoa! Lovely bathroom, grandmother!"

"Thank you, Bakhona. There are two bathrooms now, both have baths and showers. Ours is en suite. This one is for your use as our guest. And toilets of course."

We were walking outside the house when granddad joined us. He took over, and summarized all the work that had gone into renovations.

"Replacing the small windows with bigger ones added to the breezy pleasantness of each room, Bakhona. Those small windows make the rooms very stuffy." Granddad took a deep sigh as he pointed at the veranda. "Then your grandmother and I thought after all the work in the house, adding verandas, a smaller one at the back and a bigger one on the front, would truly enhance the overall size and look of this Township dwelling. Nothing fancy, really, as you can see, my child. But it's good for us. We enjoy both sunrise and sunsets here." I could tell this had been a major decision for them. Maybe an extra, when their budget was already low.

"Wonderful work, honestly!"

"Thanks, Bakhona. So, enjoy the house," was the final word from granddad.

"Now I'm here to enjoy all of this comfort!" I said as I put my arm on grandma's shoulder.

We returned to the house through the kitchen. The wooden kitchen door in two halves had already been installed the last time I visited my grandparents. They had to get this done very quickly. A sliding lock kept the bottom half of the door always bolted, so that my grandparents could talk to people, especially vendors without having to step outside.

I remember that during the height of political violence which rose into an unbearably dangerous peak in Townships, it was safe to keep both halves of the kitchen door locked. It was not unusual during those times to find oneself indirectly involved in a conflict, as a young man jumped over the main gate into the opened upper part of the kitchen door, and dashed straight to the bedroom and hid under the house owner's bed. He desperately needed protection. An angry mob was pursuing him. His life surely at its end.

After the initial tour of the house, grandmother signaled me to join her as she sat on the bed that I'd use for the duration of my time there. It was a very comfortable double bed.

The bedroom was scantily furnished. But it was very pleasant, with lots of natural light. A small round table acted as a pedestal. It was covered with a dainty white linen cloth, embroidered on the edges, with the admirable crisp and shiny effects of starch. Grandmother was proud to admit that she had made the doilies and all the linen in the dining room and lounge.

"And all the curtains in the house, grandmother? I meant to ask if you bought them ready-made or had someone make them for you." Grandmother laughed, lazily, as she pointed her index finger to her chest. I was truly surprised. "I didn't know you sew, grandma!"

"There's probably a lot more you don't know about me, my grandchild," grandmother added as she chuckled. She was just pulling my leg.

"Mother has a sewing machine. But I don't remember her using it."

"Your mother is lazy to sew, Bakhona. I taught her the basics as she grew up. But she has money we pensioners don't, to spend buying even stuff she could easily make herself."

The purple bedside lamp on the small table and mauve bedspread matched the walls that were painted a delightful shocking pink. "Very girly," I remarked. Grandma's response embarrassed me, "Well, we like it. I hope you will learn to love it too." I was a little sad to realize she assumed I didn't quite like girly colors. So I quickly corrected that. "Guess what, grandma? I've a set of a nightie and gown to match. In dark purple."

I quickly pulled these out of my suitcase. Grandma held my sleep wear close to her face and smelled the perfume. She was miserably failing yet insisting to guess the house that made that perfume. She gave up when she was wrong even with the two Elizabeth houses she was familiar with. The "secret" perfume made it into my mental list to buy grandma as a surprise, that Christmas.

It seemed grandma just wanted us to catch up, as we lay on our backs on my bed, arms outstretched, with our feet dangling. Just the two of us girls. I got the sense that my grandmother was a bit tired, though, and could do with a little rest. Well, we'd just returned from the long tour of the no longer so typical four-roomed Township house. I also felt guilty, wondering if my grandparents had overworked themselves, as they prepared for my visit.

But our catching up was short-lived as we heard, "Gertie! Bakhona! Sorry my dears. You'll have plenty of time to catch up, girls. Now it's time for tea." So, while the girls were on a tour, granddad was busy in the kitchen, for a greater part of that time. How nice of him!

As we emerged out of the bedroom, he signaled, just like a traffic inspector, that the lounge was the place of meeting. The coffee table that had a huge vase of fresh flowers on a white fancy doily had in minutes been transformed into a delightful rendezvous for a tea extravaganza. Whole wheat scones, bran muffins, a whole chocolate cake and apple crumble to help ourselves to.

The man of the house had gone to town preparing a real treat of a tea-drinking session to remember! The tea service looked very expensive. It was so light, even a two-year old could lift a cup with just the little finger. Well, I'm exaggerating a little bit!

"Your muffins came out well, Zabalaza. But my scones are not as fresh; two days old now," grandmother praised and apologized in one sentence, as she carefully took a small bite of the bottom half of her first scone, after carefully cutting it across and loading a generous helping of grated cheddar cheese on top.

I had started with a scone as well, packing my one half with lots of cream and strawberry jam. "I warmed them up a bit, Gertie, to give them some pick me up. They are still good." Granddad remarked as he took a generous manly bite of half his whole scone without applying anything on it. "Well, as long as Bakhona likes them," he added. Grandfather was looking in my direction now, expecting a comment.

Grandmother gave me a curious look, waiting to hear my response. I had a full mouth and could only nod my comment. "I doubt Bakhona can tell the difference between a fresh scone and one that's two days old, Zaba." Grandmother wore a teaser of a smile on her face. I did not respond, because it was true that I wasn't an enthusiastic flour smith by any means, and so couldn't tell the difference. Unless the thing smells rotten or there's green mold on it.

Grandmother was putting my baking skills in the limelight, questioning them. I thought the next thing these old folks would be discussing are recipes, talking about dishes and ingredients I'd never heard of. I didn't like the idea of ending up looking like I live in dog's kernel.

So, I decided to change the topic to move the spot light away from me, "You both look very well. You've been taking very good care of yourselves and each other, I must say. Both of you in your early 70s now? Gosh! When last was I here? One year after you retired? How time flies!"

This was music in grandmother's ears. She flashed her teeth. "Thanks, my grandchild. Your granddad here must be surprised to hear that comment directed at both of us."

Then she looked into the eyes of her husband, "How often do you tease me, Zabalaza, my teeth still in the tumbler there?" I waited for granddad's response. None. Grandma continued, "Bakhona, my grandchild, picture this scenario. It's Sunday morning, to be precise. I don't know why that day and time. You can ask him. He calls me to the bathroom, so we face the large wall mirror there, together."

"Come on Gertie!" Grandma mimicked her husband, succeeding very well to portray the boisterousness in his voice. "Who has woken up older today?"

She continued, "He'll cock his balding head to the side, and turn round and round. It's early. I'm hardly awake, after watching Saturday movies on Television. My mouth is like that of a goldfish, my grandchild. I call it a youth confirmation ritual."

"Too late to call it a midlife crisis, I guess, grandmother." That comment made grandmother laugh out loud. Granddad poured out tea in all the cups, and then said, "Why don't you tell Bakhona what I do for you after that ritual?"

Grandma took her time adding milk in her tea, and then stirring in the sugar. As she lifted her cup to her mouth she teasingly winked at her husband, as if she was deliberately withholding the more juicy part of his tortuous ritual.

"Of course, dear," she said as she put her cup back on the coffee table. "I was going to get to that. Don't rush me now, Zaba." Grandmother caught her breath. Pointing at him, she proudly told me, "Then this man here, serves me breakfast in bed. Never forgets! God knows. On my honour, Bakhona, as a Girl Guide." I watched grandmother stand up at attention and then make the three-finger salute of Girl Guides.

"What, grandma? Excuse me! Not once in six months or quarterly, if you are lucky?"

"Every Sunday, Bakhona! Every single Sunday. Without fail. And it's an elaborately prepared breakfast, my child!"

"Not just maize meal porridge?" They both rolled their eyes at me and my question, as if to say, "Don't spoil this beautiful tale now with your poor imagination, child. Where did your sense of aesthetics go? You are disastrously deprived!"

"But coming to your grandmother being a perfect picture of agility, Bakhona, just watch her get up from that chair. Just observe her." Grandmother gave her husband a 'guess who's talking now' look. Granddad ignored it.

To make his point, he began to stand up, painfully slowly. "It takes her ages to negotiate with this muscle and that tendon and that bone, and that blood vessel, nerve and whatever else have you. She is begging them like Ezekiel summoned those dry bones, before she's up on her two feet. She's sighing and moaning. And so grateful to be finally upright."

"Grateful for mission finally accomplished, granddad," I added fire to the teasing party thrown for grandmother. "Bakhona, she looks pitiful." Granddad shook his head in a mock holier than thou disbelief. His eyes were beginning to fill up with tears from suppressed laughter. It was easy to tell these two had become very good bosom friends.

I wanted to come to grandma's defence by saying she had so swiftly stood up at attention as a Girl Guide just minutes before. Probably granddad would have had a counter to that one. Maybe something about the time of day and how grandma's whole body had had the opportunity to thaw the aches and pains with the heat from the sun. How her entire body was now empowered by solar energy.

Grandma watched as she was being made fun of. I could tell she was biding her time. She was looking for just the right spot to land a thorough, smartly delivered upper cut, one whose impact granddad could not reply to.

But I figured out, as one who was observing the goings on, that granddad had a sense of what would follow, and decided to beat it before his wife's missile knocked him out of his better agility claim. Indeed, he was up and busy clearing the table now.

By the time I got to the kitchen to wash the dishes, granddad was already wiping them and putting them back where they came from. The special tea set was piled up safely, all ready to take to the oak display cabinet, in the dining room. This very piece of expensive furniture made me wince when my eyes landed on it. It was standing majestically in the corner, elegantly adding class to the otherwise old but forever classy mahogany dining room suite. I was obviously too late with my plans to buy one such display cabinet for my grandparents.

I watched granddad as he swayed his body slightly to the music playing on the transistor radio placed on top of the refrigerator. The man had natural grace. If he'd been a dancer, he'd easily win accolades. I admired the verve in him. What an epitome of health and happiness. "Here is a star-studded picture of swagger," I imagined some message would read on the strip of *Big Brother Africa,* were my granddad a participant.

Old age and my granddad? No doubt, these were like water and oil. He was aging very gracefully. Was he in fact aging? Hardly! It would be decades more before granddad was really spent. I thought to myself, here is an African man, born and raised during the difficult years of overt racism and all its myriad tributaries. How remarkable that in so many ways apartheid couldn't touch him. And in the new dispensation he could still afford to offer himself and his wife a reasonably good life. Grandma also looked very well. No doubt about this, despite the teasing from her darling husband.

I attributed my grandparents' good health to a number of factors. They both never had a very difficult childhood. They lived fairly comfortable lives from an early age. They were fortunate to have parents that reasonably cushioned them from much of the stress, trauma and daily humiliation; some of which could easily and most regrettably have passed as inherent, given several centuries of strife. This is all comparatively speaking, of course, in the South African situation. My grandparents also didn't do strenuous work as adults. They were school teachers, the deceptively easy profession of "talk and chalk."

Their marriage remained stable. Their love for each other deepened. They worked on keeping it tireless and ageless. No doubt, the love had grown into a great bond of friendship, over the years. Quite a smart package of bliss. How enviable!

I wondered if I could ever pull off this love thing, find my own perfect prince charming, in a modern world now heavily complicated by a plethora of problems. Even if the whole of the world's men and women in uniform could fight the challenges, there'd be no successful defeat in sight. Love!

This reminded me of my University Professor, Kathleen Jack, who liked to make a similar comment about black men, "They grow old very gracefully, looking more dignified and handsome as they age." She knew of course. She was married to a Black man.

I remembered Professor Dave, her husband. He had a head full of black and white tightly curled short virgin hair. He was always dressed in colourful African shirts. There he'd be, seated in one of the comfortable chairs in his wife's office, reading an academic journal. His long feet were in brown leather sandals. His well-manicured fingers would usually be reaching in to the packet of dried fruit he was absentmindedly nibbling, his eyes glued on the journal article he was reading.

We'd agree with female classmates that our Professor's husband was a sumptuous jam tart, indeed. This would be over dinner in the mixed dining hall, as we eyed out boys in different departments. We'd be engaged in our favourite pastime of figuring out who had class? Who was a natty dresser? Who seemed richly endowed with brain power? Who was a gentleman? Who had great eyes? Who was well-spoken?

I remember one girl who was already dreaming about marriage. She was adamant Professor Dave was her type. I always tried to deflate her spirits, so that she stopped invoking the usual 'Oh, my God' of teenage girls: "Nombizo, that man is African American from one of those southern states of those United States of America. Far away from here. There might be a lot we don't know about him and his relationship with our Professor. We need to stop envying and gawking."

We were first year students. We had many years ahead of us, to make our individual long lists of characteristics we would love our future soul mates to have. There was no rush.

But here I was, ten years after those university days, still *dreaming* of a true soul mate! "What is the formula, my grandparents?" I wished I could ask them, so that I could also be the envy of younger women, come the right time. But my grandparents' formula for enriching long-lasting love, was right before my eyes, in large font! I only had to open my mind and my eyes.

As day one in the Township came to a close, I was very proud of myself for having decided to be with my old folks that Christmas season. Before the sun set and waved good-bye, lulled to sleep by the beginnings of what promised to be a cool night, grandmother took me on a tour of the garden.

Trees were swaying from side to side. I could hear birds chirp. Were the bird parents preparing dinners and getting to tuck their little ones in their beds in home nests on tree tops? I was in a mini park. My grandparents had done a good job of self-sculpting their yard, with smart use of every available patch in that limited space. The stone paving from the gate to the front veranda glistened as those last rays of the sun beamed on it.

Pot plants of different varieties were everywhere. Climbers were riding playfully, curling and swinging around the pillars that supported the veranda. Flowers were in bloom in all the little garden patches spread out on the yard, some on the edges of the freshly cut lawn.

"What about hydrangeas, Bakhona?"

"Of course. Yes, please, grandma. It's Christmas season anyway."

"These will make a nice full vase, for enjoyment in your bedroom, my child." She continued to cut more fresh flowers for the house.

At the back my grandparents had a small but very interesting vegetable garden. It was very well-planned, with just one long row each of a wide variety of vegetables. The patch of herbs at the corner, with its mix of scents, wafted like incense from a priest's chalice.

Just being there and admiring the good choices and careful planning in this labour of love, made me truly thankful. I'd become a careful eater over the years, and this garden had all one needed to eat healthily.

The two peach trees were laden with fruit. It was easy to tell where the long line of bottled canned peaches in the pantry came from. I'd learned of course from my grandparents that children still attempted to steal the fruit, although Rex, their dog of many years, was still a very good security guard.

To all intents and purposes, it was a very comfortable home. I said as much to my grandparents over dinner of steak, mashed potatoes, butternut, spinach and fresh fruit for dessert.

"Thank you, Bakhona," grandmother responded, "except of course, this is still Siyahamba Township! No point here in glorifying plans of apartheid architects who ruthlessly and audaciously changed the landscape of our country and lifescapes of our people in this lasting manner."

Granddad continued, "We had land aplenty, to build big homes, enjoy big yards. Not this prison of a yard. And rear livestock. That was not all. Each household had a large strip of land for maize, beans, sweet potatoes and pumpkins. You know, I will always commend our old folks for choosing to settle at Masangweni. Very beautiful and fertile land!"

In a subdued tone granddad added, "And we left the resting places of our ancestors, when we were forcibly removed. We'd have taken you there to ask them to shower you with blessings and protect you. But we are here, Bakhona."

With my hand on the side of my face, I said, "Still at Siyahamba Township, granddad!" A moment's silence passed. Granddad lightly tapped the edge of the table with his fingers for a while. His exasperation couldn't be missed.

Then grandmother laughed self-consciously and reached out to touch my hand. With glassy eyes from suppressed laughter she addressed me, "And you know, Bakhona, for a couple of years after ... What was it called by the way? The negotiated what? Yes, the negotiated settlement. Your grandfather excitedly looked forward to the announcement of major changes about these Townships. Would they be demolished? Would they be developed into big towns and cities, with all the amenities and conveniences? And run by us this time?"

"Well, it's no laughing matter, really, Gertie, I honestly thought the Townships would go. And we'd have a decent alternative to this eye sore, spread out along the length and breadth of this country. Honestly, that made every sense to me." Granddad made this point as he looked at grandma and me in turn. Of course this wasn't a laughing matter.

I jumped in and added, "Not to cut you short, granddad, I attended a conference once, about three years ago now, where the government Reconstruction and Development Houses, RDP houses for short, were condemned as an abominable insult to injury." Both my grandparents nodded in agreement. "Very true, Bakhona!" Granddad commented, as he shifted a bit in his chair.

I continued, "Someone stood up at the conference to say rumor has it that the idea of building skyward instead of the sprawling space consuming RDP houses, was squashed by those who claimed to know us best. And listen to this. It was not about saving space. Guess what their rationale was? 'Africans are scared of heights!'

And our leaders caved in. They allowed themselves to be convinced that flats going many storeys up would remain a white elephant. They chose to go along with the joke that is RDP housing. A quarter the size of the matchboxes?"

I watched both my grandparents shake their heads simultaneously. As I continued with this incredulous piece of information, and clear let down by our own folks, I angrily told my grandparents that I was shocked, and immediately wrote a little note to the person who was seated next to me: *And those who consented to this untruth, our own people, they grew up climbing trees.* The guy responded: *Exactly. For both food and fun. How ridiculous for them to sell out like this!*

Grandmother added, "Bakhona, those were the beginning of the short-changing games that have become our hallmark in this negotiated settlement." I noted that grandmother had just made a very poignant observation.

"You like that phrase, Gertie, dear. *Negotiated settlement.* How it sounded good and well-thought out when it was brandished about those early days and years into our - what you call ..."

"Democracy you mean, Zabalaza?" grandmother completed his sentence and then she continued, "I honestly no longer know what that word means. Yes. That culprit and crook. Democracy. What a thug! What a turncoat! How it has defected from its inherent just cause, as our defender and champion! We are now collectively profiled as these lazy people who live on hand-outs."

Grandma continued, "Look at the young girls, using pregnancy and baby production as a lucrative business? Just to access the government's grant? Tell me, what are we teaching these girls? Any work ethic inculcated in this legal prostituting of their minds and bodies? I knew some of the girls when they attended my primary school. Who knew after all that devoted work of teaching them the basics of life, they'd end up like this? I tell you, at this rate some of them won't even see their 70s."

I must admit I had never looked at this problem this way. "And we don't hear of measures to get our girls out of grants, out of this cycle of easy but short-sighted short cut and humiliating begging, paraded as advantage. These grants are the be-all and end-all it seems." Granddad gently put his hand on his wife's lap, in an effort to calm her down. He quickly took advantage of her silence as she struggled with a piece of meat in between her teeth.

"Bakhona, you work with NGOs, am I right?" I nodded, put my fork gently on the plate, sat up straighter, and waited to hear what granddad would say about my development work with NGOs. "Tell me, is there anything else planned for these young grant ladies?" Granddad's question put me on the spot, because I didn't know of any next steps for the young girls, some with a brood of babies.

"Have you seen the long lines they form on the day they collect grants? Able-bodied women. Such a waste of human potential." That last remark by grandmother made me feel really bad. Here were thousands of women, countrywide, the hard work of making something of oneself, killed with government's love of easy fixes.

"Our people never felt dignified receiving hand-outs. With land and means, who would need 'thank you' stuff, both hands outstretched, a whole man throwing his hat on the floor to show gratitude for a half-eaten sandwich given to him by a passing white motorist? Everybody had enough. And we shared what we had."

When grandmother retired her fork and knife on her plate, and with a bang rested both her elbows on the table, I knew she wasn't done making her point, and making it very clear. Some bigger bricks and stones would still be hurled from her corner.

"Frankly, I'm tired of these balls of faeces handed to us in the name of feeling sorry for us. It's good for you. Meeting us half-way. What nauseating and sickening babble!" Grandmother just fell short of spitting out real saliva, I observed.

It was quiet around the dining room table, after this. We all appeared somewhat shocked and at a loss for words, until granddad unscrewed the tongue-tied lock jam. Deliberately wiping his mouth with his serviette, he looked at me to explore and figure out my muted response, "Bakhona, there goes your grandmother, daughter of a priest!" Granddad was flashing his teeth in an awkward grin. His eyes were blinking at one second intervals. "Gertrude, please mind your language, my dear. We are still at table, and now you are forcing us into toilet business." Then he looked at me and smiled before collecting a frown again and adding, "We also have a guest here from the city. Please behave, my dear."

I simply burst out laughing. But let me say, watching him and his demeanor, I could imagine how granddad had run his school. How he disciplined wrong doers, young and old, with a tone and look which was such a well-crafted cross between jest and seriousness.

"Well, respected dear guest and you, Zabalaza, some things need to be said. I couldn't help myself. I'm sorry. There is this perception that the poor don't understand the meaning of decency. They are so poverty numb, they can't even tell when their rights are trampled upon. They so rely on hand-outs, that they won't even notice when some-one gives them what you call ... Well, Gertie's balls. The women and girls will curtsy and the men will tip their hats to demonstrate gratefulness. It's all such shitty nonsense."

When we were done with our long dinner, I made sure to get to the sink first and wash dishes this time around. After a little while grandma called me from the lounge and asked if I was almost done. I returned to the lounge to find a hymn placed on my seat. Granddad was paging through the bible in preparation for our evening prayer.

I quickly remembered the rule of wearing something on my head and covering shoulders, during prayers. I excused myself, dashed to my room, and grabbed the long beige silk scarf I'd left on my bed. It was large enough to cover both my head and shoulders. Grandmother had already draped her black scarf around her shoulders and she had pulled her blue beret to fit her whole head. It was almost covering the whole of her forehead. How she looked a bit funny like that.

As grandma and I waited for granddad to get himself organized, I thought about how deeply grounding it is to go back to one's roots. I fitted perfectly well, back into the mold I was brought up in. Here I was remembering who I am, finding my bearings anew, and facing the reality of how far I still had to go, to usher in sustainable development to my people. What grandmother would perhaps refer to as "previously disadvantaged" - were she privy to my thoughts at that moment.

After our prayer, I could hear grandma singing another church song, her voice slightly muffled by the water from the shower. "It's truly a delight to be back, granddad. Bongani has missed out on a wonderful holiday with you here," I mentioned to granddad, as I proceeded to spend time looking at photos mounted just at the right eye level on the walls. Some were placed on corner tables and top of the side board.

Granddad nodded a response. I guessed we were all tired then. He quickly told me whose photos were displayed in the other rooms as well. Then he went to the kitchen to fix them some night caps. He offered. But I declined such a treat. I was too tired to even lift another container of beverage into my mouth at that stage.

Old photographs of mom and us children. My little brother, Bongani, and me. Our photos were everywhere. Mother looked funny in her high school uniform. So were the photos of granddad and grandmother in their younger days.

Then here were my grandparents in group photos with their respective teaching staff. Grandmother seated on the front row. Right in the centre, as the school principal of an all-female teaching staff at the lower primary school she headed for many years. Arms are crossed on the chest. Or hands are resting on the lap.

Likewise, here is a photo of granddad, seated in the same position in a group photo of teaching staff where he headed a higher primary school, with male and a few female teachers on the staff.

But the best photos were those of my grandparents' own parents! They were fading now. But their features were still well-defined. Here were the sources of my own genes, my DNA!

Sumptuous meals, every day, were one sure treat at my grandparents' home. I'd offered to prepare breakfast. But my grandparents declined my help. "You are on holiday, child. We appreciate the kind thought, but we want you to rest," grandmother had assured me as she took my face in her hands. "Read a book. Write a book, even. Sleep in and rest without guilt." Grandfather nodded. His wife was right. Then he added, with mischief all over his face, "so that you'll keep returning to visit us."

So, I'd wake up a bit late every morning, to smells of a variety of goodies baking in the oven, and something else cooking on the stove. They filled the whole house. The house was pulsating with aromas. Just the smells were undeniably full of flavour. I'd hear granddad whistling as doors opened and closed. I'd faintly hear conversations with neighbours passing by.

Days were slow and restful at my grandparents' home. Gone were the days packed with mountains of energy that necessitated that we grandchildren woke up very early to clean the house. Such obsession with cleaning! I realized this more so now that I have my own little flat to keep clean.

Mind you, it wasn't just here at my grandparent's home. It was everywhere. Some did the cleaning like puritans, so that as the sun rose in the east the house was already spotlessly clean. Missionaries and colonizers in general had labelled us as dirty. This started of course with their perception that our black skin was perpetually dirty.

As I watched these two, how they got along day by day, my mind began to wonder about their young lives. How they met. How granddad courted his lady. What made her agree to spend the rest of her life with him?

I knew a bit of the answer of course. It was from sheer common sense. I'd been around my grandparents since early childhood. For as long as I'd known him, grandfather has been a sweet quiet man. He spends his time mostly at home, busying himself with this and that, if not reading the local newspaper, listening to favourite programmes on radio or watching news and sports on Television, among other programmes that are a favourite.

As professionals, both my grandparents have always had a role to play in the community. People continue to seek their advice, even though they are retirees now. They serve on this and that committee, but of course within the parameters of a place like Siyahamba Township. Grandmother is just as amiable, with her quick wit and boldness. She definitely is a self-confident no pushover of a woman.

And so, it would have taken a secure man not to be intimidated by her. That she was the daughter of a priest, and had a profession, must have made her a sure attraction to dignified loving men like the one that finally won her heart. The man she fondly addresses sometimes as Zaba.

I'd also observed over the years how industrious granddad is. I've never forgotten the smell of freshly baked bread he proudly cut, smeared with a thick layer of butter and gave us kids to enjoy. And that industriousness has not abated.

Take the Christmas dinner, for instance. The dumplings and meat he prepared. All by himself! Before he started cooking I had asked so keenly, "Are you sure, granddad? Won't you need help in the kitchen?" Well, this was also to ease my own embarrassment. How could two women leave a man to prepare all of the Christmas dinner by himself?

Granddad was checking the spice rack, making sure he had all he needed. Before he answered my questions, grandma gestured to me that I shouldn't worry. He'd be fine. Now, listen to what grandma said, when her husband emerged out of the pantry! "I always say no man anywhere in the world enjoys cooking like Zaba does." Honestly. Why is grandma rubbing this in now? I asked myself.

"So you say, my wife. But for your information, Bakhona, it wasn't always like this." I saw grandma give her husband an anxious look of, "Don't start now!" I sensed a bit of awkwardness lacing what to me was beginning to taste like a strange cocktail. I hoped that time, the bartender, would probably clarify things for me in due course, and break down the ingredients that were in this cocktail. I could be mistaken. But the cocktail appeared to have signs of being a difficult drink to swallow. Truth be told, I had never been aware of any negative vibe between mother's parents!

Then grandma confused me more with her admission later, as we shared a pot of tea. Just the two of us. "He's right. Your grandfather didn't start off like this. Why would he be different from most men of his age and times? Of course, some are actually taught cooking and housework by their own mothers. I applaud such women, although this comes across as domestication or even emasculation in some ignorant circles. But not him! Not my Zaba! He knew how to do the simple basics. Just enough to save himself from fatal hunger."

I kept quiet and looked at grandma. My moment's silence was an indirect encouragement for her to continue. I was still very uneasy about grandma's attitude. Letting granddad handle all the cooking? Our Christmas dinner at that! And she absolutely had no qualms about this?

I sat there watching grandmother. She seemed to be studying the rich cream colour of her tea. Rather absentmindedly, though. What was up with grandma? Granddad had changed? Is this what grandma was saying to me? How did he change? Why did he change? I was hoping she'd expatiate. I was sure grandma had read the questions occupying my mind. She is smart. Without me having to ask, she could have answered them. She didn't!

It's not that we went to sit under the tree and gossip with grandma while granddad was cooking up a storm in the kitchen. I watched grandma roll up her dress sleeves, climb up the ladder, to scrape and sandpaper down uneven patches of old paint. I offered to do this for her. This was in a little nook in the house.

I was sorry I'd never held any paint brush in my hand, let alone paint some small patch. But grandmother was a very neat and careful painter, I observed. I had had trepidations when she started. I imagined the tiled floor covered with large pools of paint, which I'd have to clean up, as the younger person in the house. There was none of that. When grandmother finished it was only the strong smell of paint that we'd have to live with for a while.

Grandma was left with one wall to paint when granddad called for fresh potatoes and some carrots. He needed to add these to the beef stew he was making, so that it would be "nice and rich." Grandmother asked me to get a bunch of carrots. I pulled out a handful, quickly washed out the soil, and took them to the kitchen.

I lingered in the kitchen for a little while, as I watched granddad at work. The sleeves of his white shirt were neatly rolled up. They gently hugged his biceps and triceps. He was kneading the dough for our Christmas dumplings. He knew his way around the dough in this large basin, I observed enviously. How neat also. Just like grandma as she painted the wall. His black apron with a white photo of Mandela in the centre, remained untouched even by a speck of flour.

I stood on the side of the little potato patch and collected the potatoes into a bowl, as grandma dug out a few. It was a good crop. Nice and big white potatoes, like the kind I buy at my local greengrocer. Well, not quite, though. This was true organic produce.

Mother had taken after her parents, I'd noticed. She also kept a nice big garden where there was something fresh and ready to eat every month. But I'd left for boarding school too early to really master gardening.

As I put the bowl of these potato masterpieces on the table, clean and beautiful, I was feeling quite fulfilled. Less was truly more here. Much more! There was actually no comparison between this time with my old folks, and all the expensive stressful options I could have fallen for.

———————

Christmas and the almost dizzying buzz of shopping in preparation for celebrating the birth of Christ, had pretty much come and gone. I had noticed how Christmas

Day was the pinnacle, really, of what everybody understood as December holidays in these parts. In other places there was still all the excitement building up towards New Year's Eve celebrations. Fancy dresses, fancy parties and fancy balls.

Not at Siyahamba. To make matters even worse, this Township was far from any coastal town. The planners of forced removals made sure the residents of Masangweni truly landed in a wilderness. The usual beach visits on day one of the New Year wouldn't happen here.

Beyond any doubt, the excitement and adrenalin rush of Christmas was proving only to have been a very temporary heart, mind and soul lift, for most of the people of Siyahamba Township. Indeed, traces of the happy Christmas spirit were already overshadowed by anxiety: bills, school uniforms, school fees and school books. Neighbours who stopped by, said as much.

There were talks of borrowing from moneylenders, where interest accumulated, and became a huge stumbling block. Easily, this one desperate move could offset savings for the entire year.

So, life was slipping swiftly back to the same daily struggles, the same daily grind, the same drudgery of want and suffering, once again - all tightly bandaged by the unbearable band of heat from the sun. Of course, everybody looked forward to the beginning of the New Year, in the hope it brought something good, even something better.

There we were in the sweltering heat at midday. It was two days after Christmas. We were trying as best as we could, to manage the unmanageable. We were seated under the peach trees. It was the thick of summer. This was the only place with some decent shade, that time of day.

The two verandas were simmering in heat. The air was hot and still. With the strike of one match stick the air could easily explode into an inferno. The atmosphere was just as stifling indoors. Ceiling fans blew the same hot air. We were at the mercy of the elements. Nothing could make us fool proof from the blazing heavens.

We had just finished the last of the beef stew and dumplings we'd enjoyed on Christmas Day. I'd microwaved some frozen peas. I'd also offered much earlier to make a potato salad for our lunch. This was my moment to show off, I hoped, some of my town cooking. Well, I did receive compliments, although both my grandparents added tomato sauce to my potato salad! Who has ever felt the need to add tomato sauce to a good potato salad?

Whether the compliments were staged or well-meant, I really didn't want to dwell on that. I ironed out the creases of self-doubt and disappointment that began lurking in the dark, determined and ready to zap the confidence I'd brought to the preparation of the salad. I embraced the compliments. After all, compliments are compliments! One is supposed to appreciate them, especially those that come from doting grandparents. These are eternal gifts wrapped in ribbons of love.

I had neatly piled up the dirty dishes on the tray, and covered everything with the fancy net, to keep away the usual intruders. I was feeling lethargic from the heat and full stomach. Just when I summoned up enough strength and will to stand up and go wash the dishes in the kitchen, a teenage girl walked past. She had a baby on her back, wearing a semblance of a sun hat that hardly shielded the little tender head from the merciless sun. The teenage girl had just a small rickety umbrella as cover.

She greeted us in a decently long sentence. Nothing is rushed unnecessarily in these parts. Grandmother responded, addressing the young lady by her name. Bathokozile. Tozi, for short. "Did you have a good Christmas, Bathokozile? I have not seen you pass by in quite a while. How's the baby? Still breastfed? How old is the baby now? Is it a girl or boy, by the way, Tozi?" Grandmother's questions kept coming.

"Yes we had a good Christmas. Yes, the baby is still breastfed. It's a boy grandmother. How quickly you forget. I told grandma when he was born." Then the young mother laughed shyly. There was unmistaken fatigue in her voice. I sensed it was enveloping her, clearly siphoning out the energetic exuberance teenage girls usually display.

"I'm old, my child, and forget some things. Keep breastfeeding him for as long as you can. Your son will get all the good body building food from your breast."

"Yes, grandma. Thank you for the advice. Not that I've the best food every meal, though," the young lady commented as she looked at her feet.

"Oh, most of us don't have the most nutritious variety of food at every meal. But your breast milk is still the best for the baby."

"Thank you, grandma."

"Did you have any visitors for Christmas, Tozi?"

"Yes, father's older brother came to visit."

"Very good news! Where does he live by the way? I'm sure he brought you some nice gifts."

"Yes, he brought meat and some fruit for us."

"Did he come with his wife? She works in the kitchens, by the way?"

"Yes, she works in the kitchens. But she didn't come. Her employers had visitors from overseas. So, they asked her to stay and help. They will pay her extra, because she wasn't supposed to be at work."

"That's a pity. She'd have done all the fancy cooking and baking for you all. Next time then."

"Yes, grandma."

"How was the time spent with your father's elder brother?"

"It was okay, grandma. He's a kind man and doesn't drink a lot. Unlike my father. I don't know what they were arguing about when my father started a quarrel, and they fought. This was on the day before Christmas. But luckily, my father was too drunk to cause any damage to his older brother. They got along again."

"Very good. They are brothers, after all," grandmother commented. The girl did not respond.

"How are your other children?"

"They are okay grandmother, growing fairly well. You know it's hard. We are thankful just to see and welcome the dawn of a new day."

"It is true indeed. Life isn't easy. You father still doesn't want you to visit us here? He's a bad man!"

The teenage girl looked on the ground and didn't respond to grandmother's last comment. Then she said good-bye as she turned to ask if the baby on her back was asleep. Grandma told her his head was tipped uncomfortably to the side. He must be asleep. The mother of the baby said she must rush home then and put him to sleep, before his little neck got too strained.

Tozi had a litre of a green drink in her hand, and a packet of what looked like biscuits, the smallest packet in the shop. I had once or twice relieved my grandparents of the daily morning trips to the local shop to buy fresh milk. And I'd observed how most people bought the smallest quantity allowed for sugar, tea, bread, maize meal, flour, cooking oil, etc. How this irked me. Couldn't they organize bulk buying of some kind and save some money?

It was quiet for a while, where we were seated. Grandma began to sing a little song. It was a tune of a church hymn I knew well. I noticed that mom and grandma had the same habit of singing a little church song when they feel uneasy. Grandmother was the daughter of a priest, after all, and summoning a church service atmosphere came naturally with her. And she had inculcated that in mom. Granddad was looking far into the distance. For a moment, he was alone with his thoughts.

The teenage girl and everything I'd learned about her in those few questions and answers, bothered me. "Does she go to school?" I asked. Grandma didn't think so because her children keep coming. Grandmother further explained, "No sooner does the baby take the first step, then you notice a few months thereafter, she's pregnant again. The baby on her back is her third. All under the age of six," grandma gestured with her thumb. I think they anticipated the next question from me as grandma spoke in a low voice and told me, "All of them have the same father!"

"All of them? The three kids you mean?"

"Four of them, with the mother!"

I covered my face with the sweaty palms of my hands, as soon as I figured out what this meant. I'd never thought I'd come to grips with stark abuse in this manner. "That father doesn't know anything about family planning," I thought only. The whole thing of a father fathering children from his own daughter got me sick right in the pit of my stomach. Linking it to family planning was my way of handling the shock. This had nothing to do with contraceptives.

I immediately knew there was more to this story. But I was too shocked right then, to further pursue what I'd just heard. In these parts laws don't work the same as elsewhere, I concluded. Maybe there aren't even Social Workers around. If there are, the father has a way of stopping his daughter from reporting him, I thought. The same stance used by abusers, to isolate their victims.

But his own DNA for a victim! He may have found a way to threaten her, isolate her. And also, the poor girl might just be too embarrassed to discuss her situation with anyone else. What about the girl's mother? Probably dead, chased away or she simply left him, unable, too scared, and too embarrassed to deal with the mess? Then I finally found the courage to ask about the girl's mother.

"She ran away when the girl was still about ten years old. She has not returned since. No-one seems to know where she is," grandmother further elaborated. No doubt, she knew quite a bit about this family.

I was mulling over this situation, when the title of my Television show rang uncomfortably in my head: "What Would You Do?" I was still working on the proposal. It would be a month before I was ready to pitch the idea, find sponsors.

I felt nauseous. I was concerned I might just feel sick enough to throw up! Not that I'd have minded if the contents of my stomach landed squarely on the face of the man who fathered her daughter and then his babies with the same daughter! Not one. Not two. But three babies! And counting? Who knew? Oh, God!

Then granddad tried to calm my nerves by relating more stories of lives of people in the Township, in their church, on their street. Some stories were good and encouraging. There was a group of retired Mathematics high school teachers. They made themselves available to help students with homework. Church women took turns to visit the elderly on their streets.

The woman who won the government tender to provide lunch in all the Township schools was doing a very good job. Meals were balanced. Even the Ministers of Health, Education, and Social Development from Provincial and National Government had visited a few schools. Pictures of them seated among the school children and enjoying lunch, had made national news some months before. Other stories were bizarre. But not as mind-boggling as the one of this young lady. Unless a miracle happened.

There was the man who had three wives. He forced them to wear similar clothes, right down to their underwear and nightdresses. How could I even begin to analyze this crazy mentality, from a gender perspective? How mentally exhausting! My mind just sighed and left it alone.

Then grandmother appeared more flabbergasted when she told the story of the pseudo priest who used the hall in her former school as a church on Sundays. How he was exploiting the poor congregants.

"I attended one of his services just to see for myself, one Sunday. He was bold enough to force people to give more. 'Children of God, *Bantwana bakaNkulunkulu.* Nothing under R5.00! How does God bless you when you are stingy like that?' The offering plate had lots of crumpled R5.00 notes. Some were folded many times. You could tell these notes could have been the only ones in the house. Taken from a tin. From under a mattress. A piggy bank." I shook my head in disbelief!

"And that's not all, Bakhona," grandmother continued. He is rumoured to have a connection with drug dealers. You must see the cars he drives. That crook of a false prophet."

"Oh no, grandmother! Drugs even in Siyahamba! This is incredible. *Lafa elihle kakhulu.* [The beautiful country is dying.]"

"Indeed, say that, child of my child. My father, the dedicated priest, is turning in his grave. I tell you. If people even pose as God's messengers in order to extort, exploit and lead shady lives like this, God save us all, Bakhona. God save us all, Zaba." Grandmother changed her sitting position, and straightened her summer dress.

At that 'God save us all' moment a man in a white general practitioner's coat went past. Greetings were exchanged.

"In no time then, you'll be back at work," granddad said to the man.

"You mean on pension lines? We help a lot of people there," the man in a white coat responded, as he smiled proudly.

"I've always wanted to ask you, though, how you prescribe the right tablets for this and that kind of faulty blood pressure." Here was granddad becoming boldly confrontational, so out of the blue.

The man appeared shifty. He assured granddad, however, that he's trained to diagnose correctly. He quickly said his good-bye soon thereafter and left. Both my grandparents smiled knowingly. "On pension days, he poses as a medical doctor, Bakhona. He wears his white coat daily to rub it in that he's not a quack. How foolish he is. I'd leave you, Zaba, if you tried to earn a living by telling lies and robbing sick people."

I then asked how this man deceives pensioners. "Bakhona, he puts his stethoscope on several places on your chest while he asks you to breathe. You pay a fee. Then he gives you pills," grandmother told me. "I let him examine me once, but told him the pills he was giving me weren't the same as my GP's! He was embarrassed and simply moved on to the next person," granddad seemed to support why he was this belligerent with the thug. "That was the last time your grandmother and I joined those long lines in the sun, rain and the cold, to get our pension."

I was amazed how this quack had the nerve to still try and browbeat my grandparents with such a straight face, when granddad had already put him on the spot. He'd just lied to us, "We help a lot people!" What rubbish! I figured out it's the rouge element in him that quickly rolls in. It shields him as it also emboldens this man. So shamelessly.

"How is your pension paid out now?" I asked my grandparents, as I began to realize how people get away with so much even in sleepy places like Siyahamba. I was also concerned about grandparents' safety, as they advance in years. Losing their sense of judgment and discernment, among the apparent crooks that came in different shapes and sizes, even on pension lines at Siyahamba Township.

"That man belongs in jail," I continued. "Surely, the law will catch up with him one day," granddad assured me.

But grandmother pointed out something else. "You people are just hoping for something that won't happen. The law is right there, with those civil servants who pay us. They know what's going on. I asked one of these young men one day why they allow quacks and other kinds of crooks to exploit the elderly and disabled. He looked at me with disdain, and muttered, 'Grandmother, just mind your business. I'm not a policeman.' See that?"

"My goodness! She's not going to school," I found myself repeating this one hard fact. In all of the drama and sad tales of Siyahamba, my thoughts were on the girl, again. The answer was clear enough. Neither granddad nor grandma bothered to respond.

"Don't despair now, Bakhona," grandma had her arm around my shoulders. "Life is just like this. Maybe you are privileged to read about these shameful things in newspapers, and hear them mentioned on radio and Television news. We live them here, daily.

All we do is to be alarmed. We put our hands on our heads, wondering how some of these things can be possible. One day, *siyobulawa ukubabaza* [our awe will kill us], *mntan 'omtanami*, [child of my child.]" I could understand why such bizarre and alarming happenings could really end up sending one to an early grave.

"It's too much, I tell you!" Granddad added. "And where we are the system seems broken. Things don't work like a well-oiled machine. We are like lost people here."

"Some things work, of course, Zabalaza. Let's be fair. We can't blame government for everything, you know." Well, everything is relative, I thought, when we choose to shy away from courageously digging our teeth into the bitter fruit of painful reality. "We all understand that dear," granddad responded. "It goes without saying. But ..."

"But the truth of the matter is this," grandmother said as she signalled granddad to pass her a toothpick, "by and large, we most often feel like we are a forgotten people, that the laws and that Constitution that is praised for being advanced and inclusive, pretty much excludes us here.

How that happens, Bakhona, I wouldn't tell you. A lot still needs to be attended to. Many aspects of our lives aren't better at all. This 'better life for all' we were promised? We are still waiting for it, my child. It's our other messiah."

"I always wonder if you city people believe these horror stories," Granddad added. "Some read and sound like made up movie stories, honestly."

Grandma nudged me on the side of my hip and pointed at granddad, laughter following the pointing finger. "When last were you in a bioscope, Zabalaza?"

"Bakhona, see your grandma now, making fun of our lives here. Tell her even 80 year olds do go to movies. Me too, if I had means we'd both dress up in our Sunday best, get in our car, my old lady and I, have a fine meal in a restaurant, and do a movie. But with a semblance of public transport here, no night life is possible, or even social life, worthy of the name, really."

Grandmother nodded in agreement. And granddad continued, "Apartheid barred us from enjoying life. Now, the older one gets, the more stressful any trip into town becomes. In these kombis they rush you to get in and sit down. With Gertie's snail and chameleon movements? Forget it! Those taxi guys wouldn't care that her one leg was still on the ground. They'd pull off, I tell you."

Granddad winked teasingly at his wife. She was looking far into the distance, again. Her mind? Who knew where it was travelling to and fro?

"Movies at night, granddad?"

"Oh, yes, why not, Bakhona? We used to do matinees, up until we retired. But we all want variety. And going to matinees with noisy fidgeting children. Come on, child of my child! There's something more romantic about the evening. Not so? Honestly, though, jokes aside, here we can only yearn for such times of enjoyment. Age, geographical location and means, automatically exclude those of us who rely on public transport. We'd need to hire a taxi. Who has such money, when people elsewhere don't struggle so much to move from point A to point B, even at night?"

"Public transport is scarce for anyone, Bakhona, from early evening onward," grandmother added.

This was one reality that got me quite worked up about social life in our Townships. I began to plan in my head surprise city trips for my grandparents. While I was there, at least. Dinner, shopping, and a late movie. It caused me so much pain that there was no social life for my grandparents, when they had so much free time, and were in good health.

"And a balanced life is key to longevity and happiness. Who doesn't know this?" I was beginning to be quite angry, I noticed.

Both my grandparents shrugged their shoulders, like people who had given up hoping. I understood that a time comes when for people like my grandparents - their own dignity stops them from pestering the same issue with people who know how to fix what's wrong, but do not bother. Where were the councilors of Siyahamba Township? What about the residents' representatives in the provincial parliament?

These officials may not know this. Each time they dishonour their own, they themselves lose a bit of their humanity and dignity. Something in them dies. Something gets chipped away, little by little. I would not go to that subject again, I resolved. Maybe the earlier image of grandmother Gertie's balls, had summed up everything aptly. And that's what I'd take with me.

I finally got my agitated mind to quiet down, helped by the therapy of washing dishes. During this time I came up with the idea of survival. A four-letter word sprung up in my mind. Cope. How many times had the lady professor who taught the gender class told us she hates that word? How could the young lady cope in a dismal situation like that? Could she afford to play around with some hope? In order to cope?

Except I called the police right then and reported this filthy man! But then, would this intervention help? Would it make the situation worse? Men shielding other men? How come the father denied the daughter a visit to my grandparents? *What would I do? What would I do*, indeed, if I was in this teenage girl's shoes and lived her life every day *and* night?

My grandparents would have been worried to see me alone in that kitchen, muttering stuff to myself, and nodding my head as I wiped the dishes. For I had found some resolution.

Here, at Siyahamba Township hope was both a means and end. Here, hope was a shrine the residents had to worship, like fools with heads gutted of their normal brains. To be hopeless was to die. One lived longer in these parts for keeping the glimmer of hope alive. That lazy speck of light swaying ever so reluctantly in the stale still wind of abandonment.

But there I was, hiding now behind this other short four-letter word. Hope. I was ashamed of my cowardice. Was hope that far-reaching? Was it really a panacea? Was it that broad-shouldered to carry millions of burdened people?

Oh, young lady, you've no idea how you got me so incensed! My grandparents were right. Perhaps, reading about you would not have drawn as much ire as it has now. I've actually seen you, as well as the living, breathing proof of your continuing abuse, right on your small weak back.

One evening we were sitting at the front veranda. The stars shone brightly. The evening air was cool. We'd just had our simple meal of couscous and sour milk, *amasi*. This is our richer South African version of plain yoghurt. Couscous. I'd brought my grandparents this special gift. It is easy and quick to cook. It's thus a better replacement for the labour intensive and time-consuming preparation of *uphuthu*, the crumbled maize meal Zulus traditionally enjoy with *amasi*. We had agreed that after eating of all that meat and other sweet and fatty treats during the festive season, we needed to be gentle with our digestive systems.

After dessert of home preserved canned peaches, served with perfect custard I'd made, we spoke about the previous Christmas holiday, where we were, what we did. I had travelled overseas, of course. Then I heard, "I was here at home. And your grandmother was away, visiting a good friend." Granddad emphasized "good" in a rather deriding manner. He looked at his wife, to see how she'd react. But grandma simply kept her lips locked with a strong padlock. She seemed shocked.

"Is it okay, dear?" Bakhona is no longer a child. Besides, she loves us so much that she sacrificed the fancy city lights and overseas places to be with us this time. Maybe the time is right to talk about this thing. We've managed to keep it under wraps for decades, we hope. Who knows, though? Even that teenage daughter who has three kids by her own father, maybe family think they have the thing tightly sealed, under wraps. But somehow, we know their business."

Grandmother continued her silent protest. The awkwardness she felt was conspicuously splashed all over her. Like red paint accidentally splashed on a lady's white dress. But grandmother's Zaba looked like he wasn't gifted in simple observation of awkward and uneasy behaviour. Fancy! A whole teacher and school principal.

He waited calmly for his Gertie to give him the green light to proceed. From his look I could tell he'd force green, anyway, and cross his Gertie's red light! There was a dangerously calm determination about him. It made my heart skip a bit. It appeared to me that granddad had braced himself. He was ready for his and Gertie's mind, heart and soul collision.

I was quite taken aback, because grandmother's defence mechanism wasn't going to absolve her anytime soon, from what I observed of granddad's determination. The scenario reduced me to a little girl. I was tongue-tied and clueless about how to resolve a fight that was brewing quite fast, between mother's parents.

And yet granddad's, "Bakhona is no longer a child," imposed adult responsibility on me. I had to take over. Intervene. Break the impasse. Just do something, to move the needle of the record player by hand, stuck as it was in this one groove. I felt it my duty to uplift the mood. I needed to rise to the tricky if not treacherous occasion. How about making light of the awkwardness that was getting worse and not abating, with grandmother's silence?

"Well, I never thought such a discussion could arise while I was still around," grandmother finally responded. It was from a place that felt even to me, an emotional by-stander of sorts, like deep-seated pain or embarrassment. It was difficult to make a clean and clear distinction.

"Grandma, you are beginning to scare me now. Are you telling me something?" She looked at granddad as if to say, "The loud mouth that started this must carry on, and answer Bakhona's question." It was granddad's turn to contribute only silence, I thought, as I observed his demeanor. He was sitting so still, even a mosquito would have mistaken him for a concrete pole. So huge was his determination, in what felt like, "It's now or never."

The man seemed to know the effect of his silence on his wife. Indeed, the awkward silence propelled his Gertie to say more. "Lucky you ask me that question now. If you were younger what I'm about to tell you would have been too much for your little ears, Bakhona." Grandmother said this with a tint of playfulness as she gently pulled the lobe of my ear closest to her. There was a tinge of shame laced with pain I picked up. But I hoped I was wrong.

"Whoa! Grandma! That's heavy! It sounds like you'll tell me a crime story," I played along. I was a bit hopeful that my light-hearted attitude would finally succeed in diffusing the gridlock. Granddad had mischievously, deliberately or accidentally thrown this confused ball of wool on the table.

I couldn't wait for the process of untangling it to begin. I watched this sorry piece of entanglement roll for lap to lap, as if pleading for some-one with enough dexterity and oomph to find the lead thread. The man of the house adamantly remained still and silent like a grave.

"No. I never committed any crime, my girl. Just life. 'Ja, that's life!' You young people say it all the time." Grandmother added some Afrikaans accent to the words. I knew the whole of that statement in Afrikaans. But I did not utter it. I had to honour and respect the people of Masangweni. "The packages we come in at birth, my child," grandmother began to elaborate.

I chuckled. This was easier and safer. I also had to be careful now, and keep my mouth shut. Otherwise I'd interfere with the momentum that was slowly building up. Indeed, grandmother willed herself to continue. I was relieved traffic was moving again, and some work was being done on the messy ball of wool.

"And life you don't even know much of, Bakhona. Just because you got your first period, or received the first love proposal from a favourite boy at high school, then you think you know life."

"Well, to a degree, by high school time we know a bit about life. Come on grandma! Please grant us that bit of collective wisdom and experience. I mean some girls by that age are marriageable in other countries. Well, even here, sad to admit. Some teenage girls have already gone through very traumatic experience. Rape. Poverty. Divorced or separated parents using their offspring as weapons of war."

"Bakhona don't even mention that mad heartlessness and selfishness of parents who marry off their own twelve year old girls for cattle, which translates into money, as you know. That practice is cursed even in heaven. God knows it's just plain wrong!"

I was still agitated that granddad was alone in this house last Christmas, when he could have spent time with mom and my younger brother. So I returned the conversation back to where it had seemed to end. I asked why they did not both go to visit grandma's 'good' friend. I hoped this would take granddad out of the blanket of deliberate stillness he'd stubbornly wrapped himself in, in the last few minutes. His silence also wasn't fair to grandmother and myself, because he had started this apparently difficult discussion.

"It's a very long story," grandfather replied, as he dragged each word slowly. It felt like he was reluctantly opening a door to a painful past. Yet his resolve to go in there, could not be mistaken.

He'd noted that his Gertie had recovered from shellshock. She seemed ready to engage fully, land a helpful hand and play a pivotal role in proceeding with what her husband had kind of mischievously, thrown on the table for discussion. It appeared to be a challenging mountain to climb kind of tale to tell. There was something in the atmosphere that smelled a bit like a rotten potato. It made me uncomfortable.

I must confess that by this time, I was my own entangled bundle of unbearable apprehension and curiosity. Curiosity? I really wouldn't say. It was nothing like a child's "let me break this toy car or doll, to see what's inside it" kind of curiosity. I don't think so, as I look back to that evening which baptized me into the life of unease and uncertainty, about a lot of life issues.

"What your granddad is trying to say, Bakhona, is that every family has its little secret. Big or small. We've never felt comfortable to open up to your mother about this. But, with you, her daughter, we feel more at ease. Why is this, Zaba?"

"Maybe distance, Gertie. Distance. What they refer to as the generation gap. It's advantage, in this instance."

"Poor mom, your only child, her life of struggle after father left us. It is all coming back to me now." I muttered these thoughts in my head. For once in my life, I was happy to be mother's protector, even by proxy. I knew I needed to be strong.

A part of me was also beginning not to stand up and dance to the anxiety song, "*Every family has a secret.*" So, I braced myself for any eventuality. There were enough hints already, that what would follow would not be easy to take in.

With that firm resolve to protect dear mother, I felt I had to protect my grandparents as well. I needed to cushion them from the awkwardness of the moment. So I asked a question which to my mind would be easy to answer.

It is true that during my grandparents' years as a young couple, contraceptives were still being tried on rats in laboratories. Children, no matter how many, one to eleven or more, kept coming as long as the loving couple shared the same bed, until menopause put a break to the procreation duty or pastime.

So, this is the question I posed to my grandparents: "My lovely respected elders, can I ask you something that has bothered me for a while?" Both my grandparents looked a bit taken off guard. I proceeded to elaborate. "Why did you have only one child, when both of your brothers and sisters had a little more? And I'm talking about uncomplicated nuclear families. No polygamy. Mom grew up alone except during the times her cousins came to live with her, from time to time. Why were you two so stingy with children?"

This was a genuine question. For as long as I could remember, conjectures about possible answers had become my private pastime.

"A very good question, Bakhona." Granddad took his time to respond. And then grandmother expatiated, "As we've been talking about this and that about our government, I will tell you there's a lot we learn every day. Maybe not from government directly, as it were. But from the openness of the world at large. Our government may steal some of the credit, and claim it as theirs. It really does not matter."

The entangled ball was now jumping around as grandmother had found the lead thread. Knotty parts were beginning to be undone. I was relieved her tongue had loosened up. Grandmother continued, "Bakhona, it is true that our families were straightforwardly nuclear, comprised of a mother, a father, and children. But mine were very conservative. I'm not just picking on my parents. God bless their souls. Those days marriage was a big deal. It defined one. Generally speaking, it still does."

Grandmother seemed to have a big story to tell, judging by this wide radius that her introduction arose from. She was casting a wide net, to fish for details that were obviously long on her fingertips, however.

"Well, my parents are gone now, but from time to time I think about what my life would have been. How it might have turned out had they just let me be me, and allowed destiny to play its cards in shaping my life. As I look back at the way things turned out, maybe it was destiny's hand. Who knows?"

Apprehension began to creep in. I continued to wonder to myself why grandmother was taking such a long road just to get to where we were seated! Via government. Via her old folks. Her earlier statement suddenly loomed large in my mind. It seemed this had truly been her prayer, even more than hope; that the family secret would come out after they'd passed on!

The gravity of its content seemed entrapped in a bud, although my grandparents both knew the content had long been fully formed and developed. It was only to me that it was still an unknown quantity. How this got me sick with anxiety!

"She was a tomboy, Bakhona. She played with boys. She climbed trees. Girl things really didn't interest her." Granddad chuckled and continued with some light-heartedness, "During our times of youth, it was a bragging thing to exchange watches with a new lover." I laughed. "Don't laugh, Bakhona," grandmother chipped in with tears welling up in her eyes from withheld laughter.

Granddad continued, "I'd be wearing a lady's small watch and she'd be wearing my big one. But it didn't happen in our case, because ..." Grandmother raised her arm to show off her man's watch. "This she's done till today," granddad added. He was looking at his wife lovingly, as he pointed at her watch. I hadn't even noticed grandmother wore a man's watch!

"Yes, it didn't take long for me to make a bully of a boy or even a girl, eat the dust. When it became clear that I was not going to change and be ladylike, as my teenage years ended, mom and dad began to put pressure on me. Subtle match-making began. The old-fashioned way, you know.

To cut a long story short, the result was my being married off to this gentleman here. I was in my early twenties. Not quite married off, of course. There were hints. There was indirect coaxing." Grandmother seemed a tiny bit relieved at releasing this background to their matrimonial beginnings with granddad.

"You are jumping the gun Gertie." Granddad spoke slowly, looking at his wife as if seeking her permission to make a correction in what she had so exuberantly shared with me. "Before she was finally tied down to settle and behave, she had started a friendship with her good friend. The one she visited last Christmas."

Granddad put "finally settle down and behave" in inverted commas made of his two index fingers. Granddad's face unveiled a naughty look, in rippled phases which unfolded before my very eyes. If he'd been very fair in complexion his face would have been a huge

112

red strawberry. Grandmother's tongue seemed to be untied.

"We were so alike with Buzani. We were boyish and rather rough with everyone. We parted when she went to work in one city and I proceeded to college for teacher-training. We kept lively correspondence, though. Of course she wasn't fortunate like me to pursue a decent education. But still, she was creative, and made her life full. Her way."

"Did her parents suspect she'd be like you, grandma, and forced her to get married?"

"Actually, no. She worked for a long time. That girl had a way of getting what she wanted. Even with her parents. Well, she didn't have a stern looking father, wearing a priest's collar to subdue her. Being summoned to an impromptu meeting by my parents was always quite an ordeal. It was very intimidating. In a split second, mother could shift from being mom to being a priest's wife. Psychologically she'd put on the cloak she wore to church. It distinguished her, you see. It enabled her to command a lot of respect or distance. So, Buzani was lucky in a way, to be able to be the mistress of her fate. Yes, she made her bed. She lay on it. Comfortably or uncomfortably."

Grandmother stopped to hunt a mosquito that was circling her space. When it was a tiny speck, defeated in between the palms of her hands, she continued, as if she'd not just snuffed out a life. "Honestly, I had dedicated life or destiny brokers in my parents."

Grandma then shifted gears in this tale. It seemed on a safer road to gain up speed now. There was some escalated excitement about her. "There was a time I heard

Buzani's employers had taken her overseas with them. But she came back, many years later."

"And that's when more serious trouble began," remembered granddad. He took a deep sigh. It seemed what was coming to mind had been quite a rough patch for him. And its effects were still just buried shallowly under the thin skin of his mind and heart. "I had heard one day from one of my cousins that Buzani had been seen in the neighbourhood. What had been only a hushed suspicion in earlier years, had now become more public knowledge. In those years, Buzani would be seen in pants! No African woman dared even think of doing such. It was not even on their collective minds. And Buzani came back with not just short hair, but an obvious boy's cut!"

"Boy! How she became the talk of the town!" Grandmother added as she shook her head. It was obvious that her mind anxiously and yet excitedly, was revisiting that time in her life. "Not only that," granddad continued, "Buzani had the audacity to go to Gertie's parents and demand to see Gertie! You see travelling overseas had wizened and emboldened her. She had gotten wind of rights, now that I think about it, and knowing what we do know now."

Granddad continued, "By that time Gertie and I were engaged to be married! It was clearly a tug of war. Buzani and Zabalaza, fighting over Gertie! We were both trained teachers and on our first jobs then. Just imagine, Bakhona." Granddad seemed to be spinning in a mix of emotions.

"Teachers earned peanuts those days, Bakhona!" Grandmother added. But I hardly paid attention to the comment. All this time I was not believing what I was hearing from my own grandparents. Mother's own parents.

Neither did granddad respond to the comment about teachers' salaries. He simply said, "Don't side-track me now, Gertie! We've to get through this. I started this talk. And I'll see to it that it is finished. A half-told story will torture Bakhona for the remainder of her life. So, may I?"

Grandmother responded with a nod, as she lowered her head for a second, as if deciding what mood she must invoke, to let this difficult cup pass. "And I could tell that your grandmother here – a part of her wanted to be with Buzani! It was a rough beginning for me. I must tell you. But I had grown to like Gertie a lot. I expected and hoped that as we continued to live as husband and wife, we'd grow to love each other more. She wasn't shy and timid. And she was very smart. I liked all of that, although some of my friends felt very uneasy with her."

Grandmother rested her chin on the back of her hand, and looked at her husband as if studying him, while he spoke. A faint smile was on her face as she listened to him. Then she asked, "Who were those friends?" Did I meet any of them?"

"No, you didn't. I didn't want you to. I feared you might embarrass me, somehow."

"Oh! Like do what?" Grandma successfully put on a frown laced with a minimal smile, as she cocked her head for the answer.

"At the slightest provocation, tackle one of them and throw him on the ground. Give the guy a bloody nose. Who knows? Then I'd have to come in and separate you. This would not be a walk in the park. Then I'd have to apologize. Worst of all, I'd be the talk of the community for a very long time. Some hurtful things did land in my ears, of course. But I protected you, and kept them to myself."

"Like what, Zabalaza? That I'm a boxer?" Grandma's smile was gone. There was a curious triple mix of agitation, anxiety and self-consciousness in her voice. Her face managed to successfully display all three.

"I'll take these and the pain they caused me to my grave, Gertie." Granddad spared his Gertie the sad look, as he bent to tie up his slightly loose shoe-laces right then.

I watched grandma as she seemingly engaged her mind in what granddad had just told her, apparently for the very first time ever. I saw her holding back tears. She wore a grave look. Then like a driver controlling a car out of a slippery patch on the road, grandmother finally succeeded to pull her voice through the oily road patch of deep sadness, embarrassment and agony.

Grandma continued, as she steadily controlled the steering wheel of her vocal cords, "The problem with this condition, Bakhona, is that you don't choose it. Honestly, this is the most painful part."

I listened as grandma's voice gained strength and momentum. "As I grew up in years I began to notice that there was something different about me. Something other girls and women didn't have." There was dead silence as grandmother spoke. I wanted to interject with something to lighten her load. I couldn't think of anything appropriate to say.

Then I understood something else right then. I'm not a shrink or psychologist of any kind. But it felt to me grandma was finally making a breakthrough. She was finally engaging her deep-seated pain. She had shied away from it for many decades. It wasn't easy even now.

But she was brave. She'd firmly decided to remain in the boxing ring. Throw in the towel? Definitely not.

Granddad continued to examine his shoes as he listened. He was very present, I noticed. "Of course I'd thought nothing of my boyish behaviour in earlier years. But I'd grown up to be very self-conscious, confused, least understanding what the hell was wrong with me! I knew there was something not so 'normal'. Being Gertie, of course, I expressed my anger and frustration by engaging in aggressive behaviour."

"Something slightly off, grandma. I understand what you mean." Granddad was still and quiet like a boulder now. He was still making a ponderous study of his black highly polished shoes. So he had two pairs of the smart designer shoes.

"It is true that there were times I yielded more towards Buzani. It's an oscillating pendulum. On a daily basis, I'm not sure which is which. One day you are more of this. Another day you are more of that."

Grandmother's hand was half-way down her forehead. It partially covered her eyes, as she spoke. There was an unmistaken tremor in her voice. Granddad's shoes continued to provide an escape for him. I had to find a spot on the wall to fix my gaze on.

When grandmother's voice stopped shaking completely, she continued, "Unlike Buzani, you see. Her situation had become more clearly defined. She was rather too open about it for that society, thinking about it now. But that was just her. The girl who grew up almost free to do as she pleased, her life in her hands."

I kept looking at both my grandparents. I was hoping for an agreeable gap in the conversation to pose the question, "What happened next?" Believe me it took a lot of courage for me to even think that question. Plenty gaps became available. But I didn't open my mouth.

It's not that I was curious for an answer, truly eager to know what happened next. If I'd dared ask the question, it would have been a case of simply playing along, trying hard to go with the flow of the difficult tale, all in a desperate effort to mask how shell-shocked I truly was. Yes. I was trying to find a way to mask my shock.

As grandmother laid bare the pain of not being straightforwardly straight, this made my heart ache, deep inside. I lacked words to comfort her. I honestly couldn't even try to minimize her pain. It would also have been rather dishonest and very insensitive of me. She's smart. She would have seen right through it. My pretence would have hurt her. There was absolutely nothing I could call forth to soothe the gaping wound she had just bravely opened up and poked with a sharp knife.

So I kept quiet. There was nothing polite or nice I could say to ease the situation. I had to accept that what was, was; what is, just is. I could tell grandmother expected nothing else from me, besides both of us spread a blanket on the grass, lie on our stomachs and invite the gift of her situation, her permanent reality, to join us, opening up an opportunity for hugs of acceptance.

And of course, there was granddad who had such an unusual experience in courting a woman of grandma's disposition. They were both young in a society that had yet a very long mileage to cover, in efforts to evolve in these tricky matters of sexual orientation.

The fact that grandmother had visited Buzani, the previous Christmas, didn't make this a story with an ending yet. It was still such a work in progress. Time would tell how it would end. This was a painful acknowledgment for me. How much more for granddad who so late in life had to resume the fight he thought he'd won when he married grandma? And so many decades back?

Grandma excused herself to go to the toilet. Then it was granddad's turn. No-one spoke during those intervals. Granddad returned with a bowl of fruit. No-one reached out to take and enjoy any. The toilet visits somewhat interfered with the momentum of the sad tale. The initial awkwardness was threatening to return, served in the safety of silence. But grandmother saved the moment.

"So now that we know more about this thing, I'm sometimes thankful that mine is not as pronounced as it is with other people. Society isn't blind to there being unconventional men or women. There's a man who sells food at the bus stop here. He wears tight skirts, silver clip-on earrings and still has this man's voice. I watch as people make fun of him. I wince, knowing that could easily have been me, if I'd been born with more than I have."

All granddad contributed was a reluctant grunt. I made it out to be a cross between a Halleluiah and God have mercy! I could see his jaws tightening.

"This thing." I noted grandma's choice of the word. Thing. A thing that still lacks a proper name. Like an alien. An alien. Not a condition. Just a thing. A thing yet to be understood, long before it can be accepted. I looked at grandma, and knowing what I knew now, there was some boyishness about her silhouette. I trembled a bit. But thank goodness we were sitting outside. And the bright light from the dining room didn't directly shine onto our faces.

Granddad suggested that we go in the house. The night air was becoming uncomfortably cool. And mosquitoes were bingeing on us.

Believe me, it was very difficult for me to watch my grandparents taking turns at telling this painful story. Some parts were spoken of for the first time ever, in my presence. What was clear to me was that once the telling of the story started, both my grandparents wanted it done and over with. Actually, grandmother did say during the course of that conversation that it's important for at least one living relative, especially of a younger generation, to know this family history.

She touched the corner of the garden table close to her, and said she hoped none of her descendants would go through what she went through. I bowed my head. That added depth and meaning to this story. How family cannot shed this reality about grandmother. How I wished it was at least blue eyes we'd inherited from grandma. Drama, yes. Children teasing us at school. Weird looks from all and sundry, but certainly less trauma, for whoever got this feature added to their chromosomes.

I imagined Bongani, my younger brother, in tight skirts, dangling earrings, high-heeled shoes and fishnet stockings, leading a gay parade in Cape Town, as an older man. Would there be tolerance or mockery? Would there be cheers or rude comments hurled at him and his kind? My little brother? My only brother? *What would I do? What would he do?* How would he handle ridicule for something he did not bring upon himself?

Homophobia was still not responding too well to sermons on human rights, gay rights and free expression. Some might probably argue that homophobia still came a close second to the scourge of racism. In gender circles we might begin to speak of quadruple oppression, as we add homophobia, to oppression by race, gender and class for Black women like grandma.

My grandparents must have disappeared into their bedroom when they got back in the house. I found myself alone in the lounge for quite a while. But I had company. Thoughts. I immediately had a flash back. The light on memory beamed on Bongani. Here he was embarrassed when I caught him in the bedroom. He was applying my doll's lipstick. He was about four years old. Here he was trying on mom's high heels, at about age six. I quickly dismissed those thoughts, though. At those ages Bongani was just exploring mindlessly. Like I also did.

But I didn't want to remember what one of his friends had told me in confidence, that it seemed Bongani was mixing with the wrong crowd. He'd been seen wearing dangling earrings. His lips were painted a bright red, and he was walking funny. This was during his third year at high school. I had to confront him. So, I carefully created an opportunity for an honest eyeball to eyeball conversation between siblings. Just the two of us, with the door shut in his bedroom. It wasn't an easy conversation.

"Gees, big sister, that was for a school play. We'd been rehearsing."

"And you did not think to get rid of all that stuff before you left the rehearsal?"

"I like fooling around with what you call, "stuff" - as if you are not a girl, Bakhona. I like to make my friends and classmates laugh. What's wrong with that?"

"And why are you playing a girl's part?" I asked. The last question was silly, and he said as much.

121

"Anyone can play any part. You know that, Bakhona. What are you implying here? That I'm ...? Don't be silly now."

"Sorry Bongani, I didn't mean that." He simply shook his head and marched out of the room. He banged the door behind him. The walls shook.

My grandparents did return to the lounge. But they remained on their feet. They were holding hands. I'd never seen them do this. "Sorry Bakhona, we left you alone for a while." No explanation came forth. Not that I needed any. Some things are best left unsaid or just left alone. I had my silk scarf on my lap. Grandma quickly realized what I'd readied myself for. "I see you are nice and ready, my grandchild. But we'll not have prayers tonight. It's a bit late." She looked at her husband, as if expecting him to confirm this is how the two of them felt.

Then grandma's husband made a suggestion, "Your grandma and I will say a little prayer before we close our eyes and sleep. You could do the same, if the spirit moves you, Bakhona." I nodded my head and said I would do the same. I think both of them came short to verbalize the obvious. That it had been a very *long* day. I looked at my watch. It actually was quite late if one lived at a place like Siyahamba Township.

I remained seated and watched them walk away. Two tall straight-backed parents of my mother. Their hands had found each other again. Arms were swinging a bit stiffly, as if my grandparents were self-conscious about this display of their love and friendship, in the company of their "guest."

I took a long bath. Indeed, a bath was what I needed that night. Not a shower. I had to soak all of me. Body, mind and soul, it seemed. When I got to my bedroom and shut the door, I collapsed on the bed for a while. What I'd heard that night came tumbling down on my mind. The story barked at me to revisit it.

I prayed that I never viewed my grandparents in another light now. Especially grandma. I was now very keenly aware of what I might be carrying, embedded somewhere. Who knew? It could be lurking in the quiet and secret corners of my make-up. Dormant and defiant! *What would I do* with this streak of society-unfriendly DNA? I was a rotten bag of panic, confusion and anxiety. I thought about mom and Bongani. It was useless to think about dad. It was impossible to try and fit him in. He'd left us so long ago, it was difficult to even think of him as family.

But I immediately knew what I'd do first thing I got home. I'd ransack Bongani's room for any piece of jewelry, make-up or any girl stuff in there.

Then something happened. Shall I call it an epiphany? My anxiety was changing about Bongani. Asking me what I was implying with that line of questioning, and leaving the bedroom in anger? This gave me hope. His anger gave me a fat blob of hope. I was so glad now that my younger brother thought I was out of my mind to entertain those thoughts about him.

I stood up to go to the toilet. I sat on the seat, relishing my moment of salvation from unnecessary agony. I looked behind as I flushed the toilet. Like I usually do with people who upset me deeply, I flushed the toilet again, imagining that gene being flushed completely out of our lives.

It's not that I hated the gene. It's just that it is work to carry and live with it, in a society that isn't quite ready, and usually does not know how to handle people who have it.

No cosmetic surgery in this instance. Very much like arriving on earth wrapped in the permanent body blanket of a black skin. It's work hauling it around. You can't put it on and off at convenient times. South African champions of our Black political liberation cause flashed in my mind. What about champions of causes like my grandmother's, and those in her camp? There were none when she was confused about what was different about her.

A saving epiphany about Bongani? It wasn't gracious enough to last, unfortunately. So, for many nights after this revelation I lay awake at night. Agony and anxiety both wanted to get under covers with me! How these two pestered me, begging me for intimacy. I tried to chase them away, by giving them some homework: "I can't have both of you together. Go home and decide how we'll do this." The fools. They'd both return hand-in-hand to say, "We are twins! You can't separate us."

But a steadier voice of reason appeared from behind. It patted me on the shoulder. Then it slowly turned my upper body, so that we were face-to-face. Next, the voice of reason looked me compassionately in the eye and said, "Don't do this to yourself. Genes are genes. Just surrender."

The voice of reason advised me, as it hummed softly and repeatedly in my ear, *Que Sera; what will be, will be.* I remembered that this was mom's favourite song, especially when she was disappointed about something. The voice kept its hand on my shoulder until I became calm.

"And that will be alright. It's not what happens to us that matters. It's how we react to it," the voice repeated what I'd heard a therapist say in a film: "What is, just is. What will be, will be." I listened, half-heartedly at first to the voice of reason. But more sincere appreciation came later, as I mulled over these words of wisdom.

Despite efforts from the voice of reason, though, my sleep often suffered from horrible nightmares. One of those was not quite a nightmare, though. One morning as I opened my eyes to do the usual debriefing of how the night had gone, I almost burst out laughing as the memory unfolded. It was actually a true story that my friend, Lindeni, had told me about a year before.

We were taking a break during field work, on a very cold winter's day. Strange enough, the setting of the story was almost similar to where I was. A visit out of town. In Lindeni's case, she was visiting her parents in what towns folks refer to as rural areas. What some Africans refer to as the village.

I'd been wizened about how that designation is misleading at times, though. My Political Science lecturer convinced us that those indigenes who have stayed behind, and warded off the lie of better lives in the cities, are smarter. Not backward or uncivilized. They are actually doing us, so–called smart city folks a great favour! They are gatekeepers and savings bank of our culture. Without the defence and preservation of this basic core of who we are, we die a slow death, as a people.

As I opened my eyes this particular morning, Lindeni loomed large on my mental screen. I instantly recalled that we were huddled in my rickety car. Field work wasn't going too well. Our questionnaire clearly needed more work. Definitely not a good sign. We'd taken some time off for lunch. It was unexciting egg sandwiches. We'd wash the bread down with black tea from my flask.

Then to lighten the mood, Lindeni told me a story. On that visit home, her parents had a party in her honour. It was just to thank God and the ancestors that she was still the Lindeni they knew. She was the same daughter they had brought up to fear God. She was healthy and whole. City life hadn't corrupted her or decimated her integrity.

The main event was over. It had gone very well. Lindeni recalled that she was in the kitchen with some grannies from the neighbourhood. They were drinking tea and cupcakes she had made. She hadn't seen the old ladies in quite a while. So, they were all catching up.

One of the grannies introduced another topic after local gossip was exhausted. It was about Lindeni's love life. "So typical of grannies," I said to Lindeni. We both laughed. She assured the old ladies that when she had found the right person, worth bringing home, they would know. One of the grannies remarked, as she wagged a finger at her, "Lindeni, don't bring us trouble!"

"You mean a drunkard? A thug? Or one from a different race group?"

"Just some-one decent, my child. We'll be happy," another granny responded.

Then the granny who had been washing some dishes at the kitchen sink turned to face them all. It was granny Olga. Lindeni told me granny Olga began her question with a preamble. "We are all women here? Right?"

"Oh, Lindeni! Women are familiar with that kind of introduction to a subject matter. It's usually meant for women's ears only," I commented.

"Exactly, Bakhona! As if you were in that kitchen!" Lindeni continued the story.

"Yes," everybody responded to granny Olga's introductory question. It was punctuated by giggles from some of the women.

"Then we waited, Bakhona. We knew something off colour was following. We braced ourselves. Granny Olga took her time wiping her hands on the dishtowel. She lowered her voice. "So, Lindeni, my girl, I've always wondered, eh, eh, eh ..."

"Gosh, Lindeni, why was granny Olga stammering now?"

"Then granny Olga laughed diffidently, Bakhona, as she playfully covered her eyes with her hands. Just like a naughty child. I knew she was coming with a bombshell. Then it came!"

"Eh, Lindeni, my girl, when women are with other women, in a love relationship. How does this thing work, you know?"

"There was silence for half a second, Bakhona. It was followed by a whispered, 'Yes, Lindeni! Just tell us!' The 'yes' was quite a long-drawn subdued chorus from the whole kitchen full of women." I must say I hadn't been prepared for such a big bombshell from Lindeni's story. I exclaimed loudly, "What, Lindeni? *Hayike, labogogo!* Gosh! These grannies! What did you do?"

"Hey, Bakhona, one of them quickly shut the kitchen door in readiness. They stopped drinking and eating. They were all eyes and ears. I was truly taken off guard. But I couldn't peel off those several sets of eyes, all waiting to hear from me."

"Oh, my God, Lindeni! How did you escape?"

"Not a chance! I couldn't find a way out, Bakhona."

Lindeni told me she proceeded to explain to the old ladies that she wasn't sure herself. But she had read a bit about it. Lindeni had one concern, as she retold the saga to me. "Bakhona, I didn't want the old ladies gossiping and making up stories about me. Typical of gossip, these untruths would mutate from fiction to fact by the time the grannies shared them with my mother, you know." I totally agreed with Lindeni.

Lindeni told me that by the time she had finished, the shock on the grannies' faces made her regret the bit she'd told them. Granny Olga actually hurried out with a hand on her mouth. When she returned she'd splashed cold water on her face. Her eyes were red. She'd filled her mug with cold water from the large corrugated iron tank just outside the kitchen.

As she gathered her full skirt to seat neatly, she took a closer look at the mug, and ran her fingers on its brim. Then she turned to ask another question from Lindeni. "My girl, these people didn't come this time to speak to us about rights, and give us new mugs or other gifts."

"Granny Olga, changing the topic, Lindeni!"

"Obviously, Bakhona. Smart granny Olga!"

Lindeni recalled that granny Olga's remark prompted everybody to remember their mugs of tea, and Lindeni's cupcakes. But not one tea cup or mug reached lips, Lindeni told me. I said, "Something like, *too much slip betwixt cup and lip*, I guess." Lindeni nodded her head and a couple of times and then continued, "Bakhona, I took a glance at the inscription on the mug. It was fading but still legible. *Human Rights Day*!

Then I asked, 'You mean Human Rights Day, granny Olga?' She lifted her face and waited to hear what more I was going say. 'That date is still coming. What month are we on? Yes, that holiday is still coming.' Let's hope the people who gave you mugs last year have other nice gifts for you, as they remind you all about human rights."

"We'll see," Granny Olga responded. "I'd love another mug. They are a good size for morning tea." Still, no-one continued to drink the tea, even though they had prepared a full tea pot of their favourite brand. None of the old ladies' hands reached for the cupcakes, either.

A thought passed through my mind that morning, as I rested on my bed in my grandparents' home. Did the old ladies notice and then connect the dots between that uncomfortable conversation and Human Rights Day? Maybe not right then? But some other time, perhaps? I still wonder.

Then I also recalled an incident I'd found interesting to watch, some months before. A teenage grandson was walking out of government's pensions' offices. I noticed that he was wearing a nice shade of blue eye shadow. He was protectively holding the hand of his old grandmother.

I imagined the young man had taken time that day to accompany his grandmother through taxis, buses and busy city streets, to sort out some problem with his granny's pension. I read nothing but relief on both of their faces. *What would Granny Olga do* if this was her grandson?

That morning I thought, here was grandma, my own family, in this situation. I had absolutely no idea when Lindeni recounted that story. Life?

On the last Sunday of my visit I treated my grandparents to a very special picnic at the park in town. I'd bought wine, cheese, and lots of meat that grandpa grilled as grandmother and I prepared sandwiches. My shopping list included everybody's treat of favourite this and that.

Somehow they talked me out of making any fancy salad, besides the usual thinly sliced combination of raw onion, tomato and chilies. So, there was no potato salad.

The section of the park we went to was quiet. Just a few families. Mostly of other race groups. They were enjoying themselves. Children were playing on the swings. Some older kids were passing ball. We'd brought the small transistor radio from the kitchen. I put on soft music when we were enjoying our picnic lunch.

It had been many days since the story. I mean the one about my grandparents and granddad's former rival. Grandmother, Buzani. I was very thankful that both my grandparents didn't seem conscious around me, given what I knew now about their love life. And I'd pleasantly observed this right from the morning after the very *long* day before. At our late breakfast everybody was normal. No-one even hinted on the previous night's talk. I'd also prayed that I didn't seem to look at them differently, since the revelation.

I watched granddad on our picnic day. He seemed very happy. I couldn't quite figure out why. It could have been the wine, the outing, or more importantly relief that they'd finally shared with me this incredible story. Or maybe pride that at least one family member knew now of their hardship. Especially his, perhaps.

Here was a man in his 20s who had to learn to smartly and single-handedly manage with the expertise and experience of a pro, this rare situation. He was truly learning as he went about it all. True navigation of uncharted waters. He had no clue of what he was into.

Grandmother was less of an open book that picnic day. I couldn't read her.

After our lunch I decided to leave the two of them alone for a while. I was playing on the swings close by. This little girl and I were taking turns to get ourselves going on the swings. She was about 7 years old. We had exchanged polite greetings and good wishes for the New Year with the parents. I immediately noticed they were bringing her up well. She was very friendly and comfortable around me, although the parents kept an eye on her.

Then I left the swings to be alone in the great outdoors. It was a nice day. The sun was hidden in the clouds. The slight breeze added to the pleasantness of our natural surroundings. Given the nice weather that day, the picnic was a much better outing than the stifling inside of a movie house.

My grandparents would probably disagree of course. They seemed to have gone back to the little childish pleasures of popcorn, chocolate and coke, judging by the way they carried on about yearning for visits to movie theatres. But I'd already planned a movie night for my old folks. We had a car! We'd do the whole works the following week. An evening dinner at a restaurant. Then the movie afterwards. I'd thought this would made a perfect good-bye gift to my grandparents.

It wasn't long before I heard, "Bakhona! Bakhona!" I turned. It was granddad. He was gesturing that I come back. "What now, granddad?" I wondered in my mind. He asked that I sit down, right between the two of them. I knew instinctively that they wanted to finish the story of their love and life. I wasn't prepared for this, I must say. But I complied. Without any further ado and background frills or recap, grandfather went straight to the subject matter. He continued where they'd left of, as if only 5 minutes had passed before we resumed this talk.

"Bakhona, to come to your question of why we only had one child. Your mother. You are old enough now my girl to understand these things. "There we go again," I thought to myself, as I held back a wince they'd have easily detected. "We couldn't consummate our union. Things then were still quite fuzzy even after we got married. Buzani was still a big factor. Fight to win a woman who has a female suitor! My God, you've had it, as a man!" Granddad clapped his hands so loudly, he startled me.

"You see, grandchild, ours was a very difficult situation. There was no history."

"No template," I added, as I shook my heard. "Whatever template means, daughter of our child, you get the subtle and intricate meaning of course." Granddad continued. "I knew there was something wrong somewhere. But I would be lying if I said to you now, I completely understood our situation. Neither did Gertie. In fact it was worse for her."

With this acknowledgement by granddad, I could tell he felt sorry that his beloved wife has this mountain of an issue in her life. She hadn't asked to be born that way, granddad seemed to say. His Gertie nodded in agreement, as she cast a gaze at a butterfly that seemed to enjoy our company.

I noticed granddad couldn't figure out I was very uncomfortable with these bedroom details. He could not see my eyes and how they reacted, hiding as they were behind very dark sunshades. But I trusted my grandparents' modesty and decency to guide them, so that they knew how far they could go.

Over and above everything else, my sympathy was with them. But I quickly told myself that these sessions of sharing their secret with me, also served as therapy of sorts for them. This made me feel better. And they had made me the sole custodian of this family secret! It was in truth a great honour, although this was a very difficult revelation.

"Let me just put it this way, "I begged her. I coaxed her. I couldn't use force. I'm too much of a ...." Grandmother butted in and ended granddad's zig-zag meandering. "Finally, I yielded. Just to get it over and done with, Zabalaza. I still hate you for that." She pointed a finger at him, but with a sunshine drenched smile on her face.

She had been rather quiet as the head of household went to town with the details. Stopping and starting. "And that one time was all it took," granddad added, with his hands coming together in a prayer mode. "Mission accomplished, granddad," I mischievously added.

"It was a very difficult pregnancy. I was fighting it, totally in denial, in the initial stages. But God took over. Your mother was born. Your granddad was a bundle of nerves that entire period of nine months."

"I was worried you were going to kill the baby, Gertie!"

"Come now, Zabalaza! You really thought that? See, Bakhona, how we are talking about things we've never gone back to, since they happened, when we were a young couple.

The mother/mothering instinct can never be under-estimated, I can say. Mother Nature took over. My physiology, my body systems and functions knew what to do. Eventually, the ripples of my resistance died down. Finally they lost the fight, and gave up. I surrendered to what I was going through. Absolutely."

"What would be, would be, grandma."

"Yes, exactly, my child. *What else would I do?*" Grandmother looked up as if in prayer to the Power beyond the visible blue sky. I imagined grandma's silent prayer. "Lord you gave me an extremely difficult cup. But God, You were gracious enough to hold my hand, until You let it pass."

"And listen here, Gertie. Do you know that I had pressure from my parents to have another child? They urged me to keep trying until we had a boy? I didn't argue with them. But I knew that would be totally out of the question."

The last thing my grandparents told me was not to worry about Bongani or the future. "Indeed, what will be, will be," I thought.

"That's what has helped us survive as a married couple. Sometimes things are normal. At other times the other side of your grandmother gains the upper hand and rules for a while. I've learnt over the years to accept and not fight it."

"As long as Buzani is not around, granddad," I added. "Oh! She finally gave up and left, when your grandmother fell pregnant with your mother."

I noticed grandmother had retreated to her cocoon of silence again. How reliving this saga seemed to drain her more than it did granddad. She was taking it all hard, at times, it appeared to me, as I tried to understand her withdrawals.

Probably it was deep-seated pain she still didn't know how to deal with, and then appease, so that she could heal. I had thoughts of organizing psychotherapy for both of them. But it was just a fleeting thought. I lacked guts to further explore this possible next step. Besides, it would have been too big an adventure to escape mother knowing about it. And that was a definite no!

"Buzani did finally return from wherever she spent the rest of her adult life," grandmother spoke again. She was taking us back to how this story began. Her visit to this other lady last Christmas.

I thought of possible escapades, explorations and a myriad of love affairs for grandmother Buzani. She came across as very aggressive in the way she pursued love relationships, judging from the stiff competition she had managed to give my granddad. My heart quickly softened, however, when I considered the bitterness and pain that comes with being singled out and treated as the 'other' if not completely rejected by so-called mainstream society.

"Zabalaza could have joined me, last Christmas. I begged him. But he refused. Buzani and I are old ladies now. We are just friends. She has a number of ailments. She suffers from a weak heart and arthritis. So I helped around in the house, cleaning, cooking, washing and ironing her clothes and linen."

"So that's what you did, Gertie? Bakhona, she tried to tell me all about it when she got back. But I wasn't interested." I figured out granddad's lack of interest was his way of protecting himself from revisiting that challenging time of rivalry between himself and grandmother Buzani, as he fought to secure his Gertie.

About one week later I returned home to spend some days at mother's house, before I returned to work. It was good to be with mom again. After wishing mom a Happy New Year in person, I walked straight to Bongani's room.

135

His door was locked. I returned to the lounge where mom was watching Television. I asked where Bongani was. Mind games were at play.

"Ah! Bakhona. You forget your brother is no longer a baby. He went out." I envied and pitied mom for not knowing what I now knew about her parents. I could not bring myself to ask her who my younger brother went out with. It was nosy of me, and not my business, mother would have told me.

I noticed how mom was becoming lax with Bongani. At his age I could not even stand at the gate inside the yard and chat to friends as they passed by. Also, I thought, could it be mother had suspected something, and was forcing girls onto my brother, to flush these feelings out of him? My thoughts were running wild. Anxiety was picnicking on me.

We were having dinner when Bongani showed up with a girl. He introduced her to me. Pretty girl. I should have been happy for him. For both of them. For mom. For me. But it was still too early to tell where he intended to go with this relationship. My younger brother was still at school. He had school work to concentrate on, and to a smaller degree on his extramural activities. Let alone a social life involving girls. This was puppy love. It was still too early days to throw away my anxiety in the garbage bin, and risk agonizing trauma afterwards.

My visits home became so ridiculously frequent after this holiday with my grandparents. Mom probably thought I'd been evicted and squatting with friends during the week.

I got into the nasty habit of monitoring Bongani's mannerisms. But it was all futile. As he was completing high school I worried when he had friends over. These were boys in his class. They woke up fresh while I woke up tired from trying to eavesdrop and listen for anything that might give me a clue. Any clue.

Bongani completed high school and proceeded to university. He continued to go out with that same girl. He still brought friends home. These were boys he studied Chemistry and Physics with during their first year at Medical School.

I finally left South Africa, of course, as I'd promised myself, so that my children would not become guinea pigs of an education system that kept being changed like undergarments. I'd resigned myself to never finding a plausible answer as to why they did not get it right the first time. Once and for all.

Was I moving overseas with a husband? No. I still had to find a loving man to begin a family with! I had rumblings in my head at times about grandmother's situation, wondering if guys smelled something unusual about me.

Worrying about Bongani returned when he came to visit me for the first time in my new home in the mid-West. He was alone! I'd tried to fish for more information on his girlfriend. "Yes, we are still together, if you insist on knowing. But the relationship has become complicated."

That's all Bongani was willing to share! This secretive brother of mine. "Is she highly expectant with your first born, and as a result barred from travelling long distances? Is this the nature of the complication?"

Those would have been speculative and inquisitive questions. Bongani would have dismissed them with the quiet arrogance he had acquired, to deal with people he despised for their foolishness. I wasn't sure he was aware of this standoffishness about him. It was something he put on and off. The attitude was enhanced by his studious look when he had his white coat and prescription glasses on. I observed this from the latest photos he'd brought to proudly show his only sister.

And then Bongani insisted on spending a week in San Francisco! He asked that I help him with flight reservations. He has always known what he wants out of life, this boy. But was he also pushing my buttons? Unwittingly so?

Of course it wasn't easy for Bongani to understand our grandparents' story when I finally told him, one year after they both had passed on. What about sharing the story with mom, though? No ways! I could not bring myself to ever discussing this family secret with her. I was glad Bongani felt the same. We saw eye to eye on this one issue.

Here is a story which has continued to torment me so many years after granddad and grandma told it to me in that staggered fashion. They did not make me swear to secrecy. I suppose, just as much as they knew to trust me not to repeat the story, they also had all the confidence in my fine judgment, that I'd remain discreet in the story's vicinity. But how could I trust myself never to share with anyone else? What utter cruelty. What a high level of trust, though. Yet, what weighty responsibility. I still think sharing this family secret with Bongani, was the smartest thing.

Now we watch our children grow. You'd think we watch their every mannerism and habit. Not so. The world has changed. I have changed. Whatever genes we all come with are an inheritance and a gift.

Bongani told me on one of his visits back to the United States, that he is developing a keen interest in genealogy. He was attending a conference on the same subject.

I ask myself why this matters to Bongani. If we traced the gene that gave grandma that streak in her make-up, then what next? *What would Bongani do? What would we as family, do?*

Better let what is, just be, and probably learn by heart the prayer of St. Francis of Assisi. Especially the wisdom to distinguish between things we can change and those we can't, so that when moments of trepidation seek to throw us off balance, that wisdom is readily available.

# Poetry in Motion

"Poetry in motion it truly was, Elizabeth! Would you not say, my love?" He was up now, stopping short of stretching out his arms too wide. He suppressed a full yawn. He had yet to brush his teeth. He was always energetic. Right from the second he opened his eyes. He was a busy man of course. He always had lots on his plate. He would have a quick breakfast. And then, with his brief case swinging high in his arms, his jacket flying and his feet climbing two stairs at a time, he'd storm right into his very busy day's schedule.

Except this past night. It had been a special night. Very special. For once, he'd flopped into bed without the next day's "to-do" list on his mind. Contrary to other nights, he'd honestly felt bedtime was enjoyable.

What a peaceful respite from his daily life! Running around like a rat. Making money he hardly truthfully enjoyed. So packed with perks he'd grown to hate. A tad absentmindedly, his fingers played a little happy tune on his bare chest. For this one night, he'd thrown out the window, the curse of his house.

With that "poetry in motion" question he was ready to strike a conversation with his bedtime companion, Elizabeth. He hoped she'd also wake up glowing with happiness, contentment legibly written all over her. Definitely with no pockets of disappointment hidden somewhere, in the folds of her mind and body. This still had to be confirmed, however. He'd done a bit of personal debriefing about his performance. He had concluded there was every reason to give it a high five.

Pleasant thoughts tend to be infectious. Here he was allowing the happy little song to carry him further, deep into the world of more bliss. He daringly proceeded to pack his mind with thoughts of even more heavenly possibilities here-on.

So grateful was he to Elizabeth for re-awakening in him something beautiful. He shook his head in wonder as thoughts kept flowing, "Damn! How could I have convinced myself it was all gone? That I was now only an empty shell? But look! My verve is still here. My vim never left me. It's been lying dormant. Yes. All there. Just dormant. That's all."

He was scanning his body now, looking at it with fresh eyes. Disbelief and relief were his happy package. He slapped his knee, grateful to have tasted, once again, the buoying possibilities inherent in intimacy.

If one threw the word 'regret' at him, Elizabeth's companion would have drawn a blank. Had he actually ever heard of the word? Or, if he had, its meaning had slipped his mind. He attached nothing to it.

He was still excitedly waiting for a response from his companion, when he spotted out of the corner of his eye, some joy buster. Worry! That nasty notorious coward. The notorious spoiler and menace that no-one wants as a neighbour. The spoiler was threatening to poison his good mood. How could thought processes be such unreliable turncoats? One minute they are giving him an assuring pat on his back, "You are the man!" He feels clearly the man. It's all glorious. He's puffed up. Chest out. And then? The next minute worry shows up. How could good mood defect on him like this?

What became even worse as moments unfolded, was that worry not only showed up. It dragged a seat and sat comfortably, determined to stay. Although it was such an unwelcome guest, worry hung its jacket behind the door, kicked off its shoes and even made itself a cup of tea. So began worry's unwelcome visit in the mental home of Elizabeth's companion!

Consequently, things took a turn for the worse. With worry's negative energy, Tom's high five rating began to stand on shaky legs. How it began to mar his joy and contentment! Tom found himself caught in the sticky web of a spider. He began the stressful process of peeling off the menacing web of self–doubt. It was sticking all over his once buoyed self, and the verve he had so happily boasted of just a short while back.

He was agonizing now about Elizabeth's take on the event. Possible poor ratings of his performance gnawed at his self-confidence. How that would surely deliver his heart and mind straight into the merciless jaws of a shredder. Worst of all these negative results would be coded in evasive words. Painful all the same. At that possibility, Tom grimaced. Elizabeth, a typical woman, would not be forthright with him. He'd have to be smart and alert to pick this up.

As a young man he remembered how those quiet messages killed him for what seemed like weeks. How had most ladies inculcated the nasty habit of being dishonest about their true feelings? Half absentmindedly, Tom muttered "Always, and with all of them, from my own experiences of course, yes is spelt with an N, and no spelt with a Y! Not anymore of course. Just joking. I'm minced meat should conscious women hear me say this today."

Last night. Tom recalled how he had noticed the interesting shape of Elizabeth's lovely eyes. They were enhanced cleverly with the dexterity of a good make-up artist. Eye-liner modestly applied. And whatever else goes into making up a woman's eye area.

Tom was familiar with eye-liner of course. In the early days of his marriage his wife wouldn't leave home without it. When he jingled the car keys and insisted it was time to go, he'd watch as she completed the procedure in the car, seated next to him. She'd pull down the lower lid. Right inside it, she'd draw a line with the black pencil. He knew it was unpleasant because she'd be blinking non-stop afterwards, as if trying to remove some foreign body in the eye. Why put the foreign object there in the first place? It had taken him a long time to see the slight difference the drawing on his wife's lower lid made to the overall look of her eyes and face.

His companion had clear, milky white eyes. So like those of a newly-born baby. He'd noticed this the previous evening, as she bashfully moved her eyes from side to side. This was during times she felt he was probing a bit too deeply into the private parts of her life.

There she was seated across him, nervously clasping and unclasping her long fingers, the soft glossy light pink nail polish the evidence of a well-done manicure. Thank goodness, he had absentmindedly observed, these were her natural nails. He was scared of the long artificial ones. Done distastefully, they looked more like weapons of war, and dismally failed to present the lady as well-groomed.

To Elizabeth's amazement, the pricks kept coming, in that very expensive and seemingly exclusive restaurant. One prick on the tip of the finger that a medical officer requests, is tolerable. But several of them? "Have you ever...? How do you...? How would you...? Why, if you knew it was risky? Would you...?"

The tone was confusing, soft as if it was agony for Tom to ask these barbed questions. Elizabeth, the respondent, thought from time to time that the scenario almost resembled documentaries on interrogation rooms of the old South Africa.

Like a boxer, she had to duck and dive in the answers she provided. It was her desperate effort to protect the most private parts of her life, from the relentless probing blows that kept coming from the man seated opposite her. Most times her efforts yielded too little, if anything at all. She was not a trained boxer.

As the interrogation continued, the blows that managed to land accumulated. They began to count. Elizabeth felt her head slowly swell, like too much air being pumped into a balloon. So dizzying were the questions. So daringly embarrassing at times! Something would soon explode in her, she felt. She managed to hold onto her wits, however.

Elizabeth was keenly aware that with this vicious tornado of pricks and probes, she might end up losing the bearings of her dignity. Easily, she could be thrown off mental balance, and even divulge her best kept secrets. The pricking didn't stop. The dark stormy clouds from these heavy questions kept descending, lower and lower. She was wary of the fluffy deceit of these clouds. They were tantalizingly soft, as they came out of Tom's gentle tone.

Deceitfully, they landed on top of Elizabeth like smooth flour lands softly in a bowl, out of a bakers' sieve. But how saturated they were with the potential of a damaging heavy down pour. Sharp thorns coated with the deceptively harmless flower that was Tom's voice. How the pricks and probes feigned playfulness, accompanied as they were with Tom's gentle face.

There was a time when Tom tried to reach across and hold Elizabeth's hand. She quietly refused to surrender it. She'd been through this danger zone before, where due to poor judgment, or expert luring by the other party, she'd ignored warning signs, angrily and desperately flashing from her gut. She'd later found herself right in the eye of the storm. Battered and bashed about she'd end up confused, and unable to figure out her integrity's cardinal points of south, east, west and north.

The current scenario wasn't a typical danger zone, though. He looked decent and polished. Clearly upper class. But the pricks and probes that came out of his mouth! They spewed out like bullets. No sooner was one round of ammunition spent, then another would show up.

Elizabeth was tired. She felt like stopping the interrogation with a few hard facts. The words had longed formed in her mind. They were on the tip of her tongue. But she did not utter them, "Come on, Tom. There are risks involved. But they come with the territory, you know. Cut this interrogation session out now." She wasn't used to these marathon embarrassing preliminaries, even as a tiny bit in her understood their necessity.

"Some people are very particular and fussy. Much too particular and fussy," they'd all been told in that first orientation session. She had long gone solo of course, tired of pimps that treated them all like trash. She understood perfectly the need for vetting, as these escapades can be *life-changing*. For the sake of survival, Elizabeth had long flushed out *life-threatening* in the special dictionary that was her psyche. Adopting such an

146

attitude could hinder her in many ways. It was too defeatist.

What about viewing her line of work as *life-changing?* Not bad, actually. Carefully turned around, and scrutinized for attributes, one would smile with relief at spotting some positive connotation tucked away neatly in several folds. There was the potential to *change life.* There was the possibility for growth and gaining experience. There was the likelihood also of turning over a new leaf. And, there was the heart-warming destination of healing.

On zooming onto the larger picture, bringing it into a clearer and more detailed focus, Elizabeth understood, however, that she was playing a mind game. It enabled her to go on working. However, it was never lost to her that she lived precariously on the edge. A slight mistake could be huge enough to see herself careen to the precipice.

What carried her daily? It was the attitude that while you have life you must live it; deal as best you can with the invisible hand of destiny. On this night of probes and pricks, it was this mind talk that stopped Elizabeth from reaching for her overnight bag, tucking her fingers under the two straps of the bag, heaving it onto her shoulder, and marching out from the man and his tireless pricking and probing of her private life.

With a deeper analysis, of course, and sad to say, there was no clear line of demarcation between what was and wasn't private, about Elizabeth. The private and public spaces of her life were pretty much blurred. This was the nature of the beast. When clear thinking visited, she completely understood this stark reality.

The pricks and probes continued. They deepened with each question. Tom maintained his determination to reach out to every little corner in Elizabeth's cupboard of private life. How she squirmed in her seat as he insisted on knowing this and that very private detail about her. It was hurtful. Her companion noticed how her eyes enlarged and watered slightly, after she gave another reluctant answer, which she had to dig up and out, from six feet deep.

Elizabeth was fearfully aware that Tom's pricking and probing would eventually draw blood from her soul. This was a no-no for her. She had long decided that she'd always protect her soul with all her might. Her precious soul was the only entity that would allow her to embrace wakefulness that came with the rising sun.

Indeed, it was the sun alone and daybreak it called forth, that relieved Elizabeth somewhat, of the nightly drudgery. With her physical strength wrung out to the last drop, her soul was the only priced possession she was left with. Only her soul would enable her to still answer when her name, Elizabeth, was called. Her intact soul was her ultimate core, even if she couldn't preserve other parts of herself.

Taking cognizance of the goings-on, over a period of time, soul had risen up the ranks and taken charge. It was her faithful champion. Soul picked up, bandaged and nursed back to health the other fractured parts of Elizabeth. Soul generously provided her a true feeling of wholeness. She felt healed.

Soul invoked and re-awakened that perfect beautiful baby, Elizabeth, the nurse had delivered to her mother, bundled up and warm, in the first few minutes of her life here. Soul brought back to Elizabeth, the same baby girl clad in a long dainty white christening robe, her parents had both handed to the priest to be anointed with holy water, and admitted into the Christian fold. Elizabeth. But life comes with vicissitudes. And there's destiny which works unseen.

Elizabeth's companion was quite defiantly determined to get to the last question on that long list, though, and have it adequately exhausted before they were done. That decision to probe had been resolute. For this was going to be his debut. He had summoned up the necessary courage and determination to keep on probing. No doubt, the process was uncomfortable for him as well. But they had to go through this. His companion had to bear with him and stick it out, he thought constantly. This was certainly the ugliness of the beast.

In time the discomfort of the probing questions had finally ended. She'd known this gruelling process would end. But what an ordeal! She didn't remember ever being subjected to such a lengthy preliminary interview. No-one had ever taken so much time to get to 'know' her! Caught off guard she had been, really. But her solid armour, her saving grace, was in her handbag. She had yanked it out and put it on. And her eyes, the deceivers she'd trained to be, played along. They never betrayed her true feelings. Clad in her armour she'd easily eased into make believe mode. As usual, she had siphoned out her real self. She had protected it from the demeaning situation. She had left her genuine self, within the safe and secure walls of her own bedroom, at her home.

As was her practice in this work, she only subjected her outer self to be the dirty floor rag. Her eye was only on the price at the end of the torment. She had a vivid picture of her outer shell in a bucket of soapy water and a scrubbing brush, to bring about that temporary sparkle and joy to her users. "They don't really know me," was the line that made the separation easy and distinct, between Elizabeth's core, and her outer shell.

So she had passed the test! And here she was now. Her scrubbed outer shell was lying next to the prober. He had known that the preliminaries, uncomfortable as they were for both of them, paid dividends in terms of the protection they guaranteed.

He understood that his conscience would prick him mercilessly. But at least, the assurance that he was adequately protected, lessened the pain of guilt feeling that would slowly rise, plague and ache him, over time. Nevertheless, Elizabeth's host hoped guilt conscience would be lenient with him, because the circumstances that led to this inaugural, were well-documented. He pleaded for understanding, without condoning his decision and action.

It was the morning after the night before, as he willed Elizabeth's eyes to open. He missed already the joy of looking into them. A fine work of aesthetics they were.

Bliss is best shared. And so, he couldn't wait for a recap, to savour the events of the night before with this special guest. He had already decided he'd find the right moment during their romantic debriefing, to talk her into another "Poetry in Motion" rendition, before they parted ways. He imagined that they'd be sitting upright against the head board, hands held, as he negotiated with her, that morning.

For these imagined thoughts to take firm root, Tom quickly locked up self-doubt mind talk about possibilities of a poor rating. Indirect negative reviews, and a polite if not blatantly rude and insensitive refusal to offerings of a second helping, would demean him. They'd cut his tall well-structured form to the size of a mosquito.

Thandi's husband imagined Elizabeth gleefully capture and satisfactorily slap his face to sure self-esteem death, instead of caressing it lovingly, held firmly in her small butter-soft hands, her beautiful eyes voraciously gobbling it. Would he emerge a giant winner or a crushed paper-weight mosquito?

Well, it was just a matter of time before he'd know his fate. At the moment he thought it best to fling the key to that locked up cupboard of negative thoughts, far into the wilderness.

Tom travelled back in time to his experiences when he courted women. He had long observed the following: If she liked her beau on that first date, nothing pleases a woman more than to hear, "Let's do this again. I'd like to see you again," as he pecks a light nervous kiss on her cheeks and leaves. The gentleman is content. He knows that he has responsibly tucked the lady safely in her place of abode. But more importantly, he knows he has secured another date, and made one lady happy.

Tom was so obsessed with this part that at times, when he brought his lady to her front door, he'd make as if he was leaving, without commenting on their date. And then he'd turn and pronounce that fine heart-caressing line, just before she opened her door, and disappeared into what could perhaps escalate into a heart too heavy for her wilting body to carry. Her hopes would be dashed into small sharp glass pieces she'd drag to bed with her. A long wild stormy night would ensue.

This scenario was a constant teaser when Tom went out with his grandsons. These were the years the boys pretended to their granddad that they were still clueless about dating protocol. "Imagine a thick rich lather from a favourite cake of soap. Imagine it tantalizingly and seductively forming and sliding on your wet body, after a taxing work-out, the delicate scent filling the shower or bath tub."

His eyes would be all out, darting from one grandson to the other. "That feeling, my boys. Trust me, nothing pleases a lady more. This is apart from the dinner, the movie, what have you. Believe me. You mess up this last part on a date? You've spoilt the whole thing. And perfect timing for the right words is key."

The grandsons would smile, nod an agreement as they fiddled with a teaspoon, a fork, a knife, a sugar bowl, or serviette - whatever served as a tool to absorb the awkwardness of intimacy discussions with granddad. "My dear, what a lovely evening! I definitely would love to see you again!" This was the younger of the two grandsons, practicing. "Like this granddad? Then a kiss on the forehead?"

"Exactly! You'll love how your date responds."

This morning Tom couldn't wait for the right moment to surprise Elizabeth, treat her to this special rich lather of suggesting a repeat of the previous night's beautiful pinnacle performance of Poetry in Motion. And indeed, so many more revisits of the previous night, in the not too distant future.

More importantly, he fervently hoped she'd be willing to cross over to a more regular arrangement with him. For to him, in a few short hours, Elizabeth had metamorphosed into some-one more grand, especially after she passed his prickly pear test so impressively.

How a regular arrangement would save him. How it would make his life easier in so many ways. The more he thought about this possible arrangement, the more he concluded how perfect it would be. If she declined the humble request? Well, he was willing to understand, disappointed as he might be, though.

As a business man he knew it was necessary to respect the boundaries Elizabeth had probably set for her kind of work. He hoped she'd forgiven him for the long pricking and probing session. Were she to garner the courage to complain about it, he had a ready assuring answer, "Trust me, it was necessary, dear Elizabeth, for both of us, needless to add."

He had no clue of course how Elizabeth had, and maybe still felt about the barrage of questions the night before. How did the ordeal compare in some respects to the Comrades Marathon, in terms of its challenging and exacting nature. At the finish line she had received her medal, for passing the test with distinction!

Unfortunately, it was the kind of medal she couldn't display proudly on her nightstand at home, or wear around her neck. It could perhaps end up pencilled in codes in her private journal or personal diary, if not pinned carefully and securely on the wall of her memory.

As for the pricking of his own conscience, Tom hoped against hope that as he prayerfully fingered the beads of his rosary during early morning Sunday Mass, his eyes and those of the Virgin Mary would lock. And he would see her merciful eyes speaking to him with divine compassion, "I understand, son. Trust me, I do understand. Confession was made for such times of folly and weakness of the flesh."

It was all quiet, though. He listened carefully for faint sounds of breath from Elizabeth. The body lying next to his, with the nuisance of a bed sheet in between them, made it difficult for Tom to observe any chest movement. He was hoping to catch her rib cage actively expanding and collapsing, even slightly, typical of a content body at rest, in deep sleep.

As carefully as he could, Tom slowly began to free himself from the entanglement of the entire sheet. He lifted his upper body to get a better view of the situation. He rested his upper body on his elbows and peeped, in an effort to see her face more closely. He was aware of the silly boyish smile enveloping his face. Her eyes were shut. How he missed them!

With the back of his hand he gingerly felt her upper body covered by the sheet. He hoped to be comforted by Elizabeth's warm body. With the duvet at the foot of the bed, the sheet was rather cold and so he could only pretend to feel her body temperature.

Mindfully, he slumped back into a supine position. He was becoming more acutely aware of the panic mode he was slowly slipping into. Worry, his unwanted guest hadn't left. Tom put his hand over his heart to quiet the thumping heartbeat which strangely seemed to march in step with a pulsating headache. He moved his hands to his temples, to silence the throbbing.

All to no avail, however. How anxious he was to see Elizabeth begin to stir, out of what seemed for some reason, an awkward deep and long slumber. Not that he was familiar with her sleeping style of course.

Tom wanted a cigarette badly. He was surprised at the strange but strong urge right then. There weren't cigarettes in the house. Of course. He had become a strong 'smoke free zones' advocate. Like born again Christians who don't need to be asked their spiritual status before they proudly blurt it out, Tom was known for his, "In my younger days I'd be lighting a cigarette right now. But government and health folks pestered us so sick with second hand smoke stuff, I finally hung up my habit, and flushed my last cigarette down the toilet many years ago." To non-smokers there was no reaction. He was preaching to the converted. To smoking addicts and zealots, he was a pain, a nuisance.

But what an encouragement to those still on the road to Damascus! This crowd was looking forward to the time they'd answer to the name Paul, and automatically abandon the name Saul. They seriously yearned for the big bang moment of salvation, after the enlightening lightning struck cold the fire at the end of their cigarettes, and their smoking habit was turned into useless ash.

Tom was torn. Should he remain a good, well-mannered host and not disturb his guest in her sleep? Or should he respond to an urgent desire to allay fears that were beginning to form in his core and then spread all over him, in small ripples of a potentially nauseating menace?

Let alone tempt him to light a cigarette and smoke? As each minute passed, the plot seemed to thicken. Elizabeth's body remained in limbo, in a progressively disturbing way. He began to survey his surroundings. He was trying very hard to not acknowledge how insanely panic-stricken he was becoming.

This was his house, but not his regular bedroom. He had always listened half-heartedly to tips from his friends, some of whom appeared seasoned in the trade he was just beginning to venture into. "Never take her to the sanctity of your bedroom. That's the lowest you can get, if you got married in church and repeated those holy vows after the priest, with family and friends to bear witness."

Tom was surprised that he recalled the advice so effortlessly. The advice given had not even been directed at him. Everybody knew he didn't play the infidelity game. But something had changed. Something was about to snap. Or had it already snapped? Only time would tell. Here he was engaging in quite a sure-footed operation, as he led Elizabeth, the previous night. He was holding her one hand, playfully feeling the smoothness of her manicured nails, as if he was still a young unattached man, enjoying the company of his girlfriend as they took a long walk at the park. The long winding journey ended in the guest room, far from the vicinity of the master bedroom.

Worry wasn't done tormenting Tom. The question of violence against women was on his mind. For women like Elizabeth, where did gender experts and activists draw the line? Take his case with Elizabeth. They were consenting adults. Both had needs.

For a brief moment his mind travelled back to his primary school days. It zeroed on his English language classes, specifically feminine and masculine gender drills. Yes, they actually sounded like drills as they repeated after their teacher:

"ram, ewe
 boy, girl
 male, female
 nephew, niece."

Tom remembered how he had finally figured out how to differentiate between nephew and niece. Girls are nice, as in pretty. So niece belongs in the feminine gender.

His mind then brought back those classes to the moment with his guest. He wondered why the main bedroom is also known as the master bedroom! "Repeat after me, class:

Master bedroom, mistress bedroom."

If they were primary school kids of today who know too much too soon, Tom was sure there'd be knowing giggles! It also occurred to him that he'd never heard any comment from gender activists or read from any of their gender literature about this awkward "mistress bedroom" possibility.

Elizabeth was taking a shower. Tom's mind was quite idle as he waited for his guest to join him. His mind travelled deeper into the subject of gender. Gender activists and their selective gender "equality and equity." He recalled the point he had made at one gender workshop and the fracas it caused:

"Madam Chair, I wish to raise my concern about the difficult words and terminology used in gender discourse. The difficulty of mastering or mistressing, if you will, the difference between gender equality and gender equity, need not be over-emphasized. Not many people understand it. And does this matter?"

Tom remembered the huge number of heads that nodded as he made that point. Aware he was becoming a nuisance to the workshop facilitator, he still prided himself for having slipped in one last comment.

"Madam Chair, I have always wondered how your favourite people are empowered and helped to change their lives by this complicated jargon? I'm talking about your main constituency of concern, the so-called 'poorest of the poorest.' Sorry, 'the poorest of the poor' - I mean."

He had put "empowered and helped to change their lives" in imaginary inverted commas.

"So-called, Sir? Do you not believe in the work we do?"

"Madam, my point is this: With this gender jargon, how do you ensure that *that* constituency on the margins of society is helped to fully understand, imbibe and inhabit these new ideas, so that they become second nature to them, not a special dress they put on for special occasions, like these workshops, and then park in the suitcase suffocating in the smell of moth balls, to haul out again another distant time and put on for another special occasion, like this gathering today. Obviously, utterly useless in their daily lives. Do you get the point I'm making here, Madam Chair?"

"As a matter of fact, we do, Sir. We do make a difference in their lives. The statistics speak for themselves. The women you are referring to, do become empowered."

Incensed by the display of arrogant bogus confidence, Tom had persisted, aware that he wouldn't be tolerated for much longer as a nuisance and menace. "Let me put it bluntly, Madam Chair. In actual fact, I don't believe you. Which stats? Where is the living evidence that the poorest of the poor are now empowered? Who in this audience can boldly and proudly vouchsafe your claim?" Tom tapped the roaming microphone to ensure it was still live, and then continued to engage the audience.

"Madam Chair, a friend works in rural areas. He knows first-hand what goes on there. His activism is hands-on. How many times has he agonized about the failure to engender real change, as a gender activist?

This is his usual lament: 'Tom, I'll still ask for funding for my NGO. But we are not making noticeable progress.

Regrettably, some of our gender activists believe this work begins and ends with these perpetual and meaningless gender workshops!

And the attendant jargon, how do you explain "gender mainstreaming" and show the difference between "equity and equality" to a dedicated woman activist out in the rural areas, and with very little or no education?' Do you see what I mean, Madam Chair?"

"Ladies and gentlemen, let's break for tea. We'll continue with this discussion after the short break."

Of course that had been the end of his comment. Tom remembered the look of disappointment Madam Chair wore. During that tea-break, she had proceeded to speak to some other women speakers and government officials attending the event.

No-one took him to task during tea break. Not even during lunch. He made an effort to find a seat next to Madam Chair. But she told him that if he didn't mind she had a few important phone calls to make.

A gentle perfumed mist followed Elizabeth as she finally emerged out of the shower. It put paid to the host's wondering and wandering mind. Gender stuff quickly retreated. So did any possible thoughts that he could be violating Elizabeth's rights, as a woman. They were consenting adults. End of story!

For the first time, in the gradually discomforting quietness and Elizabeth's almost motionless form, Tom absentmindedly paid attention to the decor. How many times had Thandi raved about what she and the interior decorator had accomplished? How she urged Tom to go see for himself. But, he never really bothered to go and see the acclaimed handiwork.

He was occupied with making money, in an effort to quench Thandi's insatiable appetite for accumulating stuff. Money and stuff had become her perfect definition of a good life. And her husband had become the money-generating machine. How it nauseated him to see his wife flaunting her advantaged life, wearing money and wealth on her sleeve.

This was surely not the woman he had married. Or had she cleverly hidden something from him when he courted her? Calculated revenge? It smelled like it? Misplaced, though? It appeared so. At times Tom felt there was something else much deeper, that Thandi was suffering from. She appeared angry with the world. And Tom was the closest scapegoat to be subjected to her anger and urge.

He'd spent precious time and energy cursing his luck for drawing him to a woman clearly neck deep in baggage. Definitely a very foolish investment. How she had mastered the art of swimming in the horridly dark and dirty river water, infested with anger and hatred - crocodiles that would eat her up one day. But Tom had, over time, worked on his emotions. He'd successfully trained them to choose their battles. He had two boys to bring up after all.

MaZulu, the house keeper, knew they'd been at it again when the lady of this ice cold mansion stormed into the kitchen, arms akimbo, as she aimlessly opened and shut kitchen cupboards, buttons and button holes of her white silk gown mismatched, her long unkempt hair a carpet piece matted like the thick tops of the natural Amazon forest.

When the hour of 9 am struck, MaZulu knew to clear the table setting for one, understanding that the head of house had already left without having breakfast. The lady of the house usually had brunch, after she'd had a good long bath, perfume in her bath almost chocking the potted ferns adorning the top of the gold cistern.

This was her supposed power. To be insanely extravagant. He made the money. She wasted it. This had become their unspoken deal. Tom had come to terms with these rules of engagement, although he often wondered to himself where and how Thandi got fulfilment from sucking his blood this dry.

Had she no yearnings of going back to her profession? Engage in something useful, related to her profession - medical care? With his financial support and business acumen she could long have developed a lucrative business out of her professional training. Maybe establish a private clinic, or start a private ambulance company.

He was constantly baffled by his wife's behavior. He was disappointed, actually. Thandi had taken such a selfish and skewed stance on married life. Did she not remember who she was; what kept her happy, busy, and self-confident and fulfilled when he met her at that HIV/AIDS International Conference? How many times had he reminded her of what had attracted him to her?

A powerful, young self-assured African professional nurse, delivering a brilliant paper on that podium. And she was fielding even tough questions on gender issues, women's empowerment and men who refuse to put on condoms.

"I found a way to make you notice me, Thandi. You've no idea how delighted I was when you gave me a moment during tea break. With your business card sitting snugly among my bank cards, I knew I had the greatest news to share that night: "Mom and dad, I've found her! The search is over."

For as long as he could remember, these thoughts had become his mental pastime. They were often triggered when in the silence that had become the signature of their time in this space they shared, he heard his wife's shuffling feet, her heavy body further weighed down by the hatred and unhappiness she seemed to wear proudly like a designer garment. Where had that light spring in her foot disappeared to?

Tom usually left the door of his study slightly opened, in case Thandi pounced on MaZulu, again. He feared something small might escalate into a big thing. MaZulu would find herself carrying out the threat she'd shared with him on several occasions.

"Mr. Tom, I'll grab a frozen pack of sausages and smash her head into little pieces with it. No woman urinates on my head like this, time after time. I may be poor, but you know I proudly belong to royalty. I'm a descendant of King Shaka, Shaka Zulu! *Ungizwe kahle.* Hear me well, Mr. Tom."

He spent time pleading with MaZulu to calm down. He advised her what to tell herself if the troublemaker wife started it again. Despite this talk on how to handle the lioness, Tom understood MaZulu was only human.

When he was around, he felt it his duty to stay vigilant, so that when need arose he could jump in and save both women the trauma and embarrassment that an unbridled flare of tempers might lead to.

In the silence of the guest room, as Elizabeth continued to sleep, these all over the place thoughts, had visited Tom again, almost unconsciously.

His eyes continued to zoom in on different parts of the guest room, as he waited for signs of wakefulness in Elizabeth. Photos of their grandchildren were tastily displayed on the dressing table. The carpet was the same as in their master bedroom, he noticed. But the colour on the walls was warmer, Thandi had told him. Whatever designers mean by that.

He gazed at the photos of his two grandsons. They were in their early teens in the photos. They had those naughty looks on their faces. Their teeth were all wired up. Tom still didn't understand what for. He began to feel guilty just looking at the pictures. In their late teens now, granddad knew to be careful. He had to be exemplary.

He knew his grandsons were absorbing like a sponge his every word, said or implied. Had all the pricking and probing been enough? He was pestered by stories of damage despite guaranteed fool proof protection and precaution. One after the other, the boys' parents had died of AIDS. First, the boys' father, his only son. A year later, their mother, Tom's beautiful daughter-in-law, a woman with a golden heart.

Tom was the custodian now, the surrogate parent responsible for the boys, Bongumusa and Colin. Tom was literally bringing up the boys alone, as his wife, their grandmother, continued to spin in her own orbit. She seemed at times on the edge of a cliff. The grandkids had learned to leave grandmother alone, after many years of agonizing about her behavior.

Initially, the boys felt guilty that she perhaps found them burdensome.

Two years into this miserable life, Tom had requested a child psychologist to intervene. The boys were assured that if they noticed something odd about their grandmother, they were not to blame for it. In the depths of her heart, she loves them dearly.

"You are such adorable and loving boys, no-one in their right mind would even dare entertain hating you. For what, honestly? So, just relax. Grandmother will come around when her time is right. And do also remember this: don't you dare accept the label 'HIV/AIDS orphans', insensitively given to children like you, by a world that is losing its decency."

The boys had needed just one session with the psychologist. Tom hoped that the awkwardness of the meeting began to melt just as the boys stepped into the afternoon breeze, and he drove them home. Tom wished that by the time the sun set that day, the boys had had time to chew, digest and accept what the psychologist had told them. It was Tom's silent prayer that the boys carefully tucked the advice in the inside pockets of their Sunday jackets for safe keeping.

That night, as the grandsons filed into the study to give their granddad 'good night' hugs, Tom smiled and further impressed upon Bongumusa and Colin, "Boys, I hope the advice from the psychologist becomes your priced compass to guide and direct you, as you navigate your way through life in general, and here, in your grandparents' home."

As for the 'good-night' the boys wished him, these two words had long become meaningless for Tom, except on the night before, with Elizabeth.

Tom's eyes moved to the latest school photographs. Individual photos. Group photos with classmates. Photos of the boys with their respective rugby teams.

The mixed bag of thoughts about the boys' private boarding school haunted him. How he always looked forward and simultaneously dreaded conferences with the teachers. Meeting the other parents, some of whom still gave him and the boys a look that clearly communicated a very unwelcoming message. Never mind he was well-dressed and decent. Never mind he was driving the latest Jaguar. Never mind his grandsons were good rugby players and very well-mannered. Never mind everybody knew he was the granddad, a man who was parenting again, with the boys' parents never ever going to show up at school and deal with all the crap from some of the stubbornly unrefined, unreformed and untransformed.

Tom and the boys had long learned the unwritten rule by some parents and their sons. "Outside school premises we do not know you blacks at all." The three had been shocked at first. They'd be all excited to meet some of the parents and sons - in town, at the Mall, only to be slapped with clear messages of, "How dare you make such a claim? Have we met you before?"

Initially, Tom's grandsons had to look twice and ask each other in confused disbelief, "Isn't that so and so, and his parents?" Of course it was. No mistake about it. Tom and the boys had learned and accepted the pretence. Tom was grateful, however, for other parents and their boys who perceived and treated him and his grandsons as complete human beings.

It was natural for Tom's thoughts to gravitate to a paper he was working on. It aimed at addressing the issue of Africans in exclusive private schools. Over the years these schools had become ridiculously expensive. What was the aim? To deliberately exclude the majority? In his head he had completed the paper. He knew exactly what he wanted to put across. But on paper he had written very little, besides two items.

First, the title he had long concluded was appropriate: *"Our African Educationists Are Failing Us."* Second, was what he'd already planned to be the very last paragraph of the paper, in which he would invite those concerned to ponder on this: *Is there no alternative for us, other than subjecting our young beloved sons and daughters to the daily stress and humiliation of being made to feel they don't belong or are too inadequate to belong; that they don't and will never measure up, no matter how much they tried?*

Frustrated as Tom was, he had a duty to perform, to bring up his son's boys well, groom them to be life-smart and world-smart dignified African men. "Always put things in perspective. You can imagine how many difficult situations I've come across in my life. This is what always comes to my rescue, when life's challenges come knocking on my door, young lads. So, always put things in perspective. Never forget, my boys!"

As he liked to teach or preach to his grandsons, depending on the occasion, they'd also become familiar with Tom's, "Good manners, my boys, always. Be gentlemen. This will take you far in life. Trust me." His times with the boys, Tom thought. What a blessing! How Thandi was missing out on these precious moments.

Tom was at his wits end about what to do next, as Elizabeth's position in bed did not change. He knew he had to decide on the next step regarding his guest. But panic mangled his usually clear thinking. His mind was caught in a bind.

It was easier to carry on thinking about his boys. These were clean thoughts. And they were convenient when an ugly situation he could not understand, was fast building up in the guest room. The warm colour on the walls wasn't even coming close to easing the spasms from the cold shudder that was slowly rising up his spine. For a minute more, Tom managed to ignore the status quo, as he allowed thoughts about his boys to occupy centre stage.

It was almost a given that during every homecoming granddad and the boys would have a thousand and one issues to discuss, as they enjoyed their lunch away from school rules, school bells, school prefects and school teachers. Most were complaints about a long list of what made them mad at their school. It hurt Tom to realize that no matter how long he'd take to complete the article, it would always be relevant.

Tom felt it was his duty, however; just like his parents had done to him; just like his grandparents had done to his mom and dad; to protect the young, as far as possible, from the negatives of life. So that as was humanely possible, under any prevailing circumstances, children could manage and afford to enjoy just being children.

Tom never took light-heartedly his role as a model to his grandsons. He strongly felt it was his task and responsibility to give these boys tools that would protect and sustain them. He had to take up the banner here and appoint himself champion. He had to find ways and words to build and sustain his grandsons' human dignity and sense of self. This was his effort to assist the young men to emerge victorious over the humiliation and degrading episodes that they were becoming more sensitive to, as they grew up in years.

And his wife's' strange behaviour had not ceased over the years ....

It's strange how fast thoughts travel! All of these one hundred kilometre long thoughts covered, could be calculated in minutes by clock time.

Tom's mind finally regained current situation consciousness, as it were. It went back to real time. He collected the necessary wits and courage to face squarely the predicament in his guest room. Flashes of good times he usually had with his grandsons passed through his mind. They imposed guilt on him.

Thandi's husband was in two mind zones. While he was trying hard to numb his mind and nerves to the anxiety building up, as the form on the bed remained motionless, he also had to be alert to changes, if any, he added reluctantly. His mind couldn't imagine Elizabeth's grim condition gravitating to something worse. This was huge already.

And he was struggling to decide on the next steps. Dwelling on hope alone, clearly hadn't delivered any good results since he posed the Poetry in Motion question to Elizabeth, when he woke up. Quite a while back now, actually. Tom didn't even want to do an estimation by clock time of how much time he'd been sitting there, hoping and waiting.

He gave his neck a little massage and exercised his shoulders. It was time to brace himself, face the music, like a man. Here was a poopy situation building up, if the gods remained insane.

Tom recalled, "Boys always put things in perspective." Blah, blah, blah! It was painful for Elizabeth's companion to conclude that whatever perspective he'd come up with and employ to manage life with an unloving, selfish wife, it was this dysfunctional relationship that was responsible for the predicament he was in now. He could long have stopped Thandi's exasperating skewed stance on their marriage. So, he had to take the blame for his inaction.

Gradually, as Elizabeth's condition didn't change for the better, Tom began to see his once reasonably quiet and almost uneventful public life, taking him to places he never dreamed of. Police, court, lawyers, prison, shame and regret.

Thandi had departed to Switzerland, without as much as a forwarding address, after she had her by-pass gastric surgery performed by a well-respected Swiss surgeon. Tom had conducted the research, located this doctor, paid in advance and signed the necessary papers as Thandi's husband. "Just in case," the doctor had explained to him telephonically.

Without his knowledge, Thandi had treated herself to a first class round trip ticket. Just before he drove Thandi to the airport, Tom had noticed the second ticket, as she checked if her passport was among important documents.

As he fought the urge to confront her about the other ticket, Tom reckoned that the date for the operation could not be changed. So he assumed she intended to travel to the other secret destination after being discharged from the hospital. He had sensed it was deliberate on her part, to not divulge where she'd be going, and what she'd be doing, after her operation. But he had let that purposeful slip slide into nothing. He'd grown weary of a life without any trust and mutual respect.

Tom knew the street. He had been driving past there most nights, since Thandi's departure, observing and thinking and finally deciding the woman decently and tastefully dressed, carrying a lovely designer handbag, was going to be the one. She had been easy to approach as she seemed discreet. No heavy make-up. No extremely tight fitting clothing. No bulging boobs. Just a normal woman. Clearly, a cut above the rest.

He'd walked up to her, had a little chat, and left. The next evening they'd met at a certain spot. They'd then driven off to begin their time together. They had spent quite a while at the exclusive restaurant Tom had chosen for dinner. This is where the grilling questions had taken place. He had referred to this session as preliminaries.

They'd watched the full moon and attempted to count the stars, as they sat sipping wine. This was in one of the more private balconies in Tom's mansion. Tom understood that Elizabeth had reluctantly endured his incessant probing. He hoped the ambience in his house had fast deleted the unpalatable experience for Elizabeth. He hoped it hadn't been so rough that she neither remembered what she ate, nor appreciated the special atmosphere at the high end restaurant. Maybe Elizabeth would mention the probing when she woke up. In that case, he was ready to apologize.

Finally, Tom sighed deeply and said a little prayer. He proceeded to strip the bed of the duvet. Right off, although it was crumpled at the foot of the bed. He was resigned now to face squarely, the reality of his daytime nightmare. He prepared for the worst as he began to slowly peel off the top sheet the lady was entangled in. First the neck. Then the chest. He needed to go no further. He had to almost study the chest, in order to confirm that the Elizabeth's respiratory system was still on duty.

Bending over her, as she continued to lie on her side, he found the wrist on the arm that was lying limply across the chest. He felt the pulse. The lustre of her light pink nails seemed to have gone dull, Tom noticed. Something had gone awry with blood circulation. That much he could surmise. He had to press her wrist harder with his thumb and forefinger, willing the heart to be still pumping blood like it was duty bound to. The pulse was faint. Very faint.

Feeling a bit more hopeful and forcing positivity to ride and rule the moment, he felt her chest with the back of his hand. It was warm, heaving ever so slightly, so reluctantly. "Thank God!" He whispered as he wiped a few drops of sweat from his forehead. He knelt on the floor on the side of the bed, so that he could take a closer look at Elizabeth. He felt courageous enough now to call out her name, as he shook her body gently.

Tom, by nature, was not a jumpy and easily excitable man. He did not have to try very hard to remain cool, calm and collected, even in difficult situations. But right then, he was stunned as the painful and unexpected drama unfolded. His heart was doing a 100 kilometre sprint. "Elizabeth, Elizabeth, please wake up. What's wrong, dear? Don't do this to me, please."

Tom's cell phone rang. He knew the caller. "How is it going? Or shall I say how did it go, Tom? Briefly, now. Just the highlights. I only have five minutes." There was no response from Tom. The caller continued, "The rest I'll hear tonight, over sundowners." Silence continued on Tom's end of the line. "Okay then, if you are busy. See you later."

It was Santo, a very close friend who knew about Tom's debut the night before. Tom slowly shook his head. He was regretting that he didn't have the guts to tell Santo what was developing to be a heart-stopping "highlight" in the house. Then he received a texted message. It was Santo again.

"Sorry I cut you short. I'm so curious to hear about it all. Just sum up the experience in one sentence, while I pretend to be listening to this boring report on climate change."

Tom responded, finally, and texted back. 'I'm in a soup. The woman isn't waking up! What do I do, Santo? This is a mess!"

"Not waking up? Too tired to wake up? What exactly do you mean?"
This was the next puzzled message from Santo. He immediately left the conference hall and called Tom.

"Is she not stirring? Even a little bit? She's breathing though? Right?

"Santo. I woke up early, as usual. Then ..." Tom struggled to put words together into a coherent whole.

"Relax, please, Tom. Tell me slowly now. What's happening?"

"Her pulse is faint. Very faint. Her body is virtually still. Hardly moving."

"Have you checked if she's breathing? Is her body warm?"

"Her breathing is hardly noticeable. I've just felt her body again. It's still warm. What do I do now?"

"Just still warm? What do you expect next? Damn! Tom, what have you got yourself into? Don't waste more time. Call an ambulance!"

"Some serious condition, it appears to be. What have we gotten ourselves into, Santo?"

She was in a knee length sheer and elegant black night shirt, with matching underwear. Tom found her designer handbag and overnight bag. With one hand he reluctantly went through her handbag, feeling without looking, for her identity document. He found it. He nervously read out loud, deliberately singling out every syllable. Elizabeth Nomusa Madadeni. Born in 1986 in a town Tom had never heard of.

As he put the Identity Book back in the bag his hand felt another document. A passport. His eyes widened as he quickly scanned it for travel history, in anticipation of surprises. There were no entry and exit border stamps. The passport had been issued only a few weeks back, he learned, as he turned the pages. But glued on one page was a recently granted United States visa.

Tom had just slipped on his long pants when he heard the siren from an ambulance. He held his head with both hands and shook it hard. He was bracing himself to face the world. He quickly collected whatever Elizabeth had placed on the pedestal. Her watch and lip stick. He collected her wash rag and toothbrush in the bathroom and quickly put these in her overnight bag. The cellphone was in the handbag. But it was off and useless in terms of helping him trace a few people in her phonebook. Some Madadeni names, at least.

The paramedics were already at the front door, banging it hard, by the time he turned the lock and opened for them. Just then another car pulled up. It was Santo. He placed a hand on Tom's shoulder as the paramedics asked Tom a few questions and took his details.

The head of the group of paramedics stopped as he entered Tom's surname in the form, "Piyane. Tom Piyane. That name sounds familiar. But hey, we have a crisis here. I suspect the lady might be slipping into a coma. Let's get cracking. Where's she? Lead us, please."

The head of the crew was now feeling the pulse and examining Elizabeth briefly with the stethoscope, after the group had turned her body, and gently lay her on her back. Her head was limply turned to the side. Her eyes remained closed. As he threw the stethoscope on his shoulder, the head of paramedics resignedly announced, "Without knowing her medical history, it is difficult to speculate on the cause of this almost moribund state. We need to move fast. As I've hinted it might be a coma. But until a proper and thorough examination is conducted with necessary tests done, this is all guess work."

The head of paramedics then turned to face Tom. With a little disgust and mistrust in his furiously flushed face, he asked, "When did she slip into this condition?"

"I last spoke to her last night. When I woke up, I usually wake up earlier than anybody. This is how she was."

"What time was this?"

"I'd say about 6.00am."

The head of paramedics checked the time on his watch. He suspected something fishy. Exasperation was conspicuous on his face. And he didn't care to hide it. "Now it's 9.30am!" We've lost more than three hours." Tom kept his head bowed, to avoid another blame-packed look. He hadn't actually noticed three hours had passed! He was familiar with how medical people almost scold one for delaying to seek their help.

Tom didn't like the look that implied he was responsible for Elizabeth's sad condition. But luckily, he was too numb to absorb the implications of it all. For a fleeting moment the face of the Virgin Mary loomed large. While he silently prayed for her help, his soul was too heavily laden with guilt. He could not bring himself to find her eyes and ask for forgiveness.

Elizabeth was now on a stretcher. An oxygen mask was secured on her face. She was wheeled out of the house. They were manoeuvring the stretcher with extreme difficulty on several flights of winding stairs. They also had to be very careful with Elizabeth's body. It was almost slipping headlong onto the floor. Tom watched, panic-stricken. He wondered why Thandi, the self-appointed manager, was delaying so much in having the lift installed in the house.

Quotations had been done. An elevator contractor had been appointed. It was all her choice, because she suspected Tom would go for something cheap and old-fashioned. "This is crazy!" Tom muttered to himself as paramedics struggled so many times to keep Elizabeth's body secured on the stretcher.

Tom hoped Thandi hadn't tempered with that money. Large amounts in her hands always caused problems. The first class and second destination tickets came to mind. What happened to the money set aside for the installation of the elevator? Where would Thandi be going after her operation? But there wasn't time to dwell on these images and likely answers.

Before the ambulance got ready to pull off, Santo hurriedly brought down Elizabeth's bags. Tom put these on the front seat, as the rest of the crew were still finishing whatever they routinely had to do, to ensure the patient's reasonably comfortable on the trip to the closest hospital's emergency section.

"Please take good care of these," Tom told the driver. He returned to the back of the ambulance to give the same message to the head of paramedics. "Don't worry.

They will be stored securely. We are taking her to Mpilonde Hospital. We have your number. We'll call you with further information on the diagnosis, as soon as she's been examined by the doctor. The hardest and most urgent task will be finding her next of kin. But we'll make a plan. Thankfully, we have access to her ID book. You know, we deal with these situations every day, unfortunately. Let's hope it won't be a long while before we can effectively communicate with her."

"Tom, how did this happen? Thandi mustn't know. Hey, Thandi mustn't kw." Tom nodded in response. The two friends now had time to talk, with paramedics and Elizabeth gone. Slight relief hung in the air, with the knowledge that she was out of Tom's hands and into those of professionals.

But something bigger nagged both of them. The likely consequences and potential damage to Tom Piyane's reputation. Facing Thandi didn't bother him as much. All he hoped for was for Elizabeth to recover, and for his reputation to be protected, for his and the boys' sake, first and foremost.

With hands outstretched, palms up, Tom continued, "But, even if Thandi were to know, I'm not sure where she is now. The last time we spoke, she was going to be discharged the next day. And she would proceed to a small town in Switzerland to stay in a hotel or rented house and recuperate. She wouldn't divulge any specifics. I already suspected there was going to be another destination post op, which she chose to be secretive about. Who knows why? I don't even know if the South African embassy would have her current address. Maybe just as well."

"Who is with her, though?" She can't go through that serious by-pass gastric surgery and recuperate on her own. All alone? Come on Tom! What were you both thinking?"

"When a woman insists she'll be fine, all alone in a strange country? You leave her alone. Strange as hearing such a *laissez faire* attitude from her supposed husband, may sound. As for me, I just assumed there was something else she wasn't telling me about this trip, this operation, and her very secretive destination for recuperation, for which she had tickets even before she left, you see. Careful planning on her part, for once." Tom clapped his hands to add effect to the mockery of his wife.

"Now what did you expect me to do? Confront her and demand a forwarding address after she was discharged? No, Sir. Santo, I've lived with Thandi long enough to know better than that. I'm sorry."

Santo was quiet. He was finding it hard to believe Tom and Thandi had drifted apart to the extent that even in matters of life and death, like a delicate by-pass gastric operation, there'd be no caring, no concern, on both parties.

"Don't look at me like that, Santo. Please! Are you blaming me? Maybe there are quite a few things you don't know about my wife. I don't care about the cost. It's my duty to provide for her, although she makes me feel I'm her slave." And lightly tapping Santo on the chest, Tom continued, "And listen to this Santo, from our dear Thandi, 'Tom, Men are from Mars and Women are from Venus. See. We're different.' She must have caught that Venus and Mars line from some talk show. I bet all she loved about it was how she'd squash me with it. My wife is pretty much clueless about anything that really matters. Does she read any book? No. The Thandi I fell in love with is no more."

"You've never shared all of this with me, Tom. Why are you allowing yourself to die inside like this?" Santo could tell his friend was struggling to open up and say more. It was obvious there was a lot more he needed to hear and learn from Tom.

"When we meet, we've better things to discuss, Santo. Stocks. New investments opportunities. Golf. Soccer. Politics." Then Tom tried to make light of the chiding comment from his friend. "I've tried to put things in perspective, you know, Santo?"

"What perspective, Tom? Has it helped the situation?"

The opportunity to tell all was uppermost now. "Thandi's favourite hobby is shopping, shopping and more shopping. Clothing. The twentieth dinner service. The fiftieth tea set. The wrong food, packed with fat and sugar. You name it. Otherwise she is lazing around here at home, not even swimming or toning up in the Jacuzzi. Feet up on the coffee table. Watching Television on the big screen in our home theatre upstairs. Calling on MaZulu to bring her this, do that. And the poor lady 'yes madame-ing' Thandi all day long. That woman has deep-seated vendetta against life, if you ask me. And I'm tired of it all, Santo." Tom was surprised yet relieved to be sharing this much of his many years' agony.

"Has it become this bad, Tom?"

"Yep," Tom shamelessly admitted to his friend and continued recounting his sad tale. "I try to make her feel guilty every month end, in an effort to make her see reason. So I will say, 'Let's see the damage this month end. Let's go through credit card debt.' But that hardly works. I'll observe how she restrains herself for the first week. Then, for the remainder of the month, she's out on her perpetual spending spree. Again! The woman is sick!"

"Women talk about shopping therapy, you know, Tom."

"She needs proper therapy. Sit on a proper shrink's couch. For years of sessions? Who knows? Until whatever is ailing her so much, is flushed out. My wife is a shallow-minded lazy thinker. She takes the short cut. I'm not an abusive husband. She knows this."

"And takes advantage. She is abusing herself then, Tom. She must be suffering from deep-seated something. Something happened or is happening to her. Has she never shared anything with you, maybe some incident from her past? You know in the intimacy of your luxurious bed and bedroom? So-called pillow talk?"

"No. She has never shared anything with me. Maybe she herself doesn't know what's eating her so much inside. But she's a walking sorry robot. She must deal with it. Maybe it's something from her childhood. Who knows? She's a trained nurse, and therefore the best person to know what exactly to do."

"She has to find out, Tom."

"Exactly! That's what shrinks are for, Santo! A shrink will help her get to the bottom of her troubles."

"I agree. Why don't you find her a therapist? A psychologist?"

"She has to want to do this, Santo. Just like her by-pass gastric surgery. She decided she needs this kind of intervention."

"Oh!"

"This woman is draining me of my happiness. More than money. And I refuse to become the victim of her pre-nuptial baggage, if that's what this behaviour is about.

She's fighting with me, fighting even with MaZulu. The woman is crazy. And I've just about had enough of it all. The boys have long known to let their grandmother just be. Leave her alone. It's affecting everybody, if you ask me. This home is dysfunctional. Because of Thandi." Santo didn't respond.

"Let's go back in the house, and have some cold juice. The sun is scotching my balding patch mercilessly now." Tom playfully pulled Santo by the arm and dragged him in. They were standing by the fridge as Tom poured out some juice for both of them. He had a smile on his face. Santo put his hand on Tom's shoulder, "It's great to see you can still smile through all of this, Tom."

"Well, I told you it helps to put things in perspective, Santo. Ask my grandsons. This is what I lecture them about." Tom smiled naughtily, just a little, as he led the way to the lounge. "Listen to this, Santo. Before Thandi left, I slipped a woman's magazine in her overnight luggage, hoping she'll find it in her dear self to read the article, *Have you let yourself go? Why?*

Tom realized that going back into the house reminded him more vividly of Elizabeth and what had happened. "I'm so sorry to be talking to you about Thandi, while Elizabeth is probably slipping, God forbid, deeper and deeper into a coma. But in case this is my last chance to open up about my pain, let me continue."

"Don't speak like that, Tom. Elizabeth will recover. Send the right message to God and Mary, Mother of Jesus, and all will be well."

"You are right, Santo. Poor woman. She'll come around. Do you know what I found in her bags?"

"No, Tom! Did you really have to do that? But what am I saying? Of course you had to. But under normal circumstances, ladies' bags are no-go zones." They both forced a brief laugh.

"A passport *and* a new American visa!" Santo raised his eye brows, as frowns collected on his forehead. Tom continued, "It raises questions, doesn't it, about Elizabeth? Who is Elizabeth?"

"Exactly, Tom. I'm totally surprised."

"What were her aspirations? Did she have a dark side? What am I saying now? All of these questions are in the present tense of course, Santo." Santo excused himself. He needed the loo. He also had to find words, so long, to boost his friend's morale. On his return he found Tom in a pensive mood again.

"Elizabeth. This mystery of a woman. Where is she originally from, Tom?"

"From some obscure place I've never heard of, according to her ID book. You know, Santo, I'd hoped to open this relationship up, over time. I may be wrong. This is early days of course. But I could feel us connecting at a deeper level, as time goes on. I probably would have managed to talk her out of her current work. Make her life cozy and decent. A much better investment, for both of us, I think. But alas! That was not to be."

"You would have needed more time in order to gravitate to such a step, Tom. Don't allow yourself to be carried away now. You would also have needed," Santo chuckled, "to learn to tell fibs constantly.

Like, a drug dealer, always duck and dive. Take Elizabeth to obscure restaurants and holiday resorts. Risk Thandi finding out. Risk the smoldering fire of her ire flaring up into uncontrollable flames, as she anoints your balding head with boiling cooking oil. I'd go easy on entertaining the thought of taking things further with

Elizabeth, my friend. Maybe it's not worth it. It's too complicated. Totally unsustainable! Trust me. You are even a novice in the infidelity game, Tom."

"Desperate men do desperate things, Santo. Maybe desperate women, also. Who knows?" Santo watched his friend and listened. "Sometimes I think Thandi won't come back. But only if she is attractive again, looks after herself and finds a rich man to stomach all her wastefulness and dependency. That women's liberation thing? That women's empowerment thing? It's just rhetoric and a joke with Thandi. She doesn't believe an inch or teaspoon of it."

"Maybe she doesn't understand it deeply. The responsibility it carries for womenfolk. Her ignorance might surprise you. Freedom *isn't* fun and games."

"It's very complicated, Santo. Just ask fellow South Africans about freedom! Freedom is *lots* of work, my friend. We've slowly come to realize this. Quite a sobering fact."

A moment's pause visited both men, simultaneously. Then Tom broke the silence with a phrase they've both known since childhood, "*Kwadlul' ingelosi.* An angel has just passed." He continued the conversation. The angel hadn't come to stay, make the situation better. "And Thandi, ignorant? *My* Thandi? I doubt it. Maybe her intelligence has been eroded by that personal vendetta against who knows what? How many times have I told you about the Thandi I met, and was immediately attracted to?"

"But tell me, Tom. When did Thandi accumulate fat that warranted having by-pass gastric surgery? This is a very serious op?"

Tom laughed out loud! "Good question, Santo! But that's my wife! The surgeon told me all Thandi probably needs is a tummy tuck. From the photos we sent her, as well as from consultations on Skype, the doctor was almost certain this is what Thandi needed. We'll see."

"But even a tummy tuck, Tom? All the way from South Africa to Switzerland for this?"

"Well, that's my wife. Financially, it's no big deal. My businesses are doing well. Thank God. I've always been a gentleman. I've always understood also, my responsibility as her husband. Her welfare is my obligation. Except she gets to choose what's in her best interest."

"Waste of money, though, Tom!"

"Well, that's Thandi! The more dramatic, the more expensive, the better. For five years she'll be telling all her friends about her by-pass gastric surgery in Switzerland. Look, Santo, I've learnt to choose my battles with her, very carefully. Thandi lets herself go. Eats bad food. Avoids any exercise like a plague.

When she balloons, a surgeon's knife far away from our shores, is her best option. Thandi needed no surgery. Major or minor. Believe me. What she desperately needs is to sort out her life. Neatly tuck in the unsightly shirt that is her silent pain. Diligently work on the problematic parts, and then carefully put her life back together again."

Tom glanced at his watch and pleaded with Santo to stay for a quick lunch. Santo agreed, rather reluctantly. "Well, I wasn't even supposed to have spent this much time with you, Tom." Santo truly regretted lost networking time, especially with international conference participants. But he'd decided on the spur of the moment that here was an opportunity for a practical application

183

of the saying, a friend in need ... Santo had flashbacks right then. Elizabeth's body on a stretcher. His heart almost jumped out of his chest. He thought, "How much more for Tom? What a mess?" Santo pitied his friend, especially after learning so much about his rocky married life. Not a pretty sight at all.

They were enjoying previous night's kidney beans stew, brown rice, roasted red peppers and carrots. For a while, they ate in silence. But then Tom maybe felt obliged to end his soliloquy on a good note; sprinkle a teaspoon of sugar to sweeten the sour morning, a tiny bit. "Anyway, one thing I decided to do for myself and the boys, of course, was to spend my money on the gym in the basement. And be in charge of it."

"Very good, Tom. I'd like to see it sometime."

"Anytime, Santo. My dear wife, the Thandi I married was disappearing right before my eyes, you know. I didn't want to follow suit. I have my son's kids to father, nurture and guide through life, in this very complicated world."

"You are a very good grandfather to the boys, Tom."

"Thanks, Santo. Thandi could come along if she so chose, if on waking up one morning she realized what is good for her."

"That's true, Tom."

"Well, instead of joining me for gym fun, she accused me of wasting money. I could have bought her a second car with the money. All her rich women friends have two or even three cars now." Santo, shook his head. "Haven't you noticed? That's the trend now, Tom? The woman at the end of our street, for instance. Open your eyes." Tom mimicked Thandi's way of talking, imagining her hands firmly on hips, enhancing her fierce look.

"I simply looked at her and said, 'Woman, you don't know what's good for you. Do you still remember you were once a nurse educating other women at the clinic on how to eat well? The rules for good eating habits haven't changed, if you haven't noticed. Even for the privileged and so-called rich. As for me, my dear, I want to live well. I want to live longer. Why do you think the boys and I spend our mornings in the gym?' Santo, she was too big a madam to even take a walk with me in the park here. So..."

"Tom, I've got to go. I'm chairing a plenary session after lunch. I better show up for that. I'm with you in spirit. You know that of course," Santo said, and with glazed eyes he looked his friend straight in the eye. However, that eye ball to eye ball contact was too painful to maintain with this high school friend, clearly an abused married man now. Santo dropped his eyes to the floor instead. Then he placed his hand on Tom's shoulder, as if about to pray for him. Obviously, Santo was plagued and weighed down by what Tom had agonized about in that long staggered soliloquy. Santo mumbled, as if half to himself, and half to Tom, "I hope Thandi is recovering well, in all respects. It is also my prayer that the untidy Elizabeth saga is neatening itself out. I've never experienced such drama. And this was your first time!"

"Yes, my very first time. My debut, Santo. Elizabeth is a fine self-respecting lady. I hope she gets better soon. I don't want to be selfish, but I will dare say, she must get better for both our sakes. Everything about our date went very well. She's smart, you know. She's decent. She's knowledgeable. Tom. She reminded me of the impression Thandi made on me when I first laid my eyes on her."

Santo put his hands together in a praying mode and looked up to heaven. Tom continued, "I'm confident they will trace her next of kin. I also trust the man in charge of the crew that came to the house, to handle this matter with utmost caution and sensitivity. I'm concerned about bad publicity, especially for the boys, my grandkids. I've been a good role model for them. What will they think of me were they to hear about Elizabeth? In this house? In one of the bedrooms they occupy when they are home? Hell! No!"

Tom felt a dam of warm tears filling up. The dam quickly overflowed. Then it burst its banks, as Tom failed to hold back the tears. Neither did he care to wipe them off. The tears formed a long stream of pain down his face. Intensifying the agony with each inch covered, the stream of tears meandered down the cheeks, the nose, the mouth, the chin, the neck and inside his shirt. The stream stopped and dammed up, as it created a bottomless virtual ocean of regrets, regrets, and more regrets, right in Tom's heart.

Santo blew his nose long and hard. He put on his cap. It didn't make sense to leave Tom in such a state. Santo had never seen Tom in so much pain, his eyes that red. "Keep me posted. Things will work out. You are a good man, married to a woman who doesn't understand, let alone appreciate her luck. But, that's her show, you know. I hope she'll do some serious introspection while in Switzerland, and return trimmer and wiser," Santo commented as he absentmindedly glanced at the Eucalyptus trees right at the end of the sprawling property. The peace in nature out there. How could it be restored within the walls of this beautiful house?

"Thanks Santo," Tom gently tucked a hand under his friend's elbow, "So well-said, Santo. So well-said. Thanks a lot. Much appreciated. The sound and sight of the water from the waterfall on the front lawn failed this time to massage the agony, and soothe the difficult moment for Tom. He continued, contemplatively, "All of this? Being here with me in my hour of need, you know, Santo? And such a hell of a need!" The two friends struggled to hold back more tears. Santo bowed his head, and said not one word in response to Tom's expression of gratitude. He was weighed down by accolades which were actually nothing to him. He wished he had some more wise words to keep his friend strong and hopeful. But he had to run out.

They both slowly made their way to the front door, and then proceeded towards the main gate. Their light steps were the only sound they were aware of, as they walked through Tom's top of the range red brick driveway. Every step each friend took felt like intensive labour.

When they reached the car, the two men embraced in a long hug. It was not an easy parting. Santo assured his friend, as he held his arm, "Don't allow Thandi's foolish and misguided ways get to you. Let's deal with the matter at hand. Messy as it is. Let's pray for Elizabeth. You are going through a lot, Tom. But you seem to be holding well."

"That's exactly what leads to premature death, Santo. Priding oneself in coping well. That's a silent killer of a stance."

"I meant well, with that comment, Tom. I'm sorry."

"In fact I've not actually done anything wrong by Elizabeth. I was a man in need, Santo."

"I'd add, in fact both of you were in need, Tom. Still in need, by the look of things."

"I'd even risk being proven wrong one day, but dare say that she seems to be a woman of integrity. Look what I found in her bag!" Tom kept nodding his head.

Santo continued, "Elizabeth seems a very smart young woman. Look, she is planning already to venture into the unknown and widen her horizons. Clearly, her express purpose is to make her one life more rewarding and meaningful. Tell me, then, Tom, what sane woman with all of these ambitions would find honest fun in walking the streets every night? Elizabeth has higher aspirations than most young women. Even those in better circumstances, I'd say. She has an American visa in her bag. Come on now!"

"Yep, that's right, Santo! And our dear Thandi, of course. Something is eating her up. Something is corroding her soul."

"And whatever it is, she mustn't use it to corrode your spirit, Tom. I pray that eventually she seeks help and heals. You are a good man, Tom."

"And if she doesn't? Time is running out, Santo. Elizabeth has given me something new to think about. A new perspective. At the end of the day we all have just one life. And my marriage to Thandi has long become a burden. I've persevered enough. Don't get me wrong. I used to love Thandi. Over time, she replaced me with money. And I will give her what she desires the most. Up until ...."

"Say no more, Tom," were the last words from Santo as he started the engine of his car, ready to leave his friend behind. His heart and mind were carrying tons of agony, suspense and anxiety he didn't wish on anyone, let alone his best friend. Santo still could not believe the soup they were in. They were like brothers now, especially after Tom lost his son and his lovely wife to AIDS. Prayerfully, Santo hoped and pleaded with the Universe, that in its divine wisdom, it would find ways to trim all of the rough untidy edges and neaten the saga with Elizabeth.

───────────

"I hear a woman died in this house, Tom, while I was away sick and dying in Switzerland!"

"Who told you?"

"Never mind who told me! All I want is a yes or no answer from you. That's all." Arms were akimbo, her uncombed hair the usual matted virgin Amazon forest. She would be found only in a night dress and night gown these days. Tying a belt or anything that needed to be buttoned over her abdomen still gave her pain.

Tom took a deep breath. Calmly he responded, "If a woman died in this house, you would have known. There would have been a ritual performed. Christian or traditional, to cleanse the house. Am I right or wrong, Thandi? But go ahead. Make your own gossip. And swim in it for entertainment. You are pathetic, you know. Get a life. Get a job. Volunteer in some soup kitchen. Be busy. For goodness sake, do something worthwhile with your life.

And just for once, Thandi, how about earning yourself some money. That woman at the end of our street, runs her own business. The different cars she drives are from her car dealership. She sells good second hand sports cars. All gently used, one owner cars. She has to test drive them, before she seals a deal. Okay? There's dignity in financial independence, you know. I'll still foot most of the bill. You can't maintain all this.

But show some pride, honour and dignity that comes with independence. Until when will you remain a bedbug, sucking my blood, Thandi? You are not the lovely, industrious and driven woman I married. You know what? I'd love to have that Thandi back. Before it's too late. Yes. Before it's too late."

Tom's voice began to vibrate. He was so worked up, he was beginning to choke on his own emotions. This ended his outburst. His voice lower, Tom continued, "Please, Thandi. Do the right thing. Just for once, you know. You'll grow old healthier, happier and more fulfilled that way. That's all I will say. And the subject is now closed. The rest is up to you."

They had been standing far apart when Thandi began the duel. They had drifted further apart, in the fiery conversation, verbal swords drawn. As the heavy heat wave began to pass, Tom retired his virtual sword. He took a few steps towards his wife. He faced her. Thandi was so shocked by this gesture, her own virtual sword slipped out of her hand. Tom found his wife's hand. He felt her reluctance to let him hold it. Tom managed to secure in his hand Thandi's three fingers.

As he became acutely aware of the wedding band on her finger, he felt a sharp pain in his heart. There was one more plea Tom wanted to impress upon his wife. "Thandi, just look at me, please. Right in the centre of my pupils. This is very important." Tom opened his eyes wider, and pointed Thandi to them.

The duel appeared to have been unexpected and a bit overwhelming for Thandi. She had not budgeted for the kind of response Tom threw back at her accusation, about a woman who died in their mansion. She was at a loss, for a quick "get even" round. And Tom's last request totally confused her. They'd not been this close in a long while.

So, Thandi obliged. Her lovely set of eyes, invisibly stained by who knew what, landed on Tom's eyes. There was no distinct emotion her face or eyes displayed. Maybe just confusion. The blurred lines of emotional confusion. "Thank you, Thandi. Here is one last thing, my wife. Do yourself a favour. Find out *which* woman *really* died in this house! Okay?" Tom let go of her fingers.

Thandi stood there. This time confusion was clearly spelt out on her face. It couldn't be mistaken for any other likely emotion. She had started the war about the supposed woman who died in her house, convinced she'd win it. She'd ended up speechless instead. Thandi searched for a quick retort from her bag of wrath to get even with Tom, when what she actually needed was a visit to a sluice room to empty her bedpan filled to the brim with the soiled parts of her mind, heart and soul. Indeed, she needed to take the necessary time and effort to clean herself up.

The best she could do, however, hardly the closest to what she felt she needed to do, was engage in a mental retaliation to being dressed down like that by Tom. So, she filled up a 20 litre bucket with rotten eggs. One by one she hurled the eggs at Tom, swearing at him with every landed throw. When her puffing was done, she collected her sorry self and shuffled back to bed.

Tom had long left the scene, all worked up. He had retired to the privacy of his study to catch his breath. He realized how impatient he was becoming with Thandi. He was surprised he'd snapped at her like that. He felt a

191

sadness and deep pain in the depths of his heart. Nevertheless, he hoped she would ponder on what he'd told her. And then, more importantly *do* something about it. Otherwise their time as husband and wife was running out.

He had instinctively shut the door completely when he entered the study. So angry he was. But he'd quickly opened it just a bit, in case Thandi lashed at MaZulu. Tom fixed himself a drink, put up his feet on his desk as lovely jazz from his latest collection began to soothe him. The calm he needed quickly filled the room. This music, this drink, was the sum total of the ambiance he needed to cool down, and hopefully begin to heal for a moment, from Thandi. Then a smile took a slow walk across Tom's face. He stood up to completely close the door. MaZulu was off sick!

––––––––––

"We knew as parents that she was doing the night shifts for a reason. You know, good people, a health crisis is a health crisis. It has no regard for one's financial situation. If you need a transplant urgently; if you need urgent surgery to save your life, your health situation doesn't understand. In fact it doesn't care about the general economic situation or your financial standing. Your urgent health need will not put whatever is wrong on hold, until you have a decent job to enable you to cover the medical costs. Believe me, we had tried all we could to give Elizabeth the life tools she needed. All that was expected of her was to work hard, soar like an eagle, and enjoy a long decent life."

"What happened then? Where did things go wrong?"

"Nothing happened, out of what we could call the ordinary these days," Elizabeth's father responded as he extended his hand to hold Elizabeth's clammy hand. It was almost wet with sweat, he noticed. "These days if almost all university graduates do not get jobs, we need to stop saying that is an extraordinary situation. It has become the new normal. Sad to say as that may be."

His daughter's clammy hand bothered Elizabeth's father. He put the back of his hand on her forehead to feel her temperature. He was concerned she might be coming down with flu. Her lips moved and told him, "I'm fine, dad."

"But let me say something is failing us in this country, in this new world. The rules are changing before our very eyes. And we are not coping or catching up fast enough. I don't know which is which, honestly."

His wife nodded and studied the face of the woman conducting the interview. She was surprised she didn't look as youthful as she seems on a Television screen. Elizabeth's mother concluded that it must be all that heavy make-up that ages and wrinkles the skin.

Elizabeth's mother then addressed the Television woman after they returned from a commercial break, "As I was saying during the break, nothing is as painful and heart-killing as watching your sick daughter leaving home in the evening to do a night shift, to do something you know pains and humiliates her to the very core of her being, as this is not what we educated her for. This is not what she trained for. While I respect all jobs and all factory workers, we did not pay so much money in university fees, do without for so long, for our beloved Elizabeth to end up a factory hand, a temporary one at that."

The Television woman nodded. She seemed in deep thought. Elizabeth's father added to what his wife had just shared with the audience, "I'm the man of the house. I'd done all I could to prepare our only daughter here, for a good decent life. But life and circumstances dictated otherwise.

When she collected enough bravery to announce to us, that she was compelled by her health condition and unemployment situation to relieve a friend on her night shifts, we let her, reluctantly. We were also moved that a true friend could do this for our Elizabeth, so that she could save for her urgent medical needs. Never mind that this was a factory job."

Elizabeth's mother was satisfied that whatever else she wished to say, her husband had eloquently covered and shared with the audience. He continued, "Let me quickly add that we are not ungrateful. Please don't get us wrong. We are Christians, and would be the last family to disrespect the holy teachings. The Psalmist says, 'Praise the Lord O my soul' you know." Both Elizabeth and her mother proceeded to applaud, and the rest of the people present followed.

Elizabeth's dad seemed a little emotional. "This is difficult for me. Very difficult." He paused as he collected himself, and glanced briefly at Elizabeth and her mother. "The Elizabeth that you see here, survived a coma! We count our blessings every day, as we celebrate her life." A throng of halleluiahs punctuated his every phrase.

"There are many people who are physically challenged like our Elizabeth here now. The blind. The mute. The deaf. The list is endless, as you know. Paraplegics have learned to defy the odds. As much as possible, they are leading full lives. They engage in different kinds of sports.

Dancers, even. Some have made it to the big leagues. Others even qualify for national and international competitions. Olympics! So it's not the end of the world. And, my good people, don't they say the world is full of infinite possibilities? That hope does not exclude our Elizabeth here."

There was a more thunderous round of applause from the audience in the Television studio. Elizabeth's dad held up his daughter's hand. It swiftly got transformed into a strong fist by its owner. Her upper body made a gesture of standing up, to acknowledge the applause.

―――――――

"Dear people, you've been a very good audience I must say. Thank you very much. Lastly, as we wrap up, let's hear then from the main person on this show. Let me start with a question. Elizabeth, as we are in the 16 Days of Activism on No Violence against the Abuse of Women and Children, what can you share with our viewers? I'm sorry, but in the interest of time, please be brief."

"Thank you. For the ladies who work nights, I understand the circumstances that drive you to that type of work. But try everything else first before you take this painful decision, this treacherous road that leads nowhere that matters and counts. And every morning as you return home after the humiliating experience, make a plan, and stick to that plan, to get out of this low life."

In response to Elizabeth's brief comment, the audience grunted. There were also nods and yes responses, in support of Elizabeth's message. They shouted, "*Buwa*! Speak! You are right, Elizabeth."

Some-one shouted back from the audience. She seemed to be given a reluctant hearing by the Television woman, "Come on Elizabeth! It's a business. It pays well. I'm rich because of it! Remember the 2010 FIFA World Cup? Thousands descended on our shores. But our industry was not legalized. Guess what? We still worked and made money, anyway. Not as much as we could have, judging by the potential client base that was here. You understand what I mean?"

The applause was deafening. Propelled by the loud applause, the woman raised her voice. "The girls lost millions of money as a result. Don't come here, wheelchair bound now, and preach to us, okay." The speaker was making her way to the front now, to confront Elizabeth. But the Television crew arrested her in her seat. In an upright position one could tell she was a typical night lady.

There was a bit of a lull before Elizabeth finished her short controversial speech. She was clearly shaken. But she was determined to get her one message across. She noticed but disregarded the puzzled look on her parents' faces. She continued, as she confidently drew the microphone closer to her mouth.

"Please, people, let me make myself clear. To own yourself, to own your body, to respect this temple of the Lord is very important. But ..." There was more grumbling in the audience now. Shouts of, "We don't need your morals and temple stuff."

Elizabeth's father stood up. He felt he needed to protect his daughter in this sudden din and confusion that appeared to overwhelm even the Television woman interviewer. A tame audience had suddenly turned wild! What had triggered this? Elizabeth's father wondered. He opened his mouth to speak, but no words came out. He sat down, embarrassed.

"Connect the dots, *baba,* connect the dots, father," some other rough-voiced lady shouted from the audience. She was pulling out a cigarette now. But then put if back as she remembered she couldn't smoke within buildings. It was illegal.

*Baba* looked at his wife. Her head was bowed. Her hand was supporting her forehead. She shook her head for so long; it seemed involuntarily operated. A toddler would have cracked up with laughter at the strange sight. A human live head, battery operated. No guffaws were heard in the gathering.

Elizabeth's mother had connected the dots. And she was deflated. If the noise died down, her wailing would have been heard clearly. The question that nagged her and made her hysterical was, "How could you do this to us?"

Why did you not tell us the truth, Elizabeth? Oh! My child, to bring us here to be embarrassed and insulted by these cheap girls on national Television? How shall we face the world again?"

Unbeknown to the Television host and her guests, the announcement weeks before, of the Television topic had attracted the attention of the night ladies' fraternity. The big unions had kept delaying the process of embracing and welcoming them into their fold. So the workers had formed their own union. It was virtually toothless because it wasn't recognized. But it gave its members some voice at times.

Most importantly, it gave them all at least some solidarity, a semblance of human rights' protection and a place of belonging. This Television discussion would put them in some limelight, so that they were noticed. Organizers had gone to work. Sleepless nights. Word of mouth. Hence the full audience as the show presented "The amazing story of one Elizabeth Madadeni!"

So, the audience was comprised mostly of Elizabeth's former local workmates, as well as those from other cities and provinces. Elizabeth was shocked when she realized she was going to address a house full of the fraternity. She'd also tried without success to collect enough guts to come clean to her parents before the show. Despite the challenging scenario, Elizabeth decided she'd bite the bullet. She was fully convinced that her message was more important than anything else she'd done in her life.

So, as we say in isiZulu, "*Kwaphambana izinkomishi.*" The cups got mixed up. Things got mixed up on the Television show! The presenter watched the show change gears. It was slipping into something she'd not planned or anticipated. She was afraid she'd lose control of the audience.

Elizabeth was taking the discussion in a totally different direction! Wasn't the show about how she'd amazingly survived a coma? Wrong cup served! This was not the cup the presenter expected Elizabeth to serve to the audience. Neither did the presenter understand that her audience was not the usual one she had in mind.

Some members in the audience seemed impatient to be given an opportunity to speak. Others were being commanded repeatedly, to sit down. The Television crew was struggling to control the unexpected mayhem that was threatening to break loose as every minute passed.

"Unfortunately we've come to the end of our show. I'd like to thank ..." The woman was cut mid-sentence. She stood up to shake the hands of her guests. She took time to whisper something in Elizabeth's ear, before giving her a long hug.

"Quite a moving show," Thandi commented as they stood up to go to their separate bedrooms. Tom did not respond. They were hardly on talking terms now. But even if they were, he couldn't have known how to respond to Thandi's comment. He went first to his study and wrote out a cheque to Elizabeth Madadeni. It was for a huge amount.

———————

In a few short months Elizabeth was back on Television again, to launch her Elizabeth Madadeni Street Workers' Foundation. She got straight to the point as soon as the presenter gave her the opportunity to speak: "Through the generous gift of a sponsor who has chosen to remain anonymous, God bless you! Whoever you are. Wherever you are, beautiful angel, I am launching this Foundation in my name today, to help young unemployed women.

Especially those tired of or dreading doing the night shifts on the streets. I urge you all to stop living aimlessly. I'm pleading with you today to be mindful of cheapening life, when life seems all set to cheapen you. Believe me, I've been there. Such is life these days that with a university degree I was forced to opt for street work. I needed money for surgery, a big operation. But before I'd saved enough, the disease had taken over. I can't cry over spilt milk. No. I can't."

For a little while it looked like Elizabeth was going to fail to hold down the pain. Fortunately, she garnered enough strength to continue:

"But my plea is this: Young ladies, please, whatever unpleasant and unexpected circumstances you are faced with, hold your heads up high. Own your lives. Go proudly to your destinies. This Foundation will help you to achieve, regardless of any stumbling blocks you might face. No matter how dire. Together we will find solutions. Again, all blessings to you, dearest sponsor! God bless you! God bless you!"

Elizabeth put her hands together, as if in prayer, as she ended her speech. She wheeled herself off the stage, a very proud woman. She was later hailed down by security. "Madam, no speeding is allowed in these corridors. You'll get a ticket." Elizabeth laughed out loud!

Tom happened to be watching Television again that night of Elizabeth's big announcement. He felt lonely, although he was in the exuberant company of the boys, one of whom had just completed his University entrance examination. "Good for Elizabeth, granddad. See, even smart women put things in perspective." It was Colin. And he continued, "Look at how the world has treated her. But she has not allowed herself to sweat the small stuff."

"It's not really small stuff. I mean she's bound to life in a wheel-chair," Bongumusa, Colin's older brother, added. "But putting this hardship in perspective has pretty much minimized any adverse effect it might naturally have had on her. Wouldn't you agree, granddad?"

"Completely, my boys." Tom appeared emotionally worked up, the boys noticed. *He* seemed to be struggling to put things in perspective. Indeed, his private thoughts were tormenting him. He was thinking that he'd been right about Elizabeth, that she was a woman of substance. But he'd lost her.

---

Thandi had finally seen the need to admit herself into the Life Change House in the United States of America. Her programme necessitated that she scale down to a simple life. Out with her lavish lifestyle. She had to get by with the minimum bare basic necessities. A strict diet.

Weekly volunteer work with the homeless. Giving something of her precious self would help her. Her doctors were convinced that this was one purgative that would help Thandi relieve herself of the burdensome baggage. Bit by bit. Living one day at a time. Ultimately, she'd be set free from all the excess she hid under in an effort to conceal her deep-seated anger and pain.

Tom looked forward to the day the Thandi he met at the HIV/AIDS International conference, several years before, would be back. Sober, Thandi; smart and dignified true lover of life. He hoped Life Change House would help her learn to fill up her cup. And others would reap the benefits.

And Thandi's amazon forest of hair? It was talk of Life Change House, as she apparently got tired of half-heartedly dressing it up or hiding it in the same dark brown bandana, day in and day out. From a young age she knew how to tame her "rich lush bush," as she used to say to girlfriends. Special oils would magically upgrade her virgin hair to a beautiful natural Afro. But she had long abandoned this habitual grooming. Just scarves it was when she had to emerge out of her house.

Well, she lived at another house where she was receiving treatment, but her untidy amazon forest was totally unacceptable. She had brought two beautiful African print head-scarves with her, a staff member had noticed when she unpacked her suitcases. But Thandi seemed to have forgotten all about them.

Management at Life Change House organized a special stylist for her, with the hope this could boost Thandi's self-esteem and help her take a few steps back to life, and retrieve the better version of herself. Despite all of this, the prognosis wasn't good.

Members of staff had also hoped Thandi might begin a little conversation with the hair stylist, like people usually do; open the door into her life just a little. Not one word from Thandi. The hair-dresser asked a few "get-to-know-you" questions, and Thandi chose to be quite sparing with words in her responses. She divulged nothing.

Tom was disappointed to learn this when he called Dr. Jameson, the head of the Centre, one month after Thandi's admission there. Dr. Jameson urged Tom to prepare for his wife's long period of treatment, unless a miracle happened, and she snapped voluntarily out of the demon that was twirling her around its finger.

"What could be the worst case scenario in people like my wife, you know, so I prepare for the worst, while hoping for the best, Doc?"

"It is important for Thandi to open up, be courageous enough to open the hole to her deeply embedded pain and anger. I mean open it quite wide, Mr. Piyane. So that we can get in there and excise it all. We hope and pray for such a time and opportunity. But it's up to her."

"Gosh, Dr. Jameson! Up to her? Or up to the disease?"

"Up to her, indeed! Summon enough faith. Believe. Believe. Believe, that she can do this. That she can overcome this mountain of a boulder."

———————

Tom felt alone. But his grandsons always uplifted his spirits. "You know, boys, when I spent some time in New York City, after leaving your grandmother at the Life Change House, I travelled by subway a few times. And guess what I saw? High up above the train windows there is a strip filled up with all types of advertisements. Then there's a section titled "POETRY IN MOTION".

Somewhere in my study you'll find a small poetry book. Same title, *Poetry in Motion.* I bought it at a second hand book stall when I visited the flea market here, quite a while back. How could I have known, my boys, that I would come across the same title, thousands of kilometres away? I hadn't noticed my copy was published in the United States."

"That's so cool, granddad. I'll look for the book of poems." Colin responded. "And when you find it, read us some of your favourites! Don't you agree, granddad? And tell us why they are your best poems in the entire book." Bongumusa added jubilantly. Colin looked at his older brother, and wondered why he always finds perfect ways to spoil a fun moment. That sounded so like an English class assignment.

*Poetry in Motion!* The boys' grandfather had some other past occasion on his mind. "Poetry in Motion, wouldn't you say, Elizabeth?" He refrained sharing that still very special memory with the boys. He saw the danger of getting himself entangled when the boys' curiosity was raised, and they asked endless follow-up questions that would have made him trip all over his words bound untidily in long bales and numerous heaps of bundles of lies.

"I thought of you, while I was in New York, and missed you boys quite a bit. In truth, you are all I have. You are my pride and joy. More so the pride of your mom and dad, as they keep watch over you. This I'm very sure of."

"Absence makes the heart grow fonder, granddad." It was Bongumusa, slipping in the last perfect words.

The boys stood up, all smiles. They gave their granddad big, loving good-night hugs. They felt his tight abs as their bosoms lightly touched.

# Mildred

Bang! Bang! Bang! The scary knock was on our front door. "It's the police! Open the door! *Liph' ibhoklolo?* Where's the bully?" I heard the police woman shout. Our dogs were barking.

"I'll get it," Mildred told me as she took a few long strides out of the kitchen across the lounge to reach the front door. She was still puffing. Her unshackled breasts were dancing on her chest. Her long straightened hair was in four big plaits. The last smaller braids were coming undone at the tip.

As always, I guess she didn't believe me when I warned her that the police were on their way. It was only when she heard the loud knock at the door that she quickly ran upstairs to slip on her black calf length skirt over her long pink nightdress. She pulled the long nightdress over the skirt waist, so it wouldn't trip her or get caught in her pink sleepers as she walked.

Mildred had just added oats to the pot of boiling water when we heard the first knock. She left the plate on high. The pot of oats was now spilling over and caking on the solid plate. The kitchen was choking from burnt smell. It was making me nauseous.

I had to move slowly towards the stove, concerned not to let any blood drop onto the tiled floor. Foot traffic would make pudding of it, before Mildred bothered to clean it up, after the police had taken blood samples among other evidence they'd need.

Although we occupied the same kitchen space, I must admit for a few minutes I forgot Lungile was there. He was very quiet. The kitchen was quiet, except for the loud noise of the obnoxious smell in the ears of our nostrils. I was leaning against the kitchen counter; pre-occupied with trying to stop the bleeding from the palm of my hand. In the scuffle that had ensued that early morning, I had finally blocked the long knife from causing further damage on my body.

The knife had ravaged my soul, though. I couldn't save it. I thus had a mountain of work to salvage it, make it smile, so we could live happily again. For now it lay on the floor. It was writhing in pain. My mind was a matted ball of many thoughts. Indeed, this incident had moved things to a new level. It evoked a myriad of emotions in me. Anger. Relief. Gratitude. Sadness.

This time things had been different. I knew that the situation would lead to a new package of realities. This is what the situation demanded. No two ways about this! The police were here. Finally here. I was holding my own blood in my hands.

As I proceeded to turn off the stove I realized Lungile was just as pre-occupied as his father. We were both wrapped in our different thought worlds, I realized. Lungile's world of creative art. I became an uninvited guest. Our son was engrossed in an early morning painting session. His high chair, face and hair, were his canvas. His paint brush fingers were hard at work. The baby food and milk Mildred had left on his high chair to hurriedly put on her skirt, was all over Lungile's chair, face and hair. It was the artist's moment, best left alone.

I felt my agonized face break into a tired reluctant smile. "Oh, my boy!" This is all I could say. I was amazed and disarmed. In the midst of all the noise of that morning, this little boy had managed to carve for himself a quiet time to be in his own world.

This is how God protects the little ones, I figured out. This is how God shields them sometimes from being consciously shocked and traumatized by parents. The same people who made them. And then, the very same people who fail to provide palatable surroundings for their offspring to grow up in. I did not disturb the artist.

I resumed my pose at my station. The counter was succeeding for a while to give me the support I needed, as I listened to my throbbing head. I could feel the swelling on my forehead pulsating and thumping furiously. I had bandaged my right hand with a towel, but the cut in the centre of my palm was still stubbornly dripping with blood. The towel was slowly soaking wet. I was relieved, though, that the police had finally responded.

"We've just received a call on 10111," It was the woman's voice. I heard the male voice make the official introductions, "I'm Constable Swanepoel. This is Constable Zondo, as you can read from our badges. The door Mildred had opened half way was now swung wide open. The hinges took a strain. The two cops threw their weight around as they walked in, I could tell from their heavy deliberate steps on the wooden floor.

"Who called us? It was a man's voice," the female Constable asked Mildred. I imagined them scanning her up and down. She had no marks of any injuries. "Was it your husband or partner or boyfriend that called us? Where is he?" Constable Swanepoel was asking the questions, his heavy Afrikaans accent quite intimidating. I could tell there was panic and anxiety building up in his tone. Mildred remained mum.

"Please take seats," I heard her say in a weak voice.

"No Miss! We are on duty. Where's the man who called 10111?" The woman's voice was sterner. "You seem reluctant to answer. Can we search the house for the victim? This is the right address, we are sure: 800 Farmer Road, Thomasville."

"Constable Zondo I'll begin the search. He could be in a very bad way." There was unmistaken concern in Constable Swanepoel's voice.

"And what's your name, Miss?" Constable Zondo was asking.

"Mildred."

"Mildred who?"

"Silomo."

"Mildred Silomo? Is there a surname like that in this country? Is this the name in your ID? Were you born here? Where's your green book?"

"It's in my handbag upstairs. I could get it."

"I'll go with you. You are under arrest now. You've relinquished your freedom to move freely."

I could tell from Constable Zondo's voice that she was becoming hot under the collar. At this stage anything Mildred said could easily short-circuit something. Any utterance could be a bad thread woven in the case. I knew she could snap. Just like that! I didn't trust her to realize this and restrain or arrest her own bad wiring.

Constable Swanepoel found me in the kitchen. He shouted, "He's here, Constable!" I heard Constable Zondo's footsteps furiously tumbling down stairs, with Mildred's slower steps in tow. I could tell she was being dragged along. "My God!" Constable Zondo exclaimed as she put her hand on my shoulder. Then she slowly turned me to face them.

The whole nine yards of my messy condition was in full view for the first time to Mildred, and the police. "You need to sit down, sir. Please take a sit." Constable Zondo directed me to a seat in the lounge. I couldn't see quite straight I realized, as my body struggled to fit comfortably into the contours of the sofa.

"Lady, you'll tell us now what you've done. The rest you'll complete at the police station. And that hand needs urgent attention, sir. How deep is the cut?" I proceeded to unwrap the towel. The bleeding was slower now it seemed. But the pain was there. Sharp and furious. "It is no longer that bad. I'll need some stitches, but will do so when you are done."

Lungile was aware of the chaos now. He had started crying as soon as Constable Swanepoel marched into the kitchen. I could tell Mildred was still in a resisting mood. She was hardly believing what was happening, right before her eyes. Finally happening, I should add. She still had her usual airs about her, I noticed. Her discerning skills had never been sharp. And they were letting her down badly on a morning when they should have stepped up to the plate and protected her from herself.

As soon as Lungile saw his mother tumble into the kitchen, he stretched out his arms, as usual. He was pleading with her to get him out of the chair and hold him. He was used to hands. Being held. I'd told Mildred repeatedly that we need to begin to get the boy out of this habit. No! She appeared to want to hold him forever. It was just by God's grace that Lungile had developed affinity for me as well. I was his father after all.

Much as Mildred tried to keep me a stranger from Lungile, my son was wiser. We shared DNA, needless to say. But to Mildred, less discerning Mildred, the child had become her missile. Lungile was her weapon of war, to express her hatred for me. She was taking advantage of the gift and preserve that comes with mothering and motherhood. How I despised and resented her for this. If she had had her way, and it was humanly possible, I'm sure she could have manufactured Lungile all by herself!

From where I was sitting I could observe Mildred closely. I guess my eyes took on the task of being the additional police, as I found it hard to take them off her. She had now released Lungile from the high chair. Her face was struggling to return the smile Lungile was flashing out. So happy to be held.

Wet rings had formed around the area of Mildred's nipples. These showed as ugly marks on her pink nightdress. As soon as Mildred sat down on the most distant chair from me, Lungile's chubby little hand instinctively found his mom's breast. He was now glued to it. I watched him caress it absentmindedly with his smaller version of cocktail sausage fingers.

Mildred was fidgety. I knew she was embarrassed by the almost breath suffocating smells from Lungile's announcement of poop release. And of course the lingering smell from the burnt cake of oats. It had formed a cold stubborn ring on the edges of the burner. Quite a mixture of a perfume. It was all over the lounge.

Too much time had lapsed before the Constables got on with the main business of the morning. Therefore the diaper change would have to wait, I guessed. And so, smelly Lungile was on his mom's lap, sucking loudly on the breast. Mildred knew by now that any movement and every step she took, she had to have one of the Constables by her side. She would be escorted upstairs again and watched as she changed Lungile's diaper.

"Miss, you cause all the trouble and you are still breast-feeding this baby?" Constable Zondo asked Mildred. She had a very surprised look on her face. She shook her head slightly. "Does he take the bottle?"

Constable Zondo looked around as she waited for one of us to respond. I pointed to the big bowl with washed bottles soaked in the disinfecting solution. We could all see the container on the kitchen counter.

"Fine then. When did you breast-feed him last?" Mildred looked at me as if we were still a loving pair that could give the same answer simultaneously. "About 4 or 5am. I don't quite remember," she responded as she kept her eyes on her breast. I noticed that the dress of shame was still on its coat hanger. It was still waiting for her to claim and put on.

"We'll give you time to breast-feed the baby, as well as express more breast milk for later. I'm afraid the baby will have to survive on the bottle after that, sir." Constable Zondo doubling up as nurse, concluded the matter. This scene was unusual. I could tell from the awkwardness with which the two Constables were handling the case. It was a reversal of the usual domestic violence stories they were familiar with.

"We don't have enough room for mothers coming with small babies for now," Constable Swanepoel explained. His small eyes were staring into mine, as he shut his cellphone. "Unless of course we moved her to our cells in Appleview, about one hour's drive from here. Very bad conditions there. Very bad, sir."

A lazy smile flashed across Constable Zondo's face, as she mulled Mildred's possible destination in her head, "Appleview, Constable Swanepoel?" Half chuckling to herself, she commented. "I wouldn't subject this innocent baby to those prison cells. But for the woman here? Yes, so she meets her match, the riff raff of society." Constable Zondo took a long look at Mildred and then said, "I hope you can tell how difficult and awkward this whole thing is for us. How do we handle a woman perpetrator? Ms. Silomo is it? Do you realize what you've done?"

"With the unenviable experience of Appleview, she'd come out straight as a ruler, that's for sure," Constable Swanepoel added. "Those are some hardened ladies, I tell you. But for the sake of your boy here ..."

"On the contrary I'd actually not mind Appleview for her." Constable Zondo turned towards Mildred. "You are one of the wicked ones. Giving all women a bad name. A small, almost negligible statistic of women who abuse men. All the same, shame on you!"

"What could be planned, sir? Do you work? Is there anyone to look after the baby so long? Well, it could be quite a while of course, depending on the gravity of the case." Constable Swanepoel's questions came one after the other.

"And the queue!" Constable Zondo added. Her lips lengthened and curled on the word 'queue' – as if she was caressing it for effect. "As they say, the wheels of justice grind very slowly. Especially now that our people, the victims of domestic abuse, our waking up to the need to report perpetrators." Constable Zondo reflected on the status quo. I realized, very sadly, that we'd become a sad statistic here at 800 Farmer Road.

"How old is the boy? About ten months?" Constable Swanepoel was holding Lungile's chubby fingers now. He was squeezing them playfully. He was tickling the little boy. He was ruffling his tangled silky hair. Lungile was all smiles. He had for a while begun to play with his mom's breast. "He is ten months old," I told Constable Swanepoel. "Ja. I could tell they are about the same age. Mine is 9 months old. Mr. Silomo, is it?"

"No. I'm Nelson Nkosi," I quickly corrected Constable Swanepoel.

"Of course that was the name of the caller," Constable Swanepoel remembered.

"She is Silomo?" Constable Zondo repeated Mildred's surname in question form. I was not in the mood and this was not the time and place to give a long lecture on the history and origins of the Silomo clan. Mildred herself seemed uninterested in allaying doubts Constable Zondo had about this surname. "Are you not husband and wife then?"

Constable Zondo surmised right with that question. I threw my good hand up in the air, and shook my head vehemently. I knew that exasperated Mildred. It was a silent yet very clear, "Hell no! Just as well! With a woman like her, I'd be out of my mind to tie the knot." I was thinking to myself, much more convincingly and conclusively than ever before, after the traumatic events of that morning. I noticed Mildred wasn't happy that I made it so clear that we weren't a married pair.

And this was the bone of contention. I had had enough of pleas. They had graduated to demands, and then threats that I should marry her. I hoped she got the message this time that she would not walk down the aisle to marry me. Not in a million years now. Today, I was sure. Very sure!

A funny scenario flashed in my mind just then. There we were, in our old age. Finally tying the knot! With her mother long gone; Lungile, our son, was walking her down the aisle. Mildred was leaning heavily and unsteadily on her walking stick. It was draped in white silk carnations. There I was waiting and smiling. I was leaning on the shoulder of the priest who would finally join us in holy matrimony in our 90s. I quickly snapped out of this silly very unlikely possibility.

I watched Mildred as she sat there. Our son was embraced by the same arms that had led to the rupture of my blood vessels and the unbearable pain I was in. I imagined Mildred had a good size chunk of stuff to take in. Loads to think about. Worry about.

How she had made fun of me each time my calls to the police led to nothing. But the police world was changing. Thank God. This was clear now. I took a reluctant gaze at Mildred. I wanted our eyes to meet. I was forcing myself to search for any trace of remorse in her. None.

Lungile now appeared distracted. He was gazing around, taking in the new scene comprised of two unfamiliar people sharing space with his mom and dad.

"I suggest you attend to the diaper and express the rest of the milk,' Constable Zondo addressed Mildred. "We don't have all day."

"Yes, Constable. But can I brush my teeth, take a bath before breast-feeding the boy again?"

"Feeding him for the last time, indeed!" Constable Zondo cut Mildred short. She checked the time, and gave Mildred the look that sent the message she was asking for too many favours. "Be ready in 15 minutes. Prepare a change of clothing. It might take a while before the case is brought to trial."

"No bail?" I asked.

"I doubt it," Constable Swanepoel responded. "Not with that record in her file, I'm afraid. How many incidents of domestic violence?"

"Twenty," I reminded Constable Swanepoel. "And counting of course, if our court system failed you and us," he added. It sounded like a frustrated comment about the legal system and processes. The various constituents it let down. Constable Swanepoel continued along the same vein, "Our work comes to naught at times, I'm afraid. But what can I say? It's a new South Africa. Lots of teething problems, even so many years down democracy road. The country, especially government structures. It's all very much a work in progress."

"While we continue to suffer," I added silently.

"But look here, Mr. Nkosi. Things are getting better. There are good people who work hard every day to make our country better than it was before.
Believe me." Constable Swanepoel was right of course. There *are* good people working hard to make South Africa a better country. But who listen to that kind of reasoning when they are in distress, their lives even in real danger?

Then a call came through for Constable Swanepoel. In between static I could hear the person on the other side reporting that they'd found the file. Ten major incidents of severe domestic violence reported against one Mildred Silomo. Ten minor incidents reported against the same Mildred Silomo. "Thank you, Constable Mitchell. Is there any chance we could have room for the suspect's ten-month old baby son?"

"That's what I thought. It's a pity then."

"There's Appleview, of course," the other Constable seemed to have added, almost as an afterthought.

"Appleview? It might be good for the suspect, but ..." Constable Swanepoel couldn't finish his utterance. "Not for the baby, of course," the voice on the other end of the line trailed off. He had to attend to the next emergency.

Constable Zondo announced that she'd be upstairs with the suspect. I watched Mildred's big eyes become even wider with that new name. Suspect. A cold shiver went up my spine. Mildred, the mother of my son, Lungile, was now a suspect! She was getting ready for her "trip." Constable Swanepoel told his colleague, "I'll be taking the statement from Mr. Nkosi, so long."

The writing of the statement, was very emotional moment for me. I answered questions that clearly revealed I had allowed myself to be a victim for far too long. I was remembering the number of incidents I had not even reported. Over and above the twenty. One incident is enough, you walk out of that relationship, they advise. You pack your belongings and leave. Granted, indeed, one incident should have been enough. Done it!

How, though? An abused man leaves to go where? This was my house. And it was a woman abusing a man? Constable Swanepoel apologized for the station's negligence to act much sooner. "Luckily the old staff kept your file, although they played down your plight. You know the mentality that you are a sissy of a man to report abuse from a woman."

"They always promised they'd follow up, but never did. My partner here, grew to take it all lightly. Even to the point of deriding any calls I made or reports I went to the police station to make."

"Is it? Today, is the surprise of her life then?" Constable Swanepoel raised his eyebrows. They formed a small arc. A sly half smile flashed just below his brownish red neatly trimmed moustache. His bottom set of teeth was ridiculously perfect. He absentmindedly pinched his nostrils as he took the statement. I had stopped dabbing the hand towel I'd filled with ice cubes to control the swelling on my forehead Mildred had bashed with a pot.

It was one of our expensive ones with a very thick base. She could easily have done more damage.

We were nearly done with the statement when we heard steps. Mildred was ready. She was dressed in her new power pants suit. She looked half-dressed, though. No usual perfume. No jewellery and make-up. She left her bag by the door. Without talking, she pulled Lungile out of the high chair to breast-feed him. I watched how contentedly Lungile rested on his mother's lap.

The boy seemed to have some premonition. Indeed, his mother had committed an act of abandonment. As a consequence, he would not see her or her breast for quite a while. I felt a sharp object piercing my heart. Mercilessly and repeatedly. By the time Mildred moved Lungile to her other breast, we could tell he had had enough. He began playing with his mom's breast. He was gurgling, smiling, and looking at his mother lovingly.

For the first time I noticed in Mildred, something that looked like a pair of eyes splashing in a very shallow pool of reluctant tears. In a flash her fingers emptied the pool though. The dry bed made her close and open her eyes quite a few times. Lungile thought it was a game. He was laughing away. But his mother couldn't even fake a smile in response.

Constable Zondo suggested Mildred must express the milk for refrigeration. She handed the boy to me. "Dada, Dada," Lungile kept calling my new name. I had to carefully contemplate any movement I made, navigating between the swelling on my forehead and the cut in my hand.

I managed to put Lungile on my shoulder and lightly rubbed his back. In no time that burp was loud enough for all to hear. The two constables smiled. Constable

Swanepoel praised Lungile for burping, "Good boy! Good boy! I know all about the little gift of vomit for your shoulder that comes with the burping at times."

"I know all about that and more," I responded. I was envious of Constable Swanepoel's obvious happy life as a father, with a wife or partner that was very loving. I gave Lungile a kiss, part of it perhaps unconsciously dedicated to loving women in other men's lives. Constable Swanepoel took a few steps to play with Lungile's chubby fingers again. The boy seemed to fall in love with this very tall red head with a gentle face. How it contradicted the type of work he did.

Constable Zondo was standing next to Mildred. She constantly checked time on her watch. She had remained standing during this entire time. I watched her as she asked me a few more questions. There was a time she took off her hat. Very carefully she put her middle finger on an itchy spot in her new cornrows. She had a good shape of a head. Then she tapped the itchy spot with her flat hand. Her fingers were long and dainty.

Her finger nails were well-shaped. They were varnished with a neutral colour polish. Although it wasn't meant to show, it was a very lovely colour. Her eyebrows had been newly trimmed also. I could tell by the lighter parts where the tweezers or wax had been used to remove unwanted hair. How did I know all of this, as a man? Well, my very first girlfriend was a make-up fanatic. I'd go with her shopping for all this stuff women do to themselves to look "pretty."

Constable Zondo wore a pair of small dainty gold earrings. The hint of orange lip gloss brightened her honey complexion. She was of middle height and very slim. Her belt highlighted a very small waist. I estimated that I could easily wrap my two large hands around her entire waist. I'm tall and heavily built, of course. The handcuffs and her gun in its holster, were secured firmly around her waist. These suited her so well when she took those deliberate steps. How they made one really feel her presence!

She was still very young it seemed to me. She could pull out a very mean stare though. I could tell her profession had hardened her otherwise pretty brown eyes. I imagined them softer and kinder in other situations. Maybe she had mastered the art of acting and looking the part of a no nonsense policewoman. She had perfected the art of putting on and taking off the sternness, as demanded by circumstances. I hoped so, at least.

Unlike her colleague, Constable Zondo had not engaged in any small talk, except her smile as a response to Lungile's nice burp. She seemed more agitated by Mildred's behaviour. What was about to happen to her? The little breast-fed boy his mother would leave behind. I simply could not have imagined Constable Zondo throwing in some small talk about family, as she kept her eyes on Mildred, making sure to send the message "You've transgressed the law. You will pay."

Mildred likes to smooth talk or act her way out of nasty embarrassing situations. I'd watch her even with traffic inspectors, when she'd been pulled to the side of the road for speeding or violating some other traffic rule. In a blink of an eye lid she'd slip into this kittenish mode. How it annoyed me!

From lashing out at me about something, with her long fingers on and off the steering wheel, to stopping and getting out of the car, she'd change her demeanor in a flash. What an actress! Over the years I got tired of getting out of the car to plead on her behalf. But she couldn't pull off that kind of nonsense with the Constables who called at the house, especially with the woman Constable who was the less sympathetic with her.

Another call came through. Constable Swanepoel responded. He gave the caller a short report of what was happening. "We should be out of here in 15 to 20 minutes." He raised his bushy eyebrows to confirm with Constable Zondo. Constable Zondo made a thumbs up sign.

"Yes, Constable Zondo agrees with me. In about 20 minutes. No! We don't need back up. No need to call the ambulance either. Because of the baby here. Mr. Nkosi's hand is still bleeding. But not as profusely as at the time we arrived. He has assured us he will be able to drive himself to the nearest clinic. He is currently unemployed. But he's actually starting a home business. He will look after the baby.

He's a fine dad it seems. And believe me, they make a fine pair with his son." At that fine comment, Mildred looked at me with her usual sagging face. It's the one she usually put on when she wanted to tell me "I'm not all that. I mustn't be puffed up." I ignored her. I was surprised I felt absolutely no pain for her. Just anxiety, given the well documented stories about abuse in prison.

Constable Swanepoel was so right. Lungile and I were buddies. This was despite his mother's efforts to keep me a stranger from my own son. We had long bonded. Much to Mildred's disgust. On her return from an errand she would expect to find Lungile wailing pitifully and calling for his mother. She'd find us happy. My boy very content with his dad. And so, I had no worries about the two of us having a peaceful home. Just to ourselves. For now I didn't have the energy or guts to think about the immediate future.

Constable Swanepoel had found the long kitchen knife. My blood was now a thick solidified layer on it. "A nice exhibit, this," he commented a bit boyishly. He seemed to be gloating with that 'can't wait' attitude for the future time when he'd have to tell the magistrate about this episode. He carefully wrapped the knife and made sure it was secure in his bag. Constable Zondo assured me as they handcuffed Mildred and walked out, behind her, "We'll probably arrange for visits so she can breast feed the boy at least once a day. She's going to have a tough time with breasts swollen, dripping with milk."

"See. They are kinder with women suspects. Especially the ones with babies. Can you manage to bring the boy over at least once a day, Mr. Nkosi?" Relief couldn't be missed or mistaken for something else in Constable Swanepoel's voice.

"Yes, Constable Swanepoel. The boy's welfare is of paramount importance. Luckily it won't be a long drive. But even if it was, I'd still do it."

"Even with that injured hand?" Constable Zondo asked a rhetorical question. It appeared to be aimed at helping us all come to terms with the reality of the moment. "The photos of your injuries will be in your file by this afternoon, Mr. Nkosi. As well as the other exhibits of course." Constable Swanepoel was referring to the knife and the pot." Both were already in his bag.

"It's a pity you didn't think of all this inconvenience before letting your emotions get the better of you, lady. And it's not even the first time!" I heard anger and frustration in Constable Swanepoel's voice. He was closing the front door. He'd waited by the door a while. I suppose he soon realized I wasn't moving an inch from where I was. What? Get out of the house to "see Mildred off?" And then Lungile prompted to wave them all good-bye? His special wave, of course.

No. Certainly not. I didn't want that unfortunate landmark picture for Lungile. The sad fruits of his mother's labour. The sad story of domestic violence he was bound to hear when he was older, was enough of a point of reference for his life world and family history.

It wasn't lost to me that as a man, Lungile could possible find himself seated amidst abusive men. He'd be recounting the story that began, "I come from a home of domestic violence. I'm a victim of it. It was not the usual story of domestic violence. By that I mean it was my mother who abused my father ..."

Ah, the police vans of the new South African Police Service. Out with the apartheid yellow vans that were known in our Townships as the "Mellow Yellow." I heard the double back doors open. I imagined Langa's mother struggling to climb up and in at the back. She'd have probably needed a light push on her backside to give her the necessary lift. That must have been like another humiliation for her, deciding which foot to go in first, high heels having been thrown in first.

And then struggles with her tight pants. Trying to pull them up, hoping to get them up to her knees. And, with handcuffed wrists. Maybe Constable Swanepoel had come to her rescue, put his hand on her behind and threw her in. No, he was too much of a gentleman to do that. I imagined that the two constables simply watched and waited until Mildred figured out how she was going to find herself seated at the back of the van.

In a little while I heard the double doors shut with two loud bangs. A bit of discomfort for Mildred? Just as well. So that every step of the way she would feel the inconvenience she had caused. Look, I'd hate government to have a special fleet of vans designed specifically for women suspects and offenders. Low enough for the bad ladies to step in with some grace? Furnished with comfortable seats and even mirrors?

I imagined Mildred stumbling in and trying to find her balance as she finally sat on the hard side bench, her fingers reaching and holding tight onto the metal wire for balance. All of this drama in full view of neighbours and school children walking to school. Watching, talking, and wondering, as they passed by. It was quite an ordeal for Mildred.

Silence descended and wrapped itself softly around Lungile and me. We had the entire house to ourselves, with no Mildred's negative vibe lurking in some corner, plotting how to hurt me, again; indirectly and more implosively, hurting this young lad, Lungile. The quietness and relief was all the more noticeable after Mildred's drama.

I put Lungile in the burping position again, and took a walk around the house. It was in a bid to soothe the pain of separation, which Lungile would feel as time passed. I then took a seat in the lounge. I wasn't ready to venture out for now. I dreaded the stares and questioning eyes. But I dreaded much more actual questions from some of my neighbours.

As I sat down in the quiet of Mildred's absence, the whole early morning's drama played itself back in my mind. Mildred had remained unusually quiet, except for heavy sighs from time to time as bottle after bottle filled up with her breast milk, and as I labelled them minimally with my good hand – 1, 2, 3 4, 5 ... and then packed them neatly in the deep freezer. Gone was, "Go ahead, call the police! Call the police, Nelson," as she pinned me against the wall, looking like a mad woman, her breath stinking in my face.

She'd be gritting her teeth like she does when in the annual budget speech, the Minister of Finance announces that taxes will be raised on unnecessary health hazard items and expenses. "Oh! Taxes up again on cigarettes? Raise them all you want. I'll smoke till kingdom come, me." That morning's happenings were a long piece of confused drama. The only reliable sensible recording of this play was the file at Thomasville police station with my name on it. And Mildred's name on all the pages!

Lungile was falling asleep on my lap as I went into a solo debriefing session of that morning's quarrel. It was his late morning nap. I was still struggling to make sense of it all. How when lovers slept peacefully in each other's arms elsewhere, here, at 800 Farmer Road, death of one lover at the hands of another, was knocking hard and impatiently at the front door. A tragedy about to happen.

Then I thought to change Lungile's diaper, so that he'd have a long comfortable nap. He wasn't pleased that I disturbed him as he was falling asleep. But just a bit of bottle feed lulled him to sleep. This would be a good time for me to take a nap as well. I lay on the long sofa, and put some soft music on.

But there was a problem. The ambience I was trying to create was not in sync with the ambience in my head.

The morning's drama couldn't be easily dismissed with music. The solo debriefing of the morning's drama continued.

I had made sure Mildred didn't punch me in the face or in desperation attempted to squeeze my neck and strangle me. She was so enraged she could kill me without knowing it, if I let her. She'd grabbed the kitchen knife with the aim of stabbing me right in the heart. I made sure to be gentle, though. I know the rules. I am well-versed with the law.

I have advantage as a man. I'm solidly built. When things are normal and I'm keeping to my routine, I exercise daily, with intense muscle building at least three times a week. But besides the law, it's not in my nature to use force, to be violent, with anyone. Much more so with a woman. One that I'd professed to love at that. A woman I once loved, I must add.

The mistake I'd made with one more woman was difficult to bear. The first serious love affair had ended the same way. The baby, my first son, died at birth. Thanks to a mother who had a careless pregnancy. How I'd repeatedly warned Yakhe to stay away from alcohol. "I can't even have beers now? Come on, Nelson. You are too fussy. The nurse said it's no danger to the baby."

That was a lie. I was young. I was inexperienced. I was careless. I paid a heavy price. I'm now a father of two. One was still born. I had to agree with the thought that took a careful wise look at me. After a long uncomfortable stare at me, the thought came up with a suggestion, "Nelson Nkosi, you have to go through what is wrong with you. Yakhe first. Now it's Mildred. You keep attracting the wrong women into your life. What actually is wrong with your psyche to fall for and then stomach this unacceptable behavior from women lovers?"

I was laid off. I did not quit my job. I'd provided for Mildred since the time I courted her. I didn't want her to move in with me. I wanted to do things right. Pay my dues and plan a wedding to remember. No. Not my Mildred. As soon as she fell pregnant she insisted on coming to live with me. Her mother had no qualms with this also. My mother and father did. Over time I gave up. I ran out of excuses to make Mildred go back to her home.

Living with her showed me her worst side, I must admit. Consequently, I'd long made up my mind I'd not marry such a nasty mad cap. But I lacked the necessary guts to make this official, the African culture way. Assemble our parents and make my announcement, with all of Mildred's belongings actually packed in the boot of her car.

In the early hours of this morning as she breast-fed Lungile she thought it prudent, I guess, to wake me up and raise the subject of our tying the knot one more time. She claimed she has to be rewarded for all the hard work of being a mother, a working one at that. Marry her as a reward for being a mother to our boy? This was an injunction. The boy couldn't fall asleep with Mildred yelling at me like that. What were the neighbours thinking? I suppose they were now used to the frequent fights in our house. Facing embarrassingly all-knowing greetings the next day, has always been hard for me. The questions and sadness in the eyes and polite words exchanged.

This morning I had to make my get away, to escape Mildred's vitriol. I came downstairs to drink some water.

I had a good mind to catch some sleep in the car parked in the garage.

Then Mildred followed me to the kitchen. I did not respond to her provocation. She was pushing me repeatedly, pinning me against the wall. She left me when Lungile began to cry upstairs. That kind of scuffle and verbal abuse didn't warrant a 10111 call, I concluded. I was about to go to look for my car keys in the lounge when Mildred returned and continued to taunt me.

Calmly I told her, "You want me to hit you, I know. I will never let you drag me down to that level, Mildred." I walked out of the kitchen to the lounge. She followed me. Then she disappeared back to the kitchen. I heard a drawer being pulled out. I heard her dragging out pots and pans from the kitchen cabinet. I heard running water. I knew she was boiling water for breakfast oats. She was still hurling insults at me. I could hear them clearly. Her usual expletives. "Nelson, the dog. Useless idiot. Worst imbecile alive on this planet." And far worse insults, too vile to repeat.

Usually, insults meant she was quieting down. Now that she was getting back to normal morning routine, I assumed the worst in this morning's episode was over. I therefore felt some relief and decided to force normalcy in a morning of crazy happenings. They bore a typical Mildred hallmark. I planned to return to bed as soon as she left for work. I was distraught and in too much soul pain and agony to ponder on the depth and gravity of footprints her rage and abuse left on Lungile.

Then she returned to the lounge. I kept my eyes deliberately glued on the Television set. I was avoiding eye contact. It could probably set her off again. The woman hated the air I breathe! I was flipping through the

Television channels after watching, half listening to the news when I heard, "Be a man for once, Nelson. Just for once. You coward!" She was at it again. She came at me, banging my forehead repeatedly with a pot. I stood up and grabbed the pot.

She had another weapon. It was more deadly than the pot. It was the kitchen knife. She was gripping it with her front teeth. At a glance I noticed it was the one she'd recently bought. It was sharp. I knew instantly that with one slip on my part, I'd be dead meat. I caught the knife just as it ripped the pocket of my pajama top. I sustained a two inch cut across the palm of my hand.

Blood gushed out. The sight of blood ended the incident. It was clear that drawing blood and seeing me suffer gave Mildred a strange sense of contentment. She seemed to feel the mad satisfaction of revenge. I quickly got a clean hand towel from the linen cupboard and wrapped my hand with it. I managed to make a cold compress to stop the swelling on my head.

Mildred went upstairs for a while. I followed her, soon after. I was not going to be caught off-guard any longer. I was watching and listening and waiting for what would come next. Thank God there was no gun in the house.

I'd never seen her reach this level of rage. I was sure she could use even a gun on me, given a chance. When she went to the loo, I called the police. "Mildred, I've called 10111. They will soon be here," I told her as she emerged out of the toilet. I was leaning against our bedroom door.

She simply looked at me. Not even a faint reaction to what I'd just told her. It was like I had just uttered some disjointed words in Greek. I went back to the kitchen. I was feeling weak. She, too, soon came downstairs, with Lungile in her arms. She put him in his high chair.

Coming to think of it, we'd not even spoken about her absence from work, as the police led her away. I didn't know what to say if her boss called. I didn't want to give Mildred a bad name. But telling the truth remains the best option in all situations. That I did know, as I postponed coming up with a reason. No such call came. I concluded she found a way to report her absence. I wondered what excuse she gave.

Mom Agnes looked after Lungile and did some cleaning in the house. She knocked on the door on this unforgettable morning. I opened the door slightly and told her she could return home. I assured her she'd be paid for the day. She looked suspicious as I prepared to quickly shut the door after she left.

I didn't want to interfere with any other evidence the police might think of coming back to collect. For example, I noticed during the course of that morning, skid marks of sorts on the floor where she had tackled me. Not too obvious, as both of us were still in morning sleepers. But the marks were noticeable and traceable. This was evidence all the same. In fact, I had a good mind of alerting the Constables to this additional evidence.

I knew the old lady up the road had most likely picked up something from the police presence at our house and then told her husband. Retired, frail and bored, I knew she had already made several phone calls to her daughter in London, her son in Australia and all her bowling and church friends about the activity in my house. She'd probably also spent a greater part of that morning looking out the window for more news to gossip about.

"Stanley, here's their servant. I'll go ask her."

"Yes, Constance, their girl should know something."

"Aggie, dear, do you have a moment?"

I imagined her beckoning Mom Agnes to come in as she walked past. Not into their lounge. But just to stand outside on the veranda. That's where she usually stood to chat with me. In her quiet but smart moves she'd block me from entering. Well, the old busy body could conjecture all she wanted with her Stanley. As always, I trusted Mom Agnes to use her discretion.

I actually did not think my hand needed to be X-rayed, for possibilities of more serious internal damage. I was sensitive to unnecessary procedures which cost a fortune. Especially now that my health insurance had lapsed with the loss of employment. And with Mildred's health insurance reserved for Lungile only. Until I officially became her husband.

Lungile sat quietly in his perambulator as the doctor sutured the cut in my hand. I asked to take a video of the process and a picture of the stitches when the doctor was done.

"I see, Mr. Nkosi. You are helping the police in their investigation. Collecting extra evidence?" He looked at me through his lowered glasses, as they sat secured firmly on the strong and pronounced bridge of his nose.

"Yes, for that, doctor. As well as for this boy here," I responded with a very heavy heart.

"Don't be ridiculous now," the doctor said, almost pleading with me, "No, man. He's still only a baby!"

"Well, when he gets older. And I have to explain to him why it's just the two of us in our house. His mother long gone."

"I understand now. An important forethought," the doctor said as he fidgeted with his glasses. He had taken them off and was absentmindedly swinging them from side to side. "Showing as well as telling, Mr. Nkosi?"

"Exactly! See what I mean? So that in the future I don't sit with a teenager who is acting up, abuses drugs and/or alcohol. Let alone attracting the wrong women into his love life. Unconsciously seeking love in the wrong places."

"God forbid, Mr. Nkosi!"

"Doc, I attracted the wrong woman into my life. Abusive. Vindictive. This is what destroyed our budding family."

"Oh, Mr. Nkosi. That happens in life, you know."

"And it wasn't the first time, doctor!"

"Really? I'm so sorry, Mr. Nkosi."

"This boy must know about my repeated failure in choosing the right partner. So that he learns from my mistake."

"And the repercussions thereof," the doctor added. "I get your point."

The receptionist had opened and shut the cubicle we were in several times.

"This boy may never have to hold his own blood in his hands, like I just have. Probably no woman will ever draw blood from him. But while no physical part of his body may be caused to bleed at the hands of an abusive woman, his psychological skin may remain badly bruised and bleeding. Unconsciously, and unknown to any of us, blotches of pain are already forming on this boy's other skin. They say the first five years of life are the most formative. What he'll become as an adult is done and sealed by age five. Not so doctor?"

"How old is he now?" The doctor asked. It seemed to me an inconsequential purposeless question. I suspected it was his way of handling the bitter, messy and thorny fruit. I ignored answering the question by ruffling

Lungile's hair. I knew the hard time would come as evening set in, when his mother was usually home from work, with all the goodies for him tucked in her brassier. At times when he wouldn't let go of his mom's breast, I'd have to start dinner instead of giving him his evening bath, my evening routine.

"Mr. Nkosi, the sutures will disappear as the wound heals. So you don't have to come back here, with the little one," the doctor said as he got a red sucker for Lungile, from a large glass bottle on his desk. He placed it in Lungile's hand. Lungile was still a small baby. He had no knowledge and experience of suckers. I'd have it myself, to sweeten the rest of the day, I thought. "So long then, Mr. Nkosi. Just give it a few days. Call, if becomes septic. I doubt it, though. But you never know. Alright?"

By the time we returned home it was already lunchtime. I prepared the usual lunch for Lungile. He ate it well. Followed by the bottle. It took me a while to decide what I'd have for lunch. I could heat up what was left of the previous night's dinner, which Mildred had prepared. Recalling the previous evening made me grimace. Those leftovers would be like eating poisoned food. I decided to throw away all the food, before I threw up. I made peace with a meal of soup and bread, followed by dessert. Lungile's sucker.

I replayed in my mind Mildred's movements in the kitchen the evening before. As I recalled her silence and how she was abrupt with me, I realized, in hindsight, that her heart and mind were already entertaining very dark thoughts by that time. We hardly spoke during dinner. Instead, we both chose to cuddle with the food on our plates. Pork chops, potatoes, pumpkin, spinach and salad.

"Here, catch!" This was the only 'conversation' we had as she grabbed two oranges from the fruit basket, and threw one to me. I quickly cleared the table and washed the dishes. Soon thereafter I climbed two stairs at a time, to play with Lungile. He was now in his cot bed. I had to make it snappy. Timing was everything. Otherwise, I'd lose out! I'd learnt that in order to have adequate time to play and bond with our son, I had to do so before Mildred went upstairs. Because, once she completed her bath, she had another very long breastfeeding session. She claimed it was quality time. Just for the two of them. What about me? The father?

You see, Mildred had long found ways to impress upon me that in her life with Lungile, I would always be the third person. I'd always be the one to make their twosome a crowd, until we became a married couple. My lawyer had to intervene in order to have the boy baptized a Nkosi, although we weren't married. It was a lengthy affair of trying to convince Mildred, that while the boy's baptism couldn't wait, I wanted to follow proper cultural procedure before we tied the knot. The prices I'd paid for postponing marrying her became bigger, over time. Little did I know they'd culminate in the biggest price of all; a threat to my life. With a pot and a knife, as Mildred's chosen ammunition.

Lungile and I both took naps after lunch. Thank goodness, the boy went to sleep without the usual fuss. He was undoubtedly very tired. My nap was disturbed by the constant nagging thoughts of a to-do list which became longer each time I put some more thought on the next steps.

One thing I'd decided I wouldn't do was take Lungile to the police cells for daily breast-feeding. It was for the same reason I shared with the doctor. To minimize the spread of blotches of traumatic pain on the boy's delicate psychological skin. Noisy clusters of long prison keys. Heavy prison doors. His mother in awkward bright outfit. Several pairs of eyes all over us. Who needed this? Definitely not our son! The wisest thing for me to do as the father, was to postpone for as long as possible the scab that was bound to form from the bruises.

I was relieved that the usual family meeting did not take place. Dad had a bad bout of flu. He was on a regimen of antibiotics. Mom didn't want to come by herself; take decisions alone. I knew my father was badly hurt and disappointed in me. His "Son, this woman is wrong for you. Get her out of your life before it's too late," haunted me more than ever before, after Mildred was imprisoned.

My father was too kind, though, to give me the, "I told you so." It was too raw and obvious a point for him to belabour. Mother was sort of resigned to whatever eventuality. One with boundaries, needless to say.

There was Mildred's family to report to as well about that morning's tragic happening. It was a small family comprised of Mildred's brother, Michael, and their mother, Zippora, famously known as Zip. Who couldn't tell at first glance, that Mildred Silomo's mother lived the life of a perpetual protestor against the inevitable age machine? The way she carried herself around. The way she dressed. The way she applied make-up.

She fitted her somewhat hip shortened 'woman about town' name. She loved everybody to address her by her first name. Better still its shorter version. She had never married. The father of the two children opted out of the marriage right at the altar. The story is told that he

235

immediately left town. He began to communicate only with his children when they were older. He was a man of a quiet disposition. A man of a few words. Michael told me this before.

All concerned parties were already familiar with being called to these family meetings to address my unending problems with Mildred. But Zippora went on a blame trip. Even with Mildred taken away. Zippora was unwilling to accept reality. She told me she wouldn't show up unless and until her daughter was present. It was important to hear her daughter's side of the story.

It was mother of course who successfully talked me into taking Lungile to daily breast-feeding sessions in prison. She didn't buy fully into the fears I had of the negative and probably long-lasting effects this experience would have on the baby. Mother operated on one premise. She maintained that it would be wrong to deny Lungile fresh breast feed from his mother. "Don't argue with me, Nelson! You are a man. You can never pretend to feel or deeply understand what happens between mother and child during breast-feeding. And such a small baby!"

"Okay mom, I will go, if she's not in Appleview of course."

"I agree, son. Not in Appleview. Let them sort that one out."

Shall I dare say I was pleased to learn that Mildred had indeed been transferred to Appleview, where no children or babies were allowed? For the sake of Lungile and given my injuries, Constable Zondo arranged for Mildred to be returned once a day, to the prison close by. There was a quiet room where she could breast-feed Lungile without the vile environment of Appleview. A woman Constable in plain clothes fetched the boy from my car. She returned him to me, when mother and son were done.

When she gave up entertaining the hope that Mildred would come home sooner, Zippora changed her mind about the meeting. Typical of Zippora, I suppose. The wait was too long, she argued. So she demanded a meeting. I tried to talk her out of it, until my parents were able to travel. But Zippora insisted. A few days after trying, once again, to dissuade her, Lungile was startled from his nap by loud music.

It was from a taxi. It was Zip. As soon as she alighted she called out to me to pay the extra fare. "I persuaded this young man to bring me here. It's outside of his normal route. He was kind enough to oblige. He still needs to be paid." I scraped together some loose change and paid the driver.

By the time Zippora finally sat on the sofa with Lungile on her lap, she had made a lot of comments. Cheap choice of flowers to grow on the front garden. I wouldn't see those even in the gardens of the poorest people in the Townships, Zippora reckoned. The colour for external walls. Too gaudy. Couldn't all of this have waited until Millie was back home? "Women are better at these things, Nelson." Lungile seemed underweight for his age.

When I returned with a tray of tea and biscuits she was busy powdering her nose and applying a fresh layer of lipstick. I'd made up my mind to defer all proceedings to dad. It didn't matter what Zippora came up with. I knew that in his calm manner my father would probably succeed in convincing Zippora that it would be best to have a family meeting when all parents could attend. I imagined a conversation going as follows:

"I hear you, Nkosi. You'll let me know then when you are ready to arrange a possible date. It shouldn't be far off. Children? I tell you!" I was amused by Zip's kind of English language sophistication, as she left out the "l" in her pronunciation of "children". "Chidren," indeed, Zip!

"You have my word, Zip, dear."

"My daughter is in a bad way, God knows. And they've refused her bail. Totally unbelievable! I'm going to complain to the Minister of Justice. I can't take this lying down." I knew her mouth, heart, mind and soul would remain unzipped until she was satisfied justice had been served in favour of her daughter, Mildred.

After a short prayer, Zip left. She offered to walk to the bus stop since there was no hurry now. After she left I marvelled at how she didn't ask to see my injured hand. But it was healing well. Thank goodness. Interestingly, I also remembered how her eyes had glided over the black patch caused by internal bleeding where her daughter had banged my forehead with the pot.

The only information I received that Zip would be coming to the house again, was the short message she left on my cellphone: "Prayer at your house this coming Thursday." Typical of mother-in-law, Zippora! This was an instruction. Not a negotiable request, depending on how I felt about it, and my plans for that Thursday. I straightened the house a little bit, since Mom Agnes would be coming in the next day to thoroughly clean the house.

At the appointed time I stood outside. I was expecting Zip to alight from another taxi, anytime. What did I hear instead? Distant women's voices. They were belting out a church hymn. They seemed to have their faces hanging out of the windows, the way they were loud in the quiet of our neighbourhood. The singing was uplifting no doubt. It kept coming closer and closer. In a little while the bus was visible. Women in church uniforms of black tops with white collars, and white hats. They were waving white handkerchiefs outside the bus windows.

"Don't bother today, Nelson, son-in-law. We've paid for everything already," Zippora pre-empted any possible offer from me, as soon as she alighted from the bus.

"Please come in, sisters. This is Millie's home. This is her husband. Their son is over there." I greeted the women. They answered in unison. I brushed aside the status of husband, Zippora purposefully imposed and promoted. After a few hymns and individual prayers by four women, it was time for everybody to pray. I knelt on the carpet while holding, well, almost pinning Lungile to the sofa. He was restless.

Mine was a silent prayer. I prayed for an amicable resolution to the matter between Mildred and me. "You saved me Lord from the lion's den. I cannot be foolish now to want to live with Mildred again." Then I continued to kneel, with my eyes wide-opened. I was listening to prayers while almost running out of ideas to keep Lungile behaved.

Then silence descended in the room. All but one woman had finished their prayers. It was Mildred's mother of course. I soon figured out she was talking to me in the medium of prayer.

"You know Lord what happened to me at the altar, how my fiancée cancelled everything. Everything! The humiliation! Oh, the humiliation, Lord. But Lord you saw me through that most difficult and embarrassing time in my life.

And here we are Lord, with my church women. Only one thing I ask of you Lord. These children must come back together. They have to tie the knot sooner rather than later. I will not blame anyone for the recent unfortunate happenings in this house. We pray for your Holy Spirit to shake the walls of this home to your truth and reality.

What you have joined together, let no man put asunder. So says your word. I want Mildred married to Nelson, Lord. Please get them back together, Lord. What I went through! To be rejected at the altar? On my wedding day. In my lovely wedding gown, Lord. It was hell, Lord. It was hell, Lord."

Zip was going on and on. I was seated by now. So were most of the women, especially the older ones. I suspected they had knee problems. Several women took turns starting a hymn, while others repeated a lot of loud "Amen!" But Zip continued to pray.

I had closed my eyes again, when Lungile wriggled himself out of my grip and fell. He cried uncontrollably. Everybody opened their eyes. Zip finally stopped praying. When she realized that most women were already seated, she did the same. She wiped her eyes and continued sniffing for a while. One woman took Lungile from me. She went outside the house. She soon returned calmer Lungile back to me.

I was in the kitchen, already arranging cups and saucers as well as biscuits on a platter. I had put Lungile on the floor. Zip came in briefly to ask if I was managing. The woman assured her, "Mildred has a wonderful husband. He knows exactly what to do. I'm just waiting to take the tea tray to you ladies in the lounge."

"Well, he still owes me a lot. Son-in-law, there's still the fine for making my daughter pregnant. That's one. Two, the *lobolo*. You haven't sent a delegation yet."

"Oh! Is it so, mother-in-law?" I put on a false laugh. I was amazed at how she could talk about these family matters in the midst of all these people. Secondly, she was distorting facts. So, I put my hand lightly on her shoulder and whispered to her that pregnancy damages were paid. I also reminded her that there was still a meeting to be arranged by all parents concerned, regarding the latest saga that put Mildred in jail. Indeed, she had joined a long list of those still awaiting trial. Their respective days in court, to greet the Magistrate, as some put it.

"You are not trustworthy, Nelson, not at all trustworthy. But we leave things as they are for now." She told me as she said her final good-bye. She tickled Lungile on his cheeks. Then she quickly smelled his bums to see if he needed a diaper change. Putting my mothering skills to the test? He didn't. I'd just checked. I'm not trustworthy? I did not bother to respond to Zippora's accusations. I had no idea what she was referring to. I was the one sitting with a wound in my hand. I had a nasty black spot from internal bleeding on my forehead. The women did not wait for too long outside the house before their bus arrived and they left.

I had been having several telephonic conversations with Mildred's older brother, Michael, after Mildred's saga. He was a no nonsense fellow. The attitude of the ladies in his life towards me, did not amuse him at all.

"My sister? Hey, I love her a lot. But where the hell does she think she's going with this abusive behaviour?

Thank God you are the gentleman that you are. I'd long have broken her nose if I was in your shoes."

"I'd never be physical with a woman, Michael. Trust me."

"Just kidding, Nelson. Look. She's even more educated than I am. She has a decent job. She earns a decent salary. But her dependency, Nelson? How it kills me. Why can't my sister stand on her own two feet? Why did she feel she had to move in with you? Why did she not wait until you asked for her hand in marriage? Where's her pride, as a woman? Why did she force matters? Why couldn't she wait until processes like *lobolo* were attended to? She knows that's the custom." How could I respond to Michael? Exactly what I'd be harping upon for quite a while.

"You'd be out of your mind now to marry a woman like her. She's a potential murderer. She's my sister. But I don't take stupidly lopsided sides. Using a knife on you? Hell no!"

"Let's hope she won't do it again, Michael." I was really embarrassed on Mildred's behalf.

I must say the conversation with Michael helped me gain more clarity on my future with his sister. Loose thoughts firmed up into a more solid decision. With a boldness that took me aback I said to Michael, "I will not take chances, Michael. Prison will make her worse, and not better. Next time she might actually kill me in my sleep. Or even kill Lungile as well."

"I tell you, my brother. Some women and pining to be married. Between you and me, I don't even think she has any deep feeling for you anymore. I know it sounds awkward, coming from me, an outsider in your love relationship. And also as Mildred's brother."

"True, maybe deep feelings of hatred. The evidence is there."

I had been a bit anxious, not knowing how Michael would react. Blood is always thicker than water. But Michael was a sensible guy. He remained so even now.

I had in the interim searched for kindergartens that take babies Lungile's age. I had found one. Luckily, very close by. I was trying to organize my life, post Mildred. Mom Agnes would help with housework three times a week as usual. Lungile had begun to sleep well since his mother left. He had grown to demand less of the bottle feed at night.

Contrary to the breast he seemed to demand hourly. Most nights the boy slept through the night. He seemed to understand our predicament. Two men left to fend for themselves. He was doing his bit to cooperate fully. As a result he gradually made life easier for both of us. I was very proud of him.

The day of the family meeting was arranged. Finally! Michael called me early that week to say he wanted to come over for us to discuss a preposition he had, regarding the matter between me and his sister. On arrival he did not waste any time. He went straight to the business of our appointment. "The long and short of my proposal is that Mildred must move in with me. I have a spacious double-storey house. I'm not married. I've no children. The top floor could be all hers. That simple, Nelson."

Michael! No preliminaries so that I could ease into the discussion and make a useful contribution. Except I had nothing else to say. I truly was at a loss for words. I was very surprised that Michael had gone ahead of all my thinking. He had actually put some doing verbs as next concrete steps in my saga with his sister. I only had to make certain there'd be no flaws in his plan; for example, emotional repercussions that would take a serious toll on parties concerned. Hence my question, "Have you given yourself enough time to think this through, Michael? I'm anxious, naturally. What will the women in your life say?"

"I volunteer in a man's domestic abuse forum. *Decoding Men's Power*. I couldn't talk about it over the phone. DMP for short. Granted there are fewer cases of men abused by the women who claim to love them. But they are there."

"I think this matter is under-reported, if you ask me, Michael. I think as men we are programmed to take shit from women. Blame it on how well we are brought up. Some of us. To respect women as fellow human beings. Bad women take advantage."

"Exactly, Nelson. You hit the nail right on the head! It is faulty socialization when males aren't prepared for the other side of domestic violence. When they are on the receiving end of it. What to do when it is the women we've been socialized to protect and respect, who turn around and abuse us."

"As their protectors, Michael?"

"You are right to say it is shit, Nelson. Calling a spade a spade! There's something skewed when men aren't given tools to handle domestic abuse, when they are on the receiving end of it.

"Oh, Michael! This was a very difficult thing for me to admit. That I am the victim of domestic violence? This Nelson Nkosi? A strong, tall and hefty full grown man!"

"Exactly, Nelson."

That comment hit home. The 20 incidents in the police file loomed large in my mind. Granted, I'd done better than most. I'd identified and reported the abuse when it happened. Well and good. But then, why had I not opted out of this relationship? Honestly now?

"And men brought up like you were, Nelson. Not too many men like you yet. But the numbers are growing, with all the socialization and intervention strategies. Society is slowly changing. Shedding what's bad about patriarchy. Hence all of these structures to protect and empower women, you know. We have Gender Equality this. And Women's Empowerment that."

Michael then abruptly stopped talking. Epiphany time? I thought to myself. He pointed his index finger at me. He put on a broad knowing smile on his face. Then he chuckled and said, "Nelson, I've just cracked the code! I've figured out why Mildred wants so much to marry you. Your good upbringing, my man! You don't drink. You'll never hit her. You always respect her. There! You are every woman's jackpot."

"Gosh, Michael. Now that you say it. I've known Mildred is taking advantage, of course. But your analysis makes perfect sense, and it had never occurred to me." A flood of thoughts came. My poor parents! They brought me up to be a good human being. Of course I'm not perfect. I fall short at times. But it seems I'm now paying the price.

I felt helpless. So bound in the chains of a good upbringing. How ridiculous! Then the nagging thoughts revisited me. Why do I keep attracting women that are wrong for me, when I am so right for them? Actually their jackpot? What is it about me? Why do I keep taking these wrong paths to true love?

"Nelson, you are the brother I never had. That's for sure. Look, I cannot preach what I don't practice. I can't condemn domestic violence when perpetrated by men, and then turn a blind eye when it is perpetrated by women. In this instance, my own sister. My own flesh and blood!"

I winced. I deeply understood the pain Michael was going through. But I admired him for the courage to take a difficult decision on this dilemma. I thought to myself, how come Zippora's children are so different? Possible answers flooded my mind. Was Zippora harder with Michael, because of what the father did? Was he brought up with a subconscious guilt feeling about the man who abandoned them?

What about Mildred? Did she subconsciously grow up obsessed with finding a man who would not repeat what her father had done to their mother? Abandoning them as a family?

This was heavy stuff. It had never occurred to me before. I realized my deep conversation with Michael had triggered it. I left these beginnings of an analysis hanging. I decided I'd engage these thoughts another time, should they revisit. I noted the potential there for another enlightening epiphany.

Michael rubbed his hands together to signal that we were done with the talking. It was time for action. "I'm happy we quickly saw eye to eye on this, Nelson. I brought this big vehicle to begin to load my sister's belongings and take them home."

"What? Today? Just now? Are you crazy, Michael?" I asked, taken aback.

"That's right Nelson. Today. And, just now. Right away!" He smiled reluctantly and rubbed his shaven head vigorously with the palm of his hand.

"And your mother? Does she know about this move, Mike?"

"Why do you ask a question you know the answer to? It will take her years to understand that I'm doing this to save her daughter from herself. Zippora is my mother. I love her dearly. But at times she has to zip up and respect other people's better wisdom and judgment. So, any more questions?"

Michael stood up. He rolled up his sleeves and called the two young men he worked with to pull up as close as possible to the garage. It was time. That time! He playfully pulled Lungile's chin as he walked past me. "The young man has your wicked smile. Let's hope he doesn't inherit my sister's nasty attitude and bad heart."

Michael was a savvy businessman. He ran a very successful taxi service. He had a fleet of cars. All types. On this day, instead of coming in a small car, he had pulled up in one of his mini buses. I'd thought nothing of it. I'd understood he needed that size vehicle for some business errand that day.

Little did I know he already had this plan on his mind! All ready to execute. It was not long before several boxes were lined up in the passageway. Labelled and sealed, after I showed the young men what to pack. "Your guys are very systematic packers, Michael. They are working like pros. Are you involved in the goods removal business also?"

"Yes. I got my license a month ago. I'm still training these young men. Let's see how they put to practice what they've learned so far." Michael was standing with his legs astride. He was watching the young men at work.

"Get out of here! Are you really in this business now?" I asked as I slapped him hard on the shoulder. "As our people say, Mike. Money goes to those who already have it." Michael looked at me and smiled self-consciously. I loved the shyness I observed in him. How do I explain this? There was something very honourable about it.

I felt like starting a conversation about my own business venture. Selling live fowls in the Township. But this was not the day for such a talk. When the dust had settled, I'd make sure to pick Michael's brain on this and other possible business ventures I had on my mind.

The packing was almost done. The house indeed was becoming empty. I could feel Mildred becoming a ghostly presence. She would soon dissipate into a shadow. Thoughts of her casting a long dark shadow on Lungile and me, caused my heart to beat faster.

What about a haunting echo of her verbal abuse? I prayed it would not play in my mind for too long. "For once, Nelson, be a man." Finally there'd be complete silence; the type that comes with complete absence.

I truly was a bystander as I watched Michael's guys meticulously load boxes of different sizes. The young men were doing their work very patiently. There was a lot of concentration. Loading, offloading, re-arranging, loading, off-loading. Until all boxes were packed, neatly.

Taking things to this level triggered other questions and anxieties in me. In my mind I'd been preparing for the meeting with Zip and my parents. Now I had to shift gears. Michael had introduced a new ball game. I had not expected things to escalate to this level, this quickly. Michael definitely had fast tracked everything. I had little time to ponder on the meaning of it all. Let alone even savour the moment of parting ways with Mildred.

My mind rolled back to times gone by. I retraced my steps to the night I first laid my eyes on Mildred. We were standing in a long line, waiting to buy tickets for a popular film that time. I don't remember what it was. She was in front of me. I'd broken up with Yakhe six months before. I was enjoying my freedom again as an unattached man.

I started some small talk with the lady in front of me. I had seen her from behind. I had liked what I'd seen. She had a full figure. One of those people said to be round. She was a very well-dressed lady. She seemed to have an expensive taste, judging by the designer items she had on. No. She wasn't the type that leaves the label with the designer's name on the sleeve of a jacket. I wondered what she looked like were she to turn around, and I encountered her countenance for the first time. She was texting on her cell phone. I waited until she was done. Then I slipped in a comment, "Not a good idea this."

"What?" She asked as she turned to look at me.

"Doing such a romantic movie alone!"

"Well, it happens. I don't mind," she responded. She sounded like she truly wasn't unhappy to be at the movies, all by herself.

I'd already taken a glance as she turned to speak to me. Not bad looking at all. One of those ladies whose beauty is temporarily hidden in a dark cloud. You need to wait a while and watch as time spent with her peels off the layers of the dark cloud. And voila! Outstanding beauty is revealed. No point recalling all of that beautiful beginning now, I thought. Her belongings were loaded. She was not going to return to this house. I gave her my business card. She quickly took a look at it and repeated my name, "Nelson Nkosi."

"Yes, that's right," I responded. "And you are?"

"Mildred. Mildred Silomo." She responded as she looked for her business card in her handbag. I noticed that she was of medium height. The top of her head reached my shoulder. Michael was ready to leave. He was playing with Lungile. It was my son's favourite game. He was giggling away as his uncle threw him up in the air, and then caught him. Two days later I called Mildred. "Could we do a movie? Together, this time?" She agreed. Suffice to say one thing led to another, as they say.

I loved everything about Mildred. I loved brushing her four plaits of hair with my hands, as we lay in bed. I loved stroking the silky tips of her hair with my fingers. I loved burying my face in the middle of her chest, her ample unshackled breasts caressing each side of my face. Oh, it felt so heavenly. In a few months of committed courtship, Lungile was conceived.

"Don't worry about paying the fine for getting me pregnant. Just concentrate on getting the *lobolo* sorted out. So that we quickly get married."

"Hey, paying the pregnancy fine and talking *lobolo* negotiations are two separate issues. You do know this, Mildred. First things first, I think. I'm not even sure ...."

"What? How dare you? You get me pregnant. And now you are not sure you want to marry me! Is this what you are saying, Nelson?"

"Look, it's not like I impregnated a school girl. It's also not like I forced you into this. It was by mutual agreement, remember. No-one is a victim. Am I right or wrong, Mildred?"

"Nelson, this is how you are talking now? I'm disappointed in you. Men! You are a typical man. Untrustworthy. Cruel."

"Honey, look ..."

"Hey, don't honey me now. You devil!"

"The truth hurts, Mildred. That's what's making you boil to overflowing with rage. Look! The hot lid of your pot of anger is already rolling on the floor. I'm just disappointed that you don't want us to do things right, my dear."

I supported Mildred fully for the duration of the pregnancy. Some of the demands seemed ridiculous. They felt more like punishment. But it was my son Mildred was carrying. And he would never be too heavy for me. So I obliged. However, during this period I began to see Mildred's other selfish and ugly side. This disappointed me. Mildred was very mean-spirited. The Mildred who was now cursing me to hell and back wasn't the Mildred I'd first seen at the movies. Instantly, I knew that the experience with the first woman, Yakhe, who carried and lost my baby, had revisited me. That my father was disappointed in my poor choice, again, was very difficult to live with.

As I served Michael and his two young men some tea in the lounge, before they left, something else dawned on me. The signs were already there, I realized. Why didn't I pull out of this relationship with Mildred? Then the truth of my misfortune struck me. The glaring truth of my mistake. Careless mistake.

Twice, Nelson! Yakhe was already pregnant when she showed me her true colours. So was Mildred. Introducing a pregnancy in a relationship that had yet to jell into anything worth telling my parents about? This was very irresponsible of me. Jumping into bed with virtual strangers. *Take time to know her.* What did Percy Sledge know?

It was getting dark. But Michael had one more thing to discuss with me. "I want to applaud you for taking such good care of my nephew here, Lungile. I don't know how you feel. But don't assume the law will take him away from you. Just because he'll still so young? No! The court carefully examines all angles of the case. I'm afraid my sister doesn't have a good record. She has behaved exactly like an abusive man."

"What are you saying, Michael, seriously now? That the law sometimes is on the side of men?"

"On the side of justice and fairness, Nelson. You understand of course what I'm telling you. It's a difficult decision to accept for any mother, when the court decides the father is the better mother! See that?" Michael stretched out the palms of his hands to emphasize that point. Working at DMP made Michael very clear about processes that I was still mulling over in my head. Gingerly so. I don't think I even knew what to think. I had not even begun to stretch my mind to these court battles.

For some strange reason Mildred's abuse made me a dunderhead. I was beginning to note now. Only now! After 20 incidents of abuse. I never looked into a future without her in my life. I suppose abuse does this to its victims. They keep wallowing in the dirty bath of its slimy waters. Thoughts of escape from the situation keep slipping from their minds. Back into the slime.

Victims seem unable to find points of exit from continued abuse. But they can let out the dirty slimy water, and then climb out of this ugly life bath, to their freedom.

"Nelson, my boy, you'll have to learn to hold firm the reins of your horse, next time. Don't allow your horse to gallop unthinkingly into a dark and dangerous hole, right into a trap, most possibly to the edge of a cliff, and a sure point of no return. *Take time to know her* first. If there ever will be a next time." This was the last thought in my long post-mortem of my failed love relationships.

As he was standing up, Michael reached across to where I was sitting. He slapped my knee quite hard. A lightening of pain did the zigzag on my poor knee. He gave me a million dollar assurance. "We'll get you a good lawyer at DMP. Your rights and my nephew's, need to be protected. This is the bottom line."

Michael was so far ahead in his thinking. He had jumped some steps. The pending family meeting, for example. I had to ask him, "Won't you attend the meeting with the elders later this week? With these developments, it's going to be a very difficult meeting, Michael. You understand that. It will be important for you to come." I half assumed and half hoped Michael had thought of all this. "Don't worry about that, Nelson. I'll have time to talk to mom, so that she cooperates and zips up at the meeting."

"Are you sure about this? Your mother will see red already, once she learns you've moved Mildred out of this house. I bet you didn't even inform her, let alone seek her advice, Mike?" We were both standing up now. The young men were long waiting for Michael by the garage. He tapped my shoulder lightly. He assured me everything would go well. "I'll talk to your parents as well. With those two I won't have to harp on the same point a million times. You are lucky to have such mellow parents."

"Are you saying then the meeting here will be the second one?" Michael looked at me with pity. "You worry too much, my friend. Let me put it this way. The meeting here will be short. It will merely be a formality. Okay? Happy?"

"Thanks so much, Mike. But let's keep talking. Please."

"I've got your back. Above all, God has got your back. Apartheid is dying. Some say it's already dead. But until I see the grave site? You know what I mean? What more do you want, African man? As for my mom and sister, it's a simple well-known adage, I've got to be cruel, only to be kind. Okay?"

Lungile and I waved good-bye to his uncle and his mother's belongings. We stood at the gate for a while. For what, really? I guess I was still in a daze. It had yet to settle fully in my mind that Mildred was out of my life. Pending the Court ruling, of course. But Michael had given me some hope.

"We'll see!" I said loudly, as I tucked my hands under Lungile's armpits and threw him in the air, once or twice. As always, he wanted more of the game. "Time for dinner and your bath, my boy!" I walked back to the house, carrying Lungile on top of my shoulders. It was a very different home.

I tossed and turned in my sleep that night. I had a nightmare. I woke up in a cold sweat. Mildred was pointing a gun at me. When I realized Lungile's toy gun was on my mind, a weak smile lulled me back to sleep.

That then began a new life for me. Michael was carrying me on his very broad shoulders. He had taken it upon himself to put his sister on the straight and narrow. Indeed, for her own good. Michael had promised to find me a lawyer to ensure justice and fairness are seen to be served all round. With all of this, all I had to worry about was probably stepping on an ant by mistake. And, with my big shoes, snuffing out its precious life.

Mildred's lawyer insisted that I get only week-end visits supervised by social workers. Just a few hours to spend with my boy. The boy was still too young to be separated from its mother, the lawyer argued.

"With all the respect I have for you, your Honour, I think you have made a mistake with a judgment that favours the father of such a young child, Sir. As a matter of fact, such a small baby, Sir."

"Is that all, Ms. Jezani?"

"Yes, indeed, your Honour. This will be all."

I watched the judge take off his glasses. He leaned forwards slightly. Then he responded, almost inaudibly. "It is always a tragedy when a qualified attorney like yourself, stands before me with her ears shut. And then publicly makes a fool of herself. This is all under the pretext of representing her client to the best of her ability."

Was the judge about to rule otherwise? Mildred's camp would definitely see red. Could Mike have been right then? My heart was pounding. I continued to listen very intently.

"I have spelt out at length, why in this instance, the boy is better off living with his father, until he reaches majority age. The brutality he has observed and absorbed like a sponge during these formative years is enough. The scars of the soul are worse off than those on the skin. So, my ruling stands."

This old man, wizened by age, turned red in the face, as he began to address me. "Mr. Nkosi, the Social worker will pay you daily visits to satisfy ourselves that the boy is well looked after. That we will do, for peace sake."

"Fine, your Honour," I responded confidently, "I don't have a problem with that. I have nothing to hide. And Mildred knows I am a better mother than she is. While she has the breast milk and probably some motherly instinct, she has a lousy temperament, and a selfish streak she can't hide or control."

The judge's hand slowly went up. He was indicating that I'd said enough. Indeed, it did feel like I was probably beginning to babble, misusing my opportunity to talk directly to the judge. But I did not make myself stop abruptly like that, mid-sentence, in respect of the court.

"If you kindly allow me to finish, your Honour, Sir. And it won't be the first time that I take care of Lungile. 24/7. It must not be lost to Mildred, her attorney and this court, that while she did time at Appleview, I did not take our boy to an orphanage. I knew what to do. And I still know how to bring him up in the most honourable way."

I then turned to Mildred and her woman lawyer, "There, feel free to check everything you want. The food, cleanliness and how we bond with Lungile." Zippora and her daughter shared a large tissue box. From time to time, Mildred's mother had a little shawl she covered her knees with. Oh, yes, she made a point to give me her usual dirty looks. I knew she'd wait for me outside court. Michael wasn't in court. I knew of course how he worked behind the scenes.

"You are bad news, Nelson. You are evil. I'll never talk to you again. What you've done to Millie is unforgivable." I uttered not one word.

Mildred and her lawyer rushed past me to the parking lot. Straight into their respective cars. This war stance. How it shook me up. I'd thought Mildred and I could have a little moment. We'd had some good times. Short-lived?

Yes. But there'd been a spark. Once. I stood there for a long minute, as if electrocuted. Then I felt dad's hand on my shoulder. "Let's go, son." Both mom and dad could tell I was shaken up.

Mom looked me straight in the eye and consoled me, only like a mother can, "Look here, Nelson, it's not your fault. All will be well. Lungile will grow up well. Before you know it, he'll be at school, at university, having a job." I noticed how mom stopped right there, and no further. She avoided the marriage institution for Lungile.

Just one month later the Social Workers reported to me that they were satisfied. The child is well-cared for. They would therefore close the file. That shut up Mildred's and her lawyer's big mouths!

Of course Mildred tried to turn the whole thing around. She sold the story to all and sundry that I was a foolish man. How could I give a woman such freedom? The bogus gospel she spread around was that she relished her situation of being child free, while I took over as both mother and father.

I knew this was just a 'pick me up' pill she popped in every so often. All lies. It was her attempt to deal with the new situation. What mother can honestly boast about having ties with her only baby son so severely cut off? And worse off, severed in a court of law? Total insanity. Mildred's attitude did not bother me. It was just a stance. One big fat façade. Who wouldn't and couldn't see through it? It was from a standpoint of grapes are sour.

She didn't know, though, that her brother kept me updated on all her failed attempts at finding love again. All in all I was rather saddened that her brother's efforts, to have her learn a permanent lesson from all this, seemed to have accomplished very little. If she had a history of repeating classes at school, I truly would have understood.

Maybe dad's own analysis could be something to go by, as he told me one early evening. He and mom had returned Lungile after he spent a whole day with his doting grandparents. As usual, they returned him to me when he was ready to sleep. Bathed and fed already.

Lungile's grandmother was lulling the boy to sleep upstairs. Dad and I were in the lounge, watching news on Television. He put his hand on top of mine and said softly, "Nelson, I've applied my mind to the working of your Mildred's mind." I listened intently, letting his teaser of 'your Mildred' disappear into thin air, as soon as it formed on dad's lips. "I tell you, son, that woman has a flare for stupidity which has nothing to do with her IQ of course."

I couldn't find from my little knowledge of the English language a way to improve dad's sentence. Just for myself. So that 'mind' would not appear twice in one sentence. Apply *myself* or apply my *mind*?

Mildred could most probably have come up with a smarter combination of words to express dad's point. She was very articulate, very good with words. Except, she wouldn't have been pleased with dad's observation. About *mind* appearing twice in one sentence? Who cared? It actually didn't matter. Maybe there was no other way of expressing dad's profound observation.

Mildred Silomo. She could have been my parents' daughter-in-law. As life continued. Life after Mildred was certainly not going to be a bed of roses. But with Lungile by my side, all would be well. Uniquely well.

# Will You Marry Me, My T Girl?

"Will *you* marry me *my* T Girl? Will you *marry* me T Girl? Will you marry *me* T Girl?" The fifteen minutes he'd timed as usual on his cell phone was up. He dressed up his face with a knowing smile. He bent with a measure of unease to tie up his shoe laces. "James. What a pro shoe polisher! I should have thanked him. Why didn't I?"

He chided himself for losing a bit of his humanity as he slowly assumed the upright position again, his two hands supporting his small hips. He felt a surge of shame that made him blush a little, as he remembered the rule in their house, "Thank them every time. Even a hundred times in one day, show appreciation.

"My God, I'm losing a bit of my posture. Come on back, straighten up! I've more years of active life you know, very active life," he said to himself as he made a study of his face on the long mirror. He took a long gaze at himself and with his hand, fixed the loose strands of his hair.

"Who'd believe me I used to have a long main of pitch black hair? It doesn't matter really; T Girl believes me. That's the photo she carries in her wallet, tucked neatly in the cover of her ID book. She's such a show off. I wouldn't be surprised to learn she doesn't tell those who see my photo that it was taken thirty years ago."

He twisted his face, grinning hard to see if more deep lines formed on the sides of his eyes. There was a frown on his brow, but that was just from habit. And those furrows on his forehead were the least of his worries. "I can't do much about these," he said as the frown somehow made the furrows deeper. "I got them from my father. God bless his heart."

The big clock chimed some tune. "Okay young man, it's eight o'clock. And time to go." As he shut the front door, he looked up, and said his usual prayer, "Thank you God - for everything." The weather man had said it would be a fine sunny day. Indeed the heat was already making its presence felt.

As he pulled out of the garage he hummed a little tune. He mused to himself, "T Girl would laugh at me now, naughty girl. I don't like her comment that even birds sing better than me. Whatever! As if she herself sings like Whitney."

Traffic was lighter after 8 am. He drove on the slow lane. He was enjoying his car, the morning breeze and Beethoven. He also had time to reflect and work on perfecting his very important one line, "T Girl, will you marry me?" He went on to a minute's mental debriefing of that morning's practice in front of the long mirror. "I'm getting better every day. The day I pop the question the words will flow out like the contents of a raw egg. The question now is timing old boy. Smart timing!"

The nagging anxiety was upon him again: When do I ask THE question? What if she says no? Well that hardly ever happens. But ... you never know with women. He revisited the merits for a young woman getting involved with an older man. He knew the demerits as well. But those thoughts he usually pushed out of his psyche. "Who needs negativism? Honestly, I can't imagine T Girl turning down my proposal. Besides, women love to be married, to be Mrs. So and So. Well, well, some feminists I know might disagree. Great God, how much the world has changed?"

Humming along with Beethoven, he muttered to himself, "T Girl, I wonder what you are doing now." His left hand reached for his cell phone. But he resisted the urge to call her. Mimicking her he said, "Patrick, why bother me so early? Or is there anything wrong?"

He knew exactly what she'd look like as she answered the phone. Her voice would be so heavily laced with sleep, he'd feel sorry for her, and of course, ashamed of himself. "I've been in love so many times before, why is this thing with T Girl so special? Or are you deceiving yourself, Patrick, old age blighting reason or reality? T Girl I love you so much. Will you ..." Patrick swerved as he cursed, "Black cat don't cross my path again. I'll sure send you to your ancestors next time."

A bit importantly, as if about to stand up and make a public speech, he touched the collar of his dark mauve shirt and felt the knot of his dark navy blue tie. He was making sure everything was in place. He put on his executive look, as the security guard opened the gate. Patrick raised his hand and saluted the security guard, army style. Then he quickly lowered his window. With a broad friendly smile, Patrick greeted his worker, "It's going to be a blisteringly hot day today, Menzi. Do you think it might rain?"

"Good morning, sir, Yes, sir, it's very hot today. I hope it rains, sir."

Patrick was proud of his security team. Dutiful, conscientious smart ladies and gentlemen. Pay a little in training and your staff becomes a brilliant investment in the life of the Company. Each time those thoughts came to mind he always imagined himself teasing Donald Trump, "With all your money and business acumen, buddy, I bet you could not have come up with that smart line."

Patrick also liked the security team's new uniform. Snow white short-sleeved white shirts with a small gold

PF embroidered on the shirt pocket. The stitching was quite fancy. It looked like some experienced hands had performed this fine and perfect work.

The security ladies wore perfectly fitting knee-length black skirts that enabled them to show off their lovely legs in pantyhose, while the men's black pants were a well-cut perfect fit for them all. Pride in his staff, actually, the brilliant selection of his security staff, carried him into his office. Didn't every visitor to the Company comment on how smart, courteous and lovely they all were?

After drinking his favourite cinnamon and apple herbal tea, he quickly went through his 'to- do- list'. It was not going to be a heavy day, thank God. The urge was strong to start off by checking his email to see if T Girl had sent him a little naughty note while he was driving to work. But alas, the Board meeting would start in twenty minutes' time. And he had to be in the right frame of mind.

He had to shelve his thoughts about T Girl, imagining how she'd react when he finally asked her to marry him; how he'd take it all. The excitement would be almost unbearable, almost uncontainable, overly overwhelming, he always thought. He felt a surge in his pants, but closed his eyes as if getting ready to meditate. A few minutes later the baking powder or yeast had lost its power, collapsing and quieting T Girl's Johnny.

Needless to say, there the usual notorious spoilers of course, that at times managed to drag him to a dark alley and attempted to clog his mind with myriads of reasons why his hope of marrying T Girl was only an impossible dream. But in no time Patrick would spot these losers, lurking in the dark. He knew their mission.

"At it again! You jealous hard-headed spoilers! You don't give up, do you?" He'd slowly rise up from his brooding corner. With tiger eyes ablaze, a hand transformed to that of a karate master facing an opponent, he'd give each loser a good smack in the face, and watch with satisfaction as they all - one by one, staggered from the impact, and then fell to the ground. Once more, with his shield and armour of resolve and focus in place, he'd take long sure-footed deliberate strides back to Hopeville, again. He'd be so proud of his victory. Even peacocks wouldn't outshine him.

During lunch with Board members, he excused himself after the main meal. He was trying to shed a few kilos and would therefore skip dessert, he announced. He went straight to his office, made himself comfortable in his leather easy chair, put his feet on the matching footrest and stretched his legs.

He was about to slip off his shoes when he remembered this was office space and he was Chief Executive Officer of a big Company bearing his name, Patrick Fitzgerald. He wanted to be relaxed when he spoke to T Girl. He was grateful for the perfect timing, though, as he knew his lady was also taking a lunch break from the grueling morning lectures.

"Hi, my T Girl."

"Hey, hey, not like that, Patrick. I'm not your tea girl."

"Oh don't start now, Thokozani. Apartheid ruined your sense of humour. Anyway, don't sidetrack me now. This is a very special call."

"My apologies, my dear. That was a joke. Okay? You sound a bit grumpy. What's the matter?"

"Nothing, I guess. I'm just uptight."

"About what? Oh! Business people. I would not manage that kind of life even for a week. Stress, stress and more stress."

"Well, there's something I've been thinking about for quite some time now."

"Relating to, if I may ask?"

"Well, you and me. Us."

"Oh, I'm ready. If it bothers you to a state of grumpiness, out with it sweetheart. Let me move to a quieter spot. It's a bit rowdy here. Students and long week-end fever."

"We need to make time. It's something we can't properly discuss over the phone." Patrick knew that if he could, he would let it off his chest, right away.

Excitement and anxiety were madly in competition. He needed to call a truce and declare it's a tie, so that his heart could relax a bit. He didn't enjoy this impromptu position as referee, flanked by the two equally strong boxers, whose arms he dutifully had to lift simultaneously, and declare above the frenzied music, "We have a tie. Yes, Excitement on my left, and Anxiety on my right: they both win, ladies and gentlemen!"

Patrick did not want to take chances, however. This was too important a subject, one he strongly felt would make or break his life here on.

"Oh well, if you say so. As you know, I hate being kept in the dark. When, then? Over the week-end?"

"That would be nice, Thokozani. Are you free this week-end?" Patrick smiled as he noted how he could pretend to be in no hurry.

"Let me make sure now. I have to prepare for a Tuesday test. I have finished the first draft of an essay. Saturday will be fine."

"That's my T Girl! Thanks, my dear. You have no idea what this means to me." T Girl picked up the unusually strong emotions, and was baffled. She felt a bit sad and sorry that she was postponing this meeting.

"What's wrong, Patrick?"

"Nothing is wrong. Maybe you should ask this time, what's right? I will pick you up at the usual spot. What time shall we make it? I know you don't like waking up too early."

"Hey, especially over the week-end, my friend."

"Oh come on, it's a long week-end, remember?"

"There's really no long week-end for me. Monday I'll be at my books again, if I want to do well in the test."

"Of course, of course, T Girl. Saturday and Sunday spent together will be heavenly."

"First things will be first, though. I'll be both curious and anxious now until Saturday. You are a very bad boy, Patrick, keeping me in suspense like this."

"Oh well... I'm sorry to do this to you, my love. But ..."

"But what, Patrick?"

"It's all good. It's all good, Thokozani. Believe me."

There was silence on the other end. Patrick knew his T Girl was anxious. But he'd planned this proposal so well, and for so long, he could not deviate from the plan now.

"How about having breakfast in town, doing a little shopping and then going home? We could even add a movie early afternoon. How's that?"

"Perfect, Patrick. I see, come Saturday morning, you will still not be in a big hurry to discuss that something relating to us. Fine. I'm not going to waste my energy worrying."

"Exactly. That's my girl! Don't think and brood too much. Let me see. It is most likely to be a good pleasant discussion. It depends. I hope it will all go well. Optimism is good for both of us."

"You are determined to keep me in the dark. We've been talking for a good twenty minutes now. We'd long have discussed the matter. Lunch time is almost over. I still need to grab a sandwich. Anyway, suit yourself, young man. I'll see you on Saturday then."

"I'll call Friday night to finalize everything. You might also want to run some errands in town. We'll have time for that."

"There'll be no need to talk on Friday, really, or will there? You are not really in a big rush for us to get home and talk!"

"Bye my love, my sweet Thokozani."

Patrick's lunch time was also almost over. He was still in the love orbit and office time could be crumpled and parked at some corner. He honestly did not care. That's what Thokozani did to him - a tiny bit careless and irresponsible some times. He let the DVD titled, *The First Time I Saw Her*, slide smoothly into its slot. He pressed the play button in the mind's DVD player.

Indeed her dark skin was flawless. Her teeth sparkled. Her hair was rich and full. As she turned her back towards him to give him directions, he viewed her from behind for the first time. He'd been in Africa long enough to love and appreciate the full figure and ample posterior of some African women. He immediately knew it was a beautiful posterior he could handle and enjoy, clothed or unclothed. Oh, how lucky he felt already!

Patrick sometimes wondered how Thokozani would look in a trendy hairstyle. But he knew she was the type that would never fry virgin hair, subject it to hot combs and chemicals. Dreadlocks she'd grow maybe, one day.

The last segment of the DVD showed them leaving the general practitioner's office, all smiles, as they celebrated their HIV negative status.

In the quiet of his office, Patrick kept playing with a pen he did not even remember getting from his desk close by. He was putting the end in and out of his mouth, very unaware of the menacing 'click' sound, as he pressed the top against his lower set of teeth. "T Girl, will you marry me?" His mind indulged itself, and he let it. There was the white wedding cake. His T Girl in a glorious white wedding gown, he had had made for her. The reception hall packed with important people in their lives. He dreaded, however, spending that whole day with Thokozani's parents. They were still stiff in one another's midst. Thokozani's only sister, Sizakele, fondly known as Siza, was always nice and relaxed. It showed she'd travelled widely.

Patrick looked forward to sharing jokes with her and her husband, the big *Inkosi* [Chief]. But there'd be all the bodyguards hovering over him and his wife, not letting them have a measure of fun. Royalty is royalty, however. All these thoughts traveled to places and spaces far and wide.

It took Patrick some time and effort to retrace his mental steps back to his office, to his comfortable chair and to normal time. His mind had allowed him this pleasant trip down memory and future lanes with his Thokozani, and of course their two families.

It was way past lunch time. He had one more report to read before going home. He put on his reading glasses and then let them slide down the bridge of his nose. He made an absentminded study of the tall palm trees outside. He wished Thokozani was right there, sitting on his lap, her legs out-stretched. He wondered what she was wearing that day. Which pair of jeans? He could bet a hundred Rand her hair was a bit unkempt.

He'd long noticed she was hardly obsessed with her beauty. She didn't try too hard to look pretty. She was a natural beauty, after all. But come the time to be well-groomed, she knew how to rise to the occasion. Her African outfits always looked stunning on her, complimenting her dark skin. She made a great partner of the CEO, Patrick Fitzgerald, at business functions, holding her own among the best of them.

"I am a thoroughbred African, Patrick, and very proud of who I am," she'd told him one evening, early on in their relationship, when he'd asked her, "Thokozani - who is Thokozani? Tell me more about yourself." She was surprised she had given this mature man some space in her life, after the accidental meeting at the university library in Johannesburg, when he asked her for directions to the archives section. She was not dating anyone, pre-occupied with her studies as she was. And she had over time also managed to flush out the bad experience from her last relationship.

"Patrick is well-mannered, unassuming and funny," Thokozani had told her only sister, Sizakele, a couple of months into her love affair with Patrick, when she felt it safe to publicly make the announcement. She liked the way he opened and shut doors for her. A true gentleman. He was an amazing listener. He was sensitive to other people's suffering. How quickly it brought tears to his big gentle eyes. She liked the way he obviously took care of himself. He played golf. He worked out with a regular gym routine. He swam. He took long walks.

His trim body told this good health story. His short hair-cut made him look even younger than 50, even as his temples began to gradually turn into different shades of grey. She would have liked his moustache trimmer. But over time, she'd gotten used to its bit of ruggedness. He was a very careful dresser. It seemed every morning he dressed to prepare for that unknown moment - when he had to make a first impression, which could never be repeated.

Patrick began to think about Saturday. He wanted to make it a special moment they'd both allude to a countless times and remember, until their dying days. "Let's see," Patrick began to concretize and finalize the planned programme. "It will be a beautiful dinner at home - by candlelight of course. The day before, Margaret will have prepared the best meal. Wine - red and white, champagne, still plenty in stock. Then Friday morning I will pick up the engagement ring."

A swipe of anxiety swept over him, again, almost throwing him off mental balance. A 'what if' anxiety played games with his mind. But the remembrance of the day his T Girl playfully tried on the ring, helped Patrick onto his two mental feet again. How dazzling the ring looked on her finger. He took out his white handkerchief and carefully wiped the sweat from his forehead.

"God, please be with me."

Thokozani did not know Patrick had asked the salesman to make a note of the size and design of the ring. A few days later, he'd gone back to pay for it in full, and asked that it be kept in the store until he was ready to pick it up, when the time was right. It was still early in their relationship, so much that Thokozani did not even think much of that trip to the jewellers.

Yet Patrick had felt something different with this new girlfriend. She seemed special. He felt at home, at rest and at peace in her and with her. He had earnestly courted her, and enjoyed it. He could imagine them sharing the same bed, shower and bath, for a very long time.

It was something he had not felt with women he'd dated since his wife's passing. "Maybe Rachel is happy with this relationship. I can feel her spirit giving our thing with T Girl a nod," Patrick had told his two sons on their boys' night out, two months after Thokozani accepted his love proposal.

The twins were on a week's business trip, but they'd finally managed to squeeze in a week-end to spend with their dad, before they returned to Japan. "Boys, I honestly think your mother is looking on and exceedingly pleased with my new find, Thokozani. I truly feel lucky and blessed. She's such an amazing woman."

"We are happy for you, dad. We can't wait to see her. But you'll know, when the time is right. It's just that distance might make it difficult. Japan is very far away," commented one of the boys, the so-called older twin.

"But please keep us posted, dad," added Patrick's second son. They all gave a toast to the new woman in their father's life, and by relationship, theirs.

As a typical Zulu girl, Thokozani Sosibo let the courtship drag on and on, even when she knew she had long fallen in love with this older man. After a while, love tricked her Zulu girl nonsense. She found herself in Patrick's arms, when he dropped her off at her university residence, one evening.

As he gave her the usual good-bye kiss on the cheek, he felt a surge of something unusual from her body. Experience took over, and with one little move, she had yielded. Both were trembling as they embraced. Her door provided the support they both needed, as they stumbled and struggled to keep their feet on the ground.

Well, Saturday was going to be the day to begin the end of a boyfriend and girlfriend love affair. He was ready to take Thokozani with him on a journey of a marriage partnership. He felt deep in his heart that the right time had come, to propose marriage.

His desperate prayer now was that the time was right for T Girl as well. Patrick began to imagine their wedding day, again, as he would, a countless times. But he knew of the old wise saying. "First things first."

At that very moment he grabbed his jacket, his laptop and left. It was still a bit early for a sundowner. But he found a quiet corner at his favourite bar, and ordered coffee with lots of hot milk. He found it interesting that the soft music playing was talking to him, directly: *Don't Worry. Be Happy!*

"Thank you, young man. You know the universe has got our backs, all the time. The universe has got us all covered," Patrick said to the waiter, out of the blue.

"You may be right, sir. But I still have to digest what you are saying, figure out what it means in my life, sir."

"Do you have a girlfriend? Do you love her?"

The young man blushed a little at the questions that kept tumbling down on him. They came unawares and from a man he never thought he could discuss love matters with.

The waiter smiled and sweat beads began to show on his forehead. His eyes flashed red hot fiery sparkles as he answered, "Of course I do, sir. She means everything to me. She's truly my world. I hope we'll go places together, and never tire of saying 'I love you' to each other, as long as we live, even into and beyond death, if I may add."

"Oh yes. Even unto and beyond death. That's powerful. I love African spirituality that encompasses life after death. I must admit living in Africa has led me to tremendous growth on all fronts, especially spiritual growth. I'm so grateful to African gods that led me to this beautiful Continent. Here the essence of life is understood very deeply. This is quite remarkable."

"And you, sir, if I may ask, seeing that we are into this wonderful topic. Anyone special in your life, sir?"

"Oh yes, young man! I'll bring her here one day. I don't think I've ever loved a woman like this, since my wife passed."

"I'm sorry about the loss of your wife, sir. But it seems you've found happiness again."

"You are so right, son," Patrick responded, as he stared rather absentmindedly at his coffee. It was a gesture that belied the places his mind gravitated to, as he savoured with gratitude how lucky he was to have "found happiness again."

It was a bit quiet in the restaurant and bar. Patrick watched the young man disappear into the rose garden, hopefully, not for a smoke which was bad for bedroom gymnastics, he mused to himself. When he looked up again, the young man was speaking to someone on his cell phone. He hoped it was to the woman he seemed to be so madly in love with.

On the appointed Friday Patrick locked the office and excused himself from the regular Friday afternoon round of golf with his colleagues. "I'm feeling a bit low. I may be coming down with flu." His friends understood and excused him. Patrick headed straight to the shop that had the priced engagement ring.

The package had been stored away for months by now. The shop assistant quickly recognized Patrick. For a face like his was not easy to forget, laced with such strong emotions as it was, the day he bought the ring and had it kept safely in the storeroom. "I wish your dreams come true, sir," the shop assistant remembered saying as Patrick left, after voluntarily telling the salesman about Thokozani, and how much he loved her.

"My friend, you must remember the lovely African woman I came to the shop with, several months ago?" The shop assistant remembered him well, but not the lady in question, though. But he had to do the right thing. "Of course I do remember her. Absolutely!" He responded as he gave Patrick an interesting curious look, while checking the receipt. "Are you two still an item?"

"Well, young man, we are still head over heels in love, more than a mere item, whatever item means in matters of love. Thokozani is a woman of striking beauty and personality. You saw her that day. I could not stop thinking about her even after the first time I met her.

And the day to propose marriage has come. Talk about destiny's intelligence! You know, a friend of mine - he's been married for three decades now, but he still remembers all the details of the day, time and place when destiny changed his life forever.

Grant that these days we have Internet dating. That's well and good. But let me be honest here," Patrick briefly raised his left hand like one in a dock before the judge. "I've tried it, without much success, I must confess."

"What has been your experience, if I may ask, sir? You know man-to-man." Patrick shook his head slightly. "The bottom line is that it's a very unnatural setting. You spend all that time and money as well as your emotions in something you are not sure of. She might claim to be this age, this well- educated, but you are not sure.

You have misgivings all the time. Even if she's told you the whole truth, she could be living in Australia. Meeting her over tea or coffee will not happen anytime soon. You may, from the correspondence and occasional phone call feel there's some potential here. But no meeting will happen tomorrow, next week, next month or even next year."

"Distance slowly sucks out the enthusiasm," added the young man. "Exactly. There you go. I tried Internet dating for some time. Excitedly, I told a friend about my new found lady. Things didn't work out. Then I became too ashamed to tell my friend later, that the whole thing aborted. I'd try again. You know this kind of dating can be addictive.

I'd go tell my friend again. And he'd say, 'Patrick, I see, another woman again! What happened to the medical doctor from Rome? You will learn the hard way next time. Internet dating interferes with destiny. It's not good for anyone.' He'd almost plead with me, to simply stay out of it!"

"You eventually took your friend's advice."

"And it has worked out beautifully. Believe me."

"I'm happy for you, sir. I'm actually envious."

"But I'm so nervous. As if she'll disappoint me. Refuse my marriage offer. Come up with a plethora of excuses, postponements, what have you. Between you and me, women are an enigma. Quite intriguing. Yet can't-do-without all the same, specimens of nature ..."

"In fact, our queens," the salesman completed Patrick's thought, seamlessly.

"Have you ever tried to imagine a world without our fairer sex, young man?"

With his hands clasped on the top of his head, the salesman laughed out loud. He appeared to have a vivid picture, and dreaded to step into the mess of a womanless society. "Sir, it would be a complete disaster! We'd be at war all the time, I tell you. Finally, we'd annihilate the entire male species of the human race." The two men continued laughing animatedly, both clearly enjoying the discussion.

"My God, look at the time. These are women for you." Patrick made sure the little box, attractively wrapped, was safe in the inside pocket of his blazer. He was whistling a little tune as he gave a military style salute to the young man. The salesman clumsily returned the salute.

He followed Patrick with his eyes for as long as he could. There he was, clearly a happy man. He was immaculately dressed as usual; in his smart navy blue double breast blazer with silver buttons, designer grey flannels, a snow white shirt, an expensive designer belt and shoes to match.

"You are a lucky girl, Thokozani," the young salesman mumbled to himself as another customer walked into the shop. Patrick was still within hearing distance.

Patrick stopped and turned, "T Girl, I call her."

"T as in letter T or as in tea - in a cup?"

"Letter T of course." The deep furrows on Patrick's forehead were promptly in situ as he frowned in disgust at the salesman's comment and suggestion. He took a few more slow and deliberate steps back in. He stood in the middle of the shop. "I'm not into that demeaning crap of apartheid times. What do you take me for, young man? Some of us are civilized you know." The salesman saw Patrick's face turn into a bright red raspberry in seconds.

"I'm sorry my comment seems to be offending you, sir. I didn't ...." Patrick turned a deaf ear to the salesman's attempt to explain. To him the comment was inexcusable, and any explanation, futile. His voice rose into a crescendo.

"Let me tell you something, young man. I'm not into that demeaning crap of your apartheid times, which for all you know continues to this very day, where any African woman who happens to have the job of having to boil water in a kettle, grab a tea bag, throw it in the damned tea-pot or teacup, pour boiling water over it, warm up the milk, according to *your* preference, pour it in a jug, make sure the sugar bowl is clean and filled with sugar, neatly arrange thin slices of lemon on a side plate with toothpicks for you to lift the damned slices with and throw in your cup, bring the whole thing to you in a nice tray – you call her a tea girl? Mark you, even decent mature married men, husbands, fathers, brothers, and uncles of somebody, just because making *you* tea is part of their job description, then that 'tea boy' demeaning label, becomes their name? Racist and very reductionist, if you ask me.

"Sir, I ..."

"In the English language, I'm sure it's the same with other languages too: there are girls and there are women. There are boys and there are men. Not so? There's a clear distinction in these nouns. The female person who happens to have to make you tea in her daily routine, is a full grown woman. *And,* she has a name. If she has girl children, they are at school.

According to the International Labour Organization (ILO), maybe you've heard of it, child labour is against the law. So, no girl would be expected to work. And in the odd circumstances that she did, except maybe (highly unlikely, though) that it was the 'Bring the Girl-Child to Work' Day, and you'd succeeded, deridingly, to talk your so-called 'tea girl' into 'bringing to work little Thenjiwe you've heard so much of, and dying to meet' - with the express purpose of trying to ensure the abominable seeds of low self-esteem you think you've planted in her mother, are dispersed and land in Thenjiwe's fragile psyche, as she carves her own sense of self and place in this world.

Never mind the circumstances, sinister or not, even this little girl wouldn't deserve the dishonour of being labeled a tea-girl. And I repeat, neither her mom nor her dad, should ever be labeled by that small menial task! Am I making myself clear, young man?"

"Sir, I didn't mean ..."

"Please let me finish, my good sir!" Patrick was beginning to lower his voice now, but his speech was still deliberately didactic. "These men and women are respected members of their communities. Margaret, who helps me at home and at the office, is a decent woman. She is married with children. She is always on the right side of the law.

I never call her anything else, besides addressing her by her name, Margaret, because I've no reason to. I know better than that. All self-respecting people would and should. And guess what, son? She serves on the kindergarten committee in her community. She's a leader!

For goodness sake, there's more to their lives than this tea making thing. Who knows what their true potential is? Where would they be had destiny dealt them a better, gentler and fairer hand, and they had been exposed to decent opportunities in life?"

"Absolutely, sir. What I meant ..."

"Now, who has given us the right to dare address them by the menial jobs they do, sum up the totality of their whole decent personhood by reducing them to tea cups, saucers and boiling water? How dare we?"

Patrick's well-manicured middle finger was up in the air. Then he stopped speaking and took a deep breath. A moment's silence passed. Patrick looked at the young salesman's face. He saw agony written in big block letters there. Patrick was a bit sorry that they'd both put each other in this awkward position. Nevertheless, he had no regrets. The lecture had been necessary.

In a soft and calmer voice, Patrick had the last word, "I'm sorry, son. But some things get worse if left unsaid and corrected. Have a good day now." Patrick strutted out, as quiet satisfaction descended slowly all over him.

Head bowed, the salesman sat down on the black leather stool, just behind the counter. He was devastated, surprised and ashamed at the rage his comment had triggered in this gentleman. He was sorry he didn't get the opportunity to explain himself. However, the more he composed himself, the more he was surprised at the conclusion he was drawing from this episode.

In a weird way he was pleased that there are people of his race, out there, who will defend the dignity of black people so vehemently, who will be so highly sensitive to stereotyping, that without any hesitation, they will be quick and ready to thoroughly fight these stereotypes, as if they themselves, belonged fully in the black race and experience, or had an identity crisis.

Like the old man just did. The young salesman lifted his head when he heard footsteps of some-one coming in. The new customer had overheard some of Patrick's fury. Realizing he'd come in at a bad time, he had thought it prudent to walk out, linger outside the store for a while, give the salesman some time to collect himself, so that he'd be slightly recuperated to receive and serve the next customer.

———————

Little did Patrick know, however, that a young black university Professor was also pursuing Thokozani, his T Girl! He'd been drawn to her because of the intelligent and tough questions she always had for him, even remaining after class to further pursue her point with the Professor.

There had been of course the policy that bothered him. Love relationships between students and lecturers were not encouraged! After agonizing about this for months, he finally took the decision to go ahead anyway, hoping that by the time the news spread, Thokozani would have graduated.

"Mom, I think your prayers have been answered," he had broached the subject one Sunday, while dining with his mother, Grace, at her favourite restaurant.

"What do you mean, son?"

He only responded by moving his head from side to side, the playfulness and light-heartedness struggling to overshadow his self-consciousness. His face beamed as he anticipated his mother figuring it all out.

Grace looked at her son, lovingly, proudly. She was observing how youthful he looked. She realized she was growing to love his dreadlocks; that they could look neat and acceptable on those whose profession is engaging in serious academic discourse. In the silence that ensued, she admitted reluctantly that perhaps she'd been too "old school" about acceptable dress codes for academics, in these modern times.

She remembered how her son would simply leave the room politely, whenever she started the argument, that no self-respecting academic wears dreadlocks. She admired her son's gift of a clear skin. Even as a teenager he had never had the usual problem of acne. She observed, as he sat across the table, waiting for her to speak, that his skin was actually glowing, maybe because of her prayers he said had been answered.

As he flashed his teeth, Grace was thankful again, that by the time her boy started university studies, he had finally embraced his typical Vezi teeth. How her husband used to tease the boy, in an effort to ease his self-consciousness about the gap right in the centre of the bottom set. "Like father, like son," he'd say. "Themba, this is *our* unique gift in this Vezi house. I hope you'll grow to proudly embrace it!"

How the gap reminded her now, of her late husband, Meshack. Every year, on the day he mysteriously disappeared, just after Mandela's release from prison, she has a huge bunch of flowers delivered home. It is her ritual, to put the large vase of flowers in their bedroom. There is no grave to take them to. Meshack's body still has to be found, brought home and buried.

In his dress shirt and jeans Themba would pass for an ordinary young man. But besides his toned well-defined body, there was something about him, the same kind of quiet, wise, dignified persona that most academics carry. Just like father, like son, his mom could say, as Themba had outdone himself and landed the title of Associate Professor, by age 40, in the dog eat dog arena of universities.

That last colonial outpost in South Africa and elsewhere. As his father used to lecture Themba, "I tell you, son, this is the best kept secret about hatred and vengeance and scheming and back stabbing." It was a father's effort to strengthen and protect his son's mind and spirit from crumbling and breaking, so that he wouldn't find himself finally admitting defeat, giving up and hanging up his books and God-given intellect, as a university teacher.

"Well, let me not scare you now, son. We are in different disciplines of course. I'm in Mathematics, and promotion there is ruthlessly slow, if not well-nigh impossible for us. The Verwoerd mentality still holds sway, unfortunately. Your mother knows what I had to go through. But nothing beats determination. Here I am, Meshack Vezi, a full Professor of Mathematics!"

"And here you are, indeed, dad," Themba would respond proudly.

"But good luck, my boy. Hold your head up high, and make us, the indomitable Vezis, proud. Very proud!"

In a pensive mood and with frowns on her forehead, Themba had noticed how his mom wore an almost absentminded look on her countenance. Still without another word from her, as if a 'by the way' had flashed in her mind, she had managed to pack a nice neat morsel of food onto her fork. She was slowly guiding it into her mouth with a more steady hand this time. The concentration she had to summon to achieve this simple task, was very difficult and painful for her son to watch. And whoever else was close by. As usual, the son had taken time before the meal to push his mom's chair in. Then he'd lovingly tucked the white starched napkin neatly around her neck.

To ease the awkwardness of the moment, Themba always found something nice to compliment his mother about, when he had finished these preliminaries. On this occasion, he put his soft hand on her forehead. He gently pulled her head backwards. He planted a light kiss on her good cheek, and told her, "You are taking very good care of yourself mom. What shampoo do you use? Your hair smells divine." She simply smiled with gratitude in response, as if apprehensive about the difficult task of eating that still lay ahead.

On days the weather of her spirit was overcast, Grace concluded she had brought all of this difficulty upon herself.

When the main meal was served, Themba had cut the piece of chicken on his mom's plate into manageable bite sizes. He'd patiently separated the meat from the bones.

Themba always took his mother to fancy restaurants. Grace enjoyed and appreciated this. But she had long observed that Themba wasn't getting used to her condition, although it had been some years now since her near death experience. This bothered her.

As a result, Grace dreaded these outings with her son, more and more. They gave him ample time to see up close, the life of struggle she was living now, especially because her condition was slowly getting worse. She definitely didn't like this.

They had both eaten in silence, right through dessert. Before the waiter came by to offer them coffee or tea, Mrs. Vezi revisited the guesswork issue. She was hoping it would be the highlight of the evening. "All my life, I've prayed for so many things, Themba. Now that you are an adult, what else could I ask God for, my son? Except of course you know what." Themba nodded in approval, to show mom she was on the right track. A moment's silence passed, her son unwilling to give her another clue.

"No! Themba! Do you mean ...? Don't get me excited for nothing!" Saliva gathered in her mouth. Some dripped onto her napkin. For a second, the son was sidetracked by his mother's distorted smile. He usually managed to visualize her former stroke-free body and face. But the excitement seemed to highlight the illness. She wiped her mouth slowly, a bit self-consciously. Grace's eyes seemed to pierce her son's eyeballs.

So desperate was she for confirmation of what she assumed was the good news. A menacing concoction of disbelief and relief hovered in the air like confused clouds, unsure whether to bring rain or shine. Grace prayed for clear skies. Themba shrugged his shoulders playfully. Then his face lit up as he laughed out loud, pride and joy spread to all the cells of his body.

"That's right, mom!" He nodded his head proudly. "That's right, mom!"

"When did this happen, Themba? And who is the lucky lady?" Grace was still continuing to test the waters, with these questions.

Themba took a deep breath and cleared his throat as if about to announce the arrival of someone in the Nobel

Laureate league, "Thokozani, mom." Proudly, he nodded his head. Then he said her name slowly, "Thokozani, Sosibo."

"Oh! My good Lord! Congratulations, my boy. Finally!" Themba's mother banged the table lightly with her good hand. "Damn! Guess whose mother is jumping with joy right now?"

Themba looked at the ceiling, to hide how emotional and tearful his mother's response made him. By the time he looked at her again, he had managed to send back the slow stream of tears, back to its source. His mother's joy surprised him. He wondered why this piece of news seems to mean so much to parents!

"I'm so elated, Themba, I feel like standing up and waltzing with you around this table. Where's the waiter? Ask him to remove the chairs in preparation for an unforgettable ballroom dance show." Her speech was becoming slower and more slurred now. Excitement fatigued her. Absentmindedly, she began to play with the corners of the tablecloth, folding and releasing, folding and releasing, while Themba looked on.

"Is she pretty? Not that it matters. I must not ask senseless questions now, out of excitement. I'm just curious to see her, you know. My future daughter! Any photo on you?"

"No photo, mom. Just yet. It's all still new."

"Oh, now you tell me!" Grace looked dejected.

"Mom, just wait, please. Let me finish explaining." He braced himself, anxious not to deflate his mother's spirits that he had observed were building at the rate of a big sea wave. He wanted to leave her spirits and hopes riding the crest of this high excitement wave, while he continued to do the work with his Thokozani.

"I'm actually jumping the gun a bit, dear mother. She has not given me a definite 'yes' yet. But, the prospects look good. Quite good, I must say. I feel her in my bones. She's the one for me, mom."

"She's yours, son," Themba's mother responded with the assuring voice only a loving parent can convincingly summon and master. "I've not seen you so sure about a woman before. It will all work out as you plan."

"There's just one snag, mom."

"What now?"

"She's in my class. And university policy won't let lecturers have love relationships with their students."

"Come on now! Are you really sweating small stuff like that, Professor Vezi? There will be a way around that wimp of a stumbling block. I'm confident you'll find a way out. Don't give up easily, son. Where there's love," she wiped her watery mouth again, "excuse me, there's a way. Always, son."

Themba was sitting now with his hand just beneath his chin. He looked a bit worried. His mother noticed this and reassured him again, "Just be strong-willed. Nothing is really impossible in this world. She sounds like a smart woman. In our days, not many women took Political Science. So there you go. Good choice, my boy."

As long as they were discreet, all would be well. Thokozani was a level-headed smart woman. She'd not want to jeopardize things for both of them. And that's how Themba had put the matter to rest. He also had the backing and assurance from his mom, who, at her ripe age, was beginning to feel like an ancestor for her only son.

Themba wished senior Professor Vezi, his father, was around, to give him another crutch to lean on, as he navigated his way through this policy-tricky hurdle, into Thokozani's heart. Man to man. Thokozani's heart was a destination Themba could not wait to reach. "Where there's a will, there's a way," became Themba's pillar of strength.

As he took his mother home, after the dinner outing, Themba assured her once more, "Massive oceans of everlasting love are all I have for my girl, Thokozani. God knows, mom!"

"I know, my boy."

———————

Thokozani decided to seek advice from Sizakele, her elder sister. She always trusted her big sister's wise counsel. Earlier on, Thokozani had sent Sizakele a texted message. It was to set the scene for the phone call that would follow. "Love troubles again. We need to talk. I'll call you soon."

"I'm happy you finally called, Thokozani. I've been waiting anxiously. Believe me, I'm so happy I'm out of the dating game. And thank goodness, I made the right choice. The Chief and I are still very happy. God knows, I wish the same for you. So what's the matter this time, Thokozani? I thought you were settling nicely into a stable relationship with yours truly."

"Well, I'm a bit confused, big sister. Of course, on the one hand there is, as you rightly say 'yours truly'. An older mature guy who makes me happy. On the other hand, there's my young dreadlocked Professor, who is really my type. You know me and my Africanism. We look good together. And I love his depth of knowledge about issues. I tell you, he's a genius. I don't know what to do!"

"How come you've never told me the African guy has graduated from innocent Prof to potential boyfriend and lover? And to crown it all, that he is actually pursuing you, Thokozani? University students and crushes! The same old teacher's pet syndrome of our mother's late teenage years, when Doris Day sang *Teacher's Pet, I want to be a teacher's pet*. How exactly do you mean? What has the Professor said to you? Couldn't it be just your imagination?"

"We've only met for coffee outside campus a few times," Thokozani explained, hardly warming up to Siza's attempt to make light of her dilemma. "You should see him at lectures, talking about Antonio Gramsci and the organic intellectuals, finding brilliant ways to weave in our great African writers into it all – Ayi Kwei Armah, Chinua Achebe, Ngugi wa Thiong'o, Es'kia Mphahlele, you name them."

"I may be wrong, little sister, child of my mother, but I've not heard you say anything about his qualities. You seem infatuated with the African intellectual and not with the man himself! Very much like student ways of seeing. And what's his name? I thought Patrick was the all for you."

"Themba. Themba Vezi, a Zulu from a Township in KwaZulu Natal."

"I see. Well, we are Zulus too."

"I don't know, Siza. But it is definitely not infatuation. This I do know for sure. We connect at a much deeper level. And trust me, Siza, I have taken my time, watched developments with Themba ...."

"Yes indeed, way to go! And what's stopping you now, girl?"

"My last phone conversation with Patrick." Siza heard heavy breathing on the other end of the line.

"What now, Thokozani? Is your relationship beginning to be a lukewarm cup of tea?"

"Far from it, Siza. It's still a very hot cup of tea served in a tin cup for that matter, with every sip burning the lips and scalding the tongue and gullet." Thokozani then laughed half-heartedly.

"Oh! That's good. That's what I thought, Thokozani. So, where or what is the problem then? See? I can't even ask straight-forward questions any more. You are confusing me. But continue. I'm listening."

"I have a hunch Patrick wants to move our relationship to the next level. I hope I'm wrong, so I can buy time to think carefully now. I'm no longer that young, and can't irresponsibly blow any of these relationships."

"I agree with you there. Playing with some-one's feelings, raising their hopes and expectations only to eventually dash them into pieces, is unfair and cruel. And it's bound to cost you something, take a toll on you as well. It's the law of the universe - to tread carefully on other people's souls. I've not met Themba.

You'll remember that mom, dad and I initially had a problem with Patrick. From a different racial group, and many years your senior. But over time, he's proved to be a wonderful human being. You know how we finally completely accepted him as a family. Now, here comes Themba! This possible brother-in-law of mine, a new boyfriend who is confusing my sister? What's making you confused now? What's wonderful about Professor Vezi, if I may ask? Again!"

"Associate Professor Themba Vezi, to be sure." Siza noticed subdued excitement in Thokozani's response, as if she couldn't wait to be asked to sing her Professor's praises. So like a teenager, Siza thought to herself. "Well, he's a cool homeboy, you know. And so into Steve Biko's Black Consciousness philosophy, you know. And, he's a handsome dreadlocked well-educated dude and scholar."

"Mm, that sounds yummy, Thokozani," Siza remarked rather teasingly. "I see some potential there. Now I am beginning to feel your dilemma, and don't envy you. How do you find good ones that haven't been taken yet?"

Thokozani released a rather reluctant laugh. There was no energy in her voice. Was the dilemma taking such a toll on her? "But honestly, Thokozani, what is it that you want out of a marriage partner - say any of the two men want to lead you to the altar? Tell me, what are you looking for in a man, a marriage partner? Let's look at this dilemma more carefully and closely now, dearest." Sizakele understood that her question was bound to push her younger sister into a tight corner.

"I've been looking for men like these two fellows, Siza. As people usually warn: 'Be careful what you ask for!' Both have attributes I adore in a man, in a quality love relationship. Themba is fairly new in my life, in a sense, but he's my Professor, a true intellectual, and so adorable! He's the right age, although age for me is really just a number. You'd love him in class."

"As you know I can't make the decision for you, Thokozani. But I sympathize with the dilemma you are in, sisi [sister]. Your luck in attracting the right men should not end up being a headache for you, an albatross around the neck. Remember, you don't have much time."

"Please don't make me too anxious now, Siza."

"You know it's the truth, Thokozani. Time is of the essence here. Why didn't you share this dilemma with me a little earlier? Did you leave it all to time to make things clearer for you? You'll be with Patrick soon. Great God, I don't want to be there when you break the sad news to either man. Good luck, girl!"

"Oh, how I wish I didn't have to choose?"

"Would they want to share you between the two of them? Please. It's a tough decision to make, I'm sure. Mistakes in marriage are very costly. You make the wrong turn, you've had it. Your life has a dent no panel beater can smooth out completely."

It was quiet on the other side. "Hello, are you still there, Thokozani?"

"Yes, I'm still here." Thokozani responded in a shaky voice. "Is your voice breaking now, big girl? Don't do this to yourself now. Be strong. God will guide you. The universe will not lead you astray. Okay? Go and do your life-changing homework now. You know the usual process, when people need to make a smart decision. When it's done to your satisfaction, truthfully done, following all the steps, you'll know. You are a university student, after all. The exercise may be life-altering for you. Do appreciate the seriousness of the assignment."

"Okay, I hear you, Siza."

"I love you, Thokozani. Don't you ever forget that." Sizakele waited for a response, but Thokozani had hung up. Siza was apprehensive since the last call from her younger sister. She truly and deeply felt Thokozani's painful dilemma. A part of her was sorry for seeming to discourage her younger sister from entertaining the love relationship with the Africanist Professor Vezi. Who knows what's good or bad for another person, especially in matters of love? Siza felt she was not really qualified to rule in a sensitive matter such as this, except she was

Thokozani's elder sister, and could only give an opinion; one her younger sister valued highly, however. Siza understood that Thokozani would be the final decision-maker, difficult as that might be. Sizakele had to wait for delivery of the assignment. This is all she could do now.

Given the conscientious student that she was, who liked to do assignments on time, Thokozani went to her usual quiet corner in the main library. She drew a long line in the centre of her yellow A4 page. It was a long arduous task of comparing and contrasting, comparing and contrasting.

Those within hearing distance suspected the student in the next booth was crying. She was sniffing for a long time and blowing her nose. Yes, it sounded like a she. But, she didn't leave her seat. Not even once! Some strange determination and work ethic there.

When the library closed, Thokozani called her sister. She still had plenty of time to take a walk to her residence. She usually took a brisk walk, especially on days when she could not go to the gym, because of the heavy load of classes, on top of her 3 hours' library job.

"Here's the assignment, delivered telephonically, if that's acceptable to you, Professor Sister Siza on Love Dilemmas 101." Thokozani heard a chuckle from her sister and continued, "Are you ready, Siza?"

"Fire on, Thokozani."

"Okay. I've known Patrick for much longer. I know he loves me dearly. He might have baggage. But none that would shipwreck my emotions. Race is still an issue in South Africa. But we are used to stares by now. We also know how to handle or brush off nasty remarks."

"And Themba?" Siza asked.

A sigh was the only response. "Thank goodness I'm not seeing Siza face to face. I'm an emotional mess," Thokozani thought.

"Thokozani, don't lie to yourself, child. Are you sure you've come to a decision, and with a clear unclouded mind? Can you live the rest of your life with this decision?"

"Must I really answer that question now, Siza? Right now?" Siza acutely felt her sister's pain. But she couldn't help her.

"Thokozani, we leave it all to the gods and our ancestors, honestly. What else can we do or say now? I wish grandmother was still here. You know how she'd have sorted this thing out quickly and wisely."

"I know. That woman was a born problem solver," Thokozani responded. Siza continued, "How I wish this was not a difficult decision to make. That the young Professor Vezi is clearly a new comer in your life."

Sizakele was beginning to be weighed down by her sister's dilemma. As a woman she clearly understood how these two equally wonderful men could keep a woman mind's spinning with indecision. But Sizakele knew she had to be strong and shepherd her sister as far as she could on her tricky road. Indeed, the rest of the journey was just for Thokozani. She had to trudge on, alone. Just herself, in the close company of her heart, mind and soul.

Having to choose in a matter as life-changing as this, wasn't easy. Both sisters knew that matters of choice in love relationship were huge determinants of one's future, in fact, the rest of one's life. Who wouldn't love to get it right the first time? Could Thokozani summon a distilled mind in the process of choosing?

Sizakele continued, "Honestly, Thokozani, how I wish Themba is such an unknown quantity for you, that it won't be too difficult for your heart to release him to another woman, the universe has reserved for him. How I wish there isn't much to draw from."

"Another woman? That hurts you know. I don't know why, but it makes my heart almost sore to the touch. I guess I have to let him go. Release him to another lucky woman. This is not easy, Siza. Oh! My God. What am I going to do?" Siza was quiet. That quiet moment seemed to be helpful for Thokozani. She took a deep breath.

Then her cell phone rang. It was Patrick. But she ignored the call. A texted message soon followed:

*You have no idea how blessed I am, to have you in my life. I can't wait for our appointment this the week-end, T Girl, my goddess! Love, P.*

Thokozani took a deeper breath. She noticed that her heart missed a beat as she read the message.

"Are you still there, Siza? Patrick has just sent me a loving texted message. It's fine, my sister. It's alright now. I've collected myself."

"Are you sure, Thokozani?"

"It wasn't easy, Siza," Thokozani responded, surprised she was now suddenly using the past tense. "I don't want to lie to you."

"Everything notwithstanding, all things considered, shall we say the best man has won?" Siza asked, forcing lightheartedness in her voice. She hoped her sister would catch the bug.

"Mr. Fitzgerald has won! Yes! The man with the long surname!" Thokozani tried to fake a playful voice. Her resignation to her fate wasn't difficult to detect, however. Just a few tiny scratches on the surface of her emotions would still reveal the whole nine yards of her dilemma.

"And the one with the short surname? Is it a question of length now, Thokozani? Fitzgerald against Vezi?" Siza tried to downplay her sister's pain. She was forcing the spring in the midst of a horrid winter.

"Let's not go back there, please, Siza."

It was obvious that Thokozani's wound of indecision was still very red and raw. Expectedly so. Siza hoped time and reason would provide the smart balm to engender the necessary healing, and finally, closure. Siza felt it was time to end this conversation, yo-yo-ing in and out of this Themba Vezi. "It's been a long road. The dating game is quite tiresome, Thokozani. But it's probably the only way to learn and experience what love is supposed to be. As you know, I've made my mistakes, and learnt from them."

"I know, Siza. We've both escaped life-threatening situations as young women. Thank goodness none of the guys you've been intimate with threw any tantrum about using a condom. Your choices, overall, weren't too bad."

"As for you, Thokozani! Do you still remember the prophylaxis you took that saved your life?"

"Don't talk about those experiences. HIV/AIDS was knocking at the door. Death awaited me. But as they say, we should 'let bygones be bygones' Siza."

"I sincerely hope you'll find a way to disengage from the Professor, without hurting him. From what you've shared with me, it sounds like he's a cool brother. Don't make him resort to singing songs of lament, the blues of disappointment in love."

"Siza, that makes me sad. I don't know why. But it hurts a lot."

There was a moment's silence, with Siza searching for the right words to fill the awkward pain-ridden moment, as Thokozani still clearly struggled with the complex emotions she was also failing rather dismally to hide. The clarity Assignment 101 was to have yielded, seemed to be defecting.

"What can I do, really? Life can be so difficult if not downright unfair at times. I'll maintain our robust debates in and out of class with my great thinker and scholar. That's essential to my academic development and growth into becoming a sharp intellectual. I must make sure I still have my life as a student on my way to becoming a scholar, outside of Patrick and his sober and mature love for me." Siza noticed how her sister seemed to be resigned to her fate. That hurt. Deeply.

———————

Thokozani was lazily watching Television when a call came through on her cell phone that same evening. She did not recognize the number of the caller.

"Hello Thokozani. Is this a good time to call?" She could not mistake the voice she was now so familiar with. His mother's dejected "Now you tell me," was still ringing rather painfully in his ears.

"Good Lord, what a surprise!"

"Pleasant or not? Please tell me the truth now, Thokozani."

"Themba, why must I answer that kind of question?"

"Well, that's how students fail examinations! By not answering the question."

"If you push me to a corner like that, I will answer the question. Of course, it is a pleasant surprise. Have I told

you that you are one of my best Professors this year?"
Thokozani noticed excitement loosening up her tongue.

"Honestly? I'm flattered and elated to hear that from
one of my best students," Themba responded. The
excitement he picked up in Thokozani's voice turned up
the volume of his own excitement.

"I have been thinking that when I get the opportunity,
I will travel to Italy, to learn all I can about the life history
of Antonio Gramsci, the prison where he was held, and a
lot more." Thokozani babbled away to calm down and
control her excitement.

"That's quite interesting, Thokozani. Incidentally I do
travel to Europe from time to time. Maybe we can go
together next time. I'll take care of all the costs, including
air ticket, accommodation, travel costs at our
destination, and meals. You are my best student, after
all. We can even cover more European countries and
cities when we are tired of being in Italy, eating pizza and
pasta. Would you be happy to undertake such a trip with
me, seeing you are so in love with the Italian scholar? I
must say I'm fascinated with him myself. Maybe you have
picked this up during my lectures."

"In love with Gramsci?" Thokozani mused to herself.
She caught her strong feelings for Themba beginning to
run amuck. Her heart and mind were misbehaving. What
would she do with these strong feelings for Themba? How
would she control this pack of undomesticated mountain
dogs, running helter-skelter?

She knew she needed to chase these naughty feelings
with a stick, round them up, and lock them up! Maybe
even wag a threatening finger at these unruly wild dogs.
Command them to "stay!" And hope they'd obey, tame
their tails, tuck them in and "sit." But destroy them? No!

Thokozani didn't even dream of that possibility. So completely out of the question it was.

Themba heard a knock on Thokozani's door and people coming in. It's just what Thokozani needed, to save her from herself – the awkwardness she felt she couldn't handle level-headedly. Themba felt it logical to cut the conversation short, even though Thokozani still had to respond to his travel proposition. Maybe over lunch next time, he told himself. Definitely before the next dinner appointment with his mother, Grace.

"It sounds like you have company now, Thokozani. Let me say my goodbye then. We should go out more often. I would love us to get to know more about each other. And the Italy trip is on, my dear." He couldn't tell if that was a statement or a question. Those are nerves for you, Themba mused to himself.

Thokozani felt her legs crumbling into half-set jelly. Her mind seemed paralyzed. She was flustered. Her head was in a fast merry-go-round. She had to collect herself before talking to this man who was such trouble for her mind, heart and soul.

"That will be fine, Themba. Goodbye then. These are members of my discussion group."

"You know, Thokozani," Themba continued, his voice becoming deeper and serious, "I have been intending to call you for quite some time. Firstly, it took me some time to get your cell number from administration offices. Then, secondly, I don't know what else stalled the process of punching your cell number and talking to you. A simple process, like I've just done. Nerves, I suppose. Anyway, talk to you soon. Have a good evening now. And enjoy the discussion with the group."

Themba stared at his cell phone as if it harboured some mystery. Why had it taken him so long? This was the question he couldn't answer. But how exceedingly glad he finally made this important call! Yet he was also anxious about Thokozani's response to his invitation for them to travel together to Italy. Did she really have to think about this? Indeed, this would be the unforgettable beginning of many things Themba hoped they would do together.

The climax of it all would be sharing a bed, their souls finally and blissfully intertwined in a perfect lifelong permanent embrace. Indeed, Themba had picked up the excitement in the woman's voice. This had encouraged him to make a few confessions. He'd sensed they'd do no harm.

Themba even compared his confessions to a seed that fell on fertile ground. As he replayed his exchange with Thokozani, Themba's fervent wish was that the seed would germinate and grow into something definitely rich and sweet. How this would be just wonderful for him and his African princess! And, for Grace.

"No, the seed of my confessions didn't fall on barren soil." Professor Vezi caught himself uttering this as statement of fact, as he wrapped himself in a towel after taking a long shower later that night. He smiled as he realized he'd just invoked a parable he'd heard so many times, but never thought it could fit so perfectly in the context of love relationships.

That she did not comment on his "my dear" egged him on and gave him hope. Themba was a full-grown man. He understood how to tip-toe around a woman's feelings, while also, at the right pace and with perfect timing, becoming bolder to gradually test even deeper waters, as she let him.

Themba took a stroll to his window and gulped in the fresh air. It was a pitch black sky. The stars twinkled. He winked back. "One late night we'll be admiring the stars together. Just me and my Thokozani!"

He went to bed that night a very relieved man. A soft blanket of hope embraced and cuddled him lovingly. Here was his opportunity to take the first mile that would, God willing, lead to that final moment when the priest asked him to "kiss the bride" with everybody ecstatic for the lucky couple. They'd be walking down the aisle, and straight into the limousine waiting to take them to the airport and to their honey moon. Maybe in Sicily.

"So, class mate has a boyfriend. A Themba from somewhere. Bad timing on our part, to cut your conversation short. I have a splitting headache. Can I make myself a cup of herbal tea, Thokozani?"

The leader of the study group did not expect further explanation from Thokozani, about Themba, the caller. She knew how secretive Thokozani was about her personal life. The gossipmonger went ahead and busied herself in the small kitchen area, while the rest of the group made themselves comfortable on the few chairs, sofas, cushions and boxes, in the room.

"I do have a variety of herbal teas. I did some groceries last Saturday. So, help yourself," Thokozani responded with this generous offer to the fellow student, some on campus accused of being loudly gay.

"Well, I thought as much. Sister never shares ... Except tea of course. Thanks for this interesting variety of herbal teas. That shop is way out of town, though. How did you get there? By taxi?"

Thokozani nodded her head. She did not want to disclose that Patrick had taken her there. She had learnt that with woman friends, especially students, one has to keep personal business to oneself. After one friend tried to snatch her first boyfriend, Thokozani would not share much, besides teabags, pens and pencils.

———————

At the appointed time Thokozani was waiting at the usual corner for Patrick to pick her up. In about five minutes the gentleman pulled up. He got out to open the door for his lady. And of course he shut it gently, when she was settled comfortably on the passenger seat. The usual greetings were exchanged. Thokozani gave her man a quick hug before Patrick started the engine.

It was an awkward hug, she noticed. Her arms seemed to temporarily forget the contours of the body she was so familiar with now. The two were off to a day of shopping, followed by tea or lunch and maybe a movie, depending when they'd finish their errands. Then it would be the long anticipated drive home and to talking about the issue that was uppermost in both their minds for a while.

Margaret had prepared all there was to prepare the previous day. Patrick had given James a week-end off. He wanted just the two of them in the house for the two days. Two days that would determine his future life with T Girl. As usual, Patrick fixed some drinks as soon as they arrived home. They always had to rest after running around in town.

Patrick knew, however, that T Girl expected him to delay no further the matter to be discussed. She had been rather quiet during the day, he'd observed. The usual bubbly T Girl wasn't quite there. He knew she was anxious, and that the anxiety was killing her. He felt sorry for her. But it would not be long now for the moment of truth to usher itself in, and determine the rest of their lives henceforth. Patrick was anxious but hopeful.

The group discussion had gone to about 12 midnight. Thokozani had simply flopped into bed after the last round of herbal teas had been drunk and everybody left. There had not been time for her to call her sister, Siza, again, to tell her about the latest development with her Professor!

Thokozani knew Siza would not be impressed with her indecision, when that very afternoon they had put paid to the dilemma Thokozani seemed to face for a little while, until Siza helped her sort it out. Thokozani cursed herself for waking up a bit too late to squeeze in a chat with her sister, before Patrick picked her up.

"Maybe just as well. Siza would be confused now, wondering what I want in life," Thokozani had winced and mumbled to herself as she picked up her week-end bag and began the short walk to the bus stop to wait for Patrick.

So, with a heavy heart, the dilemma having resurfaced when Themba called, and becoming more and more burdensome as a result, Thokozani had a lot on her mind. The only relief was that the time had arrived for Patrick to broach the subject that had caused her some anxiety for a few days now. However, from what she'd observed since Patrick picked her up that morning, Thokozani had almost come to the conclusion that the subject would have nothing to do with a marriage proposal.

Thokozani knew her man fairly well by then. If he wanted to prepare her for a good night together he'd do so, way ahead of time. He'd be romantic in all manner of ways he knew - fixing exotic drinks, playing carefully chosen music with lyrics and voices to melt one in a hot love oven, or relax muscles in a bubbling Jacuzzi.

His schooled fingers would 'accidentally' lightly brush the sensitive parts of her body, playfully and lightly squeezing her ample posterior, passionately kissing her eyes and ears. These antics would increase in frequency and intensity as the time drew close to bedtime, the exotic drinks making him or both of them bolder. And his Thokozani knew how to play along.

But none of that on this day! Not even a playful slap on her knee as Patrick drove them from this to that place, in their errands spree. So, when Patrick finally broached the subject for discussion, Thokozani was convinced, by the look of things, it would be about something else. Maybe a holiday trip to Europe. Italy, perhaps. Thokozani teased herself with thoughts about Themba. Indeed, these were thoughts she simultaneously did and didn't want to shelve for later, or forever.

She was a bit baffled with the lukewarm rather very un-Patrick behaviour, for he had assured her the matter to be discussed would be good for both of them. Why did the mood in the house so loudly speak a different language, however? In his panic, Patrick had lost his usual self. Unawares, he had lost his vim and verve. The steam train was low on coal, and the fire wasn't quite enthused. The driver tried to stoke it, hoping to generate some speed on the train, but the pace remained stubbornly slow.

"A negative response from T Girl will kill me. But old boy this is the day. There's no other. No time like the present. God, please be with me. Let my timing be just right." Patrick's jaws would tighten each time panic gained the upper hand. Melancholy threatened to ruin his big moment. But the karate chop was ready to strike, if there was need.

Patrick finally summoned up enough courage to start the conversation. He hoped more courage would carry him to the conclusion of this mighty project. He prayed for momentum. He had been monitoring T Girl's every word, mood and action for a while. Finally, courage ushered in the crucial moment. It gave him a steady voice. Much to his gratitude.

"T Girl, I have not had you talk about family in a long while. How's mom? How's dad? How's Sizakele?"

"They are all fine, thanks. I actually spoke to Siza just yesterday about something that was bothering me."

Patrick frowned to learn his T girl had something bothering her. "Oh what was that about? You know you can always talk to me when you have a problem. I thought we've long agreed on that."

Patrick noticed T Girl's face and demeanor change. He knew something was wrong somewhere. So, before he could carry on laying the appropriate groundwork for his final proposal, which he'd planned to include asking about the payment of *lobolo* in the Sosibo clan, he felt he had to clear the bad energy, take care of whatever was troubling Thokozani.

He regretted in some way that asking about her family seemed to sour her already insipid mood. That had not been his intention at all. However, he'd long observed she wasn't quite herself. She was not quite present. And strange enough, asking about family seemed to make her mood worse. There was foulness in the air Patrick definitely did not need, and did not like. The stink! Oh, the stink! It was polluting the atmosphere. It seemed

304

Patrick could even smell it as he opened the front door to let in cool afternoon air.

"It's about my grandmother. We were very close. I was telling Siza I miss her a lot."

"Oh! But your grandmother has been gone for quite a while, T Girl. Hey, what am I saying now? Such moments do pounce on one, unawares sometimes. I'm sorry, my dear. Is this why you've seemed to lose your usual exuberance? Since this morning, actually."

Patrick did not want to tell T Girl it's natural to miss beloved ones, taken away from us, as he also missed his wife, Rachel, from time to time. Contemplatively he asked, "So, as Zulus, what ritual do you have to perform in such circumstances? Do you have to slaughter a goat or cow?"

"Patrick, you think we slaughter at the drop of a hat. A child fell and bruised her knee. We slaughter! A family member had to extract a tooth. We slaughter! Don't be silly now. Don't you miss your late wife sometimes?"

"Well, I don't want to drag late Rachel into our lives. This is a new page for me, as you know," Patrick responded in a subdued voice. There was a trace of exasperation in its timber.

"I do expect you to think about her sometimes. That's normal. Nothing amiss there. It's the same thing with me. Well, humanity at large, I'd say. But I take exception ..."

"Calm down, Thokozani, please. You know I did not mean it like that. You should know me better by now. Coming to think of it, you seem very touchy today. Is there something else the matter? I thought you wanted to come spend some time with me this week-end. Not so, my love?" Her eyes seemed to reflect a fiercely burning furnace; red hot anger that ebbed and flowed through her entire body. She literally saw red.

The glare from the afternoon sun did not help the situation, as tempers began to flare. His internal. And hers, both internal and external. Patrick wanted to put his hand on Thokozani's brow, and cool her down. But she was a blazing fire! He put his hand on the side of her waistline, instead.

And now that he'd instinctively come closer to her, he felt like doing more with his hand. He wanted to lower it to her posterior. But he knew the time wasn't quite right. Like a man wary of making unwanted advances, lest he be charged for encroaching into a woman's private space, Patrick gingerly positioned himself behind Thokozani. Slowly and hesitatingly he finally managed to wrap his arms around her pleasantly toned waist.

For a little while he rested his chin on her well-shaped head, draped in her short virgin hair. He gently kissed her hair in an effort to appease here. Then he turned her slowly to face him, his hands still hugging her waist, "Look at me now, Thokozani? What's wrong?" His eyes were doing a troubled dance all over her, searching for clues and answers.

Thokozani avoided the eyeball to eyeball talk that Patrick so desperately sought, lest her eyes gave her away, and opened the lid to the depth of what was really ailing her. She politely freed herself from Patrick's embrace, excused herself and went to the bathroom.

He heard her blow her nose for quite a while. Long drawn blowing. Like she had a bad bout of flu. He wasn't sure whether to open the door and check on her or not. She seemed so touchy, he didn't know what little thing would set her off again – to cry, snap at him. So, Patrick remained seated on the couch. He was confused, a bit frustrated and irritated.

"Things aren't going well at all." He muttered to himself with clenched teeth, as he mechanically paged through the latest copy of *Time* magazine on the oak coffee table. T Girl returned from the bathroom, eventually. The redness in her eyes had gotten worse. She moved slowly, feet shuffling, and sat on the upright antique chair in one corner of the very spacious lounge.

Patrick noticed the distance she was keeping between them. He took one long askance gaze at his lady, and pretending he did not notice she had been crying, he got her a glass of cold water from the kitchen.

She gulped it down without even looking at him. She got her cellphone from her bag, and scrolled down the numbers. She was concerned she might erase Themba's number by mistake.

On realizing that Thokozani did not seem to recover from the 'grandmother issue', Patrick offered a solution. "Do you want to talk to Sizakele again, my love? Go to my study. I hope she'll help you out. I'll be setting the table and preparing dinner so long."

Thokozani acknowledged Patrick's suggestion only with a nod. She walked slowly to the study, head bent all the time. Instead of calling her sister, she collapsed into the swiveling leather chair and cried softly. Patrick mumbled to himself as he went to the kitchen, "This is one of the times when women are most difficult."

Thokozani whispered, "*Sisi*, what am I going to do about Themba? God, what am I supposed to do about Themba, after what happened last night?" For a period that seemed like an hour, the questions kept coming.

They were punctuated by heavy sobs. After a while, the questions and sobs began to subside.

Thokozani rested her pain swollen head on the desk and cried softly. From time to time she'd blow her nose and gaze at the large pictures which adorned the desk and bookshelves. Enlarged photographs of herself alone. Patrick alone. The two of them together. She knew the occasions and precise times when all of these pictures had been taken.

After a while Thokozani walked out into the kitchen to get more water to wash down the pain. But she walked into Patrick's well-built chest instead. He knew he had to stop this foul-smelling spell that was engulfing his T Girl. The flames were lapping at her. They were threatening to kill her body and soul, as well as his plans for that special afternoon and night. He needed to extinguish the unwanted flames fast.

"Ah! Look at you T Girl! Still crying? Why? Are you sure this is all about missing your grandmother? Anything else the matter, darling?" Patrick asked again as he took a few paces away to study his T girl's face. He stroked her cheeks lovingly with his soft hand. He picked her up, lifted her off her feet and squeezed her tight.

As he slowly lowered her body, and her feet landed gently on the floor, he held her two hands, looked deep into her eyes and said, "Thokozani, my love, I'm here for you. I've told you I love you madly. I want to spend the rest of my life making you happy. That's my life's noble and greatest mission, my dear. Do you hear and understand that? I love you, my T Girl. Trust me to love you till the end of time, unto and even beyond death."

Patrick lowered his voice as he attempted to connect with Thokozani at much deeper soul level, "I believe in life after death, Thokozani. Even death will not do us part. Please, believe me. Will you allow me to love you forever? I promise to do nothing less, my love."

Thokozani nodded her head in response to Patrick's unrehearsed speech. He was actually surprised at himself. How did he pull off that kind of speech, at such a difficult time? Patrick's T Girl looked like a little lass, seeking comfort. She cast furtive glances at him. She knew she looked quite a sight. She was a bit embarrassed. The matters troubling her deep in her heart had transported her to a different emotional plane, devastating her.

But surprisingly, Patrick's words seemed to succeed in soothing her. She sighed loudly, and took a long deep breath after Patrick's speech. Then she took Patrick's face into her hands. She looked him straight in the eye, with her still red eyes and whispered, "Patrick, I'm back. I'm here, my love. Okay?" Patrick instantly gave her a long tight hug and whispered in her ear, "Thank you very much, Thokozani. I'm so relieved now."

When they freed each other from that embrace, it was quiet in the kitchen for a while, as they got busy getting dinner ready. To Thokozani's surprise the dining room was transformed into an enticing lovers' nest. Candles on the table. Her favourite red roses at the corner. Lovely music playing softly. It was Barry White, doing what he did best, caressing a woman with love-packed lyrics that no woman could ignore.

"Why did Barry White have to die?" Thokozani was now thinking to herself, the music and the lyrics obviously sinking deep into her heart, effectively seducing her. Gradually, she collected herself. Her mind, body and soul found one another and became an integrated whole.

The ambience in the dining room gave Thokozani a swift lift off. She began to chat. She laughed at Patrick's jokes.

As they enjoyed dinner and talked, she also found her own DVD titled, *The First Time I Saw Him*. It was about Patrick. But it had not been playing for long, when she pushed the pause button. The stop button was next. There were too many interruptions. Their conversation. The clanking of their wine glasses. Barry White in the background, a man that clearly knew what love is, and what love is capable of.

After the main meal Patrick walked slowly to where Thokozani was seated, opposite him. He bowed, took her hand and led her to the make shift dance floor. "Come, my love! Let's dance all the worries away. I have you. You have me. We have each other. Nothing else matters, I assure you." He winked at his T Girl, as they began to flow as one, to the music.

With this romantic ambiance the CD titled, *Phone Call from Africanist Professor* began to fade into the distance. Thokozani continued to hear snippets of it. Antonio Gramsci. Italy. All costs taken care of. Themba Vezi. I don't know what took me so long to call you. Nerves."

Thokozani shut her eyes for a while as she listened to Barry White, with Patrick singing along, his way. He was all smiles. Thokozani felt that somehow, her grandmother had actually spoken to her, helped her granddaughter clarify her thinking. "Come let's have dessert and more wine, my dear," Patrick suggested as he led Thokozani back to her chair, after their long cheek to cheek dance.

By the time they sat for dessert, Thokozani was Patrick's familiar T Girl again! As they finished second and third helpings of ice cream and fruit salad, Patrick felt the right moment had come! He extended his arm across the table, took T Girl's left hand as she was now talking animatedly about members of her study group.

He got hold of her ring finger, looked straight into her eyes and said, "Life has its ups and downs, my T Girl. But thank God they don't last forever. Here we are now, laughing and happy again. Do you remember what I said to you in the kitchen? I meant every word of it. Thokozani Sosibo, I want to spend the rest of my life, even unto death and beyond, making you happy. So T Girl, my love ..."

Patrick was choking with emotion. Tears threatened to create pools in and around his already misty eyes.

Thokozani Sosibo seemed to gasp for air as tears unashamedly rolled down her cheeks, and into her mouth. She was shaking. With the other hand Patrick found the box in his pants' pocket. He put it on the table and managed to open it while still holding T Girl's ring finger. "I've practiced this line for a very long time, Thokozani."

He shook his head a couple of times. "God, knows, for a very long time. And now I finally get to ask the question that has been on my mind and in my heart and soul, ever since I first met you: Will you marry me, my T Girl?"

The special moment rendered the normally eloquent Thokozani, mute. She struggled to find a response, let alone a brilliantly crafted memorable one, to make it into the Guinness Book of Records. She briefly remembered how they used to compose marriage proposal acceptance lines, and even bride speeches with her sister, Siza, when they were teenage girls.

Thokozani was speechless. She simply nodded a very unhesitating, "Yes!" Then the three-letter word came out. "Yes!" It was whispered relief. Tears continued to flow in a quiet stream. Patrick slid the engagement ring. It fit Thokozani's finger as if it was custom made, just for her. Thokozani wanted to say something. But her bottom lip quivered. It trembled quite uncontrollably, and for a long while. Patrick stood up and walked up to Thokozani.

His eyes were soaking wet with gratitude. He kissed away the tears from her eyes. Then he rested his index finger on Thokozani's trembling lower lip. He finally succeeded to quiet it down.

Patrick's lady finally composed herself and then spoke, "I don't know what came over me, Patrick. I least expected this. But what am I saying?"

"It's alright, Thokozani, my T Girl." His eyes pierced hers for quite a while. His heart was beating furiously. He waited a few seconds for it to calm down. Then he continued, "Thank you, Thokozani. God truly knows, our journey to everlasting joy has begun." He found her lips. Hers had long been ready for his.

It was a bewildering moment for both of them. In the dimly lit room, the diamond stones on the engagement ring sparkled like stars on a dark sky. Here was a glorious moment the two love birds would file and store in their sweet memory archives forever. They were ready for a life long journey. Even into and beyond death.

Just as Patrick had wished in his wildest dreams, their marriage was blessed at Saint Mary Magdalena's Cathedral, back home in London on Christmas Eve, one year after the engagement proposal. Patrick's mother was frail and in a wheel chair. But she was there. He was upset that no-one had told him about these developments in his mother's health.

Well, his younger brother, Willie, had also found love. A sad kind of love. Patrick spoke to him once or twice on the streets of London. He soon realized that there was no-one there. He was talking to a shell. Willie had long been hollowed out. He was long gone. Lost to drugs and alcohol.

Patrick privately chided himself for sort of neglecting his mother after he fell in love with Thokozani. With a broad smile on his face, he remembered words from university friends when girlfriends caught him trying to cheat on them, "You are a one woman guy, Patrick. Never try again what you are not good at." One girlfriend had told him as she patted him on the shoulder, "Cheating doesn't even suit you, Patrick. Such an adorable man like you!"

Well, those were different times. His life still lay ahead of him. A blanket of soft rose petals all the way, he'd naively hoped. But after all he'd been through now, he fervently hoped that God had that same blanket of rose petals laid out for the rest of his life with T Girl.

After the wedding Patrick felt he had to be home to take care of his mother. With the Rand becoming weaker by the day, he realized it would serve him well to start something new in England. He found willing business partners among his Company's Board members in South Africa. He also had to be close to Willie, his only brother. Patrick understood that he could not completely give up on him. By God's Grace, Willie could still save himself.

———

"How do you start a political party, and run a government as a follower of Antonio Gramsci? You are a hegemony as government! The people will accommodate and resist some of your well-meant offers. How do you survive?" Themba liked to tease his fourth year students with this question, as the semester drew to a close. He posed the same question again. It was the last day of lectures for another group of students in his Political Science class.

"Prof. Vezi, it's a delicate balancing act, in my view. It always is. It always was. It always will be." The quick answer came from the slightly older woman in the class. Cynthia. Her grades told the story of some-one who'd returned to university determined to be finally awarded her degree.

"Cynthia, you argue like a woman student I once had in my class, many years ago. I failed to win her heart, though. It wasn't long before I learned she had chosen another man to marry." An awkward smile reluctantly tarried on Professor Themba Vezi's face, and then it quickly disappeared.

He looked down ponderously, and shook his head. "I cancelled lectures for two days. I was down with a very bad bout of flu. The sad heart-stopping, heart-wrenching flu of rejection."

Waves of shock travelled from the front desks to the end of the lecture room. Themba's students were not sure how to react. One student finally braved the awkward moment and asked a question that was possibly on every student's mind, but which no one dared enough to ask.

"True story, Prof?" It was Thabani, the President of the Black Students Association on campus. He liked to weave into class discussions on merits and demerits of both non-racialism and Africanism, with the no longer so new South Africa, as a case in point. Discussions were always robust. But on this day, Professor Vezi was into "life" stuff.

Professor Vezi laughed a bit self-consciously, and then responded, "Yes, Thabani. Indeed, this is a true story." He paused for a while as he nodded his head quite a few times. Themba had not planned to open this unusual door to his students. He never let students into his very private and personal life. But to his surprise, on this last day of lectures, here he was, publicly revisiting an old wound.

Then he continued, "These things happen, even to Professors, you know." Some young men in the class shifted in their seats, but still uttered not one word. A usually shy female student who hardly spoke in class mumbled, "So sorry, Prof." Only a few heard her. Her Professor shrugged his shoulders as he looked in her direction.

This was Nandi. She was one of Themba's favourite female students. He had even mentioned her to his colleagues. Just like a sport's coach searches for talent, Themba advised them to closely monitor Nandi's progress. He was definitely sure that Nandi was Ph.D. material, although that giant academic step, was still a few years away.

Themba volunteered further information. "I learnt years later that I lost that woman to an older business man, originally from the UK."

"Sounds white!" Melusi, the outspoken male student who never combed his hair shouted from the back row of the lecture room. There was disgust in his tone.

"Well, does skin colour matter, folks?" Themba asked.

"She sold out, Professor," blurted out another young man named Delani. He had already bought his ticket, Italy bound. It was a group tour. "To visit my man, Antonio Gramsci," he liked to say. He was the envy of his course mates. Of late, he'd begun throwing in an Italian word here and there, whenever he opened his mouth to speak.

Some girl students turned to look at Delani, and said nothing. Themba responded, "She sold out? I wouldn't say so, class. Love is a strange phenomenon. Love power! Maybe as simple and as complicated as that, shall we say? The power of love. Maybe she was meant for that lucky guy."

"And maybe yours is still coming, who knows, Sir? Soft-spoken Nandi added, very sympathetically, "Maybe soon, Prof,"

Themba was sure he would not make the mistake of divulging that that one woman was still a student in this very class, when he fell in love with her. He threw in further observation for consideration, by his students. "Well, Mandela was pretty much married to the struggle!" The class grunted. Sighs were heard. Some heads bobbed. "Life deals you whatever hand it chooses. You've to accept that."

This was Themba's last comment to close the intimate session. A bit of pensive silence reigned in the class. Unknown futures that still lie ahead can be unnerving, especially for the young and ambitious.

"Party next Wednesday, people. Let's make it the best yet, in the history of the Political Science Department!" The class leader threw his weight around for the last time as course mates collected their bags, and made it out the door, some giving their Professor a warm handshake.

———————

On the day he decided the time had come to announce that he was stepping into the limelight, Themba had to flush out the nerves. He took a few very deep breaths, before he finally sat down by the phone and wiped his sweaty palms on his gym pants.

He finally picked up the phone to make the grand announcement to the only important person in his life that was within reach. His mother. "Mom, I'm doing it today." He was thinking of a great line to introduce this next big step in his life. He felt he had to practice the line.

But before dialing his mother's number, Themba had something else to clear, and get out of the way. He didn't have to. But somehow, he felt compelled. It wasn't going to be an easy task to execute, nevertheless.

There was a partner and partnership in his life. It was defunct. Although in reality it had folded and gone under even before it came into being, Themba thought it was his obligation and duty to share the big news with someone who was now out of reach. That one love of his life. Thokozani. He walked to the closest window in his lounge. He opened it wide and looked far out into the distant horizon. It was a clear day. The sky seemed bluer than usual.

"Thokozani, wherever you are with your guy, I'm sending you a very important message. I'm taking a giant step in my life. Maybe you'll be disappointed. Maybe you'll be happy. I don't know. I think you'll be happy. The rest, you'll read in the newspapers and online."

Themba returned to sit by the phone, and pondered on the other most important person in his life who needed to hear the big news. He was also out of reach. Permanently so. Themba took some steps again to the window. He was proud and excited. Yet, he was also extremely sad. He was thinking about what could have been.

"I don't know where you are, Dad. I'm not sure if you'll like my decision or not. If you are concerned and anxious, I'll understand. With you protecting me, though, my life should be safe, I strongly feel. Dad, a time comes when one has to stand up for what one believes in. That time for me has come. I know I have your blessings."

Themba reserved the rest of that speech for his mother. He had practiced the announcement already. So, he was feeling more self-confident when he made the call.

Over time, it had become clear that Grace's health wasn't going to improve to any great degree, despite continued tests and medical treatment. Her condition was what it was, and would pretty much remain so. Thankfully, her only son had long solicited the services of a highly reputable nurse aid agency. They sent one of their best nurses to live with Themba's mother.

But Mrs. Vezi was usually upbeat. She never resigned herself to complete misery. She kept in touch with family and friends. Her cellphone was always by her side. But it took her time to position it right, when a call came through. Those who knew of her condition and did not want to leave a message, always let the phone ring for quite a while, understanding she was still getting herself organized.

Themba found his mother in a jovial mood when he made the call. "Oh my goodness! It's you, Professor Vezi!" She laughed out loud. The nurse aid was close by to slide a fresh bib under her chin.

"Mom, I'm not Professor to *you!* But I'll humbly accept the honour."

"I'm always so proud of you, son." Mrs. Vezi paused to collect her breath as well as her deeper thoughts. "So is your father. Wherever he is."

"Thanks, mom. How's your day going? You sound happy."

"Well, the sun is shining. The mornings are becoming colder, you know. Winter is here. But the weather has warmed up nicely today. I'm sitting in the warmest spot on the verandah here."

"I see. Good for you, mom. Still happy with the young lady?"

"Oh, yes! So very happy, my child. She is kind-hearted, caring and so bright. She's such a voracious reader too. Do you remember your old student days' novels in the study? She's helping herself to them."

"A godsend, mom. I'm so grateful."

"Indeed, my son. How's work? How are your students? How is going with the marking? Have you finished already?

"Work? Actually I'm just about to leave work, mom."

"Leave? As in end of the semester?"

"As in leaving the profession for good, mother."

"Why, Themba? Are you out of your mind? I thought you'll be positioning yourself for the Head of Department position. Come on, Themba. Even a Deanship now, you know?"

"You are right, mother. I could have. I'm the longest serving academic in my department."

"That's what I thought. You arrived as a lecturer. Now you are a full Professor. Many long years, Themba. You've earned the most senior position possible."

"I know mom. But I feel called to higher service."

"What now? Joining the Priesthood? Well, we've never had a person of the cloth in our family. On both sides, actually."

"I'm taking the plunge into active politics, mom." The line suddenly went dead on Grace's side. Themba waited. He understood this could be quite a shocking piece of news for his mother. She needed time to mull it over in her mind, before she could swallow it. Themba regretted not even giving his mother a hint before; better still, taking time to discuss this venture with her.

But Themba had thought it wiser to spare his mother many long nights and days agonizing about whether he should or shouldn't be actively involved in politics.

When the line went live on Grace's side, there was no doubt that Themba's mother wasn't pleased. "Are you out of your mind, child? Your father disappeared. And now you want to what?"

Themba could imagine what his mother looked like at the moment. Anguish and anxiety all over her face. He was very sorry to put Grace through this.

"Dad wasn't a coward, mom. He stood up for what he believed in."

There was quiet determination Grace quickly noted in her son's voice. She realized nothing was going to deter him.

As she took a deep breath in, her voice became more even toned and subdued. It came across as such when she spoke, again. "True! I agree. Well, what can I say, Themba?" Her son kept quiet, a tad relieved.

"It's your calling, as you say. Undoubtedly, this is in honour of your dad. I understand. And you *are* a Vezi!"

"As dad liked to say, mom."

"Yes, as your father used to say." Her voice eased into a reflective mode.

"Well, I've been in politics for a great while, mom."

"How, do you mean?"

"In the safety of lecture halls and classrooms. It's time to get the show on the road. And not hide in the safety of academic freedom and free speech."

"We are the ones that fought for and truly appreciated academic freedom. During our university days with your father, there were the draconian laws of apartheid. All around us."

"I know, mom." Themba hoped his mother understood what he meant by "getting the show on the road." Somehow, she appeared to be hiding behind academic freedom memories at this moment. "Silly thought," Themba chided himself as he placed the flat palm of his hand on his forehead, and playfully banged it as punishment.

"So, what do you have in mind? Join the ruling party, son?"

"No way, mom. I'm forming my *own* political party."

"What? Get out of here!"

"Well, watch this space, mom. I'll be in the news soon." He heard his mother blow her nose hard.

"What now, mom?" He let her compose herself.

"It is tears of joy, son. Tears of pride and joy. And your father not even here to share this proud moment with us, you know? Very sad!"

"I know mom. But wherever he is …."

"Yes, wherever he is …."

There was a moment's silence on both ends of the line. The pain of permanent absence! Who or what can heal it?

"Any thought yet about the name of your party? Where's your names brainstorming list? I'll pick the right one for you."

"Well, I actually did have a list of possible names, mom."

"And then what happened? You couldn't pick one?"

"Something strange happened, mother. I was in deep meditation one evening. Then it came. Love at first sight. I knew it was the one. I knew you'll like it. I had no more thinking to do."

"Is it so? That sounds like they sent you the name in the spirit world of your ancestors. And, so, out with it now! Curiosity is killing me."

"Vezukukhanya Party!"

"Oh, Themba, that is a good choice! I like it. The party's mission is right there. So clear! Who doesn't love light, progress, development? The name is perfect, so all-encompassing."

"Exactly, mom. In every sense."

"Anyone can feel welcome in it, son. Absolutely! And everyone can pronounce it easily as well."

"True, mom. I hadn't thought about that."

"Not that easy pronunciation matters at all. God forbid, Themba, that we compromise important decisions such as this, for a silly thing like pronunciation. It's the meaning, the vision and inherent hope and aspiration in "Vezukukhanya Party" that is paramount. This is what I feel so endeared to."

"You are right, mom. Just as well the issue of pronunciation never even crossed my mind."

"Well, see it as a bonus to those who still struggle to pronounce words in indigenous languages. And after all of these years living here with us, Themba!"

"They are actually disrespecting the host country and its indigenous people, mom."

Mrs. Vezi steered the conversation back to the most important news of the day. "You have my blessings, Themba. I'm so proud of you. People will join

Vezukukhanya Party without hesitation, and in large numbers. It's just the right time!"

"I think and hope so, mom. I've been canvassing quietly, steadily and systematically for some years now, among my former students."

"That was very smart of you. Very smart. So you already have not only a following of great enlightened minds. Your leadership will come from their ranks also. Great planning ahead and forethought, son. Your dad would be so proud! So proud of you!"

"He is proud, mom. Wherever he is. Thank you, mom."

"So, we'll be seeing a lot of you on Television from now on then? I'm one very proud mama." Grace's exuberance drew a chuckle out of her son.

"I guess so, mom. I'll be registering the party soon. Then it's on!"

"On! My child. Maybe one day you'll rise to the highest office. God must keep me for that proudest day of my life. It goes without saying that my name is number one on the members' list. I'm your number one fan. Never forget this, son. Nurse, come and hear this."

"Okay then, mom, not too much big news. Do get some rest now. I'll keep you posted." The nurse came prepared to change Mrs. Vezi's bib, wipe and freshen her face.

"Mama Vezi, don't you want to go inside and lie down a bit? Lunch is almost ready. I just have to make the soup and mash the potatoes."

The day after Themba launched his Vezukukhanya Party, Grace opened her jewellery box. She kept turning her engagement ring over and over with her good hand. Then she asked the nurse to wrap it nicely, put it in a box and tie a red ribbon around it.

"Here it is, Mama Vezi. Do you like the way it looks?" Mrs. Vezi was resting in bed at this time. Then something else occurred to her.

"Oh, my child. I'm so sorry. Any more spare ribbon and wrapping paper?"

"A bit left. What now? Are you changing your mind? Another gift instead of this ring?"

"No. I forgot to enclose a message. That's all. But it's a very important one."

"Oh! What should we do then, Mama?"

"It's fine. No need to start all over, my child. Bring me the special paper and envelope. I'll write the note. It will go with the gift."

The nurse slipped out of the room as soon as Mrs. Vezi was sitting upright with pen in hand:

*Dearest Themba*

*Congratulations on launching your Vezukukhanya Party! Well-done, son! Judging by the very enthusiastic way the party is received, I've no doubt that you'll be the ruling party in the next general election!*

*There was one woman you loved. Thokozani. I never met her. But I miss her so much. God knows.*

*Here's the ring you could have put on her finger. Maybe one day she will return. Maybe in spirit. Maybe in another woman who will steal your heart, to become First Lady Vezi. You will put this ring on her finger. If no one suitable shows up, don't force matters. This will mean Thokozani was not meant for you. Take heart. Everything happens for a reason.*

*In that case, you will place this ring against your heart as you constantly listen to the heart-beat of this great nation. I know you are fully committed to keep your finger on the pulse of our people's needs. Bring forth the light. Indeed, Themba, be an ever shining example to this wonderful land of our forebears!*

*On behalf of your dearest father, and all members of the Vezi family and clan, I wish you prosperity. God bless you, dearest son. All will be well.*

*With all my love, Mom.*

———————

Thokozani had all her credits transferred to a university in London. Political Science was her field of study and interest, after all. Thanks to Professor Vezi, who had successfully sown this love of politics in her. It was fitting, therefore, that Thokozani kept abreast of world politics, especially the political scene in her homeland, South Africa. So, from time to time she searched for Themba Vezi on the Internet. "Let's see what you are up to old boy."

She read a few years later that Themba Vezi had started a new political party. She was elated to learn that Vezukukhanya Party was so strong, it was threatening to topple the ruling party at the next general elections. Thokozani did not doubt that this Antonio Gramsci scholar and faithful disciple, respected the organic intelligence and dignity of ordinary people. Patrick's wife deeply understood that a time for such a change had come.

Thokozani was relieved also, that whatever heartache she might have caused Themba, he'd be pre-occupied for a very long time, with the politics of transforming and moving South Africa to a better future. Thokozani did not doubt that as Themba was always conscious of Antonio Gramsci's wise thoughts and words as his guide, he was going to have an amazing and memorable once in a life time experience.

"God bless you my love, my T Boy. It's a mammoth task. But you are very smart. South Africa is lucky to have you at its helm during this time in its history. Our hard-won democracy will be stronger. This is very important for South Africa." So mumbled Thokozani to herself as she closed the website one day.

Unknowingly, Patrick had ended a chapter or potential chapter, for Thokozani. It would have been to his detriment. But another chapter had begun, with Themba Vezi, a fellow South African, a very special home boy at that, soon to be President Vezi, according to reliable polls.

This was a man Thokozani held in high esteem and proud to be associated with, even in a very small way, although destiny had pulled her away from him, and put her where she was now, in terms of space and place. But her spirit was free to roam! It inhabited both men. And she was at peace with it all.

Thokozani's joy was also awkwardly enhanced by a line on Themba's short biography posted on the Internet. It read, "Professor Themba Vezi, the leader of the new Vezukukhanya Party, is still single."

"Of course I would love to have a child or two with you, my dear. Never mind that when our first child is 20 years of age, I'll be in my early 70s. I'm well. I'm healthy. I take good care of myself. And our family is well provided for, should ...." Not once did he manage to complete that sentence. Thokozani always sealed his lips with her index finger.

So, time was of the essence for this couple. In a few short years Patrick and Thokozani were blessed with two healthy boys. Bhambatha Patrick Fitzgerald arrived first.

Then a mere eighteen months later, Mgabadeli William Fitzgerald followed.

"Mgabadeli? This is a Vezi clan name, Thokozani!" What would go through Themba's mind, were he to learn this sometime in the future? Oh, well ....